WRONGFULLY REMOVED

A Novel
by
Braxton DeGarmo

Christen Haus Publishing

Copyright

Dedication

This book is dedicated to all of those families that have been torn apart by capricious family courts and state child welfare agencies that believe they, not you, know what's best for your children and denied you due process, as guaranteed by the U.S. Constitution. In God's eyes, it takes a family to raise a child, not the state-controlled "village."

Acknowledgements

I realize that acknowledgments such as this might come across like those windy tributes by the winners on Oscar night. <yawn> Yet, without the people mentioned here, this book might not have made it into your hands. So, here goes.

I'd like to thank the members of my newly formed "street team"—AJ, Dotty, Gordon, Kendra, Mattie, Stacey, Sue, and Susan. These folks provided helpful feedback that improved this book, allowing it to become what you have today.

I wish to thank Gabriel Leveille of Bell Helicopter for information regarding the Bell 407 and "vetting" the crash scene which opened the story.

Of course, as in some of my past books, one or more characters are derived from and named after real folks. Detective Tammy Jahn was inspired by Tamara Jahn Pritchett, who truly was raised by her grandparents in Racine, WI and came to St. Louis for a fresh start. She was a SLMPD District 8 officer for a number of years, although from there most of my character's story is embellished. Don't you love literary license? Oh, there's one other "surprise" character, but I'll leave it at that, a surprise.

My thanks once again to my editor, Patrick LoBrutto, whose suggestions always improve the final result. And to Lenda Selph for her proofreading expertise.

And last but never least, I want to acknowledge and thank my dear wife, Paula, my awesome, multi-talented son, Braxton and my amazingly gifted daughter, Stacey, for their valuable assistance, whether it be proofreading skills, general help, or all around encouragement.

Author's Note

I first learned of the term "medical kidnapping" when I read the story of Justina Pelletier, a 14-year-old girl in Boston with Mitochondrial Disorder, who was forcibly taken from her family *not* because of anything they did. They had a team of doctors caring for Justina at Tufts Medical Center and they followed that team's recommendations. Unfortunately, when their daughter caught an intestinal virus, one of those recommendations was to seek consultation from a gastroenterologist at Boston Childrens. Thus started an eighteen-month ordeal.

A doctor at the children's hospital disagreed with the doctors at Tufts and thought all of Justina's problems were psychosomatic—"all in her head"—and that her parents were using her to gain the attention of doctors. She was diagnosed with Munchhausen Syndrome by Proxy and her parents were accused of medically abusing their daughter. Now, no criminal charges were ever brought against the parents. They had no "day in court." In fact, they were denied all due process in this matter despite the guarantee of such in our U.S. Constitution. Justina was forcibly removed from her family and placed in a psychiatric rehab facility where she languished.

Actually, I shouldn't say they had no day in court. They had dozens of days in court, fighting to regain custody of their child, all because two sets of doctors disagreed. After a year and a half, Justina finally returned home.

For more on medical kidnapping, see my Afterword.

One

"Uh-oh!"

Amy Gibbs' head jumped to attention from its half-napping position, their helicopter sliding through the sky as if a giant heavenly hand had swept them aside, like brushing crumbs off a tabletop. Those were not words you wanted to hear from your helicopter pilot.

They had left St. Louis early that morning to transport a patient to the Mayo Clinic, eager to outrun a promised weather front that would move into the region that afternoon. All had been going smoothly, and she tried to take advantage of the trip home to take a much-needed nap, as best she could manage on the Bell 407 where she attended as the flight nurse.

"Oh crap!"

Kent Howard had the reputation for being easy-going, calm, and methodical as a pilot, so even the mild expletive emerging from his lips gave Amy cause for concern. "What's wro—?"

A thump, loud enough to hear over the engine, arose from the rear of the aircraft, followed by a wobbly, slow, uncontrolled spinning of the chopper, a spin that began to accelerate.

"Hang on!" yelled Kent into the intercom. "That storm

cell popped up out of nowhere, and something just took out our tail rotor."

Amy had seen training films about tail rotor failure. The tail rotor countered the torque of the main blades and kept a helicopter from spinning around. Without it, safe flight was no longer a possibility, and most flight instructors trained their pilots to perform an autorotation to the earth. Under the best of conditions, that would be like careening down from the tallest peak of a roller coaster and hitting soft sand at the bottom. Under the usual circumstances, autorotation was more like a rock falling out of the sky. With this wind, well . . . the odds were strongly in favor of their hitting the ground, hard, and rolling.

There was a word for that, crashing.

A tear emerged from her eye at the thought. She'd become engaged to the man of her dreams less than a week ago. This wasn't fair.

"No trees, please," murmured Amy in a short, quiet prayer. "Lord, please help us safely to the ground." She donned her helmet, brushing her shoulder-length, dirty-blonde hair back inside the headgear to keep it out of her eyes. She took a deep breath but refused to close her eyes. She needed to be alert to everything happening around her.

Kent struggled with the aircraft but managed to minimize its spin. "I can't autorotate with the winds we have now. I need to attempt a running landing."

Amy saw that he had managed to align the chopper so that it had a left crosswind, which helped to reduce the spin and compensate for the tail rotor's failure. But, his airspeed remained high. A running landing at even ten knots could seriously injure them all.

Rain and hail now pelted the windshield and made

visibility impossible for those in the back. The darkened skies, making it seem as if they were flying at dusk and not late morning, didn't help that visibility. She hoped *he* could see what lay ahead in the trajectory he had chosen. Again, she asked for no trees. Landing in trees would kill them all.

A flash of lightning gave her a sense they were nearing the ground. Kent had managed to slow the aircraft. She felt him flare the main blades and watched him temper the cyclic to bring their ground speed to zero. Hopefully.

A sudden gust of wind caused the 407 to shudder, and in an instant, Amy felt the right skid hit the ground and dig in. Before she could blink, she was on her side, then upside down, her five-point restraint keeping her in the seat. They continued to roll, as she lost consciousness.

Sinead O'Malley criticized herself inwardly. Why had she told the man that she knew how to operate this blasted tiller? The April air had warmed, and she was anxious to prepare the little garden plot she had so carefully laid out in her mind over the previous couple of weeks. She couldn't afford to waste time in a town that was over an hour away from the house. *How hard could it be to operate a tiller?* she thought. *Isn't it just like a lawn mower?*

Besides, the man at the rental store seemed so patronizing. She couldn't ever recall being called "little lady" before, despite her petite stature.

She again adjusted the choke and pulled the cord for what seemed like the hundredth time. This time it caught short and about yanked her arm off. She massaged her right shoulder and took a deep breath. After a moment, she grabbed the pull cord in her left hand and placed her right foot on the edge of the machine to stabilize it. She pulled, and the old Briggs & Stratton™ engine sputtered for a few seconds. Encouraged, she eased off the choke and tried again. This time the engine came to life.

She let it run, to allow the engine time to warm up, as well as to refresh her memory on how to engage the tines. Satisfied that the tiller wouldn't die on her, she eased the lever forward and startled as the machine began "walking" forward without her. She quickly grasped the handles and fought to maintain a straight line as she worked down the 20 feet of the first row.

At the end of the row, she stopped the tines and turned back to see what she had accomplished. Nothing more than scraping off the tops of the newly emerging weeds.

"This is going to take more work that I thought," she muttered. If the town wasn't so far away and her funds so limited, she'd almost consider giving up this fantasy she hoped would become a vegetable garden. What business did she, a New England city girl, have trying to become a farmer in rural Illinois?

Suddenly, a gust of wind slapped her like a Boston Bruins player checking her into the glass. She caught her hat as it tried to escape her head and looked up expecting to see a tornado carrying off the house, as her old nemesis peddled into the clouds with Sinead's daughter strapped onto the back of the bicycle. She shook her head at the thought. Her Technicolor™ world devolved into black and white as the ominous clouds fomented toward her and seemed to swallow the sun.

The weather forecast had called for a storm front to move into the area that afternoon, but God apparently saw humor in making those weather people look foolish most of the time. How did that scripture go? "For the wisdom of this world is foolishness before God."

No, that wasn't the precise one she searched for. Mentally, she stepped ahead one verse. "The Lord knows the reasonings of the wise, that they are useless." Well, that fit most politicians, maybe weathermen, too, but it still wasn't the verse she strove to recall.

The first few drops of rain began to pelt her face. She saw that she would not have time to move the tiller out of the weather, if she wished to remain dry. So, she dashed for the back door of the house, holding tightly to her hat. She heard the noise as she reached the door.

The sound, like two cars slamming into each other head-on at high speed, came from above, but with the wind and escalating rain she couldn't tell exactly from where. She searched the sky, wiping more and more drops from her eyes as she did so. About to give up and go inside, she saw it. A helicopter spinning, in trouble, and falling.

"Mom!"

Her daughter's cry reached above the wind to catch her ears. At 14 years of age, the girl still anguished over thunderstorms. She dashed through the door, into the kitchen.

"It's okay, Ruth. It's just a storm. Why don't you go into the safe room? I need to go back outside."

The girl started to move from the kitchen but turned her head back and reached toward Sinead with her right arm. "Come with me."

Sinead walked over to her daughter and cradled Ruth's hand in both of her hands. "I will. Soon as I can. Someone's in trouble out there, and I need to see if I can help." She leaned over and gave the girl a kiss on the forehead. "Go on. You'll be safe in that room. Don't come out until I come get you."

The girl pleaded with her eyes, but Sinead knew she'd argue no more. Ruth knew her mother's grit and determination well. Once Sinead's mind was set, little could change it.

"Go on." She watched Ruth leave the room and mentally thanked her friend, Adriana, yet again for the use of the old family home. Even more, that there was a room prepared which could withstand all but the most powerful tornadoes. That reassurance had proven critical for dealing with Ruth's fear. Yet, it wasn't a fear of the storm that lay at the bottom of the girl's anxiety but fear of being separated from her parents again. Sinead sighed. The year and a half struggle to regain her daughter from foster care had been draining on them all. But the persecution wasn't over. Her husband, Jameson, sat in a Massachusetts jail cell on contempt charges, charges that the judge would drop if she and the girl would return to the state. In agreement, the couple vehemently refused to do that.

Another blast of wind caused the house to shudder. Sinead wrapped her arms across her chest and wondered what good she could do, even if she found the helicopter. Still, her parents hadn't raised her that way. She knew she would offer what aid she could, even if that jeopardized being discovered by the authorities. There were other states in which to hide.

She grabbed a poncho from a coat hook near the back door, slid it over her head, and pushed through the back door into the storm. Small pebbles of hail, mixed with cold, heavy drops of rain made her pause. She shook her head and moved into the yard where the house no longer provided a modicum of protection from the wind. She looked toward where she had seen the aircraft, not expecting to see it there, of course. Yet, it had been on a course toward the northeast. The farm on which the home sat extended that direction. The fields had been leased to neighboring farmers, but an old tractor path had been maintained to allow movement between the fields. She decided to follow that rutted road, to find whatever she might discover. If she had found no crash site by the time she reached the end of the road, she would return to the house, her conscience satisfied that she had done what she could.

Two

Richard Nichols paced the floor of the historic home where colleagues had gathered to remember three others who had died in a terrorist bombing at the headquarters of his new employer, the American Party. His boss and two others had been killed, but his emotions roiled for other reasons. Amy's supervisor had called him as he was in route to the gathering to inform him that the MedAir helicopter had gone missing. That the man had Richard's cell phone number and knew of Richard and Amy's recent engagement caught him a bit by surprise, but he appreciated being placed "in the loop."

"So, what happened?" asked Bradley Graham, the face of the American Party and its first presidential candidate. So, in reality, *he* was now Richard's boss.

Richard stopped pacing and faced the group that now gathered near him. His broad-shouldered, six-foot-three-inch frame physically dominated the group. "Some freak occurrence, they say. Radar showed a thunderstorm popping up ahead of the leading edge of the front and might have caught them off-guard. They don't know whether the helicopter crashed, landed safely but without a radio and in a dead zone for cell phones, or what. The storm cells in the area are preventing any aircraft from starting a search. I . . .

I . . ."

He took a deep breath, and his shoulders sagged. This wasn't fair. He'd finally met the girl he wanted to grow old with, and she'd said "Yes" to the most important question he could ever ask her. Now, just days later, she's missing? Was his dream about to become a nightmare?

He didn't want to think about the worst-case scenario.

Brad placed his hand on Richard's shoulder. "Let's pray for their safe recovery." He led a short prayer asking God for the safe return of the aircraft's crew, as well as for that 'peace that passes understanding' for Richard. Several others added their words for comfort, and Richard knew that all was in God's hands at that time. What more could he say—or do?

As he looked up from praying, Richard noticed Lynch Cully, Amy's ex-boyfriend and Graham's new Chief of Security, his eyes closed and shoulders quivering, across the room. Until a short time ago, Lynch had been presumed dead, and Amy had suffered the emotional discord of his loss. Richard's work had brought him to St. Louis, and a chance meeting had led to his filling that void. Yet, after Lynch's return "to the living," she had chosen Richard over Lynch. Richard could only imagine what the man was feeling at the moment.

Lynch opened his eyes and looked up. The two men locked gazes for a moment, and somehow, Richard felt the pain in Lynch's heart. And yet, it wasn't the form of pain Richard had expected. He felt no jealousy. He watched in quiet anticipation as the ex-detective crossed the room toward him.

"Richard, I'm really sorry to hear this. It's . . ." He sighed. "Amy's a special lady, and I hope, I pray she's okay.

But, I want you to know I have no hard feelings about the two of you. I've come to realize that I've changed, a lot, through my . . . my . . . whatever you want to call it. I see now that she and I would never have made it together, so I'm glad she met you."

Richard started to interrupt, but Lynch stopped him.

"I hope we can all be friends, without any awkwardness or reservations. And I want you to know that I'm here for you both. If I can do anything to help you, please, don't hesitate to ask."

Lynch extended his hand to Richard, and Richard accepted it. He saw sincerity in Lynch. There was no hidden agenda here. He'd suspected since first learning about Lynch that he'd like the man, that had Amy not been between them they could be friends. Not long ago, that issue became moot. Amy had chosen Richard and, now, Lynch had shown himself to be magnanimous and worthy of Richard's friendship.

"Thank you, Lynch. I would value your friendship."

"So, what can we do now?"

"I . . ." What *could* they do now? "I don't know. Until I hear from her boss, I don't know what to do."

"Then we wait. Together. I'm here to help."

Three

⚜

Sinead stepped out into the rain and looked again in the direction where she had seen the aircraft moving. She and her daughter had taken refuge in the farmhouse just a few weeks earlier, but she knew from her brief exploration of the farm that the rutted lane ran in that direction.

She walked toward the lane and realized she wasn't thinking ahead. If someone needed help, was she going to *carry* them back to the house? Hardly. Her lithe, five-foot-two-inch frame was muscular but not *that* strong.

She ran back to the house, and just inside the back door, she found a ring of keys. There was an old pickup in the barn. She crossed her fingers that one of the keys belonged to it and that it would start.

She unlatched the main door to the barn's garage area and struggled to slide it open. She then turned to the truck, a 1965 Chevy K10. That it had seen better days was an understatement.

She climbed into the driver's seat and fumbled with the key ring. Two keys appeared to be for vehicles. The first key didn't fit. The second, however, did, and upon turning the ignition, the truck sputtered. *At least it seems to turn over*, she thought. She pushed the gas pedal to the floor and let up. She tried the ignition again. The engine awakened and died. She let up on the gas and tried one more time.

The engine came to life. Rough, but within a minute, the only noise it released was a steady purr. She smiled, until she realized it was a stick shift on the column, a "three on the tree." Fortunately, whoever had driven it last had left it in neutral. Otherwise, she might never have gotten it started, stalling out on every attempt and never guessing why.

She backed into the gravel area near her garden-to-be and stopped. With the clutch depressed, she turned the wheel toward the lane and shifted into first. As she eased off the clutch, she stalled.

Undeterred, she pushed in the clutch and restarted the truck. With more care, she eased into gear and began to inch forward. She gave it some gas and began her slow-but-steady progress to the lane. She decided to leave it in first and go slowly, unsure that it could go any faster on the rutted path. And she didn't want to stall.

After what seemed like miles, she had seen nothing to indicate a crash. However, she could still see the house and barn in her rearview mirrors and realized she couldn't have gone more than a quarter of a mile.

Five minutes later, the lane evened out, and she debated venturing into second gear, until she slid sideways unexpectedly. That answered that question. She had noticed a big lever on the dash, to the right of the steering column, which was marked '4X4.' She wasn't sure what that meant, so she left it alone.

With the house now out of sight, she saw a tree line in the near distance. She noticed that the trees followed a dry creek bed. She crossed the creek and found herself between two new fields that had been recently plowed, or furrowed, or whatever they did to prepare fields in the spring. Some farmer she'd make. She didn't even know the lingo.

She rounded a bend and saw another set of gates. These two had been left closed, but that had barely registered in her consciousness when she saw a piece of something that looked like metal sticking up from the barren, soggy ground just over a low rise in the field. She had enough gas to leave the pickup running, and she preferred that option over the risk of not starting it later.

There would be no running in the turned fields, now more like pools of mud than firm soil. That condition would worsen as the rain had picked up again. She felt thankful that she'd left her boots on. Ahead and to her left was the long piece of metal. As she neared, she recognized it as a helicopter's rotor blade. She had found them. Straight ahead she saw more debris.

She walked and slid another 200 yards before she saw it. A helicopter, a medevac chopper from its markings, sat crumpled against the trees. A field of debris led to the wreckage. More of the rotor blades. The tail rotor and a portion of the tail section. A door. The patient stretcher.

She crossed her heart and tried to hurry her pace, a difficult task in the mud. Fifty yards from the wreckage, she stopped, and nausea rose up within. A leg sat in the mud, still clothed in its flight suit and the boot still on the foot. The metallic odor of blood mixed with the already unpleasant smell of freshly plowed earth mixed with jet fuel. This did not bode well. How many people were on this flight? What was she about to see that she'd never be able to un-see?

She trudged ahead. The helicopter lay on its left side. Before reaching the bulk of the debris, she saw the body that belonged to the leg. Lying face-down in the mud, the man was dead. Of that she was sure.

She crossed past the top of the aircraft—its rotors now gone and the quiet engine still emanating heat—and approached the front of the craft. Within the cockpit, another man sat strapped into the pilot's seat, his helmeted head cocked at an unnatural angle and a shard of metal protruding from his chest. She forced back the bile rising to her throat and climbed toward the body. Hesitant, she reached through the shattered windshield for the neck, which appeared to be broken, and felt for a pulse. Nothing. Beneath the visor, his eyes stared vacantly ahead.

She climbed past the nose of the helicopter to the right side of the debris, where the belly of the aircraft faced her. The right landing strut appeared mangled and twisted but seemed securely attached to the body of the chopper. She hoisted her body up onto the strut and tried to peer through the broken window of the bowed door. No good. She couldn't see inside.

She lifted one leg onto the strut and moved up to sit on it. She grabbed the handle of the door and lifted. *Forget the door*, she thought. She couldn't even get the handle itself to budge.

Climbing onto the fuselage, she knelt next to the shattered window and bent over to look inside. Another body, a young female hanging from a front-facing seat, its restraints holding her from falling to the side of the cabin sitting on the ground. And that would have been a good thing, if she were alive. The other side held little except sharp metal pieces that would have impaled her had she fallen into them.

Sinead saw no movement and no signs of respiration.

The woman's head dangled downward, but her neck did not appear broken like the pilot's. She couldn't see the woman's eyes through her closed lids. She started to climb back down. She had nothing to offer the dead, and her daughter needed her. She had to return to the house. Yet, something stopped her.

She realized she had not confirmed that the woman was dead. She swiveled back around and lay on her belly to reach through the window. She extended her hand to feel for a pulse, and as she pushed aside the helmet and touched the woman's neck, the woman's eyes flew open. Sinead started and almost slid off the fuselage.

Using her right foot, she began to kick at the glass that remained in the window. To her amazement, the glass gave way much easier than she had expected. The crash had stressed the glass, as well as the door, in ways no one ever hoped to encounter. She was merely "the final straw."

With the opening cleared, she first sat at the edge and then carefully lowered herself into the cabin. Standing in an open spot on the grounded side of the fuselage, she next worked on the metal objects around her. She easily flattened several of them with her boot. Others pulled free, and she took extreme care not to cut her hands on the variety of sharp edges she found. Within minutes, she had cleared enough of the cabin to ensure she could lower the woman to the ground without risk of a new injury.

Sinead turned to look at the woman and saw that her eyes were again open. She had never seen such crystalline blue eyes before.

"Hi. I'm Sinead. The weather won't let any search and rescue operations start for a while. I'm going to see if I can get you out of here. Can I take the helmet off?"

A slight nod came from the woman, who answered in a raspy, dry whisper, "Thank you."

"Your name tag says you are Amy and a nurse."

Amy nodded. "Water." She pointed with her left arm to a nylon equipment pack.

Sinead glanced at the pack and replied, "Okay, but let me get you down first."

Amy's eyes questioned that move. Sinead sized up the woman who appeared a head taller than her own petite frame.

"I know. I don't look all that mighty, and you look to have at least half a foot height advantage over me, but I can do it."

Amy's eyes still questioned, and she shook her head. She whispered, "The others?"

Sinead took a deep breath. "Let's get you out of here."

Tears began to flow from Amy's eyes, as Sinead's unstated answer appeared to sink in.

"If I put my shoulder up to your chest and hold you, do you think you can unbuckle the latch on these straps?"

"Yes."

"Good. When you do, just let your feet fall, and I'll help support your upper body. Sound like a plan?"

Amy nodded. Thirty seconds later, she was standing—wobbly, but standing—next to Sinead, who felt dwarfed by this woman who towered close to six feet tall. Two seconds after that, the woman collapsed to the ground.

"Here's that water." She unscrewed the lid to the plastic bottle and held it to Amy's lips. The woman gulped down half the bottle before Sinead pulled it away. "Hey, not too much."

Sinead saw Amy staring at the front of the aircraft. She

followed her gaze toward the dead pilot.

"I'm sorry. He's gone. The other man, too." She paused. "So, let's get you out of here."

Amy appeared unable to bear weight on her right leg but was able to use her arms. Still, the effort of pulling Amy from the fuselage was herculean, and as soon as Amy touched ground outside, the nurse collapsed. Sinead tried to revive her, but she would not waken. Sinead worried that hidden injuries would claim this life, too.

As she moved to gain leverage on Amy's body, she heard a hiss and crackle that made her heart race. She turned back toward the cabin to see smoke. Within seconds, flames followed. They had to move away now or else. With every strand of muscle Sinead possessed, she lifted Amy into a fireman's carry and walked from the crash.

Four

Richard had already made the decision to drive to MedAir's headquarters in O'Fallon, Missouri, just a 30-minute drive from the Ferguson home of Mike and Mary Southworth. The memorial gathering would continue without him, and without Lynch, who followed closely in a second vehicle. Richard had told him it was unnecessary for him to join him at MedAir, but Lynch had insisted.

As he neared the Winghaven exit off I-64 to O'Fallon, his phone rang. The Caller ID showed MedAir, and his heart began to race. Good news? Or bad news? He had no idea what to expect, and his uncertainty translated into an uncomfortable churning in his gut.

He answered the call through his hands-free connection in the car.

"Richard, it's Craig Sheehan. I—"

Richard could hear a voice in the background.

"Sorry about that. Our flight desk was just giving me an update. I wanted to let you know the weather has turned for the worse upstate. Local authorities won't fly in it to start a search, and it might be another hour before weather conditions ease enough to do so, but we have some news. Radar lost them over west central Illinois, about 100 miles east of their registered flight path. The area is all farm land so we should be able to find them pretty easily once we get in the air."

"So, no phone calls or radio contact?"

"Sorry, but no. No 9-1-1 calls from anyone living in the area either, but the population there is pretty sparse."

Craig's words did not go unheard. "You said, 'once *we* get in the air.' "

"That's right. They're in easy range of several of our crews. In fact, we have one in Springfield. And for our corporate 407 here, it's less than 45 minutes away. That's one of the reasons I called. I'm offering you a seat to fly with us."

That was a no-brainer decision. Of course, he wanted a seat. Yet, he needed something more.

"Do you have one more open seat?"

There was a pause from the other end. Then Richard heard some additional talking in the background before Craig came back on.

"Who do you have in mind? I can bump someone here, but I want to make sure there's good reason. We might need more medical personnel on hand."

Richard contemplated that. Craig made sense. If there were injuries, they'd need to move up to three patients. That also meant up to three helicopters might be required.

"How many flight crews are going?" asked Richard.

"We're mobilizing units from Hannibal, Quincy, and Springfield. Our corporate aircraft makes four, but it's not equipped for a patient. We're going to help spot and coordinate."

To Richard it seemed apparent that the MedAir bosses were thinking along the same lines as he. He didn't feel so bad about bumping someone from corporate now. Of course, that decision was still theirs to make.

"Lynch Cully is with me. He wants to go, too." Well, Richard assumed Lynch would want to go. Why else would he have insisted on meeting Richard at the MedAir headquarters?

Craig did not reply. Instead, dead air came through the speaker. After 30 seconds, Richard began to wonder if he'd lost the call. No matter, he was only three minutes from the facility, and Lynch was right behind him.

Craig's voice returned. "You *and* Cully? Um, isn't that, uh . . .?"

Richard could hear the question and the concern in the man's voice. Fiancé and ex-boyfriend. Was that guaranteed trouble?

"Trust me. It's all good. You don't have to worry that we'll start fighting or anything."

Silence took over the line for several seconds, before Craig replied, "Ookaayy."

"So, can he fly with us? He could come in handy." Richard hoped he wasn't overselling the man.

"Yeah, well . . . okay, we'll work it out. How soon can you get here? We'll take off in about 30 minutes, weather permitting."

Richard grinned as he pulled in front of their building. "Start your engine, 'cause we're in the parking lot."

Five minutes later, they were donning flight suits, but it was another 40 minutes after that before the 407 took off.

Amy awoke to a loud noise and images of spinning inside the helicopter filled her mind. Then there was a woman, as if in a dream, talking to her and giving her water.

Was she imagining all of this? Yet, as she opened her eyes, she found herself inside an old pickup truck, leaning against the doorframe.

As she became more conscious, pain in her right ankle took command of her thoughts. She looked down and saw an air splint covering her lower leg, ankle, and foot. She reached that way and noticed a bulky dressing on her right hand.

She startled as the driver's door opened. The imagined woman grabbed the doorframe and began to hoist herself inside. She hadn't been seeing things after all.

"Oh! Good. You're awake." The woman smiled for a second. "Although, with the trip ahead, and all the bumps and jostling around, you might wish you were still unconscious."

"I-I'm Amy."

The woman turned back towards her. "Yes, I know. The flight nurse." The woman pointed at her. "It's on your nametag."

Amy nodded. Of course. She hadn't thought of that. "And you?"

"Again, I'm Sinead. Do you remember talking with me in the helicopter?"

Amy wanted to shrug her shoulders, but that hurt, too. She managed to waggle her head.

"I understand. I probably wouldn't remember either." She paused and then explained how she had come to help them.

Amy glanced out the cab's back window. She saw two of their aid duffels, but no one else. That part of her dream came back to her. The others were dead. Tears submerged her cheeks.

Amy scrutinized the petite woman who had just rescued her. "Wh-where are we?"

"On a farm just over an hour northwest of Springfield. It's . . ." Sinead paused. Was she about to give away more information than she should? No. She continued, "The farm belongs to the family of a dear friend, Adriana. Well, her husband's family. She met him when he was a West Point cadet. She's a hot-blooded Texan, but he's managed to put up with her for over 40 years." Sinead chuckled. "She's as generous as they come, though, and offered me the use of the house. No one else lives there right now, and the farm land has been leased out to neighboring farmers."

Sinead reached for the ignition key. The engine tried to turn over but didn't catch.

Amy had one more question burning in her mind. "Where's the helicopter and how . . . " Her voice sounded thready. Breathing hurt and talking made it worse. Had she broken a rib? Or two?

Sinead turned to face her again. She pointed behind Amy. "The wreckage is less than a quarter mile that way. There's debris spread across a large field, but the main wreck was stopped by a tree line."

Amy closed her eyes. She remembered asking God not to let them crash in trees. They hadn't, and she survived. But the others . . . How could she thank God when the others had died?

Sinead faced forward to drive, and this time the engine started up. Seconds later, they lurched forward and began to inch toward wherever home was. Sinead had been right. Amy felt every bump.

*   *   *

Sinead had seen that look before. Amy had gone pale. If she had internal injuries and was bleeding inside, Sinead had no chance of getting her to a hospital in time. They were simply too isolated, and Amy could bleed out on the way.

Maybe it was only the pain. Pain was something where Sinead could help her. She'd found pain meds in one aide box and moved them to one of the duffels. Yet, while Amy remained unconscious she had had no reason to administer such meds. Now, that would have to wait until they reached the house.

Sinead was exhausted. She had carried Amy to the truck, as well as the duffels on a second trip, and had no idea where she had gotten the strength to do so. Every muscle in her body ached. The siren call of morphine sang from the duffel in the bed of the pickup, but she bound herself to the seat with the seatbelt and would wait for ibuprofen at the house.

At least the truck started. She took it as slowly as she could without stalling, but she knew that each and every bump affected Amy. She could see that in the young woman's countenance. A wince. A grimace. Clenching her teeth. Every jolt inside the cab elicited some facial evidence of pain.

The journey seemed to take much longer than the initial trip out from the house. Yet, soon enough Sinead arrived at the tree line and dry creek bed. Only it was no longer dry. There appeared to be at least a foot of water now running as a torrent down the stream. And the rain had become a deluge once again.

That, in itself, did not appear enough to stop them. The width of the stream was about the length of the truck, and only the central-most area carried the deeper water. The water spread across the majority of the rocks was but a few inches deep. Earlier, she had noticed no holes or drop-offs . She should be able to drive right across.

Except for one obstacle. A tree limb had washed down with the water and blocked their way. She didn't think she could successfully drive over it.

"Be right back," said Sinead, before exiting the pickup. Already soaked to the bone, she marched right into the stream and began to pull at the branch.

With the limb 90% out of the way, Sinead stopped and perked up. *What's that sound?* She continued to struggle with the bough, but the noise kept getting louder. As she dropped the branch, she turned to walk back to the truck and looked upstream.

A wall of water rushed toward them. *Flash flood!* her mind screamed. She had to get across the stream now or they would be stranded there. Or worse.

She raced for the truck, slipping once and catching her fall on the bumper of the truck. She didn't even take time to close her door.

"Sorry! This is going to hurt!" she screamed to Amy.

She threw the truck in gear and let out the clutch, as she prayed that the vehicle wouldn't stall. The pickup lurched forward in a violent jerk as Sinead gassed it. Amy gasped in pain, but Sinead avoided looking toward her. She focused her attention on the opposite bank.

The truck's rear wheels slipped a couple of times, and Sinead noticed the water level quickly rising. They were almost across when the left rear tire began to spin. Panic filled Sinead's mind as she recalled images from past newscasts of vehicles swept away by flood waters, their owners found bashed and hanging from trees weeks later.

Ruth needed her. Her other children needed her. Jameson needed her. She couldn't let the water flush her away.

The wall of water hit the rear panel behind the back wheel like a rhino hitting a safari jeep. Sinead held the wheel so tightly her knuckles blanched. She gave the truck more gas, and as the rear end began to rise and drift downstream, she began to panic. Then a thought hit her. That big lever's "4x4" label meant four-wheel drive. She had never driven a four-wheel drive vehicle, but, somehow, she managed to depress the clutch, ease up the gas, engage the front wheels, shift back into first gear, and gas it in one fluid movement, as if she had done that maneuver a thousand times before.

The truck lurched forward as the front wheels engaged and pulled them from the rising water.

Five

Amy responded to Sinead's gentle prodding and, with the woman's assistance, eased her way out of the pickup truck's seat and stood next to the vehicle outside a classic farmhouse. She looked up and welcomed the cold rain on her face as it seemed to wash away more than the grime and the salt of her tears. She whispered a quiet prayer of thanks and took a deep breath of the rain-cleansed air.

"Here. Let me get under your right shoulder and help you inside," said Sinead.

Together, they hobbled the 20 feet to the home's back door. Just outside the door sat a boot jack with brushes mounted sideways to remove the dirt from the sides of a boot. Sinead ignored it and opened the door to help Amy into what she could only describe as a mud room, a place for removing dirty clothes and shoes. On the left-hand wall sat a bench seat.

"Let's sit you down here."

Amy slid down but winced as she did.

"Where's it hurt? Belly? Chest? Do you think you're hurt inside?"

Amy sat still for a moment and tried to pay attention to her body. She watched Sinead peel off the poncho, which hadn't helped. The woman's clothes were soaked and hung limply from her diminutive frame. Using her "good" hand, Amy gently pressed here and there over her rib cage and abdomen. Belly seemed fine, but there was localized pain above her left breast, over the collar bone. That was right where the restraint crossed her body. With a deep breath, she also noted pain in her chest wall to the side of her left breast. She could reproduce that pain by pressing the area.

She began to raise her left arm, expecting pain, but found it bearable. She proceeded to move her arm through its full range of motion and found she had minimal pain with the use of that arm. A sense of relief flooded her. Her clavicle seemed intact, and the odds of having broken ribs fell to where they would make a bookie cry.

"I don't think I have any internal injuries. Ibuprofen should be enough."

"I think you might need something more. *I'm* the one who's going to need the ibuprofen."

"No, I should be fine with—" The pain from her ankle brought the tears back.

Sinead looked up from below where she had deflated the air splint over Amy's ankle and leg.

"Sorry. So sorry. I thought we should get your flight suit off, and we can't do that with the splint on."

Sinead inflated the splint again, but Amy felt no relief. She started to rethink the desire to limit herself to the anti-inflammatory. She reached into a pocket over her left thigh and retrieved a pair of heavy-duty bandage scissors.

"Cut it off. Please."

Amy took a deep breath and worked to control the pain.

"Mom."

Amy and Sinead both looked up. Amy saw a skinny,

teenage girl in a wheelchair holding out a white terry spa robe. A second robe sat in her lap. On a second look, she realized the term "skinny" was too generous. The girl bordered on emaciated. Yet, something about her seemed familiar. Amy wracked her brain as to why she might recognize this girl. A reason evaded her, but she noticed that the pain had lessened.

"Amy, this is my daughter, Ruth. Ruth, this is Amy. Thanks for the robes. It's raining cows and horses out there."

The girl giggled.

Five minutes later, both women were out of their soggy, outer clothes and nestled into dry, terry robes. Sinead had only cut a portion of the leg of her flight suit in order to help her remove it. Amy glanced at her bandaged right hand. She started to ask about it, when Sinead spoke up.

"It's just a bad abrasion, but, yeah, we should clean that better." Sinead looked about. "Oh, shoot. I left the duffels in the truck."

Sinead slipped her bare feet into her boots, whipped off the robe, and ran out the door in just her underwear. Seconds later, a wet duffel flew through the doorway, followed by Sinead and the second duffel a moment later. She stood inside the doorway, dripping onto the floor as Ruth pointed at her and laughed.

Sinead smiled. "Yeah, bad hair day."

Amy found Ruth's joy infectious. She looked so ill, yet so happy. Her familiarity still puzzled her. A smile crept across her face, too. Sinead did, after all, look like a bedraggled pet after a bath, with her wet hair matted around her face. On further scrutiny, she still wondered just how this elfin woman had managed to carry her across nearly a quarter mile of mud. Had God answered another prayer?

Sinead donned her robe and cinched it tightly around her. "Ahh, that feels much better. But I'm looking forward to a shower and dry clothes . . . after we clean that hand, Amy." She turned toward the kitchen. "Right in here. Let me help you."

Amy put a hand up to stop her. "I think I can manage, if I can hold onto Ruth's wheelchair." She smiled at the teen.

"Sure. You can even use it if you need to. I'm getting stronger, now that I'm back on my medications and the right diet."

Amy saw Sinead give her daughter a look that said, "Don't say too much."

"Thanks, but I'll hang on to the handles, like a walker."

Ruth's eyes lit up. "Hey, we have one of those, too, if you need it."

Sinead nodded. "It's in the den. Ruth's been able to use it a bit more each day as part of her therapy. And she's walking short distances on her own again."

As the three women gathered at the kitchen sink, Amy wondered what exactly were Ruth's medical problems and why had she stopped her medications. Sinead unwrapped the dressing on Amy's hand. Dried blood and dirt had crusted over the back of her hand.

As Sinead started the water, and tested its temperature, Amy held her hand up closer to her face and inspected it. "You know, I think once it's cleaned up, it might not be so bad." She placed it under the water and watched as the dirt and blood softened and began to flow away. "The tan duffel should have our cleansing solution and more dressing material."

Sinead nodded. "That's where I got the first supplies."

Amy winced. The water had worked its way to the raw wound. The sting was bearable. So far.

"Here. You want me to do it?" asked Sinead, as she handed the bottle marked Shur-Clens® out toward Amy.

Amy shook her head and proceeded to cleanse the wound. As she thought, once clean, the damage wasn't as severe as one might have guessed. She patted it dry with the clean towel handed to her by Ruth. The towel had a Tuft's Medical Center logo on it.

Tufts? Amy wondered. Again, she had a sense of déjà vu, like she knew the story behind these two. Yet, it was a story that escaped her at the moment. At least the towel's origin matched the duo's accents. They both sounded as if they'd stepped off a "lobstah boat in Bahston hawbah."

Sinead extended a tube of Bactroban® antibiotic ointment toward her. As Amy finished applying a thin layer of the goop over her wound, Sinead's hand held out a non-stick pad, while her other hand held gauze wrap.

"Wow, you'd make a good E.D. nurse. Do you have a medical background? You seem to know how to handle injuries pretty well."

Ruth grinned. "That's Dr. Mom for you."

Sinead ran a hand tenderly through her daughter's hair. "Call it O-J-T. When you have kids with health issues, you learn quickly."

Amy's thoughts battled within. Again, these two looked familiar, but she couldn't place them. "So, you have other children? Are they with you?"

Sinead looked wistful and began to tear up. "No, Ruth's brother and sister are w-with their grandparents. It's just the t-two of us here." She wiped a tear from her left cheek.

Amy frowned. "That must be hard for you."

Sinead nodded. "And for Ruth. They are her biggest cheerleaders."

Amy took her turn to nod in acknowledgment. With her hand wound redressed, she hopped on her good foot to turn around and lean back against the counter. "So, why don't you go get that shower and clean up? I need . . ." She took a deep breath as she thought about the enormity of what she needed to do. "I need . . . to contact my base . . . and give them the bad news." Amy teared up at that thought. She had thought she'd be able to handle it. "C-could you get me my cell phone? From my flight suit. I-It's in the right thigh cargo pocket. And I need to know just where we are."

Ruth turned toward her mother with a look of fear. Sinead, in turn, gulped and took a deep breath. "I'll get it for you, but it won't work here. There's no service here."

Amy felt her gut drop. She needed to get help. "Can I use your phone then?"

"Umm, we don't have one. Well, I should say the house has one. That's obvious." She nodded toward the phone on a nearby wall. "We just don't have any service. My friends only keep electric service here, but as far as anyone else knows, there's no one living in this house. In fact, only my friend Adriana, and now you, know we're here. I really, really need to keep it that way. Please."

Ruth started to sob. "P-please, Ms. Amy, I d-don't want to go back. Y-you can't t-tell anyone—"

Sinead placed a hand on the girl's shoulder to stop her.

Amy felt a sudden surge of sympathy for this girl. Something had happened to these two that had forced them to run. What? An abusive spouse and father? The other kids were with grandparents, not the dad. Maybe that was it. She had seen enough victims of abuse in the E.D. that she knew she could keep that secret. Now, as she witnessed firsthand the love these two shared, and the fear Ruth had about going back, she knew she would be Ruth's ally.

"Sinead, look, I don't know who or what you're running from . . ."

A look of fear now crossed Sinead's face.

". . . but I want you to know I'm on your side. I want to help, but right now, *I* need help. I have to contact my company. And I need medical attention for my ankle. If I *have* broken both bones in my lower leg, it could compromise the blood flow to my foot. I don't want to lose my foot."

Sinead hung her head but nodded. "I-I understand that. I, uh . . ."

Amy could tell that the woman wasn't sure about trusting her. Yet, she did not seem to be the kind of person who would deny Amy the care she needed. She had, after all, taken a risk helping Amy from the crash scene.

"Yes, you do. But that doesn't change the phone situation." She paused. "Let me get cleaned up. I won't take long. And then, I'll drive you to the closest phone." Sinead turned to leave the room but spun back. "What about you? We need to get you something to wear. I can't take you out in just a robe."

Amy looked at the two. There stood no chance that either of their clothes would fit her tall frame. "If I have to go in a robe, then so be it."

Sinead nodded and left the room. Ruth looked up at Amy.

"You will keep our secret, won't you?" Pleading filled

her eyes.

"Cross my heart," replied Amy, as she did just that. "Do you have someplace I can sit down?"

Ruth smiled and twisted her wheelchair around. "This way."

A minute later, Amy plopped down into a comfortable upholstered chair and used her hands to lift her leg onto the matching hassock. She sighed at the relief she found by elevating her leg, even as limited as that relief was.

"Be right back," said Ruth as she turned and wheeled away. Two minutes later, she returned and tossed something at Amy.

Amy unfolded the clothes Ruth had delivered. A pair of men's overalls and a plaid, button-down shirt.

"Those might fit," said Ruth, with a sly grin.

Amy chuckled. "They just might." She was about to make a reference to the old TV show, *Hee-Haw*, but realized Ruth would have no idea what that was. Truth be told, Amy only knew it through reruns.

Five minutes later, with minimal struggle, she sat there dressed like a farm hand. And she didn't have to remove the splint. The pants leg was wide enough to allow the air splint passage through it. She noticed her reflection in a nearby window. In reality, she looked like a scarecrow that had lost most of its stuffing. The clothes were easily two sizes too big. Still, that was better than a terry robe.

She turned to find Ruth stifling her laughter. Amy threw her hands out to the side, palms up. "Farm chic. What can I say?"

"Homeless high fashion?"

Amy turned her head toward the voice. Sinead had been quick, and she cleaned up well.

"I guess we're both ready." Sinead addressed Ruth. "I won't be long. Would you like to start dinner?"

Ruth looked excited. "Sure. I'd love to." Ruth turned to Amy. "I love to cook, but it's hard from a wheelchair, and I can only stand for so long before tiring out."

"And this will be her first attempt solo. How about spaghetti and meat sauce? Think you can do that? I should be back in half an hour. Forty-five minutes max."

Ruth nodded eagerly. Sinead grabbed her purse and retrieved her keys.

"Okay, let's go. We'll use my car, not the truck."

The rain had slackened but not stopped. Sinead moved the truck and pulled her car as close to the back door as she could. She helped Amy to the car, where she parked herself in the back seat. That allowed her the room to extend her leg, but the activity had retriggered the pain.

Sinead headed down the gravel drive at a slow speed. "Is this okay? Not too bumpy?"

"I'm fine. You can go faster if you want."

Sinead accelerated. "Let me know if it gets uncomfortable."

"I'm fine," Amy repeated. "After I get fixed up, I want to come back. I can help you with . . . with whatever you're running from. Would that be okay?"

Sinead didn't reply right away. "Why don't you leave me your num—?"

The car screeched to a halt. Amy lifted herself in the seat and looked out the window. All she could see was the rushing, muddy water of a flooding creek.

"Well," said Sinead. "Looks like you're coming back earlier than you thought. The flash flood we almost got caught in, took out the bridge."

Six

Lynch held on for dear life. When he had agreed to help Richard in the hunt for Amy, he hadn't anticipated flying. His previous two flights had been with Amy, in the Cessna 172 Skyhawk that she co-owned with her father. During the first of those two flights, she had performed a few aerial acrobatics that had made him swear he'd never fly again. Of course, he hadn't kept that oath, and they flew one last time together hunting for the "monster" who later almost killed them both.

Flying now produced a Pavlovian response in Lynch. His heart rate accelerated. His breathing became a shallow panting, and he knew that if he didn't control it, he'd start experiencing all of the "fun" symptoms hyperventilation had to offer. Why hadn't he spoken up and insisted on helping from the ground?

Why? Because it was Amy they searched for.

"We're in the area where ground control lost contact. That was the last contact with the aircraft. Keep a sharp lookout. We're going to start a grid pattern at a lower altitude."

Craig sounded so calm as he dipped their corporate aircraft closer to the ground that Lynch tried to absorb the man's cool composure. At least he felt confident in the man's ability as a pilot. An ex-Army aviator with hundreds of hours of military air-evac experience, Craig Sheehan had kept the flight smooth despite the weather. Fortunately, the front had moved east and left the search area with calmer skies.

The Bell 407 seated seven in its standard configuration. With Craig and a flight nurse, Lora Marler, in the front, Lynch sat in the starboard, front-facing seat, while Richard sat on the port side. They carried medical supplies strapped into the two rear-facing seats.

Lynch caught Richard looking at his white-knuckle grasp of the seat's armrest and saw a grin develop. Richard reached up toward his headset and keyed on the microphone. "Hey, Lynch. If you want the real feel of flying in a helicopter, we need to open the doors, strap in, and sit on the edge with our feet outside on the skid."

Lynch felt his stomach lurch at the thought. He heard Craig and Lora chuckle. He obviously had not succeeded in hiding his distaste for flying.

"That would give you a much better observation point, too," said Craig.

"Thanks, guys. I think I have a pretty good vantage point already." Lynch turned and focused his gaze out the large window in the door. If they passed by a grounded helicopter, or crash site, on his side, he would see it.

The aircraft flew on, but the group remained mostly silent, ignoring the earlier attempt at levity. Lynch could feel the tension in the others. He and Richard knew Amy. Yet, Craig and Lora knew the entire crew as if they were family. Lynch could identify with that. As a police officer, he had been a member of the "thin blue line," where every fellow officer had been part of that extended family. He'd only been back "from the dead" a month or so and already missed that.

After dozens of passes across their grid, Lynch checked his watch. Including the time it took to fly from the company's headquarters, they had been flying for just over three hours now. He had no idea how long they could stay in the air, but he suspected they were nearing the end of their cruise endurance. So far, they had seen nothing, and the two other MedAir choppers had made no sighting either.

A couple of minutes later, the aircraft veered off the course they'd been taking.

"We need to refuel," said Craig through the intercom. "We're going to fly into Springfield to do that."

"Isn't Quincy closer?" asked Richard.

"It is, but we're going to get assistance by the State Police. I'm not sure yet in what form, ground or air, or both. Anyway, I need to coordinate with them in Springfield."

Twenty-some minutes later, they were on the ground, and Lynch felt so much better, even though he knew he would be back in the air shortly. Craig and Lora had disappeared into a nearby building, while the flight services ground crew handled the refueling.

Richard stood next to him. "I'm going to stretch my legs and follow Craig. Wanna join me?"

"Sure."

Lynch thought it felt good to walk, like God intended man to do. They entered a single story building identified by a sign saying McClelland Flight Services, Flight Operations. Inside, Lynch saw everything needed to handle flight crews, passengers, and maintenance staff. They followed Craig into the weather room, which held maps, computers for weather, and more.

He and Richard listened in as Craig briefed two members of the Illinois State Police Air Operations. The ISP's fleet consisted of five Cessna 182's, two of which were available to assist in the search. He watched Craig pointing to a paper map on the wall, as he outlined the grid his teams had been flying. Something caught his attention.

"Craig, excuse me. Umm, something's not right. Could you show me where traffic control lost contact again?"

Craig tapped on the map coordinate with his index finger.

"And what was their original flight plan?"

Craig traced the rough path with his finger. "This is the path we tracked. We use a company called Flight-Trax to satellite track all of our aircraft in the air. We use a two-minute interval between pings. The last ping was here, and air traffic control lost them here, just a few seconds later." He tapped the map again. "That means they were coming down, because the controllers only lose them under a certain altitude."

Lynch saw a different pattern emerging, but he needed one more bit of information.

"Can anyone show me what the weather was doing at the time just before and at the time we lost contact? In particular, can I see what the wind was doing then?"

One of the ISP officers raised an eyebrow but nodded. He motioned for Lynch to join him at one of the computers.

"Okay, I'll start at a point four hours ago and move forward in time."

Lynch nodded. "That should work."

He watched as the radar looped ahead in time until just before radar contact was lost. In his head, he saw the aircraft being carried by the wind. They had been looking too far west.

"We've been searching the wrong area. They have to be at least 15 miles farther east."

"That would put them just northwest of us here in town, east of the Illinois River," said the officer. "Our computer model doesn't agree. We think they're west of the river, probably less than a mile from where contact was lost."

Lynch shook his head. Walking back to the wall map, he put his finger on an area of land and circled it. "We've been searching west of the river and found nothing. I think they're somewhere in here."

The officer shook his head again. "I don't see how that could happen."

Lynch thought about what he saw in his head. He had a gift for seeing patterns but not for explaining how he saw them or for explaining what he saw. How could he explain it now?

"I don't know if I can explain it, but look at the flight plan. That plan would have taken them along this path." He moved his finger across the map, following the expected movement of the helicopter. "And you said the last satellite ping had them here." He tapped a spot on the map. "Then, within seconds, they're way over here." He points to the location of last contact. "That wasn't just a slight drift off the flight plan. They had to have been hit by a pretty strong wind, and if that wind still controlled them, they wouldn't be just a mile or two away. Within the two-minute span, before the next expected ping, they could be at least ten miles farther east. I think it's more than that."

The second ISP pilot half nodded and addressed his

peer. "He could be right, Joe."

Lynch could see that Joe didn't want to accede easily to Lynch's reasoning.

After a moment of reflection, Joe said, "Okay, maybe. Tell you what, I'll pick up the grid where you left off, west of the river." He looked at his fellow officer. "And why don't you fly the river itself. We can't ignore the possibility that the aircraft went down into the water." Then, he turned to Craig. "And you guys can check out your hunch, or join one of us."

Lynch held his tongue. The pilot wouldn't call it a "hunch" if he believed Lynch to be even half right. He never understood why some people held on to their beliefs even when facts showed them otherwise. But then, Lynch couldn't say he had facts on his side, just sound reasoning and his "gift."

Lynch could see Craig vacillating as well. Richard stepped forward and placed a hand on Craig's shoulder.

"Let's go with Lynch's plan. I've been told he can see patterns where no one else would suspect one, and his gut instincts saved a lot of lives when that terrorist bomb exploded at the American Party headquarters last week. That's one of the reasons I asked to bring him along. My bet is on him."

Craig took a deep breath and sighed, before nodding. "Okay, we'll focus east of the river." He stepped up to the map. "Lynch, show me again where you think we should search."

Fifteen minutes later, they were back in the air—and Lynch held on for dear life. Yet, that didn't stop him from reflecting on what *wasn't* said during the briefing. The next satellite ping never came. Worse. Every aircraft had an ELT,

Emergency Locator Transmitter. It, too, never activated.

Detective Tammy Jahn saw the exchange 100 yards down the street as she made the jog past St. Matthew the Apostle Catholic Church on Kennerly Avenue in her unmarked car. The two men must have seen her as well and made her as a cop, because they bolted in opposite directions. She couldn't tell who was dealing and who was buying, but one man jumped a chain-link fence and ran north through an empty parking lot, while the other headed south past an abandoned building. She wasn't about to get out and chase one or the other, with only a 50-50 chance of getting the dealer, and better-than-even odds of becoming a target for somebody with a grudge against the police. Sadly, the latter scenario had become more and more common in those parts of St. Louis controlled by gangs.

She glanced down at her handwritten note. The object of her patrol had been reported in this vicinity.

She drove slowly down Kennerly, a street of modestly kept homes with abandoned and boarded-up houses and empty lots interspersed between many of them. There was more of such openness now than when she had patrolled these streets in uniform. As a rookie fresh out of the academy, she had been assigned to District 8, part of the city's North Patrol, whose headquarters had a sign above the door, "North Patrol—Home of the *Real* Police."

One had to be a pretty "bad ass" kind of cop to work that district. The "armpit of the city," as they called it, required special fortitude, as well as people skills that most would find amazing. Back then, 80% of the people you encountered were unemployed—and unwashed—with no lack of time on their hands and an astounding creativity for getting into trouble. The remaining 20% were old, retired, and trapped in deteriorating homes they had no hope of selling. Drug dealing, prostitution, theft, assaults and worse took place on these streets daily. Some of the things they had witnessed on patrol were so bizarre, the old timers joked about being willing to work some days for free just for the entertainment.

Today, 15 years and one redistricting later, these streets were part of District 5. Most of the abandoned homes had been torn down, and the crime had diminished. Well, it seemed less. At least the hookers no longer performed their services in cars parked openly on the street, pulling their toothbrushes and mouthwash from their bags as they left the car. Tammy had often wondered why these "ladies" even bothered, with the toothbrushes, that is. Combined, the two dozen or more that she had booked while there didn't have enough teeth to fill one mouth, courtesy of their meth habits.

Tammy watched the two men disappear from view. She didn't have time to bother with a small-time street dealer anyway. Let the Feds deal with the drug problem. Of course, the "War on Drugs" had produced rampant drug use, and now marijuana was legal in several states. And the "War on Poverty" resulted in ever widening income disparities and more families living below the poverty level. The government's "War on Terror" had shown similar dismal results to date—the loss of rights and privacy for its citizens, thousands of illegal aliens flooding across the country's southern border, and the formation of close to three dozen paramilitary training camps for jihadists across the country, to which hundreds of those illegals had flocked. If you want negative results, just ask the federal government to take the lead.

Tammy could say, with pride, that she had been successful in her war on gangs, in her own small way. As a detective assigned to the Juvenile Division of the Metro PD, she worked with the GREAT Program—Gang Resistance Education and Training. She could personally claim over four dozen young men that she'd helped to avoid gang involvement. All of the older ones had graduated from high school, and most of them were now in college or vocational school.

The one young man who now seemed ready to tarnish her so-far-unblemished record was the target of her search this afternoon. She found the address she'd hastily scratched onto a scrap of lined notebook paper. Yet another abandoned brick home, although this one had gang-sign graffiti spray-painted onto the wall facing an empty lot. She found that disconcerting.

"1534," Tammy spoke into her mic.

"1534." The dispatcher sounded out of breath.

"I'm at 4006 Kennerly and request assistance."

Most of the local gang members knew her and gave her begrudging respect, but she knew better than to take an unnecessary risk. A new recruit with an itchy trigger finger was all it might take to create a new statistic and one more dead officer. Over 500 police officers had been feloniously killed over the past decade. Nearly 52,000 officers had been assaulted in the same time period, with 28 percent of those officers receiving injuries.

She listened to make sure her request went out. Now, she just had to wait for backup and watch the building.

Until the 1950s, The Ville neighborhood had been one

of two areas in St. Louis where blacks could live. During the 1960's, they began to spread out, and by the 1980's, the Crips and Bloods had moved into the district. The Ville and other NorthSide neighborhoods had since become the most dangerous areas of St. Louis. Gunfire was a nightly occurrence, and those brave enough to wander outside after dark never knew if one of those bullets had their name on it.

Kennerly, although sitting squarely within The Ville, sat between established gang territories. The Bloods and Crips danced tenuously back and forth over adjacent areas just six blocks to the north, while a stronghold for the Crips sat four blocks south. To see the Bloods seeking control between two Crips territories meant one thing only—trouble.

A two-man patrol car rolled up behind her, and both officers climbed out of the car. She exited her car and walked back to meet them. She knew and liked both men. Rogers was white, late thirties, and a training officer of good standing. He'd been in District 8 about the same time as she and had transitioned to District 5 with the changes. She often wondered why he hadn't parlayed his time there into a better job, but he had once told her he was a street cop and would always remain one. Williams was black and in his mid-forties. He had grown up on the north side and had found his way to give back to his community by becoming a police officer. He had helped her on more than one occasion by using his ties to the neighborhood to connect her to the right person. Both men were experienced and usually rode with younger officers who had less of that precious commodity.

"Hey, how'd you two end up in the same car?"

"Your Daddy thought he needed retraining," said Rogers, pointing his head toward Williams.

"I drew the short straw and lost," said Williams simultaneously.

They also grinned in unison. Cop humor was rarely *self*-deprecating and more commonly a game of one-upmanship, like siblings poking and teasing one another. And only in the city did the officers call their sergeants "Your Daddy," not usually meant as a term of endearment.

"So, what's up?" asked Williams.

"Lookin' for one of my kids, Montez Johnson. Age 15. He's been a regular at our GREAT meetings until about two weeks ago. He stopped coming around, and a cousin told me the Bloods were riding him hard to join them. I started asking around, and about half an hour ago I got an anonymous tip that he was holed up here. Just want to check it out."

"Let's do it," replied Rogers.

Together with the men, Tammy walked toward the boarded-up building, hand on gun and eyes scanning the windows for any sign of movement. Williams tested the front door. Secure. They moved to the right of the house, and something caught Tammy's eye behind the house across the empty lot. She glanced that way and saw a little girl, maybe six, bouncing up and down on a "ghetto trampoline," an old mattress. The youngster appeared to be having fun, until she saw them. In an instant, she stopped and ran into the house. It was not uncommon for kids that age to be used as spotters.

"Keep an eye on that house across the lot. Little girl just ran inside," said Williams. He had seen her, too.

The trio rounded the corner to the back of the house,

and Rogers put his hand up for them to stop.

"Shh, someone's inside. Careful." He pulled his gun as Williams nudged the plywood over the back door. It wasn't secure, just leaning up against the frame, and toppled backward smacking the ground.

At that, the loud noise of wood shattering hit them, coming from the side of the house. Gun drawn, Tammy raced to the corner of the building in time to see two young black males jumping from a side window, its plywood cover splintered and in pieces on the ground, and racing away from the lot. Neither one was Montez, and she wouldn't give chase. Besides, they were running in front of both patrol cars. Odds were good that one or both dash cameras caught a look at their faces. They'd find them later, if necessary.

As she returned to the rear door, she found that Rogers had already entered the building, and Williams waved her inside as well. The obvious signs of people living, or hiding, there were everywhere—fast food wrappers, empty water and beer bottles, and ragged blankets littered most of the lower floor's rooms. The doorway to the basement stepped off into nothing. She could see the rotting remains of the stairs eight feet below. The stench of urine and feces assaulted them as they approached the front room, where they found two orange Home Depot 5-gallon buckets that acted as the occupants' makeshift latrine.

At the base of the stairway to the second floor, she saw droplets that appeared to be old blood. As Williams took to the first step, ever wary of someone having the advantage of high ground, they heard a loud moan from above. With the first floor cleared, she and Rogers covered him as he climbed the stairs. He ducked around the corner in the hallway above, and then returned, waving them up. Rogers remained at the base of the steps to cover their rear.

She and Williams cleared the first bedroom quickly. Another groan. In the second room, Tammy saw a body on the floor, a trail of blood droplets leading to it. She remained in the doorway as Williams cleared the remaining three rooms.

"No attic. We're clear," he said.

Tammy moved to the body as Williams covered her. Although she could not yet see a face, the size and frame of the young black male lying there seemed familiar and a shiver went through her. As she neared she could see that his breathing was erratic. She felt a weak pulse in his neck as she turned him onto his back.

Montez.

She saw a stab wound below his sternum but no sign of active bleeding.

"We need EMS."

Williams keyed the lapel mic of his radio. "1512."

"1512," replied the dispatcher.

"We need EMS. Expedite."

"1512, we have you at 4006 Kennerly. EMS is being dispatched and expedited."

Montez stared at her, his eyes pleading for help. And then they turned dull.

Seven

Upon returning to the house, Amy settled back into the upholstered chair. Her leg ached along with her spirit. She needed medical care. She needed to contact her company. She needed to get word to the families of the others, despite it being bad news. Had a search started for them? How could she get word to MedAir? Her emotions roiled with each throb in her leg.

She raised her head to the sound of hissing coming from the kitchen. At first, she thought maybe it was hot water boiling in a teapot, until the tones became an anemic attempt at the melody of a song. Was that Ruth whistling?

Amy grabbed the walker that Sinead had placed next to the chair and pushed herself upright. Her leg didn't appreciate that decision, but Amy tried to console it internally by thinking that the pain meds were in the kitchen. Sinead had been correct in stating that ibuprofen would not be enough.

"Hi. Is that you whistling?"

Ruth slowly turned toward her and smiled. "Pretty pathetic, isn't it? I used to be able to really whistle, but then I got worse. For a while I could barely pucker my lips or even suck on a straw, so I'm happy I can do what I can now."

Amy thought about that. The girl seemed upbeat and

optimistic. Yet, she had to have her worries, too. Amy still wondered what Ruth's underlying medical condition could be. She didn't look like someone with cerebral palsy. Muscular dystrophy perhaps. She hesitated in asking. That was personal info, and she had no right to know.

"What song?"

"Taylor Swift's 'A Place in This World.' The lyrics talk of moving on, not knowing what's coming, but staying strong, even when you're wrong. I used to sing it a lot. Not so much now."

"Why not?"

"Cuz the chorus talks of being alone and on my own." She paused. "Well, I used to be alone, but then my mom came for me and I don't feel that way anymore."

Another clue? A tear came to Amy's eye, as she nodded in acknowledgment. Whatever this teen had been going through must be like a nightmare. For parents and siblings, too. She eased her way to the opposite counter where the bottle of pain medication sat. She struggled with the adult-proof cap and finally popped it off the bottle so she could retrieve one capsule. She would take it with lunch, not on an empty stomach.

Ruth half-sang and half-spoke another phrase from the lyrics but stopped. "My mom and me really are on a mission. I may not be ready to fly, but I *am* getting stronger."

Amy smiled. "I think you're right about that." She paused and contemplated those words. A girl on a mission. "I can see why you connect with that song."

Ruth shrugged. "Yeah. I guess." She used the countertop for support as she stirred the sauce for their lunch. "Are you hungry? I made plenty. Actually, I hoped you'd stay long enough to eat, but I know you need to get to the doctor, too."

"Smells good. And I am hungry." Amy contemplated the wisdom of eating right now. If her leg required surgery, she'd have to be NPO—Latin for 'nil per os,' or nothing by mouth—for at least 12 hours. But then, she had never yet encountered an orthopedic surgeon who insisted on immediate surgery, unless the total loss of the limb was a risk. Eating now seemed unlikely to delay her care. Finding a way out to get to that care remained her main obstacle.

"Good, 'cause it's almost ready." Ruth stirred the pasta and pulled out a piece to test.

"Guess I'm right on time, then."

Amy and Ruth both turned at the sound of Sinead's voice from the doorway.

"I'll get plates and utensils. We can eat in the dining room. That way, there's room for you to put your leg up. I already moved the cushioned hassock in there for you." Sinead addressed the last two comments toward Amy.

At that moment, the sound of a helicopter flying overhead caught Amy's ears. And the look of her hostesses frozen in fear flashed into her eyes. In that instant, for a reason she didn't understand, she shared their anxiety.

Lynch gazed across miles of stark, muddy farm fields as they flew. He knew in his heart that he was right about the location of the helicopter, but so far, they had yet to find it. The heavy rains had prevented the farmers from working their fields, but they passed over a dozen or more homes, along with their outbuildings. Since they flew at such a low altitude, he saw people working on equipment, dealing with their livestock, and attending to storm damage. A few waved, but more as a courteous greeting than as a way of getting attention, as if they had helpful information. Apparently, none of these good folks had seen their downed aircraft, or if they had seen it in the air, perhaps they didn't recognize that it was in trouble.

Richard looked bleak. With every unsuccessful pass they made, he seemed more distressed. Lynch could understand that, but he refused to give up emotionally. He *knew* they'd find it. It couldn't be far away.

Their flight grid took them along a north-south pattern. After a few more passes, Lynch would suggest re-flying the area on an east-west pattern. He had learned from a previous case that trees had an uncanny way of hiding what one wished to find from the air, even something as big as the 40-foot motor coach he and Amy had sought months earlier. With the trees leafing out, they could hide more than that. Changing the viewing angle could mean the difference between finding the target or not.

And despite the acres and acres of mud he witnessed as they flew, tree lines separated many fields and lined the creeks and watersheds. There were even a few small forests, although he suspected that once on the ground, those woods would not seem so minute.

"That house looks empty," said Richard.

Lynch couldn't see the building from his side of the aircraft and suspected that Richard was simply trying to start a conversation. This second portion of the flight had been mostly silent since leaving Springfield, with all four of them focused on the ground.

"Maybe," replied Craig. "I've seen some other buildings that appear empty or abandoned. Looks like the creek is flooding and the bridge is gone. You may be right. It'd be hard to get in and out of that place right now."

Lora seemed focused on something to their starboard side. She craned her head to look again.

"Do you see something?" asked Craig.

"I'm not sure. Thought I saw light flash off something metal or glass. Out in a field to our east. It's gone now. It might have reflected off a pool of water, too.

"We'll catch it on the next pass."

Lynch strained to look back behind them, to the point where the nurse had seen something. Did he see something metallic in the mud, too? In thinking about it, a piece of farm equipment could have been left in the field. He knew that DOT road crews often left their mowers where they stopped for the day, to pick up on the following day where they left off. Did farmers do the same thing?

A sudden bright flash of light made him look away for a moment.

"I just saw something, too," he said, after keying on his mic. "Too big and too bright for reflection off a puddle. Besides, any water standing in these fields is likely to be too muddy to reflect much sunlight."

"True," replied Lora.

"We'll be back over that area in about ten minutes on our grid. Or do you think I should go back and investigate?" asked Craig.

"Keep flying," answered Lynch.

"Go back," said Richard.

Lora looked at Craig and shook her head. "I'm not breaking that tie. Up to you."

The helicopter maintained its course for a minute and suddenly veered back. "It's the first suspicious thing we've seen since we got here. We can always get back on the grid if it's nothing."

"And if someone's hurt, every minute counts," added Richard.

Despite his earlier "vote," Lynch couldn't disagree with either statement.

Lynch could now see the empty house that Richard had noted. He, too, saw nothing to indicate anyone lived there.

Craig keyed his mic, "We should—"

"That's it," yelled Lora and Richard at the same time. Lora pointed repeatedly to the spot.

Craig slowed and circled to land. He shook his head, but Lynch noticed he said nothing. Richard, too, stared at the location, said nothing, and then dropped his gaze to the floor. As they circled, he now could see what they saw, and it didn't look good.

Most distressing of all . . . no one stood there to greet them.

"Hey, maybe they've hiked out to find transportation," said Lynch, but his attempt to brighten the outlook fell on deaf ears, until Richard pulled out his cell phone.

"Maybe so. I'm not getting any cell service at all here. If their phones wouldn't work, they'd have to hike out to get help."

"Gonna be real muddy," said Craig as they landed. No one seemed to care. As soon as he gave the okay, Lynch and the other two were out the doors. Lynch could see the other MedAir helicopters in the distance, converging on the scene.

Muddy wasn't the word for the glop they landed in as they emerged from the aircraft. There'd be no running to the crash site. The field was better suited for a mud wrestling competition than anything else.

Lora appeared lighter on her feet than any of the guys, and she made good headway toward the downed chopper. About halfway there, he saw her stop suddenly and fall to her knees. As he neared, he saw that she was crying.

"Lora?"

She answered only by pointing. Lynch saw what had stopped her. A male body, one lower extremity torn away, lay face down in the mud. Richard caught up to them, and Lynch put his arm out to stay his friend.

"You might not want to go any farther."

Richard's face turned ashen upon seeing the dead crew member. He pushed Lynch's arm away.

"I've pulled pieces of friends together for body bags. I dragged crushed bodies from downed helicopters. I've tried to comfort little girls who had acid thrown on them for the 'crime' of wanting an education. Afghanistan was no picnic. I've seen the worst of it." He started to step past Lynch, his face set in grim determination.

Lynch again raised his arm to stop him. "Maybe. But you weren't engaged to any of them. If bad turns to worst, what image of Amy do you want in your head for the rest of your life?"

That stopped Richard.

"Let me go on. Lora, you, too. Let me go first. I'll call you in, if your skills are needed."

Lynch felt his heart pounding. He tried to detach his emotions, but realized that he, too, had to consider what image of Amy he wanted to live with. Yet, someone had to be first. He seemed to be the best candidate, the one with the least attachment to the crew.

"Don't touch anyone or anything. NTSB and the ISP will need photos," yelled Craig, as he emerged from their aircraft after shutting down the engine.

That wasn't likely to happen in any reasonable timeframe. The National Transportation Safety Board had "Go" teams located all across the country, but it still might take them a day or better to arrive on scene. Lynch figured the ISP would take whatever photos they might need and allow MedAir to transport the bodies to Springfield. That could still take a few hours. This was not going to be pleasant.

He forced his legs to start tramping toward the main wreckage. Along the way, he saw various pieces of the chopper and remnants of medical equipment—a shattered defibrillator, a duffel torn in half with boxes of medications and fluid bags littering the ground around it. But no other bodies—or parts.

Lynch arrived at the body of the helicopter and noticed its condition. It lay on its port side, its rotors missing. He recalled seeing what looked to be part of the main rotor embedded in the field a distance from where they landed. Craig had made a point of not landing anywhere along the path of the crash or within its debris field. Other bodies could lie along that path. Yet, first, he needed to clear the main wreckage. As with automobiles, a person's chances of survival were greatest if he stayed confined within the vehicle. Bodies ejected from a vehicle had a 95% mortality rate. For one crew member here, that had been 100%.

He found the pilot strapped into his seat. He saw no signs of life. His neck appeared to be broken, and he had been impaled by what appeared to be a broken piece of metal fence post. To be thorough, Lynch checked for a pulse and, as expected, found none. The man's body was cold to the touch. Ambient temperature.

Only Amy remained unaccounted for.

He smelled the rancid odor of burning plastic, but he saw no smoke or flames. He could see no one else inside the main compartment, but his view was hindered in several places. He made his way to the exposed belly of the bird and hoisted himself onto the right skid. He moved to a point where he could see inside.

Empty, but he saw signs of fire and the remaining passenger seat had charred to the point only the frame remained intact. A quick inspection found the fire extinguisher still sitting in its bracket near the pilot's seat. The heavy rains must have doused the fire. Fortunately, helicopter fuel pods were designed to be rupture-proof in a crash scenario such as this aircraft had endured. The fuel line connection to the pod, as well, was made to break free and self-seal. If not, the odds would have been in favor of their finding a burnt-out shell and nothing more of this chopper.

Sliding back to earth, he strained to see any sign of life around him. The understory of the tree line appeared largely clear. The shrubs had not leafed out as fully as the more exposed trees, so he could see through them easily enough. The debris field indeed stopped right here. He stooped to inspect under the chopper and then climbed the strut once again to scrutinize the inside. The port doors had been ripped away, so raw earth could be seen through most of the area under the aircraft. Unless Amy's body was directly under the main engine, he saw no evidence of a body trapped beneath.

As he looked once again at the dirt around him, did he see traces of other footprints? He claimed no tracking expertise, but for a few feet, there appeared to be one set of footprints, small and much deeper than he would expect from someone with a foot that small. Once they emerged from the limited cover of the trees, the rain appeared to have washed them completely away.

He returned to the front of the aircraft and back along the path he had already taken. He wanted to minimize any changes to the scene on his part.

Craig had joined the other two, who had moved no farther from where Lynch had left them. All three held a look of defeat. He had expected nothing else. After all, he hadn't called them for help and that meant only one thing.

Tears flowed from Lora's eyes, and Richard choked on the question he appeared to want to ask but couldn't.

Craig finally broke the ice. "Well?"

Lynch took a deep breath and replied, "Your pilot's dead."

Richard cocked his head as if to ask, "And?"

"No sign of Amy. There might be a single set of footprints leading away from the scene. They're washed out once they get into the open field, so I could be imagining them." He saw the look of hope flash onto Richard's face. "Look, they were too small for Amy and too deep for someone who might have a foot that size. I think we need to trace back along this debris field, but along its margins so we don't compromise any investigation. She could be out there."

"She's alive. I know it." Richard put both hands up to his head and rubbed his temples with the palms of his hands.

"Maybe, but we need to check the field."

"I understand that. But she's alive. Someone rescued her. I've seen that overseas. The footprints are deep because someone was carrying a heavy weight. Amy. Well, not that Amy's heavy. Don't you ever tell her I called her heavy. Now, we just have to find her." He grinned.

The change in Richard bordered on manic. Lynch could understand the man's feelings. Despite two deaths, Richard now focused on Amy as his main and only concern. To Lynch, this didn't come across as disrespect for the dead crew members but as a new urgency to find the only remaining crew member who might be alive and possibly injured, needing assistance. Nothing would bring back the deceased, but their efforts could possibly prevent one more death.

Richard turned and began to walk back along the debris field, taking care to stay on its periphery. Lynch turned to Craig.

"He might be right, about the footprints. It makes sense."

Craig nodded. "And if he's right, then he's also correct about our needing to find her. Lynch, you go help him. I'll get one of our other crews to do a low, slow sweep of this field in the air. They can cover the area faster than any of us on the ground. The State Police should be here shortly."

Lynch nodded, turned, and slipped as he tried to catch up, his rear landing with a distinct 'splatt' as he hit the mud. He quickly looked around to see if anyone else saw him. They all had.

He muttered to himself as he stood, not without difficulty. At least he was in a flight suit and not his civies. It, like the boots, would be cleaned on someone else's dime and time. The slight stain in his pride, however, was his alone to deal with.

He called to Richard. "Hey, wait up!"

Richard stopped but continued to scan the area around him. A moment later, one of the other MedAir choppers eased past, about 20 feet off the ground, moving slowly along the debris field. Lynch wished he had a portable radio to communicate with them.

"I see the guy's leg, over there," said Richard as Lynch joined him. "There's the patient stretcher and a bunch of other stuff. Must have come out when the port door ripped off. There's the door."

Lynch nodded and pointed farther out. "There's one rotor sticking up out of the dirt."

Together they walked, stopping every ten or so feet to scan the area. About 30 feet beyond the rotor, Lynch noted a huge gouge in the earth and pointed to it.

Richard nodded. "I'm not an expert, but I saw a few crashes overseas. Looks to me like a skid caught and dug into the dirt. Probably caused the chopper to flip and that put that one rotor into the ground. With the momentum, the rotor broke off and they probably rolled once or twice before sliding into the trees."

"Still no sign of Amy, though. And if the aircraft was intact at that point of impact, we should have, unless—"

"Unless she somehow survived and someone rescued her. I keep telling you all, I know she's alive. I just know it."

Lynch felt a new confidence that they would find her. Yet, he knew they still had to search the opposite side of the debris field. He had seen automobile crash victims ejected farther from their vehicle than most people suspected could be possible. Had she been ejected during the rolling of the aircraft, she could be far across the field from their current position.

"We need to canvass the other side of the debris field," he said. "She could have been ejected."

Richard stopped walking. Lynch could see that he didn't want to consider that deadly possibility, but he took a deep breath and nodded. "Then we should also widen our search on this side."

The man was correct. "Let's get some help. You keep going. I'll go let Craig know what we've found so far." He looked up at the sound of another helicopter. "Looks like the ISP folks are arriving. I'll need to brief them, too. We'll get all the manpower we can muster to spread out the search."

"Thanks." Richard glanced at the dirt and returned his gaze to Lynch. "I mean it. Thanks for all your help. I appreciate it, and I know Amy will, too. When we find her."

Lynch nodded and clapped his hand on his new friend's shoulder. "We'll find her."

Lynch returned to Craig and within minutes, the other crew members had formed a search line that spread out 90 feet across that side of the field. With a searcher every ten feet, they could systematically cross the field and theoretically not miss anything of importance, certainly not a body. However, Lynch now felt that inner voice—a still, small voice he had begun to trust with more assurance—affirm to him that they would indeed find Amy alive.

As the sounds of additional helicopters permeated the dwelling, Amy could see the anxiety mount in mother and daughter. They were so close to being discovered. And when that happened, what would take place next? Amy's heart went out to Ruth. How would she have reacted if she had been in the girl's place?

She saw Ruth begin to tremble. Amy found herself praying to remain hidden, along with Sinead and Ruth. She subjugated her own condition, even the risk of losing her foot, to the well-being of this family. And with that decision of sacrifice, she felt a wave of peace wash over her. She knew God would care for them all.

"So, let's eat," she exclaimed. She saw uncertainty on their faces. "Look, two things. They just found the crash scene, and it will take them a while to process things. Yes, it won't take them long to realize I'm not there, and then they'll start spreading out their search. That alone gives us time to eat and strategize. I'm on your side. Remember? Secondly, if we can't get out, they can't get in. Right?"

Sinead shook her head. "Not exactly. It's true they won't be able to get here by ground until the creek recedes to a passable depth. But, they have helicopters. They might not be able to land next to the house here, but they could land in the adjacent field and walk to the house."

Tears formed in Ruth's eyes. That tore at Amy's emotions.

"Okay, so we need to eat quickly and form a strategy as we eat." She looked at the pill in her hand. "Right now, I need to sit down and take one of these." She closed her eyes and took a deep breath. Yes, she really did need to sit down and put her leg up.

As Amy moved to the table, Sinead did not hesitate to dish up lunch for them all. As she finally sat down to join Ruth and Amy, she bowed her head and closed her eyes. Amy surmised she was praying for more than the food. She followed suit but spoke out loud. "Lord, we bless this food in your name, but more importantly, we need your inspiration. We know that your hand is upon this situation, so Lord, I pray that *Your* will be accomplished here. We know that you have only our best interests at heart. Thank you, Lord."

As they ate in silence, an idea formed in Amy's mind. It wasn't a great plan, but in its simplicity, it just might work.

"Not much strategizing going on here," she quipped. She smiled. The pain pill was working its magic. "Well, I have an idea. Tell me what you think."

Sinead nodded. "Good, because my mind is a blank. All I can think about is getting caught."

"So . . . folks around here think this house is unoccupied. So, then, we need to make sure it looks that way. Power off. Heat off. Rooms cleaned. The kitchen has to look unused."

"What about our car?" asked Ruth.

Amy hadn't thought about that. She scratched her head. "We need to move it to the barn or a shed. Take off the license plates so no one can trace them and cover it somehow to make it look like it's being stored."

"That could work. I pulled an old tarp off the pickup truck. I could use that. And there's room next to the truck to park it."

"Good. If the place is locked up and looks unused by anyone looking through the windows, they're unlikely to break in. You can hide in that safe room, the storm room, you told me about at one point. They won't find you."

"But if they're looking for you, they might break in," stated Ruth. Amy could see the concern still etched on her face.

Amy smiled. "First off, they'll realize I couldn't get in with the doors locked, and if I'd broken in, the door would show that. Second, I won't be here."

"What?" Now Sinead showed a new concern.

"I'm going to put my flight suit back on. You only cut the one leg open to help me get it off, so I can put it back on. And I'll be out in the barn, with the duffels. They're likely to search the outbuildings before ever considering breaking into an empty house."

Amy could see that Sinead thought this might work. Ruth didn't look as convinced.

Sinead inhaled sharply. "Then, we need to get busy. Ruth, you start on the kitchen. Clean up our lunch mess and put away everything on the counters that wasn't there when we got here. Leave any trash under the sink, and we'll just have to hope they don't go looking into the trash. I'll deal with the car and hope it cools off before anyone examines it."

"I'll change clothes and repack the duffels. Ummm, anything else?"

"Yeah," said Ruth. "How did you get here, along with the duffels?"

Yeah, how will have I gotten here, thought Amy. *There were no crutches in the 407.* She sighed. "Good question. I had to have walked here. Maybe crawled part of the way. So, I'll need something convincing as a crutch."

"And in the rain, so you'll need to be soaked and muddy."

"And the duffels, too. You couldn't have carried them, so your only option would have been to drag them behind you. They'll need to be muddy, too."

Amy wasn't sure she liked where this was going, but

she liked that these two were thorough.

"Maybe you could have used a couple of rolls of long gauze as a tether with one end tied to the duffels and the other around your shoulder. We'll have to fashion the tether, then soak it and get it all muddy, too."

Yes, quite thorough. And she was about to spend hours in a barn—wet, cold, and muddy—while hoping they even come to the house looking for her. What if they do all of this and the search crews don't even show up, thinking the place abandoned? She could be out there for two days, working up to a case of pneumonia, to no avail.

However, something told her this would be the first place they looked, after combing the crash scene and nearby fields.

Thirty minutes later, the car was stored in the barn, the house looked abandoned, the duffels looked like something from a mud volleyball game, and the tether straggling from the duffels looked well-worn and filthy. Now, it was her turn.

Re-dressed in her flight suit, Amy stepped outside into the 50-degree weather and wondered if there was an alternative.

"Let me help you," said Sinead.

With the woman's assistance, Amy sat down into the mud of the tilled ground and began to scoop up handfuls of the glop to cover her knees and lower torso.

"Do you mind?" asked Sinead.

Amy shook her head. With that, Sinead dumped a bucket of ice-cold water, freshly hand-pumped from a nearby shallow well, over Amy's head. Her body shook violently from the cold. She looked up and glanced toward the house. Ruth stared from the closest window and started to laugh.

At first, Amy refused to see the humor in her situation, but as she reflected on it, she smiled. Maybe this was her ice-bucket challenge. Now muddy and wet to her core, she must look a sight.

"If anyone asks, you don't know if this well is safe to drink, but you did anyway."

"I thought there were water bottles in the one duffel."

Sinead looked sheepish. "There were. I hope you don't mind, but I took them. They weren't in there to begin with, so I thought someone might wonder where they came from. I had to scavenge them from around a spot you would have had trouble getting to. Plus, we might have to stay in that storm shelter for a few days, and the water is turned off now."

Amy nodded. Having one bottle would have been nice, but she was right. In all likelihood, Amy was but a few hours away from rescue. She wouldn't need them.

"Want me to help you to the barn?"

Amy shook her head. "Nope. We've gone this far to make it look like I did this on my own. I'll make my own drag marks from the well to the barn."

Sinead nodded. "Sorry."

"About what?"

"All of this. I wish I could have driven you out. And I know you wanted to know more about Ruth's condition."

"Let's consider it a rain-check, in the true sense of the word. I might not be able to find my way back here, but you have my address and number, if you need it. Now, get inside."

Amy watched the woman return to the house. She then took a deep breath and worked her way to the barn. The old branch they'd found made a convincing crutch. The whole story, however? Well, she wasn't convinced the police would buy it. But, it would be her story, and she'd stick to it.

Eight

Detective Jahn sat in her car, close to tears. Had no one else been within view, she knew the tears would be flowing freely, but other police officers, as well as Montez' family, were 15 feet away in the front yard of Gloria Taylor, the mother of Montez Johnson. Only her District 8 "breeding" and its inherent machismo kept her from the emotional display that tried to erupt.

She had held it together long enough to inform Ms. Taylor of her son's death and, after some words of consolation, had retreated to her car. The anguish that only a mother could feel now showed from Ms. Taylor's every pore. The woman's sister held her tightly. Other family members, however, displayed anger and distrust of the police officers there, as if *they* had killed Montez. Why was it that even when the gangs, or a rival, or even someone just mad at the way you drove, murdered the young men of the neighborhood, it somehow became the fault of the police?

Tammy laid her forehead on the steering wheel and fought the emotional currents inside. She had worked so closely with Montez that she thought he had moved beyond the peer pressure. He had talked of vocational school, even though his grades and intelligence merited something more. She had talked to him about college, but for whatever reason, that possibility had been ingrained in him as an impossibility. She thought she had planted a seed of optimism within him, to see beyond what his family kept telling him.

Why had he died?

A growing anger filled her. She would find those responsible, along with their reason, and deliver justice to Ms. Taylor.

The opening of her passenger door startled her. Had she forgotten to lock it? In the city and certain surrounding communities, leaving a side door unlocked was an invitation to trouble. A Maryland Heights police sergeant had learned that the hard way. He had been on a stake-out when a young thug popped open his passenger door, thinking he could carjack some unsuspecting white guy. As soon as he realized it was a police car, he fired his stolen handgun at the officer and ran. The slug caught the sergeant in the face, but he survived. Officers throughout the metro region had learned from that incident.

Montez's aunt stooped down into the doorway.

"Detective Jahn, we know you did all you could for Montez. He was a good kid. Never got in trouble."

Tammy nodded. The woman's statement had become cliché. So often, when a young man, often black, was killed, his family described him as a good kid who never got into trouble, despite the fact he was killed in the commission of a felony, or by rival gang members. He never owned a gun according to his family, despite social media posts of him holding multiple handguns and bragging about how he obtained them. Was a mother's love always so blind? Tammy wondered how she would respond when her children became teens and the peer pressure increased logarithmically.

And yet, this time the statement was true. Montez *was* a good kid. He hadn't deserved this.

"He liked you. You give him hope. He says, one time, you says he was good 'nough for college. Gloria hold on to that hope, too. Wondered where the money would come from for it, but she prayed you be right." The woman couldn't reach in over the car's computer equipment and the debris accumulated on the passenger seat to give the hug that Tammy felt coming, so she reached across toward Tammy, to shake her hand. "Thank you. God bless you."

Tammy responded in kind. "Please tell your sister that Montez wasn't alone when he died. I was holding him. And again, I am so, so sorry. I'll miss him, too." The tears flowed easily now, as she reflected on the pleading in the young man's eyes before they became lifeless.

The aunt's hand lingered in Tammy's, and then she withdrew. Tammy could see the tears in the other woman's eyes as well. She bent forward to look out the passenger window as the door closed. She wanted to make eye contact one more time with Montez's mother, but that wasn't going to happen. She could see a male member of the family escorting Ms. Taylor into the house. She wiped both eyes and blinked a few times. She started to turn the key in the ignition when she saw her sergeant rushing up to the car.

"Follow me. We have a lead on the two punks who left your kid here to die."

Tammy nodded but wondered why she hadn't gotten the call as well. She glanced at her radio and saw that at some point she had accidentally hit the volume button and lowered it to an inaudible level. That could become another dangerous oversight, if she didn't correct it now.

Five minutes later, they converged on another abandoned home, one that could have been the mirror image of the house where Montez died. Its brick walls also displayed gang signs, but curiously, from the same gang. Tammy would have expected the murderers to be rival gang members.

Two more squad cars pulled up. The sergeant gave instructions for those officers to cover the back, and with caution, the men positioned themselves to do so. With his own gun in hand, he placed himself behind his car and motioned for her to join him.

"We ID'd the two bangers who took off at the other house from the video on Williams' car. One of our CIs tells us they're holed up in here."

Tammy had her own line-up of confidential informants, but she'd not had time to make contact with any of them. She wondered who had worked this miracle, because that's what it was to get a lead so quickly on these guys.

She double-checked her vest and gun, hoping to have no need for either. She saw movement in a downstairs window where the plywood had fallen askew. More of a passing shadow than anything.

Her sergeant popped his head above the car, and yelled, "Hall! Robinson! Throw your guns out and come out, hands above your heads." Nothing happened. No response. No guns. "We know you're in there. Come out where we can see you. Let's do this the easy way."

"We did'n do nothin! What's the po-po want wit us?"

Tammy thought that voice sounded familiar. She looked at her sergeant. "Which Hall?"

"Antwan." He turned his attention back toward the

house. "Montez Johnson!"

She could hear murmuring from the building. "Let me handle it."

"Not on your life, because that's what I'm trying to save here. If these guys killed that boy, they aren't going to invite us in for a fireside chat."

Tammy shook her head and stood up. "Antwan, this is Detective Jahn. I'm coming to the door." She holstered her gun, took a deep breath, and stepped out from the behind the car.

"Jahn, get back here!"

She held her hands out to her side in full view and slowly walked to the door. She could feel the glare from her sergeant penetrating her back. But that would feel like nothing compared to what would be chewed up when this was over. As she neared the door, she could hear another voice inside.

"Antwan? Cuz, that copgirl call you Antwan? Whasup wit dat? You gonna make her your biatch or sumpin?" The voice started laughing.

"Shuddup!" Antwan wasn't amused.

"C'mon, ODawg, talk with me or my sergeant's gonna call SWAT, and you know where that'll go."

The front eased open about six inches. She moved to the side closest to the opening. She wasn't going to tempt fate by standing right in front of the door.

"What?"

"You two were with Montez just before he died. We caught you leavin' on video."

"Montez dead?"

"Yes." She heard some guttural swearing, but no immediate reply came. "I'm pretty sure you didn't do it. We want to know who did."

"I'll talk, but not givin' up my nine."

"I didn't ask for your gun, but my sergeant's gonna probably insist on it. You're a felon. Not supposed to possess a gun." Again, no reply. "Who's in there with you?" She already knew, but what they didn't know was whether or not there were more gang members besides Isaiah "Big C" Robinson with him.

"Nobody."

"Well, tell nobody to deal with your nine while you come out and talk with me. Show me some good will and cooperation and maybe my sarge'll let it slide." That wasn't going to happen, but the young man didn't need to know that. "I'm sure you got a clever hiding place for it in there."

She heard some movement and the sound of something dropping, and saw her sergeant beginning to move up. She held up her hand to stop him. His face showed clearly that he didn't like that. The door opened and Antwan stepped out, hands visible.

"Have a seat." She pointed to the stoop and prepared to join him. Her sergeant looked anxious. "Hey, my sergeant's getting nervous. You might want 'nobody' to come out, too."

At that moment, yelling and the sound of scuffling arose behind the house. Antwan jumped up and prepared to run, but Tammy surprised him, tripping him at his first step. She was on him before he could take another breath, pulling his hands behind his back. Her sergeant was there a second later.

"Antwan, I told you we could make this easy. Why don't you guys ever listen?" His hands secured by a sturdy zip tie, she helped him to his feet. "C'mon, let's have a seat in the car."

She let him simmer for a few minutes in the back seat of her patrol car. One of the other officers escorted Isaiah "Nobody" Robinson to his patrol car. Two more officers had arrived, and they entered the house. She had no doubts that they'd find whatever weapons might have been stashed there.

Joining Antwan, she said, "You really could have made this a lot easier on yourself. You know that, don't you?"

He glared at her and turned his face away. "You tricked me."

"I did no such thing. If your boy 'Nobody' hadn't tried to bolt out the back, we'd be having this conversation on those steps over there. Now? We're going to find whatever guns you stashed inside, and check 'em against both your fingerprints. Odds are they'll be covered with 'em, and you could get booked on gun charges, your parole canceled, or all of the above. So, talk to me, and maybe I can get my sergeant just to take the guns off the street and look the other way as far as you're concerned."

"Yeah, right. Just another example of the poh-lice hating black men."

"Naw, just the police hating crime." She saw that he had calmed down but would he cooperate? "So, give me the lowdown on Montez."

He lowered his eyes, and she could see the gears working overtime in his head. Every gang had its own code to live by, and one of the consistent rules was never to be a "busta," a snitch. Even the most secretive informant got discovered eventually and paid for his "crime."

"Slobs did it," murmured Antwan.

"The Bloods? Why? Montez wasn't even a member of

a gang, any gang." This made no sense.

"Thought he was a zoomer."

Was that a tear in his eye? It was, but Tammy would never embarrass him by acknowledging it.

"I found Montez bleedin' outside of St. Matthews. Big C and me carried him to that house. I tried t' stop the bleedin', but he keep gettin' worse."

"Why didn't you call an ambulance, or get help?"

"Nobody answer at the church. My phone was dead. Thought we could stop it. Then the po-po shows up, and we get scared, so's we bust out and run. Montez still alive then."

"I know. He died in my arms."

She caught Antwan staring at her. As soon as he saw that she had noticed, he glanced away.

"Montez, he like you. Says you always fair wit him. Straight up. That the only reason I'm talkin' wit you."

Did she sense something more in Antwan? Maybe he'd be willing to carry on a different conversation. But, whatever new openness she thought she might be reading into that last statement, his comments on face value encouraged her. Yes, she had lost a young man in whom she had invested a lot of time, but she knew now that her time had not been wasted. Between the words of his aunt, and now Antwan, she knew that was true.

"Why'd they think Montez was a zoomer, selling fake drugs?"

The young man shook his head. "He give out Tylenol to a bunch of homeless. Some were crackheads. Slobs think he givin' them drugs, on their turf. Ain't nuthin' but Tylenol, but they shank him anyways. Totally wack."

"Do you know who did it?"

He shook his head. "But we gonna find out."

"And when you do?"

He didn't answer.

"You're going to call me with a name. Right?"

Still no reply.

"Right?"

"Jahn, I need to talk with you."

The voice of her sergeant from behind did not settle well. Even Antwan gave her a look of sympathy. She climbed out of the car and shut the door to keep Antwan from "bustin' out."

She approached her superior where he stood, ten feet away. "Sarge?"

"That was irresponsible and dangerous. You could have been shot. A minor war could have broken out. And you disobeyed my order."

"What? What order?"

"I ordered you to get back behind the car."

"That was an order? C'mon, Sarge, I knew I'd be okay. I'm not stupid . . . or irresponsible."

"How? How could you know that?"

"Because Antwan Hall is Montez Johnson's half brother. They grew up together. I knew he wouldn't have killed Montez." Well, she had a strong belief in such. Brother killing brother was as old as mankind.

"That's not the point. He wasn't alone. We had an unknown situation. And you went out on your own, put yourself at risk. If anything had . . ."

Tammy knew the tirade would continue without some intervention.

"The Bloods killed Montez, but they don't know who exactly. The Bloods thought Montez was a zoomer, selling fake drugs to their clients and giving them a bad rep."

Sergeant Barkley stopped his rant and paused. "Okay, I'll pass that on to the anti-gang unit. See what they can dig up." As he turned back toward his own car, he stopped, looked at her, and said. "And we aren't done with our little talk."

Nine

Richard pushed beyond whatever limits he thought he had. Emotionally, that morning had been like riding the world's worst roller coaster. The great plunge at the beginning of the ride started with his call from Craig and continued through their failure to find the helicopter. But the discovery of the crash site lifted him up, until the dead crew members were found and the next descent began. He rose again with their failure to find Amy and the possibility of footprints that supported her survival.

Now, the next fall into a helical spin grabbed him.

"Richard, we've been all over this field. Nothing. And no signs of any footprints. I told you I might have simply imagined them."

Lynch looked as fatigued as Richard felt. Trundling through the muck—sliding, falling, catching himself before hitting the mud, slipping in every direction on a 360-degree plane—had been difficult and tiring. They both needed a rest and nourishment, but Richard refused to stop, and Lynch had stayed with him every slip and slide along the way.

"So, how else do we explain not finding her? Either someone rescued her or she's trying to find her way out to get help."

Lynch started to say something but stopped.

"What? What were you going to say?"

"Nothing."

"Look, don't think I haven't thought of the worst possible scenario, because it keeps replaying through my head. But, we're going to find her."

Lynch nodded. "Okay, so with either of your assumptions, they, or she, would have to have a way out. And the most likely way would be the same way a farmer gets in. There must be a lane or road nearby."

Richard agreed. He'd already thought of that. "And we know that there's a solid tree line in those two directions. So, that means we should head . . ." He paused and twisted his head about, looking for the most likely route. ". . . that way." He had settled on a route to his right and behind him a bit.

"Alright then, let's do it. We find her, or we collapse in the process." Lynch smiled, but not convincingly.

They crested a small rise in the field and could see a fence line in the distance, maybe 300 yards away. Richard pointed.

"Looks like a fence. That means there's a good chance of finding a lane there."

Lynch took a deep breath and moved ahead of him. Fifteen minutes later, and having found a gap in the fence, both men found their feet on more solid, less muddy ground at a rutted tractor lane. Lynch squatted and gazed at the dirt around them.

"I don't see any sign of footprints or tires. Looks like the rain washed away any tracks that might have been here." He emphasized the word "might."

Richard looked both directions along the path. They

had a 50-50 chance of choosing the same path as Amy and her "maybe" rescuer.

"Which way did we come in to land?" he asked.

Lynch shook his head. "Not sure. With Craig circling to land, I lost any bearings I might have had."

"So, which way?"

Lynch shook his head. "Flip a coin."

"Don't have one, so I'm . . . just . . . gonna pick . . ." His head rotated back and forth as if he was watching a tennis match. ". . . this way."

He started along the lane and kept scrutinizing the dirt for any sign of recent traffic, on foot or otherwise. Ten minutes later, they came to a gate and what appeared to be a widened area in the drive. To their left, the fence line stopped and opened to a wide entry area into the field. A budding vine on the nearest fencepost appeared recently broken.

"Looks like a turn-around, where a truck or tractor could turn without having to go into the fields on either side. The closed gate might mean the border of the property. What do you make of this?" Richard pointed to the broken vine.

"Looks recent to me."

"Me, too."

Lynch tried to slide open the latch in the gate. "Stuck pretty good. If I can't move it, I doubt Amy could. And, it doesn't appear this gate's been opened in years." He looked over the galvanized metal top rail. "Looks undisturbed on that side, too. You know, if Amy's walking and on her own, if she went this way, I think she would have left some clue, a mark, something to point us that way."

Richard gazed over the gate, too. He had to agree that

the immediate area looked untraveled. Looks like they had lost that 50% bet. They should have gone the other way. Lynch must have read his mind, because in unison they turned and began to retrace their steps.

Fifteen minutes after passing the spot where they found the road, they came to a swollen creek. Richard felt the next dip in the roller coaster.

"No one's going that way, on foot or in a vehicle, unless it's a tank."

Lynch was correct. The flooded waterway was impassable until the water receded.

"Hey, isn't this the same creek Craig noted when we flew over, the one with a missing bridge?"

"Must be. We didn't see any others," replied Richard.

"Then, that abandoned house must be down this lane. What if she managed to get across before the flooding?"

Amy tried to nap, to no avail. The smell inside the barn reminded her of a decaying body, and the recurrent noises of something, or some*things*, scurrying around her brought images of foraging rats to her mind. Several times, she began to fall asleep only to jerk awake and elicit pain in her ankle. Why had she ever agreed to this? Agreed to it? The plan was hers to own.

The sun had passed its zenith overhead, not that anyone could tell with the heavy overcast skies. That also meant whatever warmth she could count on the sun providing had reached its peak as well.

The flight suit's dense weave and protective layers usually made it warm. In fact, she had complained at times during the previous summer about its being too hot. Not today. She shivered. Its dense weave also prevented it from drying quickly, and the moisture wicked away her body heat. Few people realized how dangerous the combination of being cold *and* wet became. A body in water lost heat 25 times faster than one in air, and while simply being wet wasn't quite the same as being immersed, she needed to consider her options.

What if no one found her before nightfall when the air temperature would drop into the low forties? Or into the thirties if this storm front ushered in a cold, high-pressure system. She couldn't start a warming fire without risking the barn. Was there another choice?

She used her homemade crutch to push up onto her good leg. She felt a bit lightheaded, so she stood for a moment to let it pass. Then, she began to explore the barn and discovered the garage area. She reached out to take a tarp that appeared to cover some boxes but realized it was hiding Sinead's car. She didn't want to disturb that and aid in its discovery, but it helped move her mind into a higher gear.

The old truck! If she could get it started, she could run it for heat, enough to warm up anyway.

She hobbled to its driver's side door and opened it. The seat was too high. She couldn't bear weight on the bad leg, and yet, she also couldn't use her good leg to hop up into the truck. Struggling, she tried to pull her body into the cab with her arms, but her leg hit the lower edge of the frame and the pain shot up into her hip and lower back like an electrical arc between two contacts. She caught her scream before it could escape her mouth. She didn't want Sinead to hear and come running, risking discovery.

She panted and focused on good thoughts. Anything to

help wait out the flare of pain as it slowly subsided. Recovered, she scrutinized the situation and realized that if she could elevate her position by a measly six inches, she could place her torso along the bench seat and then pull herself into the cab. Maybe.

She limped across the barn, assisted by the heavy branch she used as a crutch, toward a dusty workbench covered by cobwebs in the adjacent room. She found a few concrete blocks. Too heavy and maybe not tall enough. An old bushel basket already looked as if someone tried stepping onto it, its bottom crumpled inward as it sat upside down. There were aged two-by-fours and other lumber, some rough cut, but nothing useful. And then she saw it, an old milk crate. That would raise her up to a sufficient height, if she could somehow hop onto it with her good leg. Or maybe use a piece of lumber like a short ramp.

With some effort she managed to clear a pile of debris that blocked her from retrieving the crate, but she succeeded. Up close it appeared sturdy enough. She used her staff to scoot it out into the open and flip it upside down, and then slammed the end of the branch onto it. The wood slats held, so she bent over to pick it up. The weight of it surprised her compared to the modern, plastic versions of a milk crate. How could she use her crutch and carry it at the same time?

Amy lifted it over the staff so that the crate sat upside down on top. With one hand on top of the crutch and the other holding it farther down, she hobbled one slow step at a time toward the truck. Once she made it next to the driver's door, she placed the crate into position. She gazed at it and decided that with the aid of the crutch she might, just might, be able to hop onto the crate with her one good leg. However, the thought of failing also scampered through her mind. The thought of falling and inflicting more damage to her injured leg coerced her into a new plan.

After one more trip to the workbench area, she now had a sturdy ramp from the floor to the top of the box. After all of her efforts, sweat rolled down her forehead. Sweat? Then why was she shivering?

One more task to complete. If she needed something from one of the duffels, she didn't want to have to climb down and back up again. She dragged each duffel to the truck, hoisted them onto the floor on the passenger side, and then closed that door.

She stood there for a moment, exhausted and out of breath. As a women's basketball player in high school and college, it would have taken multiple wind sprints up and down the court to feel so short-of-breath. Was she that out of shape? Besides being winded, she realized she was already hungry and thirsty. Lunch hadn't lasted very long, and perhaps she should have insisted on keeping a couple of those water bottles. She hoped someone would find her soon.

Well, that was water under the bridge. She needed to rest—inside the truck. She worked her way back to the driver's door, hopped up the ramp to the top of the box, and gazed into the cab. *Now or never,* she thought. She leaned into the truck and with one push of her good leg, plopped on top of the bench seat, her abdomen hitting the edge of the seat with a resultant sharp, abdominal pain. The pain in her splinted leg was more tolerable than this new pain. She used her arms to pull her body deeper into the truck and then pushed herself into a sitting position and moved her legs inside as well. She suddenly felt lightheaded again but worse. She gave it a minute, and it seemed to pass, but the pain in her belly hadn't subsided.

Now seated behind the wheel, she pulled the door closed and reached for the key. There was no key. Why hadn't she thought to check that *before* all of this effort? She wanted to cry, but she was so tired, the tears refused to budge. The lightheadedness returned, and her fatigue became agonizing. Maybe she needed to lie down. She stretched out across the seat, trying several positions to make her leg most comfortable. Soon she fell into a deep sleep.

"Craig, all we need is a lift to the other side of the creek. It's too high to pass."

Lynch saw the pleading in Richard's eyes and the refusal in Craig's. Craig had already explained that they could stop and check out the house as soon as his crew was ready to fly. The other MedAir choppers had departed with the remains of the pilot and paramedic. They were low on fuel again, and he didn't want to fire up the helicopter simply to enable them to hop over a creek to check on a hunch.

"I heard you the first time, Richard. What are the odds that Amy is over there? How would she have gotten across that creek? Besides, NTSB is supposed to arrive any moment, and I need to be here."

A scowl crossed Richard's face. "You've given up on her, haven't you? The other two crew members are dead and you just assume she is, too."

Lynch watched Craig closely. The look on the man's face confirmed that Richard might be correct.

"Richard, no, I haven't given up. Look, if she was in good enough shape to walk out of here, cross that creek, and get to that abandoned house, another 20 minutes won't mean life or death."

Lynch hadn't thought along that line of reasoning, but Craig had a point. He waited for Richard's next volley.

"How do you know that? That's making a pretty big assumption. For all we know she might have gotten just beyond the creek, before the water rose, and is lying there, collapsed on the lane."

Lynch nodded. Another good point. He felt pleased with himself that he had decided to stay quiet and not to get into the middle of this one.

"What do you think, Lynch?" asked Richard.

Rats, thought Lynch. So much for staying out of it. "Craig, you make a good point about Amy's likelihood of being there and that you need to be here for the NTSB folks, but Richard is right, too. We don't know where she is or what condition she's in. Can we afford to make any assumptions at all? As a detective, the next place I'd check is the other side of the creek and work toward that house."

Craig's resolve seemed to cave in. He was about to answer when the sound of rotor blades approached in the distance. All three men perked up to listen.

"Look, if that's the State Police with the NTSB, we can ask them to take you over, and I can stay with the NTSB guys. If it isn't, I'll do it."

Richard let loose a loud sigh of relief. Lynch, too, felt the tension ease.

Within two minutes, the ISP helicopter came into view, and two minutes after that, it settled onto the mud 50 feet away from where they stood. Three men hopped out and leaned back into the aircraft to retrieve their gear. As they cleared the rotors, Craig approached the pilot and yelled something to him. Lynch couldn't hear the conversation but saw the pilot give a thumb up. Craig waved them over.

Lynch followed Richard, and they climbed aboard. Lynch, his Christian faith still new, had not yet found confidence in praying for many things, but as he buckled in for the brief flight, he quietly prayed that they would find Amy alive and well. As the last in, he donned his headset after Richard and felt the rotors accelerating as soon as he did so.

"There's a farm lane behind us and about half a mile west is a swollen creek," Richard said into the intercom system. "We need to get onto the other side and as close as possible to the lane so we can check it out for our lone survivor."

"Sure, but if you want, I can just skirt along over the lane and save you some walking."

Lynch decided that was a good idea, and replied, "Sounds like a plan. Ultimately, we want to check out the house and buildings we saw from the air. We think they're at the end of this lane."

The pilot gave another thumbs up. "Got it. And you're correct, there is a house at the end of the road. I checked with local law enforcement, and it's currently unoccupied. The owners went to a nursing home last summer and their son and daughter-in-law from Kansas City have leased out the farm land to the neighbors. The family stops by the house periodically to maintain it, but no one is there now."

A moment later, they hovered over the lane just across the creek, and the pilot slowly flew along it, about 20 feet above. He dodged the occasional tree and amazed Lynch with his flying skill and ability to canvass the area along and around the lane with such ease. Vegetation was sparse along the fence, so they had no concerns about missing a fallen body.

"End of the road. I can't get any closer to the house," said the pilot.

"Hey, before we land, could you go up and give us the lay of the land? I want to see what ways there are out of here, in case we need to keep looking," asked Lynch.

"Sure."

Lynch felt his stomach hit his feet as the pilot shot straight up faster than any high speed elevator Lynch had ever ridden. He began to wish he'd prayed for a safe flight, too. They circled the house and adjacent property twice. Lynch saw only one road into the place. Otherwise, the home was surrounded by muddy fields.

"Looks like that flooding creek took out the only bridge to the house. I'll have to check with local law to see if that's recent," said the pilot.

Lynch heard the man radio the locals as he settled the aircraft back toward earth. Once again, Lynch looked forward to solid ground beneath his feet. A minute later, they landed near the lane where they had started their search. The pilot powered down.

"I'll wait for you here. Shouldn't take you long to check out the place."

"Thanks," replied Richard.

Back on the lane, Lynch looked at Richard and said, "What if we don't find her here? What next?"

"We'll find her here."

Lynch felt a flash of guilt. Where was his faith? Hadn't he just prayed that they would find her alive and well here?

As they neared the first outbuilding, Richard ran ahead.

"Locked up tight. She won't be in there."

Lynch found the next small shed empty. "Nothing in here."

The other three small buildings revealed nothing as well. Together, they approached the house. Lynch checked the back door. Locked. Glass intact.

"You head around the house that way, and I'll go this way."

Richard nodded and headed toward their right. Lynch moved left and checked each window. He found no breakage and saw nothing inside to suspect someone lived there. He passed around to the side of the house and met Richard near a front porch.

"Front door's locked and all the windows are intact. She would have had to walk through the wall to get inside."

Lynch agreed, and they began to retrace Lynch's path around the house, when he noticed a small tiller and earth that seemed disturbed. He started to mention that it looked like someone was creating a garden, but something stopped him. It felt like what he used to call a hunch, but stronger.

"All we have left is the barn," Richard said, as he veered toward the largest building on the property.

They approached the main doors, and Richard became excited. "Look! Something was dragged across here since the rain."

He ran toward the man door, and Lynch ran to catch up and stop his friend. "Wait!"

"Why? She's got to be in here."

"It might not be her. Look." He pointed to the tiller and broken dirt. "This place might not be abandoned after all, and whoever's living here could be on the other side of this door, not wanting us to discover him and waiting with a shovel or something."

Richard paused, looked contemplative, and nodded. "So, let's see if we can open the big door."

"Sure, and if he has gun, you become a clear target. Let's see if there are any other doors."

Richard frowned and shook his head. Instead, he yelled, "Hey! If anybody's in the barn, we aren't here to hurt you or report you! A helicopter crashed in the fields to the east and we're looking for a woman, the only survivor! We just want to check the barn!"

No response.

Lynch shrugged. That was one way to approach the problem. Not his choice, but one option.

A minute later, the silence continued.

Lynch took his turn. "If anybody's in the barn, we're coming in!"

The two men looked at each other, and Lynch moved first, pushing open the door. Nothing happened. So far, so good. He craned his head to look inside at an angle. Clear. Richard mimicked him and checked the opposite line of sight. He held a thumb up.

Lynch moved quickly through the door, followed by Richard, and found himself in an open area surrounded by mostly empty hay loft space. The place seemed cavernous.

"Anybody here?" No reply.

"Looks like the loose hay over there has been disturbed, but I can't say how long ago."

Lynch nodded as he walked around the space. "Basically, just your typical hay barn. There's got to be some work space somewhere."

"Over there." Richard pointed to the back right corner of the barn, where a double-wide door led to another section of the barn. As they entered that space, Lynch saw a workbench cluttered with debris. "Looks like some of that junk has been moved very recently. Look at how the dust is disturbed. It's still floating in the air." He saw nothing else in the room.

"There's another room through there."

As they entered, Lynch said, "Looks like garage space. Probably a car under that tarp. And look at that old Chevy truck. Early sixties maybe. Might be worth something if it was fixed up."

Richard lifted the tarp. "This car's a late model Honda. Wonder why it's in storage here. No plates."

Lynch stood admiring the old truck. Needed a good cleaning. In fact, it looked as if the mud splashes were recent. He furrowed his brow and looked toward the cab. *Odd*, he thought. *I can't see into the windows.* And then he realized why.

"Richard, over here," he whispered. He pointed to the windows. "Look, they're all fogged up, not dirty," he continued in a whisper. "Someone's inside."

Richard smiled. "We found her."

Could he be right? Or was their gardener and trespasser hiding inside? "I hope so, but just in case, you open the driver's door, and I'll open this side. If it's someone else, I don't want him jumping out and getting away."

Using hand signals to coordinate their timing, they pulled open the doors simultaneously.

"Amy!" yelled Richard. "We found you."

She didn't move.

"Amy?" Richard rushed around to the passenger side

as Lynch reached for her head. She felt cool. Her carotid pulse seemed weak and her complexion pale. Something was wrong. He noticed the splint on her leg, but that wouldn't account for her being unconscious. Would it?

Richard pushed him aside and checked her. Lynch watched as he took her pulse and listened to her breathing. He ran back to the driver's side, checked the splint, and returned to the passenger's side. Lynch realized the man's experience in the battlefields of Afghanistan had kicked in as Richard pulled the duffels out of the truck and began to rummage through them.

He looked up at Lynch with pleading in his eyes. "You have to run back to the helicopter. We need a medic, IV fluids. We'll need a stretcher to get her out of here. Her pulse is 130 and her breathing is off. She's going into shock. She must have internal bleeding."

Ten

੭৹◆◆৹੭

"Your Honor, we have a situation that requires your immediate attention."

Diane Westlake, a senior social worker for the Massachusetts Department of Children & Families, or D.C.F., had taken a seat across from the judge's desk in her quarters. Her dated blouse and below-the-knee skirt seemed to speak of a woman older than she, matronly and imposing. She had once been called "the school marm" in a way that wasn't meant as flattering, but she embraced the image. Deadbeat dads, junkie moms, abusers and the like had all felt the "rap of her ruler across their knuckles." She had little use for them. As the saying went, it takes a village to raise a child, and she was glad to be *her* village's truancy officer and chief enforcer.

The judge lowered her glasses to the end of her nose and peered across them at Diane.

"Ms. Westlake, I believe I fully understand your *situation* here. That is, after all, why we're about to have this hearing."

"And if Jameson O'Malley refuses to relinquish the whereabouts of his daughter? She is in grave danger, and we are obligated to protect her. Her parents have been medically abusing her for years now. You've read the reports. She has Munchhausen Syndrome by Proxy, and who knows what her mother is putting her through as we speak. She needs our help."

The Family Court judge sighed. "I think you exaggerate a bit, Ms. Westlake. I have interviewed the other O'Malley children, as well as the grandparents, and I don't find any reason to consider abuse, as you put it. Plus, that was only one doctor's opinion." She took off her glasses and laid them on top of the dossier in front of her. "However, until all of the findings are in and the many doctors involved in this come to some resolution, I am obligated to keep Ruth O'Malley as a ward of the state."

"And as such, Your Honor, the family must give her up, allow us to regain custody."

The judge nodded. "True. However, I can't force Mr. O'Malley to talk. If he again refuses, my only recourse is to keep him in jail for contempt."

Diane gave up a rare smug smile, as she thought, *Yes. We'll see how well he's handled the last two weeks in jail. Another month would serve him right.*

"Yes, Your Honor."

The judge stood, as a signal that this meeting was over. "The hearing starts in ten minutes. I have some items to attend to first. I suspect I'll see you in your customary seat inside the courtroom."

"Yes, Your Honor."

Diane stood and exited through the front door. She held no vain imagination of privileges and would never expect the judge to allow her to enter the courtroom through the judge's own door. Still, it seemed a waste of time to have to walk around to the main hall to enter the court, when in reality, it stood a mere ten feet away, through a short antechamber adjacent to the judge's chambers. Yet, walk she did, and a few minutes later, she took her seat behind the railing, opposite the State's table, where she would be available to testify on a moment's notice, if needed.

"The Court is now in session. All rise."

Diane watched as Judge Kathleen Waverly entered the room from behind the bench and took her seat. Typically, such family and custody cases were small, private hearings, since juveniles were involved. With today's public docket, however, she had expected to see the usual gaggle of lawyers and clients filling the seats waiting their turns. Instead, the room was standing room only with reporters filling every available space. This case had received more national attention than Diane felt comfortable with, particularly since she was a central party to it.

Jameson O'Malley sat with his legal counsel at one table. That legal team had increased from a single lawyer to a team of three, supported by their team of paralegals and backed up by a collective of pro bono conservative attorneys who proved to be more meddlesome with each week. They represented the entire O'Malley case, as that family fought to regain custody of their daughter and shed light on the growing threat of medical kidnapping by the state.

In response, however, she had concern that the state's representatives had not grown to match. In outward appearance, they would not be outdone in numbers. So, while three lawyers sat at the State's table, behind the scenes, only one worked the case. They did not match the legal expertise or cunning of the defense. Still, the law was on her, their, side.

Judge Waverly sat down and gave a terse greeting to those present. She then nodded toward the defense team. The lead defense lawyer stood. "Your Honor, we again move that the State and this Court do away with all charges against Mr. O'Malley and grant him his freedom. He—"

The judge had only to raise her hand to stop the attorney. "Yes, Mr. Pfeiffer, the Court understands your position fully. However, I am trying to resolve this to everyone's satisfaction." She turned toward the state's lead legal representative. "Mr. Wesley, what do you have to say?"

"Your Honor, the O'Malleys have yet to produce their daughter, Ruth, who is a legal charge of the State. We, too, have been trying to resolve this without escalating the issue, for the benefit of Ruth, who remains our primary concern."

"Yeah, right," murmured Jameson. Mr. Pfeiffer put a hand on his shoulder to quiet him.

Diane gave a smug smile. She hoped the abusive dad would keep talking and cook his own goose. It would serve him right to serve hard time. After all, she and the other caregivers involved were trying to help that poor teenager. Her parents had put that poor girl through so much turmoil that somebody had to step in. Diane was proud to be that somebody, and she had made sure Ruth received care in the best facility under D.C.F. contract.

Judge Waverly turned her attention to O'Malley. "Mr. O'Malley, you have been directed to return your daughter to the Brookline Rehab Center, and as far as I've been informed, that has not happened. Where is your daughter,

Ruth, and when can we expect her return?"

"That place has been a slow death for Ruth, and you know it, Judge Waverly."

"Jameson, please," said Mr. Pfeiffer, again placing his hand on O'Malley's shoulder.

Anger flared across O'Malley's face. "No! My wife and I have had it with this system. A year ago, we were accused of child abuse, by that *witch* sitting over there . . ."

O'Malley pointed to Diane, and her eyes widened as she took affront at his words. Her back stiffened, and she took a deep breath while cautioning herself to remain silent. He was, indeed, locking his own cell. But then, she wondered, why wasn't Judge Waverly stopping him?

". . . and you took our child away from us. Since then, you have seen well-documented evidence that we never neglected or abused any of our children, and that the case comes down to a disagreement between doctors. We chose to believe our original doctors because under their care, Ruth remained able to walk, go shopping with friends, and enjoy her teen years with minimal restrictions. Under *her* care . . ."

Again, he pointed toward Diane, and she fought to remain professional and dignified.

". . . and that of the other doctors, our dear Ruth has lost 20 pounds and become confined to a wheelchair. So, just *who* has abused our daughter?" He paused. "And now, you lock me up in jail for contempt, when all I want is to start the long process of healing and restoring our daughter. There is no *village* that can replace the care and love of family."

Judge Waverly glanced at Diane, but the look on her face was one of contempt, not frustration or anger. Diane turned away from the glare. Certainly the judge didn't blame *her* for this, this mess. Did she?

"Mr. O'Malley, I will ask again. Where is Ruth, and when will you return her?"

"When will *you* return her to *us*, Your Honor?"

Mr. Pfeiffer appeared about to clamp his hand across his client's mouth. "Jameson, don't."

O'Malley stood to his feet. "I don't know where she is. I get one phone call a week in jail, and my wife and I agreed that she would not tell me where she went. As for the contempt charge, Your Honor, you are correct, I have nothing but contempt for a court that would steal a child away from her parents without due process." He snapped his wrists together, as if cuffed. "So, lock me away. Make me a charge of the state, too, with a cot and three squares on the taxpayer's dollar."

Diane watched the media eating up this display of theatrics with relish. Despite the ban on cameras, a dozen cell phones surreptitiously recorded the drama. Diane ducked her head when she caught some of those same phones trying to take her picture.

Diane looked to the bench. Had the judge forgotten her gavel? Why was she allowing this to continue? The judge had only to bang her gavel once, or speak a word, to quiet the room. The judge turned her attention toward the state's table.

"Your Honor," spoke Mr. Wesley. "I'm not sure what this little display is all about, but since Mr. O'Malley has made it clear they won't comply with the court order, we have little choice but to take the next step. The state will formally file kidnapping charges against Sinead O'Malley."

The judge now glanced at the defense table and raised

her brow as if questioning Mr. Pfeiffer about his next move.

"Your Honor, with all due respect, my client is telling the truth. He has no idea where they are. His wife has not been in contact with him since she left with their daughter. You can cite him with contempt if you wish, but nothing this court does will enable him to divulge information he doesn't have. The State Police will confirm that none of her credit cards have been used, her car has not been sighted, her cell phone remains inactive, she has not contacted my client, and so on. For all intents and purposes, she has gone off the grid and did so without the foreknowledge or agreement of her husband, who expected her to keep in contact and is worried for their safety as well. I think my client has also made it clear that he has no concern about remaining in jail for what he sees as a just cause and overreach by a state agency. I again ask that you reconsider your action based upon that action's ability to effect the outcome you desire."

Judge Waverly lowered her glasses on her nose and furrowed her brow. Diane had seen that look many times, not just in this case, but also the many others she had been party to. The defense attorney had gotten to her.

Diane wanted to stomp her feet in protest. Was this guy gonna get off?

"What about the potential kidnapping charge against Sinead O'Malley?"

Mr. Pfeiffer replied, "Your Honor, Mr. Wesley has every right to file whatever charges he deems necessary. But again, will that bring about the outcome he desires? Do we want this to become another Meecham case?"

Why? Why did he bring that case up? Diane wanted to crawl into a hole in the wall as all eyes within the room seemed to focus on her.

The defense attorney turned to face the prosecutor. He placed his hand upon a foot-tall stack of paper on the table. "This pile represents close to 100,000 individuals from across the country who have expressed outrage over what has happened to the O'Malley family. We receive more every day. The news media, for the most part, has turned against the state on this one as well. If our goal here is to bring resolution to this case, might I suggest that filing kidnapping charges simply adds to the antagonism and fuel to the fire? Perhaps a little sugar is in order instead."

Diane watched Mr. Wesley, indeed his whole table of lawyers, slump into their chairs. The defense had them on the run. Where the defense team couldn't argue the law, they had succeeded in turning public opinion against the state. Pfeiffer had them over the proverbial barrel. By law, as long as Ruth O'Malley remained a ward of the state, the prosecutor had little leeway. The law required him to file those charges. And after Pfeiffer's little spiel, that was going to make the prosecutors look like ogres. And of course, the judge, by law, was in no position to return Ruth to her parents. And that, in turn, made her look like the Queen of the Ogres.

Diane began to dread the following morning's headlines. She prayed for an Islamic uprising, a freak storm, a race riot, the death of a major politician, the sudden eruption of the Yellowstone super-volcano—anything that would force this story to the back pages of the national newspapers and off the front page of the online news sites.

The scruffy, bearded man knew he looked out of place

when he entered the courtroom before the proceeding. But it was a place that had been all too familiar—once upon a time.

He sat behind the defense table, in the back corner as far as he could go. He did not wish to bring the slightest attention to himself. His role was to observe. That was all.

And yet, at the mention of the Meecham case, he jumped up and made his way from the room as quickly as he could through the crowd of journalists who had filled the back of the court. As he reached the aisle, he scowled at Diane Westlake. She showed no indication that she had seen him, and that was fine. In due time, she would have that chance.

Eleven

Tammy had slept fitfully, snatching moments of unconsciousness between memories of Montez. She couldn't quite discern why this young man's death hit her so hard, but it had. She had seen dozens of gang bangers go down in her precinct and more than a few good kids caught in somebody else's crossfire or as the victim of indiscriminate gunfire during a drive-by. Yet, while each of those lives mattered and each of those kids had untapped potential to contribute something positive to their families and communities, she hadn't worked with them as she had with Montez. She didn't know any of them like she knew Montez. In her mind, she could see his face light up with a smile, a smile she would miss.

Of course, it hadn't helped that before retiring to bed she had received four private messages on Facebook from colleagues warning her that Your Daddy, Sergeant Will Barkley, had returned to their station fuming. About her. Their initial concerns ranged from "was she still alive" to "was her butt smaller from the chewing out." They left asking for ringside seats when she reported to duty the next morning. Cop humor. With friends like that . . .

One thing was widely known about Wilson Barkley. His bite was worse than his bark, a trait many had speculated grew from the all-too-frequent jokes about his Napoleonic stature. And he never forgot. Until he worked your transgression out of his system, you never knew what lurked within the next assignment, which junker car you'd be provided, or worse. She could pay dearly for her insubordination and for making him look bad, even though she had produced results. In hindsight, her success is likely what nailed her coffin. If she hadn't produced the lead on the Bloods, Barkley could have simply written her off as inexperienced, or worse, as one of those 'bossy female' types who thinks she knows more than anyone else—especially anyone of the male gender—only to have been knocked down and proven wrong.

As she dressed for work she wondered if it was time for a transfer. Maybe to the mayor's protection detail. That was bound to be beyond exciting. Yawn.

Tammy walked into the detective's squad room for roll call and made a beeline toward the coffee pot. She hoped the brew was leftover from night shift—strong, bitter, and concentrated with caffeine. She needed a jolt of stimulant, like Navy coffee in a mug that was never washed. She made a face after her first taste. The coffee was freshly brewed and much too weak to keep her going for the next several hours. She foresaw a can of Monster Energy drink in her near future.

"Hey, heads up! Barkley's coming down the hall," whispered a detective on the fraud unit as he passed by her.

"What the. . ." she muttered. Had *everyone* heard about yesterday's incident? She realized in an instant that, yes, they probably had, and they all wanted to witness the fireworks.

She rushed to her customary seat for the morning

meeting and sat down, trying to look nonplussed but feeling the anxiety mount. He had the power to remove her from the GREAT Program and assign her to something like routine auto larcenies. The closure rate for those cases was dismal. Items disappeared from vehicles as soon as the owner looked the other direction, and no one was willing to talk with the 'Poh-lice,' to become a 'busta.' She'd spend most of the day filling out paperwork, not making any difference at all.

Sergeant Barkley entered the room and headed straight to the front. Once there, he addressed the detectives. "Okay, folks, take your seats. Let's get started."

As he waited, he fixed his eyes directly on her. His face seemed passionless, but she knew better. She could feel his stare penetrating to her soul, and the intensity of that gaze seemed to heat up the tension she already felt.

Fifteen minutes later, they had their assignments, their questions answered, and their brief reports on open cases made. Except her. She could feel more than the sergeant's eyes resting on her now, but she sat upright in her chair and held her head high, even though that fully exposed her neck to Barkley's blade. And like her favorite cooking show, *Chopped*, the room seemed to go to commercial before the loser was announced.

After an obvious minute of silence, Barkley spoke up. "Jahn, you're with the GREAT Program today." He paused, as everyone in the room seemed to deflate in disappointment that the fireworks had been canceled. "But be back here by 15:30. You and I have a meeting with the lieutenant."

Whhizzz! Boom! Boom! The first aerial explosion lit up the sky.

Twelve

Diane had left the courtroom and now drove toward Boston Children's Hospital for her first client appointment. Her cell phone rang as she drove west along Storrow Drive past the Charles River Basin.

She clicked on the hands-free receiver in her car. "Hello."

"Ms. Westlake, this is Helen, at Commissioner Fitzsimmons' office. She would like to meet with you this morning, as soon as possible."

Her first thought was that she wished to compliment her on the job she was doing with the O'Malley case, but something in the woman's tone suggested that compliments might not be in her future. A sudden sense of dread flashed through her mind.

"Well, I have an important client meeting at Children's. That's where I'm heading right now. But—"

"Yes, well, that's been taken care of. In fact, your whole morning has been cleared. She'd like to see you right away."

Her sense of impending trouble plummeted first to her gut and then, along with her stomach, fell to her feet, as if she'd jettisoned upward in a rocket. What could she possibly have done to warrant the Commissioner's clearing her work schedule?

"I see. Umm . . ." She glanced around to get her bearings. "I can be there in 15 minutes."

"I'll let the Commissioner know. Good-bye."

At her first opportunity, Diane turned south and picked up Boylston to reverse course back to the offices of the Department of Children and Families. By the time she arrived at the building and found a place to park along the street, she had but a few minutes to rush to the Commissioner's office. She had told the woman 15 minutes, and she never liked being late, even when circumstances, such as traffic, were out of her control. The old Washington-Essex Building was in the middle of a minor face-lift, and as she raced past the plywood facades along the sidewalk, she reflected on her dislike of coming to the Central Office for meetings. Inconvenience, for things like parking, went against her need for order and timeliness.

She noticed a digital clock in the window of the Dunkin' Donuts on an opposite corner and picked up her pace. She would make it in time.

She stopped outside the door to the Commissioner's office and took a deep breath while adjusting her clothing and smoothing her hair. With a second deep inhalation, she opened the door and marched into the front office as she exhaled. The nameplate for the woman at the reception desk identified her as Helen, the person who called her. Despite the more traditional name, Helen appeared younger than Diane had expected.

"Helen, good morning. I'm Diane Westlake. Right on time." She smiled, but the emotion behind the facial gesture failed to support it. In her rush to get there, she had buried the feeling of dread from earlier, but now it returned. Helen's curt look of greeting now assured her that doom sat beyond the next door. The smile flattened, but she regained control before it contorted into a frown.

"I'll let Commissioner Fitzsimmons know you're here." Helen picked up the phone and keyed in an internal number. "Ms. Westlake is here, ma'am." She nodded to the answer.

Diane watched the woman's every move, from the four-digit intercom number to the way she turned away slightly when announcing Diane's arrival. She watched as Helen hung up the phone without even looking at the console, knowing exactly where it was, like someone touching her nose with her index finger while keeping her eyes closed. She realized she was staring at the woman when Helen's voice broke the spell.

"She'll be with you in a few minutes. Please have a seat."

Diane looked about the room to find the austere furnishings in line with most state government facilities. She chose a hard-backed chair next to a side table and lamp, both of which had seen better days. On the table sat a collection of dated magazines that made her doctor's waiting room seem current. She took the top magazine, *People*, but spent the time watching Helen go about her duties. Very efficient, she noted. She liked that.

The "few minutes" stretched into 20 before the door opened, and Diane saw her boss' boss' boss in the doorway. Erin Fitzsimmons, Ph.D., had started in the D.C.F. much as Helen had but nearly a decade later. Now, she was the Commissioner while Diane remained a mid-level social worker. The unfairness of that had not gone unnoticed by Diane in recent years.

"Diane, please, come in."

The Commissioner stepped back to allow Diane into her office and pointed to a grouping of chairs across from her desk. At least they looked comfortable. Diane took the seat to the right and waited as Commissioner Fitzsimmons reclaimed her seat behind the desk. This, evidently, was not to be an informal chat.

"No doubt you're wondering why I asked you here on short notice."

Diane nodded, her mouth becoming acutely dry, as if she had taken a mouthful of silica gel desiccant. "I have a morning full of appointments at Children's."

Dr. Fitzsimmons shook her head. "*Had* a full morning. Your office called to inform us that all of the parents today *and* tomorrow have canceled their appointments and refuse to work with you. They all asked for someone else."

Diane raised her brow in surprise. *Wha . . .?* she thought. "Oh my! I, I don't know why that—"

"We have a good idea. Have you seen this?"

The Commissioner turned her computer screen around to face Diane. A photo of Diane leaving Judge Waverly's office filled the screen under a headline: "Social Worker Tries to Influence Judge."

"Or this one?" The Commissioner hit a key and the screen flashed to a new page. "Do You Value Your Children?" read that headline, followed by her picture and a caption stating, "This woman wants to take them away."

"Why, that's not true," protested Diane.

The Commissioner produced a new website on the screen. MedicalKidnap.com. Diane hated that website. It ridiculed every good deed she tried to do, saying she "stole" children from parents whose only offense was wanting a second opinion on their child's medical condition. The website highlighted dozens of cases across the country where children were placed in foster homes because the parents objected to a doctor's judgment or treatment, refused immunizations for their children, or committed some other infraction. Sometimes, as with the O'Malley case, other doctors sided with the family, but still the state children's agency used the courts to take control of the child or children.

Nowhere on the website did it show the social agency's heartfelt need to protect the child, Diane's sincere belief that she was only doing what was best *for the child*. The village's children needed their guardians, and she and like-minded social workers filled that need. What could those parents know? They weren't professionally-trained, especially those homeschooler types.

Diane scrutinized the first paragraph of the lead article. In it, she was again reported as having left Judge Waverly's office after trying to sway the Judge. How had they gotten that picture and posted it so quickly? And didn't they need her permission to use a picture of her? The writer went on to show that among the zealots in D.C.F. and D.F.S. offices across the country, she was the de facto leader, the primary kidnapper, a "home-breaker far more dangerous than any mistress."

The Commissioner turned the screen back to its usual position.

"I've talked with Judge Waverly, and she confirmed that you insisted on meeting with her before the O'Malley hearing. She said you were quite adamant that an example should be made of Jameson O'Malley. In fact, the first article I showed you has a picture further down of you smirking in apparent delight when the prosecutor announced he might file kidnapping charges against Sinead O'Malley." She paused. "Why were you there? You had no role in this morning's hearing, and the judge confirmed that you had not been called to be available."

"I-I thought I might be needed. My concern is for Ruth O'Malley and I wanted to make sure progress was being made in locating her, so we could help her."

"Well, you weren't asked to be there, so you had no official standing. Yet, you attended during your scheduled work day, taking the time on the taxpayer's dime."

The Commissioner pulled a file from the side of her desk. "These are various complaints we've had about you over the years. You've been counseled about maintaining your professional role in these cases and have been formally reprimanded twice about the same. This time . . ." She let out her breath, almost in a sigh. "This time, you've created a major PR nightmare for this department as well. I have no recourse but to let you go. I've already discussed this with the employees' union, and they see no violation of your terms of employment or your rights under the bargaining agreement. When you return to your office, you will be escorted in by security, given time to collect your personal items and say goodbye to colleagues, and then escorted out."

Thirteen

Sinead trudged along the gravel drive, stopping every ten or so feet to knock the mud and loose gravel from her rubber boots. The rains had made a mess of the place. The bridge was gone, leaving only the low water ford across the creek. She pondered her predicament.

And she worried about Amy. She reflected on the previous day's events. The helicopter landing nearby. The men checking the buildings and barn. She had no doubt they'd already found the other crew members. The images of those poor men remained seared into Sinead's mind. She would never forget them, as much as she longed to do so. She had said a quiet prayer for their families.

A few minutes after entering the barn, one of the men came running out and sprinted toward the helicopter. Sinead's heart leapt in fear at the sight of his urgency. Minutes later, she'd lost track of the time by then, she heard another helicopter. More men. Running. Carrying bags, like the ones she had retrieved from the crash site. One man had a portable radio, and he stood in the gravel drive talking.

Fifteen minutes later, a third helicopter. More men. More supplies. A stretcher. Something bad had happened to Amy inside that barn and Sinead chastised herself for her selfishness. She should have insisted that Amy stay with them in the house, where she would have been safe. No matter the consequences.

A moment later, four men jogging with Amy on the stretcher headed for the aircraft. She watched all three choppers lift off and speed away to the southeast, toward Springfield. Sinead spent the night flooded with guilt, crying, and praying for Amy's recovery. If only she hadn't been so reticent about taking Amy to get medical care. They might have left before the bridge washed out. Amy would be okay now.

The new morning brought relief from the deluge but also new concerns. How long until the water subsided? Had one of the men noticed the tiller and become suspicious? Would the county sheriff come snooping around today or the next? More importantly, what if something happened to Ruth? How would she get out to take Ruth for care?

The loss of the bridge meant one thing. They needed to move on. But where?

Sinead walked back to the house. She would need to call Adriana to let her know about the bridge. Adriana would likely offer for them to come stay at their home just a few hours away, outside Kansas City, but Sinead didn't want to put them in jeopardy. She *wouldn't* put them in danger.

She kicked off her boots at the back door and walked inside. Ruth sat at the kitchen table and as soon as Sinead entered she sat upright and wiped her eyes with her sleeve.

"What's wrong, sweetie?"

"I've been thinking about Amy. I hope she's okay. I like her."

Sinead nodded. "Me, too." She paused. "Hey, I've been thinking. I know you like it here, but I feel we need to move.

Go somewhere else."

Ruth nodded in return. "Really? Me, too. This has become a sad place now. Let's go find Amy and cheer her up."

Sinead took a deep breath. "Well, that's not quite what I had in mind."

Ruth smiled. "I know. Too many people, too many police. But why not? Like in the movies, hiding in plain sight. We can dye our hair, get fancy sunglasses, and no one will know who we are."

Sinead laughed. "A *real* adventure, right?"

Ruth's grin widened. "Yeah, like we talked about driving here. Besides, I really want to know how Amy is."

Sinead did, too. She mulled over the idea. Maybe it could work.

"So, what color hair do you want?" They both had reddish brown hair, bordering on being certified redheads, true to their Irish roots.

Ruth tossed her head back a little and replied, "Well, I want to have more fun, so I want to be blonde. You'd look good with ink black."

"Black? Really?" Sinead had never imagined herself with black hair, despite having several raven-haired friends as she grew up.

Ruth gave a curt nod. "Yes. Dark and mysterious."

Sinead laughed and made a short curtsy. "So be it, m'lady. We shall make it so." She walked to the sink and filled a glass with water. "But first, you need your medicine. And then we need to pack, get the car ready, and close down the house for the second time. We'll have to take the tiller back on the way. And, as long as we don't get any more rain, we might be able to cross the creek by early afternoon."

Ruth perked up. "So, let's get moving."

Diane had never been so humiliated. She felt like a common criminal to have security follow her step-by-step from the front door to her office and throughout the building. Why, the female guard even stepped into the ladies' room with her. What was she going to do there? Stop up a sink with paper towels and leave the water running to flood the place? The faucets had automatic turn-offs.

The worst of it was that no one knew she'd been fired. So, to be seen clearing out her office with security in place, made it look like she'd been caught with her hand in the till or something.

Yes, humiliated. But as the experience weighed on her, she became more indignant. She had been doing her job. She was protecting a minor whose parents had failed her. Why should *she* be the one treated like scum?

A box that once held reams of paper for the copier was provided to her, and she began to fill it with personal items from her desk. There wasn't much. A few family photos in frames. Two coffee mugs. One read: Warning! Social Worker with an Attitude! The second listed the "work" of a social worker: Feed the Hungry, Shelter the Homeless, Protect the Children, and more. That was her favorite mug, and she took her "work" seriously.

"Diane? What's . . ."

Diane looked up from her desk to see her friend, Kiandra, staring at her, questioning. She also glanced at the guard near the doorway and decided to hold her tongue.

"What does it look like? I've been . . ." Which euphemism did she want to use? Dumped? Thrown under the bus? Pushed off the bridge? Or just the real term, fired? "... let go. Sorry, if you have to pick up some of my cases. If you do, the paperwork should all be in order."

"But why? What . . ."

Diane used her eyes to point to security and Kiandra understood.

"Hey, let me treat you to lunch. Our usual place. Say, eleven-thirty."

Diane thought about that for a moment. Kiandra was her closest ally in the office, but she was also the same age as the Commissioner and had known the woman since they both started at D.C.F. Maybe she could help make the Commissioner reconsider this decision.

"I'd like that. Might be our last time to chat face-to-face."

Kiandra frowned. "I doubt that. But we'll talk over lunch. See you there." The woman turned and left the office.

Diane opened the bottom drawer of her desk where she kept her case files in hanging folders and pulled them out. She resisted the temptation to glance through them and couldn't help but wonder what would happen to the children involved. The security guard stepped forward.

"Don't worry. I have no intention of taking them. I just wanted to make them obvious for my supervisor. Who, by the way, I thought might be here."

The sarcasm in her voice was obvious. Winona Clark and she had butted heads on more than one occasion, so she was certain the woman had been part of the decision to terminate her. Yet, she apparently didn't have the chutzpa to face Diane now, even though she should be the one taking claim of the case files.

Diane finished clearing her desk and glanced about.

She saw nothing on the bookcases she wished to take with her. The break room? *No*, she thought, *nothing there either*. She couldn't think of anyplace else where she might have something she should reclaim.

"All done. Do you want to check the drawers, count the paper clips? The stapler is still there." The guard gave her a look of disgust, and Diane realized she was venting to the wrong person. "Sorry. You're just doing your job." She picked up the box and said, "I'm ready. Let's go."

The emotions that filled her as she left the office surprised her. This had been her space, her home away from home, for nearly 18 years. Now? The office was prime real estate in the overall scheme of the larger office. Would the others fight over it? Who would get it? Suddenly it bothered her that one of several co-workers she didn't like might get it. Yet, she had no authority to "grant it" to a specific person of her choosing. The fact that she now had *zero* authority dawned on her, and that distressed her more than losing the office.

The guard stepped out of the office, into the hallway and gestured for Diane to precede her. But, in a quick scoop, she palmed her ID badge and slid it into the box when the guard looked away. Diane then complied, refusing to look around or to acknowledge anyone else in the building as she left the premises.

Fourteen

The Woods Hole considered itself a dive by any standard, pun intended. Situated in the Back Bay area of Boston, it was a "locals only" kind of place that had yet to be discovered by any of those online groups known for ruining a place by outing it to the traveling public, a.k.a. tourists. It had survived a legal challenge by the famed oceanographic institute of the same name on Cape Cod and continued to serve the best clam chowder, fried lobster, and raw oysters in the city. In Diane's opinion, anyway.

The line for lunch had already oozed onto the sidewalk when she arrived. Had they planned on a time closer to noon, the line might be 50 feet longer and delay their meal by another 45 minutes. That was always a risk when attempting lunch there.

She checked her phone for the time. Ten minutes early. She doubted Kiandra would be inside. If anything, she would be late, not early.

Texting wasn't her strong suit, but she pecked a message on her phone: "Already here. Check inside if you don't see me." After sending it to her friend, she settled in for the wait. The skies were overcast from a storm moving in from the Midwest where the winds had done serious damage to several communities and taken down a medevac helicopter. Aerial scenes of the crash site had made the previous night's national news. However, the rain hadn't moved into the area yet, so the wait outside was tolerable.

By the designated meeting time, Diane had moved inside, with just two parties ahead of her for seating. She glanced around. Still no sign of Kiandra.

"How many?"

The hostess' voice startled her. She turned toward the woman. "Two, please. My friend should be here any minute."

The woman picked up two menus and stepped away, looking into the back of the restaurant. Diane followed her gaze and saw two people stand up to gather their belongings.

"Right this way, please."

The hostess started to walk toward the departing couple, and by the time Diana arrived at the table, the place had been cleared and cleaned. A waitress stepped up with water and a place setting, which she set before Diane.

"I have a friend meeting me."

"Okay, hon. Be right back."

Diane's phone vibrated. She glanced at it to find a message, "I'm here." With that, she looked toward the front door and saw Kiandra trying to move past the waiting patrons, nodding her head right and then left to say something to people she passed. Once near the head of the line, she looked up, Diane waved, and Kiandra acknowledged her. She quickly made her way to the table.

"Hi. Sorry I'm late. I was trying to get the dirt from inside the Commissioner's office. Can't say as I found much." She took off her coat and sat down. The waitress promptly provided water and utensils.

Kiandra continued, "Word spread quickly after you left. Needless to say, everyone had their opinion as to what happened."

Diane took a sip of water. Then, she replied, "No doubt. And no one was close I'm sure."

Kiandra waggled her head back and forth. "Actually, most figured it had to do with this O'Malley case. You were all over MedicalKidnap.com and other websites. Did you really try to tell the judge what to do?"

Diane thought about that for a moment. In hindsight, she could see how the judge might interpret her action that way. But to lose her job? She was *supposed* to be an advocate for the children.

When she didn't respond right away, Kiandra continued, "Well, if you did, good for you. They need to find that girl ASAP, before she dies in the care of her mother."

Diane nodded in agreement.

"So, what are you going to do now?"

"I don't know." Diane spoke that in truth. She didn't know. The realization that her career might be over had come to her as she drove to the restaurant. For over 20 years, she had worked in child protective services. The vast majority of that time had been as a state employee. Who would hire someone the state had fired? After all, a government job was like getting tenure at a university. No one, however incompetent, lost their job. Look at that gal from the I.R.S. who went after conservatives. Even the misuse of her office didn't cost that lady *her* job. She was allowed to retire with full benefits. What did Diane's situation say of her?

"You know the Commissioner pretty well. Can you find out if there's any way I can get my job back?"

Kiandra leaned forward. "I called over to the Central Office, and they are hush-hush over there. I mean, I couldn't get anything out of anybody. That's unreal. You can always find somebody who wants to talk dirt."

They ordered and sipped on iced tea. Diane wanted to make hers the Long Island variety.

"Are you going to be okay?"

Diane wasn't concerned in the short run. She lived frugally, in the small Cambridge home she'd inherited from her parents. She had saved for retirement but would have to investigate what her dismissal would mean to her government pension. In a pinch, if she had to move, the sale of her house alone might provide well for her. She hoped that would not be necessary. She'd known no other home.

"I'm fine. Obviously, I didn't anticipate this turn of events, but I've saved a reasonable nest egg."

The food smelled wonderful. Diane hadn't realized how hungry she was. The stress of the morning had taken more energy than she expected. Over the meal, they talked of other things, but her mind did not stray far from her current situation. As she finished, she decided on dessert. She'd had Boston Cream Pie many times at The Parker House Hotel, where an Armenian-French chef had first created it in 1856. However, The Woods Hole pastry chef could compete with any at the Omni Parker House, as it was now called.

"Dessert? You never eat dessert."

Diane looked up after her first bite. "Comfort food."

Kiandra gave her a wry smile. "So, getting back on topic, what are you going to do?"

Diane thought about that, the seed of a plan beginning to form in her mind. "Well, I don't know if I should be job hunting right away. It's become quite clear that I'm toxic right now. No one would hire me at the moment, so maybe I need to lay low for a while and let this pass by."

Kiandra gave her a suspicious look. "What? That doesn't sound like you."

Diane could feel her friend's stare penetrating her mind. No, it wasn't like her in the past to back down, and it wasn't going to be her nature in the present. Could she trust Kiandra?

"You've got something in mind, don't you?" Her brow narrowed as she focused on Diane. "You do. You have a plan."

Diane remained silent.

"I can see it in your eyes. What? What are you planning?"

What was she going to say? That she intended to find Ruth O'Malley, prove herself right, and make the Commissioner regret firing her? No. Diane made the decision not to trust her friend.

"I'm thinking that if I want a job like this one, I'll need to leave New England. Maybe Chicago or Phoenix. Someplace where the courts are sympathetic to what we believe in. Here in New England, all the state department bosses know Commissioner Fitzsimmons too well." She frowned. "Yeah, I hate to say it, but I think I'm going to have to leave the region."

The truth of that statement hit her hard. Could she really leave the only home she'd ever known? The reality of her situation made her all the more determined. She needed to find Ruth O'Malley.

Tammy felt the urgent need to pee, again. She had

emptied her bladder after lunch just three hours earlier and then had sought out the restroom 30 minutes ago, prior to returning to the precinct building. Now, she sat outside the lieutenant's office waiting on Barkley and wondered if the urgency was just nerves or the onset of a bladder infection. She'd never had a urinary tract infection before, but her grandmother had them frequently, a problem only partially resolved by bladder suspension surgery.

Born to a teenage mother, Tammy's grandparents had raised her in southeastern Wisconsin. She never knew her father but that didn't matter. Her grandparents had loved, encouraged, and supported her without condition. She had been devastated when they both died in quick succession when she was a freshman in college. Not yet being of legal age at that time, the state's Department of Children and Family had stepped in briefly to make sure her real mom was capable of caring for her. She hadn't been, but Tammy successfully convinced the D.C.F. otherwise. She had wanted nothing to do with their alternative.

The relationship between Tammy and her mother had always been strained. Even today, Tammy played the responsible mom to her mother's irresponsible child role. And Tammy had learned long ago not to trust her mother. Her grandparents had left everything to Tammy, but her mom and mom's siblings had stolen cash, jewelry, and other things of value from the house before Tammy could even get home from college. They then challenged Tammy's inheritance and succeeded in getting her grandparents' estate divided between the four of them, squeezing out Tammy.

In some ways, that had been a blessing in disguise, since the incident made her resolve to move to a new city upon graduation. She found her way to St. Louis and never looked back.

Still, as she sat outside the lieutenant's office, she wondered if he would be more like her grandparents or more like her mother . . . and whether or not she had time for one more run to the restroom. Before she could decide, the door opened.

"Jahn, get in my office. Will's tied up and won't make it back in time."

Well, that answered her question about where Barkley was. Maybe this wouldn't be so bad after all.

She sat in the worn wooden chair across from the equally distressed wooden desk and sat at attention. She placed her hands in her lap and forced herself not to fidget. She continually told her three kids not to fidget, and now she was reminded how easy it was to do.

"So, let's cut to the chase."

Tammy refrained from rolling her eyes, another "talent" she realized her children had inherited from her. Or, was it the other way around? Either way, the lieutenant's habit of using clichés—cop movies were his favorites—typically produced a similarly clichéd physical response.

"Will told me what happened, from his perspective. So, give me your side . . . and don't tell me it isn't what it looks like."

She refrained from answering, "If I tell ya, I'd hafta kill ya." As tempting as that was, she knew he wouldn't appreciate that answer.

She related her actions with Montez Johnson's mother at their home and how Sergeant Barkley—she made sure to use his rank and last name—had approached her about finding the two guys with Montez. She proceeded to the point where her sergeant called the men out, with no response.

"Lieutenant, as soon as I heard who was inside, I knew my risk was minimal. I knew Antwan Hall and that he grew up with Montez Johnson. I knew he was not the killer, or Isaiah Robinson either. I had my vest on, watched the door and windows closely, and I was confident I could get Hall to talk with me."

"Yeah, that's what Will told me. But, you don't get it, do you? You didn't know who else was in that building. You didn't know if they were high on crack or lean or anything else. If they were having a bad day, they might not have cared what kind of history you had with them."

She frowned. "I knew that. I'm not a rookie, Lieutenant. As I said, I felt my risk was minimal, not that there was no risk at all. And I was right, we now know who did it and why. Well, we don't have a name, but we're a big step closer to getting it."

Ever since becoming a police officer she had found the need to defend herself on repeated occasions. She wondered whether a male cop who had done the same thing would be questioned like this. Yet, deep inside she had known to expect it. For Barkley, maybe it was a male superiority thing. She knew the lieutenant pretty well, too. For him, dealing with the female officers was more like wanting to protect his little sister. More chivalry than chauvinism. For that, she couldn't fault him.

The lieutenant shook his head. "Look, Tammy, I don't want anyone here dying on me. We gotta watch each other's six or we might leave a scene in a body bag, not a cruiser. If your sergeant tells you to get back, do it. Don't do anything stupid." He paused. "Look, I know you're no rookie. You've done a great job, and I want to see that continue. We're not so different, you and I."

She almost snorted in laughter at the last line. She'd read somewhere on the internet that the "We're not so different . . ." line had been used in over 30 well-known movies.

"Go on. Get outta here."

She didn't hesitate in jumping up and leaving the office, relieved that this "ordeal" was over and hadn't gone badly at all. But then, the lieutenant wasn't the one who worried her. Barkley still made the assignments—and he was the one known to hold a grudge.

Fifteen

Sinead couldn't help but absorb Ruth's enthusiasm and optimism about their upcoming adventure. The girl's infectious outlook showed in her eagerness to pack, her energy level, and even a willingness to wash dishes. And when Sinead discovered that their departure would be delayed because the creek remained too high, Ruth brushed off the news with the simple comment, "Then we'll get a fresh start in the morning."

When had her daughter begun acting so grown-up? What had happened to her little girl?

Morning was now upon them, and before finalizing packing the car, Sinead ventured out while Ruth willingly made breakfast. She drove as far as the creek and got out of the car. She walked up to the edge of the water, which was a fraction of the flow she had seen when trying to take Amy to get help. Still, the water was muddy, and she could not see the bottom all the way across the ford.

She understood the danger that still existed. The apparent depth of the water seemed passable. Even her small car could clear the water itself. However, if a hole had been washed out underneath that water, it might be large enough that a wheel could fall into it. Or worse, if a rear wheel encountered the hole, the damage could include a broken rear axle. Then, they'd be stuck, without cell service to call for a tow. Her only option then would be to carry Ruth's wheelchair, and then Ruth, to the opposite shore and hoof it to the nearest home.

She looked down at her boots. They had been tough enough for her attempt at tilling a garden. Plus, she had dry shoes packed in the back.

Before stepping into the water, she searched the nearby stream bank and found a sturdy limb to use as both a walking stick and probe. With a suitable branch in hand, she stepped into the water and moved about a quarter of the way across. *So far so good*, she thought. Using the stick to check the stream bed all around her, she found solid ground. She took another step forward and repeated the process.

Ten minutes later, she had surveyed the ford from one bank to the other and back again, spanning a 20-foot width to make sure that no matter where she might cross, she could do so safely. At one spot in the middle, the water ran over the top of her boots, and she squealed at the cold water flooding over her foot. Yet, otherwise she felt pleased to find it so shallow. She said a quiet prayer of thanks and trudged back to the car, where she slipped out of the boots and donned dry footwear.

Minutes later, she entered the house to find Ruth pouting.

"The eggs are probably dried out and the toast is cold. I didn't think you would take so long." She started to cry.

Sinead rushed over to her. "What's wrong, sweetie? I'm sure the eggs will be fine. Or, we can stop for breakfast along the way."

"I-it's not the eggs. I-I thought you got hurt or

something. You were gone so long." She wiped her eyes and sniffed.

Sinead squeezed her daughter and smoothed her hair. She hadn't been gone *that* long, maybe 20 minutes at most. Yet, she hadn't considered the depth of Ruth's separation anxieties.

"I'm sorry, Ruth. I had to wade through the creek and check it for holes. If a tire gets stuck in one, we're out of luck. I just needed to make sure we could get across. I guess I should have warned you first that it might take a little while."

Ruth nodded and wiped her eyes again.

"And guess what, I don't think that creek is going to delay our adventure any longer. So, let's eat some dry scrambled eggs on cold toast, pack up, and get out of here."

"Okay." Ruth's voice was timid, but as she moved to the table, her optimism rebounded. "So, you really had to wade the creek? That sounds like an adventure already."

"It was cold. A lot colder than this toast."

Ruth laughed. "Good thing you didn't slip."

Sinead smiled. "That's for sure."

Thirty minutes later, the dishes were washed, dried and put away. Their remaining belongings were packed in the car, and Sinead had secured the small utility trailer to the temporary trailer hitch. Ruth emerged from the house walking behind her wheelchair as Sinead wrangled the tiller onto the trailer.

"Need help getting into the car?"

"I got it."

Ruth maneuvered to the passenger door, opened it,

and climbed in. Sinead secured the tiller with the straps provided by the rental store, and then folded up the wheelchair and slid it behind Ruth's seat. She made a quick tour of the house, double-checked thermostat settings, and made sure they'd forgotten nothing to prepare the home for being empty yet again. She locked up and slid the key into a padded envelope addressed to her friend Adriana.

As she sat back into the driver's seat, Ruth sighed. "I liked this place. Too bad we have to leave. Do you think maybe someday we could move back here, as a family?"

Sinead patted her daughter's knee. "Probably not, sweetie. There's no work near here for your dad. Who would support us?"

As Sinead started the car, Ruth replied, "Oh. I guess that's true. Too bad."

As soon as they reached the creek, Sinead broke into a big smile. "So, you ready to go swimming?"

Ruth looked out the window and made a disgusted face. "Not in that water. Yuck."

Sinead eased the car into the water, shifting down into first gear. "Just like riding the ducks in Boston Harbor, eh?"

"If we start floating, I'm going to get worried."

Two minutes later, the creek was only a sight in the rearview mirror. Yet, Sinead grew tense. They had a ten-mile stretch of road to clear. Anyone passing them now would know they had come from the house. And if that "anyone" was a sheriff or state policeman, they would get curious about a car driving out from the property.

Sinead resisted the urge to speed, but her white knuckle grip on the steering wheel belied her anxiety. She was so intent on the goal she didn't realize Ruth had been talking to her until she felt a punch in her upper arm.

"Earth to mom. Earth to mom. I've been talking to you."

Sinead released her breath and eased her grip. "Sorry. I guess I'm a little nervous."

"A little? I think you bent the steering wheel."

Sinead smiled but proceeded to tell Ruth her concern.

"Oh. Well, we'll be fine. You'll see."

Forty minutes later, Sinead walked into the hardware store where she had rented the tiller. The same man who had rented the machine to her worked the store today.

"Well, little lady, how'd that tiller work for ya? Didja get your garden done before those storms? Probably a mess to work the ground now."

Sinead gritted her teeth at the "little lady" remark but realized he probably wasn't being as chauvinistic as she imagined. More likely the term was simply something he used out of habit. Back home she might have said something to correct him. Here? She wasn't about to create a scene that might make her more memorable.

"No, I'm afraid I didn't. I managed to get a couple of rows tilled. That's all. I can't afford to just keep it until the ground dries enough to use it again, so guess I'll be back to rent it later." Or so she wanted him to believe.

He headed out the door and Sinead followed.

He nodded. "Say, didja hear about the helicopter that crashed in the storm? On one of the farms off that way." He pointed to the southeast. "Heard it was a medical chopper. Mighty sad about that flight crew." He pulled the tiller off the trailer and began to unhitch the latter.

Sinead took his comment at its worst, thinking Amy must not have survived or he might have mentioned it. She needed to know, to prepare Ruth if that was the case. Yet, she also thought it best to lie and hoped God would forgive her for another little white one. "That's awful. I hadn't heard. Any survivors at all?"

"Not that I heard. My friend with the state police said everyone at the scene had died."

At the scene? she thought. Amy wasn't at the scene. Maybe she *had* made it. Ruth would be devastated to learn otherwise.

"That's sad. Say, I'm curious, if someone had a serious injury out here and needed to fly into a hospital, a trauma center, where would they go?"

"Springfield Memorial. Closest trauma center. You'd hafta go to St. Louis for the next closest. Least, that's what I've been told. Say, if you're livin' out here now, you outta sign up for MedAir's membership deal. Kinda like insurance. You pay an annual premium, but something happens and you need them, they fly you at no cost. And no matter where you need to go."

"Thanks. I'll keep that in mind."

He finished unlatching the temporary trailer hitch. "Looks like everything's in order."

Sinead followed him back into the store and completed the transaction, getting her cash deposit back. She would need it.

Ten minutes later, on the road to Springfield, Ruth again began to quiz her.

"What's wrong? That guy call you 'little lady' again?"

Sinead gave her a wry smile and shrugged. She didn't want to upset her daughter over speculation or rumor about Amy. Yet, the guilt had returned. If Amy did indeed die after leaving the farm, how could Sinead forgive herself for not having helped more?

"Well? What's wrong?"

"Yes, in fact, he did call me that again. But, I forgive him. It's probably just something he says without thinking about how a woman might receive it."

"Oh."

With a quick glance toward her daughter, she saw Ruth scrutinizing her. How well her daughter had come to know her through this ordeal. Ruth could "read" her better than she could "read" Ruth.

"There's something else, isn't there?"

Sinead took a deep breath. She had promised not to keep secrets or hide anything from her daughter when they started their "adventure" in Boston. Obviously, this turn of events couldn't have been foreseen, and Sinead resisted telling her daughter what the man had said.

"We're heading to Springfield. The man said Memorial Medical Center there is where the EMS folks take injured people."

Ruth continued to stare at her, as if she had turned purple or her nose had grown. Not that she had lied.

"Did he say something else?"

Sinead took a deep breath. "He said he'd heard all the flight crew had died." She glanced at Ruth and saw the tears beginning to form. "Well, he said everyone at the scene. Amy wasn't at the scene. She was with us."

Ruth made no comment but turned to stare out the window. After a few minutes of silence, she turned back toward Sinead. "I-I know we agreed to no secrets. But sometimes that sucks. Maybe sometimes, I don't want to know everything."

* * *

An hour later, Sinead parked in the front lot of Springfield Memorial. She retrieved Ruth's wheelchair and helped her daughter into it. The last half an hour of their trip had been a quiet one, with Ruth acting more subdued than usual. Even now, she gave Sinead a look that questioned, "Do I have to go with you?"

The silence continued as Sinead pushed Ruth to and through the main doors to the information desk. An older woman with more-salt-than-pepper hair and wire-rimmed glasses looked up to greet them.

"Good morning. May I help you?"

"Yes. Good morning. We're looking for a patient named Amy Gibbs. We were told she was flown in here by helicopter two days ago."

The woman moved her gaze to the computer monitor in front of her and typed in several keystrokes. She looked up. "You said Amy Gibb."

"Gibbs, with an 's.' She was in that helicopter crash. She's a flight nurse and a friend." Sinead wondered how much information she should reveal, but she, and Ruth, really wanted, no, *needed* to find out what happened to Amy.

The woman removed her glasses and shook her head. "Wasn't that awful? Those poor people. They served so many people in need, and then something unexpected like this happens. We have a MedAir crew stationed here in town and they knew them all. I hear they're taking it pretty hard."

Ruth looked up. Her face told Sinead that she, too, was reading between the lines, to what the woman *wasn't* saying—a room number. Sinead's own countenance fell, and the woman must have noticed.

"I'm sorry, but we don't have an Amy Gibbs here as a patient. I heard that everyone on the flight crew had died."

Ruth began to sob, and the woman held up a box of tissues for Sinead, who found her own eyes tearing up.

"Are you sure?"

"Again, I'm sorry. All I have is the information here on the computer. And what I've heard through the news and grapevine."

"Could she have gone to another hospital?"

"We're the only trauma center here. St. Louis would be the next choice. That's all . . ."

Sinead didn't wait for her to finish as she pushed Ruth back toward the doors and car. They had nowhere else to go. St. Louis made as much sense as anywhere. They'd find the answer there.

Marcia Holmes had volunteered at Springfield Memorial since the age of 16 and was only two years away from being honored for 50 years of service. She took pride in her work there. More importantly, since being assigned to the information desk, she took pride in being alert and observant of those who came through the front doors, whether they stopped to ask for information or not.

Just a year earlier, her keen intuition had stopped a man intent on killing his ex-wife. His actions had already sent her to the E.D., where she had been admitted for multiple injuries. The police had been searching for him, and she had recognized him from the nightly news. Security managed to subdue him before he reached her room, and the police found a hunting knife strapped to his leg.

Now, she had the same feeling. Something just didn't

seem right about the younger woman and her daughter in the wheelchair. That helicopter had been out of St. Louis, so how was it they were here in Springfield asking about a possible survivor? And who would have told them to come to Memorial when the local news had reported all crew members dead at the scene? Something didn't add up, but Marcia couldn't put her finger on it.

She used her computer to search for updates on the helicopter crash story. Sure enough, the original story had been corrected to mention there had been one survivor, the flight nurse, who was currently hospitalized in St. Louis. That, too, puzzled Marcia. If the internet now reported the nurse as being hospitalized in St. Louis, why would the woman be looking for her here? Unless, of course, she didn't have access to the internet. But, who these days didn't have access to the internet?

As she pondered the situation and tried to wrap her head around what had made her "antennae" tingle, she scrolled back to the Fox News portal. There she saw a new listing for a story she'd been following about a child taken from her parents by people at the Children's Hospital in Boston. There had been alleged abuse, but two sets of doctors disagreed. The whole thing sounded confusing. Yet, the last thing she'd read about it said the mom had taken the child from a rehab center and disappeared. They remained fugitives. Curious about any updates to the story, she clicked on the story's link, and this time the item showed a picture of mother and daughter.

Marcia quickly picked up the phone and dialed security.

Sixteen

Amy awoke from another awful dream. Men had kidnapped her, carrying her away into a woods. And then she was in an Emergency Room, one like *her* E.D., the department where she had worked for years. Then the scene shifted again. A man in a mask hovering over her, silhouetted by bright lights. The imagery was disjointed, surreal. Just like a dream.

But, was it? It seemed so real.

Sounds and smells penetrated her consciousness before she opened her eyes. Familiar sounds and smells but not from her home. No, these were the sounds and smells of her profession.

She opened her eyes, and the blurry scene around her slowly came into focus. Was she in an intensive care room? It looked like one, but not any I.C.U. she had been in before. Or had she? She had visited a lot of intensive care units in her role as a flight nurse. They all began to look alike. And the clearer her head became, the more this room looked like one at Mercy Medical Center. How had she gotten there?

" 'Bout time. Welcome back. You had us worried."

Richard? she thought. She turned her head toward the voice and saw him, smiling and scooting closer to her bed. *Her* bed? He reached over and took her hand. His touch warmed and assured her.

"What?" Her voice was scratchy and her throat dry.

"Here. Just a sip." Richard extended a foam cup toward her, with a straw extending from inside.

She knew the drill. How many times had she been the one extending the cup toward an accident victim? *Wait a minute*, she thought. *Accident victim.* The helicopter crash. Sinead. Ruth. The barn. The pain she felt climbing into that truck. Her thoughts circled back to Sinead and Ruth. Had they been discovered? What happened to them? She began to worry that something bad had happened to them.

"Where . . ." Her voice sounded better. ". . . are we? And for that matter, how did *you* get here?"

"To answer the 'where.' We're at Mercy Medical Center, the I.C.U. As to the rest of it, Lynch and I flew up with Craig to help search. The state police were searching the wrong area, and Lynch figured out where the wind had probably taken you. We found the crash scene, but we couldn't find *you*. So, Lynch and I started looking around the area and came across this abandoned house and barn. How you managed to get there is beyond me, but we found you unconscious in an old pickup truck in the barn."

Amy glanced around. Mercy Med Center was good. But why didn't she remember arriving there? Would they have accepted her straight from the crash scene when Springfield had a trauma center and had been much closer?

And then the rest of what he had said sank in. Maybe the bad dream hadn't ended. Or someone was punking her. Richard *and* Lynch? Where was the camera hidden to catch her reaction?

Yet, it also hit her that he had said *abandoned* house. Maybe Sinead and Ruth remained safe in hiding. All the unanswered questions made her head swirl.

Richard continued, as her mind tried to process that he and Lynch had somehow bonded.

"Initially, we headed toward Springfield Memorial, but a bus accident on the interstate had overwhelmed their E.D. They still would take you but care might have been delayed. You had stabilized with some fluids, and the flight was only like 15 minutes longer to come here, so Craig made the decision to divert, pushed it to max speed, and here we are. You were in the E.D. just long enough for some labs and tests, and then taken to surgery. Your spleen was torn, but not badly, and your leg was broken in a couple of places. You were in surgery for a couple of hours. But we've been worried 'cause you hadn't woken up yet."

"W-what did they have to do?"

"I don't know. They wouldn't tell me anymore because of the privacy laws. The doctor should be here shortly. I let them know when you started waking up."

Amy began mentally to list the potential treatments for both areas of her body. A ruptured spleen could heal itself with a minor tear. Anything worse than a Grade II injury would lead to a splenectomy. A lot worse could have happened. Having her spleen removed really only had minor health implications later.

But her ankle? Her mind jumped to the worst case scenario. Why did it always do that? Probably because she was a nurse, an E.D. nurse at that, trained to think the worst and be prepared for it. Still, she couldn't help but wonder. Did she still have a leg and foot? Would she play sand volleyball or a pickup basketball game with her brothers again?

She tried to look down, toward her feet, but the sheet

made it impossible to visualize them. On the bright side, however, she saw that sheet rise up in two places where her feet should be. She sighed in relief.

"Ummm, tell me. You said you . . . and Lynch. Ummm . . . ."

He chuckled. "I know, sounds really strange. Especially to you, I imagine. But over the last 24 hours, we've gotten to know each other pretty well. He's a great guy." He paused. "Look, I don't think you have anything to worry about. I think that anoxic brain injury thing he went through, well, it affected him to a point where he sees you as a great friend, nothing more. If not, he's one A-list actor. He's not going to become some stalker ex-boyfriend."

She had never even thought of Lynch becoming a problem for her. But if there was ever an ex- she wouldn't want to become a stalker, the vengeful type, it would be Lynch.

A knock at the door caught her attention.

"Ms. Gibbs? I'm Doctor Torres, the critical care doctor today. Glad to see you looking so alert." He walked up to the bed and extended his hand. She shook it.

"So, how are you feeling?"

She shrugged her shoulders. "Okay, I guess. I'm not sure how I should feel. Belly's a little sore, and my ankle doesn't hurt nearly as much as it did."

"Good. Well, . . ." He paused and looked at Richard. "Can I talk freely in front of your guest?"

Amy nodded. "Sure. He's my fiancé."

"Okay then. Well, you had a minor spleen laceration, but there was enough bleeding internally to drop your blood pressure and cause the unconsciousness. The surgeons decided to explore your belly because of the severity of the accident you were in. They couldn't be sure that injury was the only problem. All that blood in your belly made it hard to read the scans. Fortunately, they were able to repair the spleen and didn't need to remove it."

Amy felt relieved at that news. "I think I actually might have injured it, or maybe made it worse, when I tried to climb into the pickup truck to stay warm. I hit my abdomen on the edge of the seat and felt pain for the first time then."

The doctor signaled his agreement. "That's very possible. Your ankle . . ."

He went on to discuss the severity of the injury. A comminuted fracture of the tibia, needing a metal plate and screws, and more, but Amy focused on the conclusion.

". . . so, you'll be laid up for a while, mostly on crutches. Ortho thinks that in six months, with therapy, you'll be good as new, other than your new hardware setting off airport metal detectors."

That's what she wanted to hear. She didn't want or need any more medical leave from work. She liked her job.

"So, when can I go home?"

The doctor laughed. "Well, that might be a couple of days yet, but your vital signs have been stable and you look good, now that you're awake. We were beginning to think we'd missed a head injury, but your scans were normal. Your surgeons would like you to stay here for a couple of days, to make sure there's no further bleeding. We'll be able to transfer you to a surgical bed shortly, I think." He grinned. "Oh, and a nurse named Macy, from the E.D., keeps asking about you. I'll let her know you can see visitors now."

Amy laughed inside. As if Macy had ever needed permission to visit. Macy knew places in this hospital even the architects had forgotten. If someone ever needed to pay a stealth visit to a patient, Macy was the one to call. She had, in fact, arranged such a visit the last time Amy had been a patient there. From another helicopter crash. Amy began to think that maybe she should give up flying. Well, in helicopters anyway. She'd never had an incident in her Cessna.

"That is it," added the doctor, who stood to leave the room. "Any questions?"

Amy nodded. "Can I eat? I'm hungry."

Dr. Torres laughed. "I guess you are doing much better. We'll start that process."

The process? That's not what she had in mind. With "the process"—starting with clear liquids and advancing her diet as tolerated—she'd be lucky to get green gelatin and bland chicken broth for lunch. Oh boy.

Seventeen

Sinead and Ruth had no sooner settled into the car when a hospital security car entered her field of vision on the left. The guard appeared to be looking for someone, or something, and Sinead's heart rate began to accelerate. The car slowly drove past them but stopped 100 yards away at the end of the lane. Sinead saw the backup lights flash on, indicating he had put the car in reverse.

She knew there could be only one reason for that.

She quickly placed her own car in reverse and backed out of the parking slot. She turned and headed the other way, trying hard not to speed and make it look as if they were fleeing, which they were.

She glanced into her rearview mirror and saw that the security car had stopped, but now accelerated forward, speeding into the next lane and heading her way. He appeared to be trying to cut her off and block her exit from the lot. Sinead sped up in response.

"Mom?"

"Shhhh! I need to focus on driving."

Sinead concentrated on the exit. She would beat him to it but what then?

"Mom!" The distress in Ruth's voice made Sinead glance her direction. Flashing lights! A police car had just entered the far end of the lot.

Sinead buzzed through the stop sign and turned the only direction she knew, toward the roads heading back to the farm. With a few more turns, she no longer saw signs of their being followed, but that wouldn't last long. If that security officer had made a positive ID on her license plate, the Springfield Police would quickly act on the nationwide AMBER Alert that had gone out three weeks earlier for Ruth—and her "kidnapper."

Sinead tried to think, but her mind wouldn't calm down. She saw a public parking garage a block away. If she could get there without being spotted.

She pulled into the gate, grabbed the ticket, and entered the structure as quickly as she could. As they pulled into the deepest shadows the building had to offer, a police car whizzed by the entrance. A minute later, convinced the officer hadn't doubled back, she found her way to the second floor and pulled into a spot in the darkest area there. Before getting out of the car, she looked around for cameras, and seeing none, she emerged and headed for the closest source of artificial light. She couldn't do anything about the sun, but this bulb would need replacement in short order. A small chunk of concrete and a solid upward heave made sure of that.

She ran back to the car and dropped into her seat. Ruth's face revealed that she understood what had just happened. They'd almost been caught . . . and they weren't Scot-free yet.

"Diane, did you hear?"

Kiandra sounded more animated than at any time in

their friendship. Just the excitement in her voice stirred Diana as well. But, what? What had Diane not heard?

"I guess not. I've been busy trying to make some sort of plan to move ahead. Not to mention, I'm no longer in the loop anymore. So, what's up?"

"They've been spotted."

Diane suspected she knew who "they" were by the tone in her friend's voice, and the grip on her home phone's handset tightened in anticipation. Still, she asked anyway. "Who? Who's been spotted?"

"Ruth O'Malley and her mother. Who else would I be calling you about?" Kiandra sounded miffed but plugged ahead with her report. "Springfield. Springfield Memorial Medical Center. A volunteer at the information desk recognized them, called security, and they positively ID'd the license plate."

"So, they have them in custody. Good. I knew they wouldn't be far away."

Diane debated how to handle this news. The small mid-state city was an hour and a half drive from Boston. With a bit of luck, the authorities would have mother and child back in Boston, and the mother in jail, by nightfall. Did she want to try to make herself available when Ruth was delivered back to the rehab facility? She wanted to see firsthand how badly the girl had fared in her mother's care. She desperately wanted to say, "See! I told you so."

"Well, I didn't say—"

That's when Diane realized that Springfield didn't have a Memorial Medical Center.

"Wait a minute," she interrupted. "Do you mean Baystate? There is no—"

Kiandra shot back, "Sorry. Springfield, Illinois. Not

Massachusetts."

Well, that threw a wrench in Diane's slowly evolving plan for redemption.

"And they didn't catch them. They're still on the loose, but the State Police and others are on high alert. They have reason to believe the pair is heading to St. Louis."

Now the wrench had jammed between two gears and threatened to destroy the whole works. Diane needed to think, and act, quickly. She saw her pilfered ID badge on the nearby counter and wondered. Could she? Hmmm. More importantly, would she? She had never broken a law knowingly before. The next question in her head was would the local authorities check on her credentials if she tried to pass herself off as still being a D.C.F. employee? She so wanted to prove herself right.

"Hey, thanks, Kiandra. Will you keep me in the loop? I'm going to be out of town for a few days. You can always reach me by cell. Gotta go."

"Sure, Diane, but don't you want to—"

Diane hung up. She had much to do. If she was going to do this, she needed to start in Springfield, with that hospital volunteer. She grabbed her laptop and began searching. So many options. Flying to Springfield through Chicago. But then she'd still have to rent a car to get to St. Louis. In reality, it was cheaper to fly into St. Louis, rent the car, and drive to Springfield and back.

But cheaper was a relative term. That choice would still set her back hundreds of dollars. Money she'd have to take from savings. Savings she now relied upon for living expenses.

Pulling up a map website, she discovered that Springfield was 1,200 miles away and would take a good 18 hours of driving time, including pit stops. That would be the cheapest, but did she want to take that much time, only to arrive there fatigued? If she hurried to the airport, she could be in the Gateway City by mid evening, get a good night's rest, and drive to the Illinois capital in time for breakfast.

She went to the airline's website to make reservations but hesitated. Somewhere on her desk was her latest statement from her money market account. She found it under a pile of to-be-filed papers and looked at the bottom line. She looked again at the cost of tickets and car rental. Was this so urgent she had to be there in the morning? Would one more day make a difference? Besides, she only had ten dollars cash in her wallet after lunch. She'd have to go to the bank first. Maybe she didn't have enough time to do that and get to the airport through rush hour traffic.

She hated the indecisiveness. That wasn't like her.

She took one more look at her account and then at the costs of flying and a rental, and decided one more day would make no difference. She would gas up her car on the way back from the bank, get a good night's rest, and leave in the morning. She grabbed her ID badge, stuffed it into her purse, and headed out the door. She would calculate her cash needs on the way to her bank.

Sinead awoke to Ruth's punching her arm.

"Mom, it's getting dark. Are we going to sit here until we die of starvation?"

Sinead took a deep breath and glanced around to catch her bearings. That's right, the parking garage. She glanced at her watch. It was after six and the sun appeared ready to disappear below the horizon.

"I think the heat is off by now," said Ruth. "You know, in the movies, now's the time the fugitives take license plates from another car and put them on their getaway car."

Sinead chuckled. "You're right, but do I need to add another broken law to my developing rap sheet?"

Ruth laughed. "Great. My mom has a rap sheet now. I'm the daughter of criminals." She tried to lean over to kiss her mom on the cheek, but struggled. Instead, she sat back and blew her mom a kiss. "And I wouldn't want it any other way." She started to sing, "a girl with a plan" to the tune of that Taylor Swift song.

Yes, a plan. Sinead sighed. She sure could use one right about now. How could they accomplish their mission without a plan?

She pulled out her cell phone and looked at it for the first time in weeks. She debated turning it on, which would allow the GPS to ping the phone. That could help authorities pinpoint them.

Ruth must have read her mind again. "Might as well use it. They already know we're in town."

Sinead couldn't argue that logic. She powered it on, only to find it almost dead. She would have to turn on the car to power the charging cord, but she didn't want to attract any attention by sitting there with the car idling. Not to mention, not wanting to waste the gas when her cash reserves were dwindling much too quickly. She would have to rely on what reserves the phone had until they started moving.

She opened Google Maps and located their position. "Look, we're going to take some back roads to St. Louis. Our greatest risk for discovery would be the interstate." She expected Ruth to roll her eyes at the mention of a longer road trip, but the girl surprised her.

The girl gestured with her hand and index finger, saying the words, "Let it be."

Sinead laughed.

"What?"

"I think you got your celebrities mixed up. The hand signal is from Star Trek's Captain Picard, whose line is, 'Make it so.' 'Let it be' is a John Lennon lyric."

"John who?"

"Never mind." Sinead felt officially "old," but then she saw Ruth turn away with a smirk on her face. She knew who the Beatles were, and John Lennon, and was pulling her chain.

She studied the map briefly. She could find her way back to Highway 125 easily enough. That would lead back toward the farm. She would follow that back into the hinterlands and gas up at the first small town about 30 minutes away. She found a combination of state and county roads that would lead her to a U.S. highway that went straight to St. Louis. She would use the time on those back roads to recharge the phone, hoping they ran through out-of-service areas much like where the farm had been.

Perhaps with the police focusing on the Springfield area, they'd make it to St. Louis uneventfully. She said a quick prayer for invisibility and started the car.

Jeremy removed the headset and sat back in the chair that occupied the back of what appeared to be a plumbing company van. So, Diane Westlake had been fired and sought information that might redeem her. For the first time in over a year, he felt a taste of optimism. He had spent the better part of two years learning new skills, talents he put to use even now. He had a debt to pay and that due date was coming soon.

He reflected on his 28 years of life. For the past four, he'd been unable to hold a job, not because of a lack of skills. Talent and experience he had overflowing. Even his newest abilities in electronic surveillance, when added to his IT training, made him marketable. In fact, his resume made him a highly sought employee. That didn't matter. He never found a job that filled the void he felt in his life.

Jeremy anticipated Westlake's next move and opened the screen on the laptop computer sitting on the makeshift table in front of him. Sure enough, she had taken to her computer. Her unimaginative password had allowed him access to her home Wi-Fi network months earlier. Even before that, he had entered her home and bugged her home phone, living room, and bedroom.

His guess had been correct. She was thinking about going to Springfield and St. Louis.

"I'm surprised," he said to the empty van. "I thought you too cheap to spend money on flying." He calculated the time and costs to drive to St. Louis via Springfield. He monitored her actions on the computer and smiled a few minutes later. "Guess I was right after all." She had not booked a flight.

He placed one muff of the headset up to his right ear and listened to papers rustling and keys jingling. He leaned toward the front passenger window and watched her leave her house, climb into her car, and back out of the drive. *Ten-to-one odds she's going to the bank*, he thought, because that's what he'd do if he was about to embark on a cross-country trip.

As soon as she drove out of sight, he jumped from the van and walked casually to the side door of her home. On a previous excursion into her home, he had taken time to pick the lock to gain access. Once inside, he had found a spare key and made a clay impression. That led to a 3-D printed key and access to her home since then had been easy. He raced from the living room to the bedroom and retrieved the bugs he'd used until now. He doubted he would need them again.

Back at the van, he accessed his laptop one more time. The GPS device he'd placed on her car confirmed she was at the bank. A few minutes later, she was on the move again. He noticed one more stop. A gas station, her usual. Yes, she was so predictable.

He glanced up at a rumpled photo of a young woman and her daughter, both smiling and happy. Christine, their daughter, had his hazel eyes and chestnut hair. His pride and joy.

"I'm doing this for you, sweetheart. Both of you."

Eighteen

Lynch stood in the lobby of Mercy Medical Center vacillating between going upstairs to the surgical floor where they had moved Amy and turning around and driving home. The fact that he'd already driven to the hospital and had been standing there in the main lobby looking lost for going on 15 minutes didn't seem to sway him into staying.

What revolved round and round in his head was what he had said to Richard three days before. He said he had changed and knew that he and Amy weren't meant to be together. He said that he was glad she had Richard in her life. He had reached out to Richard as his friend.

All of which were true, except maybe the part about his not being meant for Amy. Seeing her near death had stirred something deep inside him. He had spent the better part of the previous 60 hours trying to figure just what that was.

Yes, he had been seeing Danijela since helping to free her and the other trafficking victims from Darko Komarčić's clutches a few months earlier. She had stayed behind because of him when her family returned to Bosnia. And yet, her homesickness became more evident each day. The overseas phone calls home grew more frequent. The stress this created on their relationship had become a subtle fissure for which he had no answer, no fix.

And yet, he had to admit that there were two sides to that growing discontent. As beautiful, and caring, and loving, and generous—he could go on with the compliments—as she was, the bond they had formed under duress had not matured, and the removal of that duress now weakened the bond. He expected her to break free from him, too, at any time. He wondered even now, as he stood in the hospital lobby, whether he might return home to find a goodbye note under the door, although he thought her too classy to leave without a personal goodbye—and an explanation.

He turned for the outside doors and took a step, when something, almost like an invisible force, caused him to do a 180. Moments later he found himself in the back of the elevator, with a crowd of people blocking his access to the door, and the car rising toward whatever was about to happen.

He was the last person on the car when the doors opened to the surgical floor. He stepped out and walked toward the nurses' station. A sense of déjà vu struck him. How many times in the past had he taken this same path to interview a crime victim—or the perpetrator? Only this time, Amy was at the end of the path.

He knocked on her door and fully expected Richard to greet him. He felt surprise, and relief, that Amy's voice alone answered.

"Come in."

The door opened as if on its own and there stood Macy. Her brow flew up as her eyes widened, and she quickly turned back toward Amy.

"Nope, it's not him. I, uh, I think . . ." She faced Lynch and, in a quick staccato, said, "Ummm, hi Lynch." She quickly turned back toward Amy. "I think I'll be going now. Bye, girlfriend."

Lynch caught her mouthing, "Awkwaarrd," to Amy. She looked up at him as she rushed past. "Bye, Lynch."

He watched her bound around the corner and turned back to see Amy sitting in a chair next to the bed. The bedside stand held a tray on which sat a disposable bowl of broth, that looked untouched, and a plastic tub showing the remnants of green gelatin.

"Hi."

"Hi, Lynch. This is a surprise."

"Um, sorry, if I'm intruding. I can . . ."

"Not at all. Come in and have a seat." Her voice sounded uncertain. Her body language confirmed her reticence in that invitation.

Lynch started to sit in a nearby chair but stopped. The item in his coat pocket hindered his movement, so he pulled it out and extended it toward her.

"H-here. Don't know if you're allowed to have it, but . . ."

She smiled at his gift of a bottle of Starbucks Frappuccino. He knew it was one of her favorites. Before handing it to her, he removed the plastic seal around the lid.

She took it, popped the top, and held the open bottle to her nose. With her eyes closed, she inhaled deeply and then sighed. She gave a quick glance at the door and took a quick sip.

"Mmmmmmm. You have no idea. Have you ever tried to eat hospital chicken broth?"

He kinda rolled his eyes and nodded.

"Oh, yeah. I guess you have. Sorry. I think my blood sugar is low or something."

Lynch counted back. Had it really been two months since he'd been in the hospital recovering from the gunshot wound and collapsed lung? She had visited him then—to break up. Well, to him it seemed like breaking up. She had made it clear that his months-long absence had forced her to move on, assuming he had died at the hands of the L.A. Rapist. And indeed she had moved on, getting engaged to Richard.

She savored another sip. "I'll have to take this slowly and hide the bottle. I'm still on clear liquids, not full liquids. I'm sure you remember the drill."

He did. He also knew that his situation had differed from hers. "The drill" was different and more cautious after abdominal surgery.

She placed the top back on the bottle and gave him her full attention. "Thank you."

"It's nothing. I remembered it's one of your favorite drinks."

She smiled. He liked seeing her smile. "Well, yes, for the bootleg drink, too. But that's not what I was referring to."

"Oh."

"Thank you for convincing them to fly a different search pattern and for finding me. I'm not sure I would have made it until the next day."

"Then you don't know."

"Know what?"

"About the fire. Well, there was a brief fire in the helicopter. I think the rain put it out. Anyway, if you hadn't gotten out when you did, you would have been in it. Your seat was destroyed by it when I got there."

Lynch reflected on Amy's appearance when they found her. She looked that way now, pale. She appeared to realize that she *definitely* wouldn't be there talking with him had she not gotten out.

"Thank you," she whispered again, as the full impact of what he had told her seemed to strike home.

 If this had been a male buddy, he likely would reply that now they were even. She had saved his life when that fake nurse had given him a drug to paralyze him when *he* was in the hospital. But, that wasn't the message he wished to convey.

"That's what friends do, and I want you to know that I'll always be your friend, Amy."

"Thank you, Lynch."

"You already said that. Several times." He smiled.

"I know, but this time I mean for not making all of this, well, awkward. Richard likes you, too."

"But too awkward for Macy, eh?" He grinned.

Amy blushed. "Oh. You saw that. Well, you know Macy. When it comes to inserting her foot in her mouth, there's no place that foot hasn't tread."

Lynch laughed, but in reality, his recalled memories of Amy's best friend were scant. He doubted he'd get another opportunity to learn more about the woman.

"So, how've you been? Still working for Mr. Graham?"

They made small talk for about 20 minutes, and Lynch finally stood to leave. He wondered if he had overstayed his visit. She had to get her rest. And yet, he felt comforted that the conversation had not become contentious. They had talked as friends would do. And for him, that was the best way to start renewing her trust in him, a trust he had broken too many times in the past.

Amy watched Lynch leave the room and felt surprise that she had wanted him to stay a little longer. She admitted to herself that she had been shocked that he had come to visit, but not as shocked as she had been when Richard had told her of Lynch's involvement in finding her. *That* had left her speechless. Well, as speechless as she ever became.

She glanced again at the door and sensing no one there, she took another drink of the Frappuccino. The bottle would be empty shortly and already she wished he'd brought a second.

An unexpected rap on the door made her stuff the bottle under the blanket covering her legs. Her nurse for the shift must have been Nurse Ratched's daughter. So cool on the exterior, but "the Big Nurse," not one to be messed with, through and through. The blow on the door sounded just like her authoritarian knock. And just like her, the door began to open before Amy could answer.

"Hey, girlfriend. Scare you?"

Amy laughed. "Not at all. You know I can hold my own against Nurse Ratched Junior."

Both Amy and Macy had dealt with the woman before, having had to transfer patients to her from the E.D. Macy still had the 'enjoyment' of those encounters from time to time.

"Maybe. I figure she was enjoying payback for all the patients you sent her way in the past."

Macy was dressed in her civvies, her shift now ended. She walked over and sat down in the chair vacated by Lynch just a few minutes earlier.

"Perfect timing. Lynch just left."

"I know. I had the clerk call me when she saw him leaving. No way was I going to interrupt *that* conversation."

Amy shook her head. "We had a very nice conversation. He even brought me this." She held up the Frappuccino bottle. Macy's eyes darted to the door.

"Don't let the Big Nurse catch you with that. Here. Finish it off and let me take the bottle."

Amy obliged her. She had tolerated it just fine, as she had everything given her so far, but it would take some doing to convince her doctor to move her to the solid foods she now craved.

"So, truth. Nothing weird about Lynch visiting?"

"Nothing at all. We had a nice talk. He, well, he seemed different."

Macy stared at her. Amy had seen that look dozens of times.

"Macy. Really?" The woman didn't back off. "He just wants to remain friends."

Macy sat back and relaxed. "If you say so."

"I do say so. I don't know, maybe it's because he's not a policeman anymore, but he seemed more easy going, more attentive. You know, just like friends are supposed to be with each other."

"Oh boy."

"Seriously. I'm engaged to Richard, Macy. I love him. I'm not going to change my mind and get caught up in some love triangle of my own making. Geesh!"

Macy simply looked at her, but that didn't faze Amy. Yes, Lynch seemed changed, just as he'd told her when he asked for a new chance months earlier. But she had moved on, just as she had told him. She knew what she wanted. Didn't she?

Jeremy pretended to pick up some trash as he wedged the nail against the car's tire. A measly six-inch roll backward in reverse would force the nail into the rubber and result in a flat tire. He couldn't predict how long that might take, but the tire *would* lose air. He doubted the resultant flat would occur immediately. In fact, he hoped it might occur somewhere in the next 50 miles where their mutual journey traveled through the most remote part of the trip.

He stood up and walked to the nearest trash can to throw away what he had "collected." From there, he proceeded to the rest stop's men's room to relieve his bladder of its eleventh and twelfth cups of coffee that day. Yet, despite the caffeine boost, he still had had difficulty keeping up with Diane Westlake.

Back outside, he stretched his five-foot, ten-inch frame that held about 20 pounds of extra weight. He wasn't used to driving such distances, although in recent years his life had become more sedentary. Without motivation to stay fit, he had allowed his body to soften. Looking toward the future, he saw no reason to change.

Jeremy hadn't wanted to leave Boston without confirming that Westlake really was going to head west in an effort to find the O'Malleys. Still, he was prepared, taking his car instead of the van for better mileage and a more comfortable ride. He waited to watch her leave and then followed her from a safe distance. Once he confirmed that she was indeed leaving town, he had expected to stop and grab some things for the trip.

However, the woman drove like she was on the NASCAR circuit. He had almost lost her GPS signal when he stopped for gas. The last thing he needed was to be stopped by a state trooper along the way just because he'd been attempting to keep up with her. He needed an opportunity to get ahead of her, and this pit stop for a restroom break gave him that opportunity. Hopefully, he would also have enough of a lead to get some dinner. They hadn't stopped to eat since leaving Boston.

He knew where she was headed. In fact, he'd already discovered who she wanted to see and question. He hoped to be able to talk with that volunteer first. So, his goal was to get to Springfield late that night, crash, and get up in time to find Ms. Marcia Holmes *before* she arrived at the hospital. His cell phone was set to alert him as soon as Westlake's GPS signal entered a 20-mile radius around him.

In fact, thanks to that technology, he hoped to stay a step ahead of her for the remainder of his trip. When the time was right, he would make himself known to her.

Nineteen

Diane had arrived in Springfield just after lunch *two* days after deciding to drive, not fly. She had underestimated her endurance to drive any distance and had made better time than she'd expected, despite the mysterious flat she discovered at a rest stop in the middle of nowhere. That two-hour delay had cost her precious time.

The past 48 hours had been like one of those amusement park rides where you spin faster and faster and then the floor drops out below you. Even now she felt as if she was clinging to the wall for her life.

Having not eaten since dinner the night before, she decided to stop at a buffet-style restaurant for food before searching out the hospital. She loaded up her plate and sat down near a window. As she looked out toward the eastern horizon, past the two large smokestacks of a power plant, she noticed for the first time that it was a lovely spring day. She hoped nothing would change that.

Despite her lack of meals, and the full plate staring up at her, she realized her appetite was off, as had been her ability to sleep. Not that she had a restless night, just one where her mind raced a thousand directions with no clear destination for its musings. What if this? Could she that?

Would she that? And if this happened, what about . . .? Sitting alone at the small table, she nibbled at the food that filled her plate abundantly to satisfy longing eyes and a growling gut without acknowledging the mental lack of desire.

She caught a waitress staring at her, the woman's countenance speaking loudly. *Don't let me catch you throwing all that away. Such waste.* Not that the woman would ever say anything to a paying guest. Yet, that spurred Diane to eat. Besides, the meal was paid for, and the timing of her next meal remained uncertain.

She cleared her plate, grabbed a second cup of coffee to go, and nodded at the now smiling waitress as she approached to clear Diane's table. Diane walked to her car and took off for the hospital just ten to 15 minutes away.

As she entered the hospital she saw no one at the information desk and worried that she'd come all this way only to find the woman taking the day off. She stopped a woman with a hospital ID hanging on a lanyard around her neck.

"I'm looking for a Ms. Holmes. I was told she's a volunteer here."

The employee smiled. "Oh, Marcia? She's more like a fixture around here. She predates this building and everyone but a handful of people working here." She glanced at her watch and then the unmanned desk. "She's usually here by noon, but she was overwhelmed two days by policemen asking about her spotting the victim of some AMBER Alert from the east coast. She didn't come in yesterday. I don't know if she's coming in today or not. The Volunteers Office would know." She turned to face the hallway behind her. "Go down this hall, take a left, then a right, and it's the third door on the right."

Diane repeated, "Left, right, third door on right."

"That's right, er, correct. Like I said, they should know. Marcia would never just not show up."

"Thank you."

Diane began walking and was several yards down the hall, when she heard the woman behind her. "Ma'am! Ma'am!" She heard hurried footsteps and felt a touch on her shoulder to which she reflexively jerked away.

"Sorry. She, Marcia, just walked through the door. She's at the front desk now."

Diane smiled. "Oh, thank you. You've been a great help."

Diane retreated along the path she'd started and saw an older woman taking off her coat behind the desk. She let the woman settle in and then approached.

"Ms. Holmes?" The woman nodded. "I'm Diane Westlake, with the Massachusetts' Department of Children and Family." She flashed her ID badge just long enough for the woman to confirm her name and check her photo. "I was hoping to have a few minutes of your time."

Marcia sighed. "Okay. Didn't expect anyone else after the other day, but sure."

"First could you verify that this is the woman you spoke with?" She extended a photo of Sinead O'Malley for the lady to see.

"That's her. And her daughter was in a wheelchair."

"Thank you. Now, could you simply relate to me the interaction you had two days ago with the O'Malleys?"

"Well, it was just the mom. The girl didn't say anything but seemed upset. They were asking about a nurse in a helicopter crash not far from here. That's what caught me as strange to begin with. Got my antennae tingling." She went on to describe the conversation as close to word-for-word as she could, and it seemed to Diane that she had it memorized pretty well.

"And how did the girl seem to you?"

"Well, as I said she seemed upset but mostly about the nurse. We'd heard that everyone died in the crash and, like I said, that's what I told them. That got her crying. Thinking about it now, she seemed like a happy kid when they came through the door. I always make a point of watching for kids coming in. You know, to try to cheer them up if they need it. Hate to see kids with medical problems. Anyway, she got upset *after* I mentioned everyone dying in the crash."

Sounds a sure way to cheer up a child, thought Diane. "How did she look physically?"

"Well, thin, but good skin color, I guess. I have to admit I focused more on the mom than on her."

Diane felt a sense of relief that Ruth didn't appear any worse. She had been gaunt when Diane last saw her. Yet, that condition could change at any moment, so it remained imperative that they be found and Ruth returned to a proper care facility.

"And what was the name of the nurse they were looking for?"

Marcia shook her head. "Sorry, I meant to write it down, but I got so excited after seeing their pictures on that AMBER Alert, the name totally skipped my mind. It started with a 'G.' That I'm sure of, but the name still escapes me. If it comes to me, I can contact you."

They talked about Marcia's feeling that the pair would head to St. Louis, and Diane found no fault in her logic. She thanked the woman for her caring about children, her alertness, and her time. After writing down her cell number for the woman, she left.

Once back in her car, she pulled out her cell phone and tried to locate information on the helicopter crash, and the nurse. All she could find in the related stories was a comment that the flight nurse had survived and had been flown to St. Louis. There was no mention of her name or the hospital she had been taken to. As she turned on her vehicle and began the trip back to St. Louis, she realized the easy part of this trip was over. The hard part lay ahead. She had to find the proverbial needle in a haystack.

Diane was closing in on downtown St. Louis when she decided to stop for coffee. She needed to create a game plan . . . and work up the chutzpa to, well, break the law. Just a little. It had been one thing to flash her illicit credentials to an unknowing hospital volunteer. To use them with another hospital's social services department, or even security, would take her actions to a new level.

The exit signs for the small town of Troy, Illinois, promoted a Dunkin' Donuts, whose coffee she preferred over "that other" national chain, so she left the interstate and found the shop. She took advantage of their free Wi-Fi to connect her phone to the internet and search for trauma centers. As she sipped her large black coffee, she discovered that the city had three Level I centers, any one of which could handle the victim of a helicopter crash. Yet, as she thought about it, she saw nothing in the news to indicate the nurse had major trauma. They might have flown her to any hospital, where she could have been treated and released, not admitted. She knew she'd have to visit all three to start, and spread out from there if unsuccessful.

From the map, it looked as if the trauma center at Barnes Hospital, near downtown St. Louis, would be easiest to find right off I-64. She would have to backtrack a little bit to find the Saint Louis University Medical Center but that wouldn't be an issue. They were only three miles apart. She plotted out her route, put a lid on her cup, and headed toward the door.

The ringing of her phone stopped her. Her heart began to race as she wondered who would be calling her in Illinois. Had someone caught on to what she was doing? And then she mentally chastised herself for being paranoid. It could be any one of her friends or a family member. Her concern resurged when she saw the number listed as her old office. Were they looking for her ID badge, wanting to claim it?

"This is Diane." She started to sit back down at the table nearest the door but reconsidered. The call might be better taken in the privacy of her car.

"Oh, good, you answered. Hey, I know you're out of town looking for a new job, but you also asked to be kept in the loop."

Diane let out a sigh of relief. It was Kiandra.

"Hi, and that I did. What's up?"

"Well, you know I've got this good friend who's a police detective and has friends in the State Police. I sorta asked him to keep his ear to the ground and let me know if there's anything happening on the O'Malley hunt. Well, he's the one who told me they'd been spotted in Illinois. He called me a minute ago to let me know Sinead O'Malley's credit card had been used, twice, last night. They still think she might be headed to St. Louis, but they're having to look at another option. The second hit suggests she's heading north or northwest, away from St. Louis."

Diane felt her gut sink. After all of the time and expense to get where she was. And, yet, thinking back on what Marcia Holmes had told her, that same gut said 'Hang in there.'

"What's north of St. Louis?" She could think of no place north of St Louis. But then, why Springfield, Illinois? Was she going to disappear into the hinterlands?

"Heck if I know. We live in Boston. That's all fly-over land out there. It's just corn fields and buffalo and stuff."

Diane didn't want to say anything more that might tip her hand. She didn't want Kiandra to know where she was, much less what she was up to. The less said, the better. So, she laughed at the comment.

"Spoken like a true New Englander."

"Well, it's true, isn't it?"

"Thanks for keeping me updated. Um, changing the subject, can I use you for a reference?" She didn't want to get her friend in trouble. However, having Kiandra back up her story would sure make things a lot easier.

"Sure. Anytime."

"And maybe, just maybe, if someone were to call you to verify that I worked for the D.C.F., you could just say 'yes' and not go into any details."

There was dead air on the line.

"Diane, what are you up to?" Kiandra's voice oozed with suspicion.

"Out of town, just like I said. I, uh, just, ummm . . . I am just too embarrassed to tell someone I got fired. I figured it'd be easier if they thought I still worked there." Diane felt satisfied at how that came out. She hadn't lied to her friend.

She hadn't shared the whole truth, either, but what Kiandra didn't know couldn't come back to bite her.

"Hmmm, I'll have to think on that one a bit. I wouldn't want to lie and potentially lose my own job. Sorry, I wouldn't do that. But, maybe, depends on how they worded the question, I guess."

"Well, it might not come to that, but I sure could use your help."

"Again, I'll think on it. Hey, I got to go. Keep me posted on how the job search is going. I'll help however I can, as long as it's legit."

They exchanged a few more pleasantries and then hung up. She began to feel more secure that her plan might actually work.

Twenty-five minutes later, with her car parked in a visitors' garage at the medical center, she found her way to the Social Work Services main office at Barnes Hospital. The place felt like home. A world-class medical center much like she was used to. Yet, would she ever work at one again?

"May I help you?"

"Hi, I'm Diane Westlake." She flashed her ID badge. "I'm here following a lead on a child that was taken from state custody a couple of weeks ago, outside of Boston. There was a nationwide AMBER Alert issued for her. We have reason to believe the mom has come to St. Louis with her daughter."

"I see. I think you might want Children's Hospital. It's right next door."

"Oh. Well, yes, I'm planning on going there next, but we believe they're looking for a woman, a nurse, who was involved in a medical helicopter crash a few days ago. I don't know if the woman was flown here to Barnes or not, but they might come looking for her here. I wanted to alert your staff to be on the lookout for them. They would likely inquire about this nurse at the front desk. As a social worker myself, I, well, felt more comfortable coming here to this office for assistance since I don't know how your system is setup. At home, we'd alert security and anyone who might work the information desks, including volunteers."

"Oh yes. We'd do that here, too. We could also alert the operators to pay attention to any calls coming in for the patient they're looking for. Do you have that nurse's name?"

"No, I'm afraid I don't."

"Well, we can ask around, I guess. Tell you what, let me call security right now. I assume you have the names of the mother and daughter."

"Certainly. Here's a copy of the AMBER Alert and photos of the two. The daughter will be in a wheelchair." She dug the two sheets of paper out of her purse and handed them to the woman.

The woman held up one finger as her call connected. "Hey, Dan. This is Kimberly in Social Work Services. We . . ." The woman went on to describe the situation. ". . . and she's given us photos and a copy of the AMBER Alert . . . Oh? You found a copy there . . . Okay . . . I'm sure she'll appreciate that. Thank you." She hung up.

"Alrighty. He's going to swing down here to get those papers. He said he'd make copies and make sure they get to where they need to go. He's also going to get them to the right people at Children's, so unless you have other business there, I think he just saved you a trip." She smiled.

"Oh, thank you. And please thank *him* for me as well. That *will* save me a trip." Diane felt a huge wash of relief inside. That meant one less group to pull her ruse upon, one less chance of discovery.

"He did have one suggestion, though. He said you should touch base with the local police precinct. Here's the address." She slid a piece of paper across the desk toward Diane. "He said they need to know what's going on since they would have to get involved. Also, they would be able to alert all officers about the car, to increase their vigilance in looking out for it. He said he'd call ahead for you, so they can expect you."

Diane smiled and hoped she looked natural. However, that was the *last* group in the city she wanted to contact. The police would be the *most* likely to verify her identity and claim of working at the Massachusetts Department of Children and Family. And yet, she really hadn't made that claim here, had she?

"Thank you, for all your help. Here's my cell number, should they be spotted here." She wrote her name and number on the sheet with the photos. "I'll be in town for a little longer." She didn't want to say "until they're found," even if that was her plan.

"I hope the girl's okay. You say she's in a wheelchair. What's wrong with her? I hope we find them."

The woman appeared eager to chat now, interested in details. Diane needed to move on.

"I do, too. Hope she's okay and that we find them. I'd love to talk, but I'm short on time and need to get moving. I hadn't anticipated needing to go to the police."

The woman smiled. "Sorry. I understand. I probably need to get back to work, too. Good luck."

Diane nodded and smiled. Minutes later, she was seated in her car and debating the wisdom of going to the police. Yes, they would become involved if Sinead and Ruth O'Malley showed up. Yes, they might help in spotting her. And, yes, they could arrest Diane for impersonating a state official.

She sighed. If only that security guy, Dan, hadn't told her he'd call ahead. Now, she felt as if her hands were tied. If she didn't show up at the police station and ask for their assistance, would someone get suspicious? That might prompt a call to Boston sooner than if she played along.

She looked at the address for the station and plotted it on her map app. The building didn't appear too far away.

Five minutes later, Diane began to worry that she'd made a bad decision. She had been in some bad parts of Boston before, but the communities she drove through now looked rougher than any place she had ever encountered. Abandoned homes. Litter-strewn lots. Small groups of young, mostly black, males hanging out on a number of street corners, watching her closely as she drove past. In Boston, if she had been called upon to enter an area like this, she might have been provided a police escort.

Before she could reverse course, she found herself at the District Five Police Station. She located a place to park, where she hoped her car would remain until she returned, and glanced about before getting out of the car. She hurried inside.

"Can I help you?" The officer at the front window sounded bored. No, he sounded more like someone expecting the same story, just a different day, different face.

"Yes, my name is Diane Westlake, and I was just at Barnes Hospital. One of the men in security there, Dan somebody, said he'd call ahead for me. It's about a nationwide AMBER Alert that went out a few weeks ago, and the good chance that the mom who took her daughter is heading this way."

"Okay. Give me a minute." He left the window only to return a few minutes later. "Sergeant Barkley, from our detectives, will be with you in a moment."

Diane looked at the chairs in the lobby and decided there was no way she was going to sit in any of them without a healthy dose of disinfectant first. She stood toward the back of the space, hoping to stay out of the way of the itinerant sorts who came through the front door with a variety of complaints for the officer. Petty thefts. Someone's music was too loud next door. Someone keyed a car. There's a stray cat on her street. Really? She came to the police for that?

After ten minutes of observing the variety of people and their complaints, she wondered if the desk officer held a degree in social work himself. Or then again, was he being punished by being assigned to the desk? One way or the other, if this was the daily routine here, she could see it quickly becoming a social worker's worst nightmare.

She glanced at her watch. Fifteen minutes. But as she looked up, she saw the desk officer waving for her attention. She approached the window and could now hear him through the tinny speaker.

"Ms. Westlake, the sergeant will be at that door in a moment." He pointed to one of the two doors leading to the interior.

"Thank you." She wondered how long *this* particular "moment" might take, but just then, the door opened.

"Ms. Westlake, I'm Sergeant Barkley. I understand you have reason to believe the victim of an AMBER Alert might be heading this way. Could you give me more information?"

He ushered her inside and to a desk.

Diane informed him of the O'Malleys being spotted in Springfield and asking about a nurse involved in a crash. She gave him every detail she had, that she had gone to the medical center simply to alert them, and that she hadn't expected the police to help. But, at the urging of hospital security, she was there now, with the sergeant, and would appreciate any help offered.

"I heard about that crash. Real shame. And you're right, that crew was based here in St. Louis. Tell you what, we can certainly help you out." He smiled, but there was a devilish nature to it. "In fact, I have just the detective to help you."

Jeremy pulled up short of the woman's destination and turned back. For the first time since he'd begun surveilling her, Westlake had surprised him. She had some real brass ones, going to the police for assistance. Was she presenting herself as an agent of the D.C.F.? Surely, the police would hold no interest in helping her if she came to them as a private citizen. Sure, they'd take a report, be polite, and assure her they would look into the matter, after which it would be added to a long list of issues they promised to investigate.

However, she would know that. Despite her failings, the woman wasn't stupid, and she had worked with the police in the past. She knew the drill. His mind drifted to the time she and two police officers came knocking on their door. No, knocking *down* their door was more accurate.

AMBER Alerts were treated by most law enforcement officers as little more than a BOLO—be on the lookout—

unless an actual sighting had occurred. He didn't expect the local authorities to offer her any true aid. There was no proof that the O'Malleys were in the area.

Still, he was in no position to get tangled up with the local police. They would only get in the way of his plans.

As he drove back toward the medical center, a thought hit him. Maybe she was beginning to feel desperate. Yes, that had to be it. She was taking a chance at being discovered because she realized how big a lake she was trolling for one specific tagged fish, a nurse named Amy Gibbs. She had no hope of hooking that prize-winning fish without some help.

He smiled as he reflected on his brief meeting with Volunteer Marcia Holmes. She had proven herself much shrewder than he had anticipated. He had to give up a C-note to convince her to "forget" his visit with her as well as the nurse's name.

He pulled into a parking slot along the main road, across from the hospital's Emergency Department. Her car, with its GPS tracker, remained within range. He could wait.

Twenty

Sinead had always been taught to be careful in what you pray for. You might just get it.

Such was the case the night before. They had been "blessed" by covering rural territory without cell phone coverage, so she had been able to charge her phone with minimal risk of someone pinging and locating it. But that also meant she had no map and somewhere along the line, in the dark, she not only missed the turn she wanted, she found herself heading north, away from St. Louis.

She discovered her error as soon as they reached the first small town with cell coverage, and she was able to chance using her phone just long enough to check their location. They had gone so far out of the way, she had to stop for gas again to ensure she'd have enough to make it through the night.

Jameson had always called her "directionally challenged." In fact, Ruth had been her trusty navigator on the trip from Boston to the farm. Not so last night. Ruth slept through most of the trip. Sinead should have kept her awake, but she knew the girl needed her rest. Ruth had been pushing her physical limits over the past several days, and Sinead hadn't stopped her. The exertion would help strengthen her daughter, but it also tired her quickly.

Sinead sat in the motel room's sole chair and watched her daughter sleep. She smiled as she reflected on the many times she had done the same, for each of her children, when they were younger. How much she missed the other two. Had they been faring well at her in-laws' home? And how were the grandparents handling the whole situation? Their stress levels had to be close to her own. Her thoughts drifted longingly to her husband. He bore the weight of her actions on his shoulders. How would she ever pay him back? Not that he expected her to do so.

"Mom?"

Sinead refocused on Ruth.

"Good morning."

"What time is it?"

"A little after nine."

"I'm hungry."

Sinead smiled. "Me, too. Get yourself ready, and we can go find something to eat."

As Ruth pushed herself to a standing position and wobbled for a moment, Sinead stood and took a step toward her.

"No. I've got it. I have to start doing more on my own. Right?"

As a mother, Sinead struggled with the idea of not helping, but her daughter was correct. She sat back down and turned on the television. She hadn't seen the news in weeks. Russia's take-over of the Crimea still made waves, with the U.N. General Assembly voting to condemn it in a symbolic vote. A judge in Egypt had declared over 500 people guilty for the murder of a policeman during a riot, and sentenced them all to death. The war in Syria raged on. Close to home, a massive fire had killed two firefighters in the Back Bay area of Boston, and the funeral of Lt. Edward Walsh would be today.

Her breath left her with the next story. Her picture and Ruth's filled the screen.

"Authorities in Boston have reissued a nationwide AMBER Alert for . . ." Sinead turned to see if Ruth was still in the bathroom. She didn't want her to see this. The door remained closed, and Sinead turned her attention back to the television. The news story told of their being spotted in Springfield and appeared to be heading west.

"We're going to get caught, aren't we?"

Ruth's question caught her off-guard. Sinead sighed. How much had she seen and heard?

"I hope not. When you're strong enough to march into that courtroom on your own and show the judge that we've been right all along, then we'll turn ourselves in. But, until then we just need to stay at least one step ahead of them."

She walked over to her daughter and hugged her, not knowing which one of them she wanted to reassure the most.

"Is that why you went the wrong way last night?"

Sinead raised her brow. "What? I thought you were asleep."

Ruth shrugged. "Off and on."

"As much as I'd like to take credit and say that was planned, I got—"

"Lost again. Sorry, Mom, I should've stayed awake."

Sinead drew Ruth's head toward her and kissed her on the forehead. "My best navigator needed her rest. Besides, I took advantage of the wrong turns and, hopefully . . ." She crossed her fingers. ". . . hopefully, I've thrown off anyone tracking us through my phone or credit card."

Ruth rolled her eyes. "Oh, Mom, you didn't." She stared into Sinead's eyes. "You did."

Sinead walked back toward her small suitcase on top of the motel's folding stand. "Well, we're getting low on cash, and we needed gas, so I charged it. And then, when I realized I was going the wrong way and heading north, I figured it was the perfect time to confuse anyone tracking my credit card." She rummaged through her bag and retrieved two small boxes. "I bought this and used the card again." She held up the two items.

"Really?"

"Really."

It felt good to see Ruth smile. And even better, to hear her laugh.

"Are you ready to become a blonde?"

Amy would never admit it to her brothers, but she was ecstatic to be passing gas. So unladylike, and yet so full of promise. If she had to spend another day on clear liquids, she would pass out. And yet, the doctor wouldn't advance her diet until he was convinced her bowel was functioning normally after her laparotomy and spleen repair. She said a short prayer to have a bowel movement.

A curt knock on the door stirred her from her daydreaming.

"You decent?"

Richard. She hadn't expected him so early.

"Come on in."

He walked in holding something behind his back. "I had to hide this once I got off the elevator. Your favorite nurse was roaming the hall."

He held out a covered plastic cup, and she began to drool.

"Iced caramel mocha from the Golden Arches. With whipped cream on top."

First, Lynch with the Frappuccino, and now Richard with a mocha. She made a mental note to become less predictable.

He handed her the cup and then went back to close the door. By the time he returned to her bedside, she had gulped down a third of the drink and whipped cream covered her upper lip.

"Whoa, take it easy."

She smiled before licking her lip clean.

Richard laughed. "I won't ask if you're hungry."

She rolled her eyes.

"Lynch caught up with me at work this morning. He said he stopped by last night."

His gaze was intent on her for a few seconds, but then he seemed to relax. She had nothing to hide, so if he was expecting something from her body language, her body wasn't talking.

"We had a nice visit. I thanked him for helping you find me."

"He certainly played a crucial role in that. I've thanked him multiple times, and he keeps brushing it aside as if it was nothing. He certainly seems humble about it."

Humble? Well, that had never exactly been the old Lynch. Not that he'd been prideful or arrogant or anything like that. Very confident? Yes. As she reflected on his visit, he had seemed, well, more selfless. She wasn't sure how to term what she'd seen.

"He, uh, brought up something that's been bothering

him since we found you."

Richard looked uncertain, even nervous about bringing up whatever it was that concerned Lynch.

"When we were looking for you at that house, there was a nearly new garden tiller and a trailer outside the house. But the house was supposed to be abandoned. And . .." He paused. ". . . one other thing. We saw drag marks from the duffels you dragged from the crash to the barn. But, we only found them from a certain point heading to the barn. Nothing in the field or along the road."

Amy felt her appetite disappear. She felt a bit guilty that her concerns for Sinead and Ruth had taken a back seat to her own condition. She knew now that the woman had truly saved her life. She was running from someone and needed protection. Now, it appeared that their ruse hadn't fooled everyone. The last person she needed tracking them down was Lynch.

"Was there someone else at that house? Did they help you get from the crash site to the barn? But, if there was someone else there, why didn't they just let you into the house? I-I'm sorry, but I'm confused now, too. When he first brought it up, I didn't care. We'd found you and that's all that really mattered. Yet, he's obviously puzzled and questioning. I guess it's all his police training and experience. I know *he* won't ask you, so I am. Is there something you're not telling us?"

There it was. The whole deck was on the table. Now, which cards would she turn over?

Her mind tumbled into a quagmire of moral issues. She and Richard were engaged. She couldn't, didn't want to, lie to him. And yet, what about Sinead and Ruth? Amy had been a volunteer briefly at a refuge for battered women. Of all the things she couldn't talk about, the top of the list was the secret of its location. In her mind, that farmhouse was just like that refuge, except that its location was known, to a few. The secret lay in the fact that they didn't know it functioned as a refuge.

Still, that raised another question in Amy's mind. She had been nagged by the familiarity of Sinead and Ruth's faces but still hadn't placed them. Who were they? What if they weren't hiding from an abusive spouse or boyfriend? What if they were fugitives from the law? Did they really deserve her promise of secrecy?

She took a deep breath and let it out slowly. "Richard, I won't lie to you. I don't ever want to have to lie to you, but I . . ." She glanced away for a split second. ". . . I can't talk about it. Please don't ask me any more. There will be a time when I can tell you everything. It just isn't now."

She watched his face intently, but the scrutiny he gave her surpassed that. "Sweetheart, whatever happened, I'm here to help. You can trust me to keep a secret, if that's what it takes. I can help. I won't say a thing to Lynch, either. I just want to be here for you."

She grabbed and squeezed his hand. He leaned over, kissed her, and then chuckled. "You taste like mocha."

She lifted up from the bed and kissed him again. He could have started a game of Twenty Questions, but he didn't, and she loved that he trusted her and wouldn't drag this on. And, that he would be there when she needed him.

He glanced at his watch and said, "Shoot, I gotta run. We have a big meeting in 20 minutes. Also, I wanted to tell you I have to leave town with work for a few days. Might last up to a week. I had wanted to be here to take you home, but I can't. If your dad's unavailable, Lynch said he'd be happy to give you a lift and make sure you're home safe and sound."

"Thanks. I, uh . . . I think my dad will be able to help out. Where are you headed?"

"The D.C. area. We're setting up a satellite social media office for the Party there. I'll call you from the airport and after I get there." He leaned over the bed and kissed her again. "Love you."

"Love you, too."

She watched him leave and realized the iced mocha languished on the bed stand, in plain view should Nurse Ratched Junior check in on her. Rather than have any incriminating evidence to give that woman cause for a lecture, she picked up the cup and finished off the drink. As she bent over the edge of the bed to throw the cup into the trash, she began to wonder if she had pushed things a little too fast. Her gut grumbled, and a sudden urge told her to get to the bathroom pronto, or else.

The problem was that, with crutches, speed was not in her repertoire of movements.

Ten minutes later, she crept back into bed. That had been close. And, yes, she probably had advanced her diet too quickly. But, she could claim to have had her first bowel movement.

After informing the nursing staff of her achievement and asking for something more substantial for a diet, she retrieved her laptop computer and powered it on. She no doubt had a zillion emails to answer just from work alone. She logged into MedAir's network and discovered a flood of new emails from that morning: Get well soon! Hope to see you back at work! Is there anything I can do to help you? Let me know.

A few expressed their condolences about the loss of the other two crew members, although she had received many more of these over the prior two days. Tears began to flow as she read those, as they had the day before and the day before that. She knew there would soon be a day when she'd have to face both men's families—to tell them what happened firsthand and become a reminder to them that *she* somehow survived. She tried to shake that thought out of her mind. She would not succumb to survivor's guilt. She'd been down that PTSD road before. Not this time.

An email from the front office came next. The reissue of a nationwide AMBER Alert. Most first responders received these on a regular basis. She clicked on the email and sat there, stunned.

Twenty-One

Lynch busied himself with the mundane aspects of moving to a new place. During his absence, his lease had lapsed on the condo he'd rented, but fortunately his parents had a level of faith in his return and chose to store all of his belongings until he returned—or until a body was found. He'd been living at his parents' home, tolerating his mother's insistence in calling him by his given name, Carson, and balancing a demanding new job with the task of finding a new place.

His job as Chief of Security for the Bradley Graham campaign had been on a hiatus of sorts after the bombing of its headquarters in the building it shared with the American Party. He had used that time to get aggressive with the home search. The effort had paid off. He had found a great three-bedroom ranch not far from both the new campaign office and new American Party headquarters. At his suggestion, they had separated. Being located in the same building had provided their common enemies a much-too-easy target.

The home was definitely more than he needed, but he had decided it was time to invest in a real home. Plus, the salary he now made, as compared to what he'd made as a police officer, made the decision a much easier one.

"Okay, cable's all hooked up. You're set to go. Hundred mbps of internet speed. Not too late to sign up for TV as well, while I'm here."

Lynch shook his head. "No thanks. Don't have much use for the drivel on television these days, unless you have a package that includes only Fox News, CNN, Al Jazeera, and the networks."

The cable guy smiled. "News junkie, eh?"

"Not really. All work related. I need to keep up on a wide variety of news reports for work."

The man nodded. "Gotcha. Sorry, but the cheapest package comes with 200 channels." He paused. "Well, if you find you need it, it's easy to install yourself." He held out some paperwork for Lynch to sign. "Thanks. Have a good day."

Lynch closed the door behind the installer and turned back to face his living room. He'd read that minimalism was trendy now, but the place looked empty, not simplified. He sighed at the thought of having to fit furniture shopping into his schedule.

In fact, his mind was elsewhere. Something didn't fit right with Amy's recovery at that farm. He had talked about it with Richard, but he hadn't been able to bring himself to ask Amy about it. He knew that if he didn't get an answer, it would continue to bug him. Yet, the last thing he wanted was to confront Amy over it.

He'd thought about going back to the farm to investigate, but time was an issue. Plus, there was a better than even chance that he'd find nothing. With the activity there, whoever had been there would have cleared out by now. Yet, he did have one avenue to explore. The trailer had an equipment rental company sign on it. He hadn't paid much attention to it—his mind had been focused on Amy—but the name started with an 'A.'

Now that he had his internet connection and home Wi-Fi set up, exploring that trail shouldn't take much time at all. He connected his tablet computer to the Wi-Fi and pulled up a map of western Illinois. He then searched for 'tool rental.' Nothing. 'Equipment rental' had the same result. Even 'rental' didn't help, finding only a few car agencies. His next choice, 'hardware stores' found a number of hits, but none of the stores started with an 'A.'

He began to pace. What was he missing? Most farmers would likely have their own garden tillers, not rent them. *Of course,* he thought, *a farm store of some sort.* He typed in 'farm store' and came up with hits in almost every small town in the region. He smiled at discovering one, Atkins Farm Supply, but questioned it. The store was nearly an hour away from the farm.

He shrugged and grabbed his cell phone. He'd make no progress if he didn't try.

"Atkins. May I help you?"

"Yes, do you rent garden tillers?"

"One moment."

He could hear the woman yell in the background, "Charlie, line one."

Lynch felt surprise that they had more than one phone line.

"This is Charlie."

"Good morning. I was hoping you might rent garden tillers."

"Most folks in these parts own one, but we have a

couple for rent."

"Have you rented one to anyone in the past week?" Lynch realized he needed to clarify his reasons for asking. "I'm investigating the helicopter crash not far from you and was one of the men who found the survivor." He felt strange calling Amy a survivor, and yet, the term fit in every sense of the word. "We have reason to believe someone else was on that farm, and I'd like to find them."

"Sure was a shame, that crash. It's been the talk of the town." The man paused. "You know something, I've actually been wondering about one of our tiller rentals. They don't go out often. Like I said, folks here own theirs. But we had a woman come in and rent one the day before the crash and return it three days later. She didn't get any tilling done 'cause of the storms. She had a daughter in the car."

"So, you said you were wondering about her. Why?"

"Well, at first I didn't think much about it, and there was nothing that would've made me connect it to the crash. I mean, that was an hour away from here. But the day after she returned it, the news carried pictures of a woman and her daughter. One of those AMBER Alert things. The woman was spotted in Springfield. I'd swear it was the same woman. I didn't get a good look at the girl, so I can't say it was her, but the mom, yeah, I'm pretty sure that was her."

"Did you notify the authorities?"

"Nah. Now, if she came back for the tiller like she said she was gonna do, yeah, I'd call. But I figured my call would just cause a snipe hunt for the staties. When I unhitched the trailer, I noticed her car was packed to the hilt. She looked like someone movin' out, not staying in the area."

Lynch agreed with that assessment, but the State Police might still have found it helpful if it corroborated any other info they had.

"Do you have her name?"

"In fact, I checked the rental form after I saw that news report. Somehow, I don't think Jane Smith is her real name. Should've, but I didn't ask for a driver's license when she rented it. My bad, but I was busy, and we tend to trust folks around here."

"Well, thank you for taking the time to talk with me. This is helpful, even if we don't find her."

"You're welcome. Good luck."

Lynch's gut told him that the woman was at that farm. The place would have been perfect for hiding out. And renting a tiller from a place an hour away would shift anyone looking for her away from the farm. Yet, this raised a new question. How did she know the place was abandoned, and how did she get in?

It wouldn't be difficult to find the farm's owner, but first, he needed to know more about this woman. Within a minute, he had the AMBER Alert displayed in front of him. Armed with a name, he retrieved as many articles as he could on the woman and her daughter.

Thirty minutes later, he sat there rooting for them. A major injustice had been inflicted on this family. The state should have no right to take a child from her parents because of conflicts over medical care. Actual physical abuse or neglect? Sure. But to take custody of a girl with significant medical problems, a child who needed the support of her family, because two sets of doctors disagreed on her care? That was wrong and yet another example of government overstepping its role.

He made a mental note to raise this issue with Bradley Graham. He knew that a core plank of the American Party platform was that family, not government, was the foundation of society. He had recently learned that this had a Biblical basis, that God stressed the importance of family throughout his Word.

His phone pinged with a private message. Stan McGonagle, Graham's campaign manager, had texted him. "Know you're busy moving into the new place, but something's come up. Will need you in Washington. Call me at your convenience but sometime today."

Twenty-Two

"Wow, you look cute. This is a good color on you." Sinead admired her daughter's hair as she combed it out, drying it with their blow dryer as she did so.

Ruth smiled as she watched her mom in the large mirror located over the room's dresser. "Oh yeah. Time to have more fun." She began to 'dance' with her shoulders.

"Well, do you like it, or not?"

"I love it. Now all I need is a pair of fake glasses, and no one will ever recognize me."

Sinead laughed. "That *is* the point, isn't it?"

Ruth grinned. "Okay, time for the big reveal. I want to see. Now."

Sinead turned off the dryer and put it down, along with the brush. She cradled the towel covering her own hair but hesitated to unwrap it.

"Nope, not yet. If this is to be a *big* reveal, I think I should do it right. Be back in a few minutes, and no peeking."

She picked up the dryer and brush and walked into the bathroom. She had been amazed earlier, when she first saw her image in the mirror after rinsing out the excess dye. The transformation was incredible.

With her hair dried, brushed, and styled to her best

ability in a motel room, she called out to Ruth.

"Okay, I'm ready. Are you?"

She laughed as her daughter began to sing, "Heeerrrre she is . . . Mrs. Ameeerrica . . ." She stepped into the room, and Ruth's eyes widened in . . . what? Shock? Surprise? Joy? Sinead wasn't sure until the girl began to squeal in delight.

"Mom, you're gorgeous. I loooovvve it. Wow."

Sinead sidled up to her daughter, and they gazed at their images together in the mirror. Ruth's siblings would never recognize them. Jameson and his parents would require double, maybe triple takes. Surely, no one local would ever suspect.

"You called it, sweetheart. Hiding in plain sight might just work."

Ruth slowly nodded as she stared into the mirror. Yet, she wasn't looking at herself.

"You know, Mom. A couple of tattoos and a pierced lip might work. Add a skin-tight latex superhero costume, and you could probably get a role as an Avenger or some other kick-ass—" She paused. "Sorry, that kind of slipped out."

Sinead shook her head slowly. "Forgiven. And let's not go overboard. I doubt I could hurt a fly with my kick."

She never expected perfect language of her children. She knew that would be hypocritical, but she had tried to stress to them the importance of controlling one's tongue. Just as the Bible instructed.

"Are you kidding me? You carried Amy from the crash to the truck, didn't you?" She leaned her head onto Sinead's shoulder. "Mom, you'll always be a superhero to me. I love you, Mom."

Sinead leaned her head onto Ruth's and smiled. "And I love you, too." She popped her head straight up and said,

"So, trusty sidekick, are we ready to face the world, protect the innocent, and get some lunch? We never got breakfast. I'm hungry."

Ruth laughed. "Now we need superhero names. But, lunch first sounds like a plan."

"Lunch it is, and then we'll head south and try to find Amy."

Superhero status or not, Sinead still worried about getting caught before the time was right. And to her, Ruth was the superhero. The ordeal she had faced—might still face—would push most people into depression. Yet, Ruth remained upbeat and optimistic. Her joy seemed infectious and Sinead wished she could bottle it for use during those down times, the times when she felt overwhelmed by the government's oppression. Yes, Ruth was the real superhero, and she was the sidekick.

Tammy looked at the Caller ID on her vibrating phone to discover Barkley wanted her. That alone was troubling because he rarely called her on her cell. In addition, he knew she was to be involved in a special outreach project that day and would be tied up until after her shift had finished. The mayor's chief of staff was personally invested in this one, and was, in fact, speaking to the group at that moment. This was not a good time to answer her phone.

Her male counterpart on the GREAT Program, Detective Sam Wellston, must have noticed her fumbling with the phone because he glanced at her with his brow furrowed. He gave her a subtle shake of his head.

She mouthed, "Barkley," to him, and he rolled his eyes before returning his attention to the politician. She struggled between her choices. Which would create the least havoc in her life? Slipping out of the presentation to call her sergeant back and risk offending the CoS, maybe even being volunteered for something while she was out of the room? Or to ignore Barkley until a break and risk weeks or months of torture wondering when the payback would come? And then there was also the form of that payback to consider.

She brought her attention back to the meeting to find the room in complete silence and the CoS looking at her.

"Detective Jahn, is there a problem?" asked the CoS.

"I-I don't know, sir. My sergeant is calling and he usually doesn't do that. He knows I'm in this meeting."

"Tell you what, folks. Let's take a break, say ten minutes, and we can continue."

Tammy sighed in relief. *Thank you, thank you, thank you,* she thought. She wanted to rush to the other side of the table and give the CoS a hug.

Outside in the hall, after a quick, but much needed pit stop, she returned Sergeant Barkley's call.

"Why didn't you answer the phone, Jahn?"

"Because Chief of Staff Raintree was speaking, just ten feet away from me." She wasn't about to tell him that the CoS knew he'd been the cause of the interruption. Maybe something "good" might come of that. She could only keep her fingers crossed. "I called back as soon as I could."

"I've got a special assignment for you. How soon can you get back here?"

She didn't like the way he said 'special.'

"You know this is an all-day thing. I sure don't want to leave before Raintree. That would not be cool. This is one of his pet projects."

There was no quick reply. Even Barkley understood that such a break in protocol, except for something dire, could cause cascades of "stuff" coming down on his head, too.

"Yeah. Okay. But call me as soon as you have some idea when you can leave."

Her colleague walked up to her pointing at his watch. She nodded.

"Will do, Sarge, but this is likely to go past shift change as it is. Hey, he's about to resume talking. Gotta go."

Sam asked, "What's that all about?"

"He wanted me to leave for a special assignment." She said 'special' just as Barkley had.

" 'Uh-oh, smells like payback time, don't it."

She nodded. It certainly did.

Twenty-Three

Amy hadn't felt this upset in a long time. True, she had been emotionally distraught when Lynch had gone missing at the hand of the L.A. Rapist, but that was different. Her emotions then had been those of grief and loss. Now, she felt anger and indignation.

A knock at her door took her mind off what she'd been reading. Macy's head popped in.

"Hey, girlfriend! Thought I'd stop in on my lunch . . . whoa, maybe I should just go back to work. You look ready to lash out in an MMA fight."

"I'd love to use mixed martial arts on some of these people I've been reading about." She forced herself to relax. "Sorry, Macy. Come on in."

"What's got you so riled?" her friend asked as she sat in the chair next to the bed.

Amy knew she couldn't say anything about Sinead and Ruth, at least not about her direct connection with them. Still, she could talk about them using the AMBER Alert as the seed to her comments.

"I was going through my email from work and saw this nationwide AMBER Alert. So, I started researching the story. The government is so intrusive and wrong sometimes, it makes my skin crawl. Have you seen it?"

Macy shook her head. "I mean, I get these alerts all the time, but what are the odds of my seeing them? Maybe I should pay closer attention, but I don't."

"That's not the point." Amy went on to tell her about the details of the case. "And then, there are two young girls in Phoenix, ages ten and twelve, who were forcibly taken from their parents because some doctors convinced the state that the sisters needed to participate in some study about their rare disorder. A study. Not even treatment that's confirmed to work. Or the young boy in Indianapolis taken for the same reason. And what about this 17-year-old girl taken from her mother by force and literally tied down to have chemotherapy she didn't want? I tell you, it's . . . it's . . . ." Amy stopped. If she kept going, her blood pressure alarm would soon go off and her chance of a discharge home the next day would dissolve.

Macy's lips squeezed to a fine line as she nodded. "I have a cousin who's a social worker. She's always telling us the best way to do this or do that for my other cousins' kids. She doesn't think highly of a lot of parents, and I can't say as I blame her. Lots of screwed up people having kids these days."

"Maybe so, but the parents in these cases aren't. And what gives the government the right to take someone's kids just because they disagree with a doctor about care? It's just wrong, plain wrong."

Macy didn't look so convinced. But when it came to the role of government, she and Macy had had differing opinions before. They had agreed to disagree.

"So, when they going to spring you from here?"

Amy knew it wouldn't take her friend long to change the subject.

"I'm hoping for tomorrow. I've had a bowel movement, and they gave me a soft diet for lunch. I've tolerated it just fine so far. So, tomorrow would suit me. I'm sitting here going crazy."

Macy made exaggerated nods to the last statement. Amy punched her in the arm for agreeing so readily.

"Hey, you're off tomorrow, right?"

"Yeah. Need something?"

"Maybe a ride home. My dad is supposed to meet someone in Jeff City tomorrow, and I'd hate for him to cancel those plans on account of me. He'd do so in a heartbeat, but I, well, you know me. And Richard will be in Washington. Lynch volunteered, but that seems awkward."

Macy mouthed 'awkward' in unison with Amy.

"Sure. If it happens, give me a call. I don't have any special plans."

"Thanks, Macy."

They talked awhile longer before Macy had to head back to work in the E.D. Amy debated whether to chance a blood pressure spike by returning to the internet and chose to risk it. The term "medical kidnapping" had evolved from the cases she'd been reading about. The problem was far more widespread than the vast majority of people knew. Hundreds of children every year were forcibly removed from their families for reasons as absurd as a father having a non-F.D.A.-approved, but legal, supplement in the house, for *his* own use. Or a parent requested a second medical opinion. And the problem worsened each year.

As she read more and more on MedicalKidnap.com, she came across the story of Sinead and Ruth, as well as several on the Massachusetts D.C.F. social worker labeled as that state's leading "kidnapper." Her resolve to help the

O'Malleys grew with each news story she read. But how could she help?

Her thoughts focused on that. As she pondered the situation, she knew from her brief exposure to Sinead that the woman's goal was to make her family complete again. She didn't think Sinead would stay on the run forever because she risked her husband's remaining in jail, and she had other children she undoubtedly longed to see and hold. Still, what could Amy do?

She closed her eyes to say a short prayer. "Lord, if I can help them somehow, please bring them back into my life and show me the way."

Amy's phone whistled that a text message had arrived. She viewed the text and her heart skipped a beat. This was not good. Hadn't she just prayed about helping Sinead and Ruth? No, he would never understand her position. He had always been too "by the book," and he would turn them in to the authorities if he crossed paths with Sinead. This really complicated matters.

The message from Lynch simply stated, "We need to talk. I know who was at the farm with you."

Twenty-Four

Diane sat in the police office for what seemed like hours, and each passing minute saw her anxiety increase. She felt downright paranoid. Would they find out she had no legal standing to ask for their assistance? That she'd been fired from the D.C.F.? That she held what amounted to stolen credentials? Every moment she sat there increased the risk of that police sergeant making inquiries about her with the D.C.F. in Boston.

Of course, she had never actually *stated* she represented the Department of Children and Family. As she thought about it, she had flashed her old creds for just a second to the social worker at Barnes Hospital, but she hadn't said anything about being there *for* the department. The police sergeant hadn't asked for anything more than a photo ID, and she used her driver's license for that.

Yes, she was being paranoid. The worst that could happen would be that they would refuse to work with her. And even then, she might be able to appeal to their sense of duty and help resolve the AMBER Alert based on her credible information. Assuming she could gather that information and find Sinead O'Malley. Right now, that remained a big "if."

"Ms. Westlake, I'm sorry for the delay."

The sergeant surprised her from behind in the waiting area where she sat. She stood and turned to face him. As she glanced at his face, she saw nothing there to concern her.

"I'm going to have Detective Jahn assist you, but she's tied up in meetings at City Hall. I don't think she's going to be able to break free this afternoon, and the day is getting late. Rather than have you wait, it might be easier if you came back tomorrow morning. She'll be available by, say, nine o'clock. Does that work for you?"

Diane nodded. "Yes. Thank you, sergeant. I can return then."

"Great. I'll make sure she's here. Have a good day."

Diane walked from the station and felt relief to find her car where she'd parked it and intact. She glanced in all directions as she walked toward it. She didn't wish to be surprised by any panhandlers, or worse.

As soon as she started moving, she reversed her course to find her way back to the large medical complex that included Barnes Hospital. But then what? She still needed to alert the right people at the other two trauma centers but that wouldn't take the rest of the day.

She needed an ally. She suspected the detective would take her number, make a few calls, and tell her she'd call if anything came up. She couldn't see the detective taking time for what most people would call speculation about the O'Malleys heading toward St. Louis, as much as Diane was convinced. She needed boots on the ground and eyes on the prize.

Immediately west of the hospital complex lay Forest Park, the home of the 1904 World's Fair and now the location of the St. Louis Art Museum, the Saint Louis Zoo, and other cultural venues. Diane found a turn-off leading into the park and meandered around looking for a place to park and think.

She drove past something called the Boathouse, realized it was a restaurant, and turned back. Her growling stomach needed assuaging. She had expected St. Louis weather to be like that in Boston and was surprised to find the warmth of this early April day pleasant enough to warrant an outside seat overlooking the small lake where, during the summer months, paddle boats plied the water. Those boats sat stacked along the shore to her left.

Hungry for a taste of home, she ordered seafood and corn chowder. Then, remembering that St. Louis, or was it Kansas City, was known for its bar-b-que, she followed the chowder with a pulled pork sandwich. Admittedly an unusual combination, but she found both tasty and satisfying.

But now that her stomach no longer competed for her attention, she turned her thoughts to the problem at hand. Finding an ally.

Her phone rang. Kiandra. She hoped her friend had a concrete lead.

"Hey, Kiandra. What's up?"

"You tell me."

"Huh?"

"The office grapevine says you failed to turn in your ID badge. Most folks are saying it was just an oversight, but I know you. You're too much into every picky little detail. You wouldn't have just overlooked that. So, where are you and what are you up to?"

Diane blanched. She had worried that local authorities might discover her "secret." She hadn't considered being outed by former co-workers. Well, Kiandra wouldn't do that. She could trust Kiandra. She hadn't been forthright with her because she didn't want to put her friend in any sort of compromising position.

"I, uh . . ." How much did she want to say? "I *am* out of town, hunting. Just not job hunting."

"And?"

"Look, I didn't want to put you in an odd spot."

"Oh? And yet you asked me to cover for you if anyone called about you? Let me guess. You're looking for the O'Malleys. So, are you in Springfield or St. Louis?"

Diane hesitated. "St. Louis."

"Have you passed yourself off as working for the D.C.F.?"

"No." Diane realized she hadn't said that convincingly. "Well, maybe." She explained that she'd flashed her ID just once but didn't elaborate on what that led to.

"Diane, you're too much. I think I can understand why you're doing this, but I never once figured you'd abuse our friendship, for any reason. I hope you don't get into trouble but don't expect me to cover for you. We're going to have a long talk when you get back, if you value my friendship, and I'll probably visit you in prison, if it comes to that. But right now, I'm really pissed at you."

Diane started to apologize only to realize her friend had hung up.

She hung her head. She wanted an ally and yet had alienated her best friend. She felt more alone now than at any point since the commissioner dismissed her. This O'Malley case had become an albatross around her neck, and the urge to vindicate herself strengthened. Kiandra was correct, and she regretted having asked Kiandra to provide cover. Now, she had to prove to Kiandra that she wasn't being reckless by hunting Sinead O'Malley and that she was worthy keeping as a friend.

She lifted her head and stared across the still water. She still needed help, but with or without it, she *would* find Sinead O'Malley and see to it that the woman ended up in jail.

Twenty-Five

"Are you sure you want to do this?"

Ruth looked up at her mother and nodded. "Yep. I know I can make it."

Sinead felt unconvinced.

"It's a long walk. I could let you off at the main entrance, park, and then join you."

Ruth contemplated that for a moment. "Okay. Maybe you're right."

That's better, Sinead thought. While at lunch, they'd used their new "burner" phone, another of Ruth's *As Seen on TV* ideas, to get the number for the MedAir headquarters. Then Sinead called, stating that they wanted to send flowers to Amy Gibbs in the hospital but didn't know which hospital to send them to. She explained that she had Amy's cell number and could call her to find out, but that they wanted to surprise her. After confirming the last four digits of Amy's phone number, the secretary told her Mercy Medical Center. And now, two hours later, they waited at a stop light to turn into that medical center complex.

A minute later, Sinead allowed Ruth to exit the car on her own, without the assistance of her wheelchair, and watched her walk into the hospital's main door. She quickly drove to the parking garage but finding a spot in short order proved exasperating. A full five minutes elapsed before she turned off the car and ran toward the entrance.

It dawned on her that her own separation anxiety matched that of her daughter. She envisioned walking through those doors to see security surrounding Ruth and waiting to take her, Sinead, into custody. Maybe surprising Amy hadn't been such a good idea after all.

She cleared the doors and searched for Ruth. She saw her sitting in a nearby chair, looking nonchalant, holding a *People Magazine* in her hands. Sinead smiled as she approached her daughter.

"You might have pulled it off better if you didn't have the magazine upside down. Did you even look at it?"

Ruth quickly glanced at the glossy rag she held in her hands and laughed as she flipped it around. "Some spy I'd make. Hey, where're the flowers?"

Sinead felt like she'd taken a punch to the gut. "Oh, shoot. I-I was so concerned about you, I totally forgot them."

Ruth rolled her eyes. "And you wonder where I get that from. I'll wait here, with my magazine."

Sinead sighed. "Okay. Be right back."

She made a beeline for the door, rushed to the car, and with flowers in hand, ran back, taking care not to destroy the bouquet in the process. Forty feet from the door, she came to a full stop, almost jumping backward. Her heart leapt into her mouth. Sweat began to bead up on her forehead.

Entering the building in front of her was the subject of her nightmares. Not security. *Her*. The witch responsible for tearing her family apart. What in the world was she doing here? How could she possibly have known that Sinead and

Ruth would be there?

Maybe she didn't. Maybe this was purely coincidence, but as such things go, there couldn't have been any worse time. Sinead was outside. Ruth was inside.

Sinead glanced around for another entrance but saw no other options. Her mind raced. How had Ruth been sitting with respect to the doors? Did Westlake already know Ruth was inside? Had security already converged on her daughter? What would happen when she, Sinead, walked through those doors?

But then other thoughts also caught her mind. If Westlake being at this hospital was pure coincidence, and she was *unaware* that Ruth was there, what would be more conspicuous, the two together or Ruth alone? Would Sinead be better off waiting her out? But if Ruth saw her, would she panic? No, Ruth panicking would not be good. And she definitely did not want Ruth to feel she had been abandoned. Never again.

Sinead tried to think about the layout inside. The information desk was straight ahead from the doors and the seating area where Ruth waited was maybe 30 feet beyond it. Ruth's back would be toward the desk, unless she had moved. Sinead could slip along the far wall to get to the seats. Whatever she did, she had to remain calm and act as if she did not recognize the social worker. And if she could avoid direct eye contact, she should. Could she create a character in her mind and become that character, like an actor being immersed in a role?

She chastised herself when the first character to come to mind was Forrest Gump. Run, Forrest, Run. Instead, she focused on the superheroes of Ruth's imagination. She would exude confidence and power. Her attitude would be one of "owning the place." Then, she saw her reflection in the glass of the nearby windows. Mom jeans were as close as she was going to get to a skintight costume.

She fumbled for the sunglasses in her purse and put them on. Taking a deep breath, she told herself, feel and look confident. No matter what.

And with that she marched through the front doors.

Diane had not found the people at Saint Louis University Hospital all that helpful. Their attitude was one of, "Well, we take all AMBER Alerts seriously and keep a watchful eye out for them," as if Diane had asked them to do something extraordinary.

Again, privacy laws prevented her from learning whether the nurse from the helicopter crash was admitted there. She had been unsuccessful at discovering the woman's name. She had even tried to contact the helicopter company but got brushed off without a name. She had to admit, though, that she sounded like someone fishing for information. Had that receptionist been her, she wouldn't have offered any information either. Yet, she didn't know any other way of approaching it.

She had one more trauma center to check out, and as she walked through the door at Mercy, she hoped they would be more helpful. Only one person appeared to be in front of her at the information desk. She glanced around but saw no one familiar and returned her focus to the task at hand.

Her turn.

"How may I help you?"

Diane explained the purpose of her visit, stating only

that she was there in conjunction with a nationwide AMBER Alert and that there was reason to believe the targets of that search were looking for a nurse involved in a crash.

"Do you have the patient's name?"

"I'm sorry, but no."

"Well, I'm sure you understand privacy laws, so we're limited in whatever information we can provide, *if* you have the patient's name. Without a name, well, we don't have any way of knowing who might have been admitted due to *any* kind of crash. Did you try calling the patient's company, the owners of the helicopter?"

"I did. They have their privacy rules, too. Well, I thank you for the help you could give. By the way, here are photos of the mom and girl. Is there a way of posting them to alert people to watch for them? Oh, and the girl would be in a wheelchair."

The woman at the desk took the sheet and gazed at it.

"Well, I haven't seen these two, and I've seen no girls come through those doors in a wheelchair today. But I can put this in our log book, for the others to see."

"Thank you and have a good day."

Diane turned to leave and noticed a dark-haired woman walk into the building. She noted how this person had the right stature of Sinead O'Malley, but of course the hair color was wrong and sunglasses covered her face. And she pushed no one in a wheelchair. Still . . .

Sinead's heart raced as she walked into the building and saw Diane Westlake at the information desk. Yet, she saw that Ruth had not changed her seat, and, hopefully, had not seen their nemesis. That gave her a glimmer of hope and strengthened her resolve to act out her part. She ignored the woman, who seemed to be turning to leave. She kept her head looking straight down the hallway and walked on in confidence.

As she arrived at the seating area, she stopped and looked at her watch, and sat several chairs away from Ruth. Ruth gave her a funny look and started to stand, but Sinead gave her a subtle shake of the head and pointed with her eyes. Ruth looked puzzled but remained seated.

A minute later, Sinead stood and walked over to sit across from her daughter in a chair where she faced the door and could maintain her vigilance.

"Mom, you're making me nervous. What gives?"

Sinead didn't want to tell her that the social worker from Boston, Ruth's real kidnapper, had just left.

"Remember a couple of days ago, when you told me that maybe you really didn't want to know everything?" Ruth gave her that puzzled look again. "Well, this might be one of those times. Maybe later, after we leave here."

"Mom?"

"Later, sweetie. You sit right here, and I'll go ask for Amy's room number."

Sinead went to the information desk and inquired about Amy.

"Hi, what room is Amy Gibbs in, please?"

The woman typed the name into the computer and looked back up at her. "Are you family?"

"No, just friends."

"I'll have to call and ask if it's okay. She's listed that only family be given her room."

"Oh. Ummm, is there any way we could get around that? She's a nurse and *very* special to us. I have her cell number and could have called her directly for the room number, but we wanted to surprise her with these flowers." Sinead showed off the bouquet. "My daughter chose them."

"Daughter?" The woman sounded suspicious.

"Yes, right over there. The blonde." Sinead waved to Ruth, who had been watching the exchange. The woman glanced at a piece of paper on the desk. She looked at Ruth, who stood up without effort and smiled. Sinead became nervous as she saw that the paper held pictures of them both, with the words, "girl in wheelchair," handwritten underneath.

The woman's friendliness returned. "What the heck, sure. They're beautiful flowers. We wouldn't want them to get spoiled."

Armed with Amy's room number, Sinead returned to Ruth. Together they walked to the elevator bank, with Ruth holding Sinead's arm for support.

Diane walked through the doors and stopped outside. Maybe she was so focused on Sinead O'Malley that any woman even vaguely close to her stature made Diane look twice. She had done so with the raven-haired woman. The woman had walked by with zero signs of recognition.

Still, something nagged at Diane.

She stepped to the side and watched through the large windows along the front entrance. The woman was at the front desk now, talking with the volunteer Diane had spoken to but moments earlier. As they talked, the volunteer glanced down at her desk. That was where Diane had watched her place the photos. And then the look on the volunteer's face softened and became friendly.

Diane chastised herself for overreacting. She was about to turn away when she saw the woman approach a young girl, a blonde. She shook her head. That obviously couldn't be Ruth O'Malley. She stood and walked on her own power.

Yes, Diane now felt convinced that she was officially obsessed. She shook her head and walked on toward her car. The last thing she needed now was to start seeing her prey in every mother-daughter pair she encountered.

Twenty-Six

Amy looked up at another knock on her doorpost. Richard had called from the airport and informed her that Lynch had also been called to join them at the last minute. Her father, too, was on his way out of town, at her urging, to Kansas City. Macy was still working, but it was unlikely she would have come to this floor with a patient. And it was too early for "dinner." Suddenly, Amy felt a tinge of excitement at having a new and unexpected visitor.

"Come in."

A bouquet of flowers appeared first, followed by the head of a young blonde girl. The girl walked in, followed by a dark-haired woman Amy could only assume to be her mother.

"Surprise!" The girl extended the flowers toward her.

"Umm, I'm sorry. Do you have the right room?"

The girl glanced at her mother and they laughed.

"Amy, it's us," said the girl.

Amy's eyes widened. "Ruth? Sinead?"

The two nodded in unison.

"Quick, come in and shut the door."

Amy became flustered. These were the last two people she expected to come visit her, and now that they had, she didn't know what to do. She remembered offering to help, but these two were wanted by law enforcement, whether or not Amy agreed with the reason they were wanted. Under the circumstances of their situation, Amy wouldn't think of turning them in, but she also didn't want to get into trouble. *That* kind of trouble could threaten her nursing license and career.

But then, she remembered her prayer about bringing them back into her life if she could help. She would have to trust in God for Him to show her how.

"How do we look?" Ruth struck a couple of poses and laughed.

"Well, I sure didn't recognize you. Hey, look, you two shouldn't be here."

The smiles disappeared from the mother's and daughter's faces.

"I know who you are now. There's a renewed AMBER Alert for you, and hospitals take those seriously. They said you were spotted in Springfield and possibly coming here, to Saint Louis. You run a big risk of getting caught here."

Sinead pulled the chair over and motioned for Ruth to sit.

"I know," she replied. "It almost happened in the lobby."

Ruth glanced up and her eyes questioned her mom. "Is that—"

Sinead patted Ruth's shoulder. "Yes. If we hadn't changed our looks, we would have been caught." She went on to explain what had transpired in the lobby. "I'm just glad you didn't see her, Ruth. I don't think you could have controlled yourself, and that would have given us away."

Amy noticed that Ruth's anxiety level had increased at the mention of the social worker's name, and her heart went out to the young teen, again. Amy couldn't imagine the anguish of being ripped away from loving parents. Sinead and her husband had done nothing wrong. They had not been accused, much less convicted, of a crime. Where was their due process as guaranteed by the Fifth Amendment of the U.S. Constitution? Murderers and rapists were assured of the right of due process but not parents who were at odds with a state's child protection service.

"So, why did you risk coming here? You both look great, by the way. Love the hair changes. I did not recognize you until you called me by name. And you walked in. I'm impressed."

"Mom was worried about you. Well, we both were, but I knew you'd be okay."

Amy caught Sinead glancing up in her adult form of eye-rolling, and chuckled. "Well, seems you were right, but I did have a small setback out in the barn." She explained what had happened and how she'd ended up at Mercy.

"I am *so* glad you're okay. I felt so guilty, not taking you out before the bridge washed away. I don't know what I would have done if they hadn't found you when they did and had the helicopter to take you out."

"Hey, don't feel guilty. Nothing was your fault."

"I should have let you just stay in the house. You would never have climbed into that old truck on your own, and your spleen wouldn't have torn."

Amy reached out for Sinead's hand and squeezed it. "We're good. It's all good. Except for your being here. We have to figure something out."

Amy racked her brain for an answer but nothing came to mind.

"Look, I can get us a motel room for a night or two, as

long as it's someplace fairly cheap. I have limited cash, and I don't want to use my credit card here. I used it up north of here, hoping to throw off anyone looking for us."

Amy thought about that for two seconds before remembering Lynch's text.

"I'm not sure that helped. One of the men who helped find me, texted me earlier to let me know that he knows you were there, at the farm."

Sinead appeared troubled, but Ruth gave her that wide-eyed look again. "How? How could he know we were there?"

Amy focused on Ruth. "This man used to be a police detective. He's really good at detecting. My fiancé mentioned that Lynch, that's his name, had commented on a tiller and trailer outside the house, when the house was supposed to be abandoned."

Sinead sighed. "Of course. The farm store's sign was on the trailer. All it would take is a phone call there. I used a fake name, but with our photos being on the news in Springfield, if 'Little Lady'-man Charlie saw them, it wouldn't take a super detective to add up all the pieces."

Ruth snickered at the mention of the farm store guy. "He kept calling Mom 'Little Lady.' "

Sinead shrugged her shoulders.

Amy couldn't help but like these two. Ruth's optimism and love for life was infectious. And Sinead willfully risked everything to protect her daughter. Amy felt blessed to have had them come into her life.

"Can you grab my bag there?" Sinead pointed to one on the window sill. "Yeah, that one." Amy rummaged through her bag to find her keys and a pen. She pulled a house key off the ring, and then wrote down her home address and two series of five digits.

"Richard, my fiancé, and Lynch are both out of town for several days. I think you can safely stay at my house. The first numbers are used on a keypad outside the garage, next to the door on the side. That'll open the garage door. My car's still at my work parking lot, so there's plenty of space. This key opens the door from the garage into the house, and the second set of numbers deactivates the alarm. The keypad for that is just inside the door, and you have 30 seconds to do it."

"No problem. We have an alarm system, too, so we're both used to using it."

"Then you're probably better at it than I am. I had it installed a month ago, after two guys broke into my house. I still forget to set it, or turn it off in time. I'm on a first name basis with the guys at the security company's call center."

"Wow. Did they get anything? The two guys, that is," asked Ruth.

"Not before I shot one of them." Ruth's eyes bugged out with that revelation. "Long story. Somebody ought to write a book about it."

Amy continued, ignoring Ruth's mouthing, "You shot someone?"

"Oh, and there's a good chance I'll be coming home tomorrow. If that's the case, I'll need a way to contact you."

"Oh?"

"Yep. I'll need to call you to give you warning to clear out of the house until I call you back. My friend Macy will be bringing me home, and I don't know what in the world she would do if she discovered you there. She works in the E.D. She's seen the AMBER Alert."

Richard's emotions twisted as he watched the plane in which he, Lynch, and half a dozen others from the American Party and Bradley Graham campaign sat, begin to speed along the runway at Lambert International Airport. The commercial airliner shuddered and rose from the ground, and everything below them began to diminish with distance. Too bad he couldn't leave his concerns on the ground to shrink along with them.

The timing of this trip was lousy. While he recognized the need from the perspective of the campaign, he wanted to be there to assist Amy. It had been but three days since he'd almost lost her. He shuddered as he reminisced of that day and, yet, rejoiced at her recovery. He wasn't ready to continue life, and especially work, "as usual."

Lynch, sitting across the aisle from him, cleared his throat and caught his attention. Richard turned to see what he wanted and noticed the man's clench on the armrests begin to ease. He thought it odd that Lynch could hunt down killers, face down thugs, and even protect others in a bomb blast, but turn white and weak-kneed when it came to flying in any form. We all have an irrational fear of something. For some, it was obvious. For others, they had yet to be put into a position to learn what they feared.

"What's on your mind?" asked Lynch.

"Who do you think?"

"Yeah, figured. I'm a bit worried about her, too."

"Oh, I'm not worried about her. I just want to be there to help right now."

"Ah." Lynch finally let go of both armrests and settled back into the seat.

"No, really. Why should I be worried? She's tough, self-reliant, and surrounded by friends and family. I mean, what could happen in a hospital room or her house?"

"All true."

Richard now wanted to punch his new friend. With one brief sentence and the tone of his voice, he'd erased all of Richard's efforts to convince himself that he had no reason to worry.

"Look, I know you two are engaged, so I'm sure you'll find out soon enough. Amy is . . . how should I say it? Um, a poop magnet. She attracts more trouble than bees to a sugary drink. So, it's a good thing she's tough. She keeps her guardian angels, the whole squad, working overtime."

Richard thought about that for a moment, only to wish the topic hadn't come up. Now, more than before, he wanted to be there for her. Yet, Lynch's comment rang true. Between things she had shared with him and things he had witnessed firsthand, Amy had been through more "situations" than the Situation Room at the White House.

"I can identify with you. I don't want anything to happen to her either. I just hope she's not getting herself involved in the case of the people who were at the farm."

Richard's breath caught. "What? There really was someone else at the farm?"

"Yep. Pretty sure of it anyway." Lynch explained what he had discovered.

Richard slumped into his seat. Getting involved in a case like that had Amy written all over it. And Lynch's theory that someone had helped Amy from the crash site had always seemed more plausible than her limping to the barn on her own, dragging two duffels behind her. That would make Amy more inclined to help them.

"I need to call her as soon as we get to DC."

"Yeah, well, I thought about that, too. She already

knows that I figured it out. If she learns that I told you, she's more likely to get bull-headed about it and not let either of us help. Plus, I read up on the case. I'd be on their side, the family's side, too. I think the court stepped way over the line in taking that girl from her parents."

"So, what do you think we should do?"

"Well, like you said, how much trouble could she get into in the hospital or at her house? I wanted you to know what's going on 'cause she's more likely to call you than me. Way more likely. But right now all we can do is wait and see. After all, I have no physical proof that I'm right, just strong circumstantial evidence. And we don't know that this mother and daughter will make contact with Amy again. I don't think we need to cause trouble, or get Amy upset, on what amounts to speculation."

Richard mulled that over. Lynch was right again. Making an issue of it, even a minor one, could get Amy's hackles up. He'd seen that side of her a few times. Plus, he would be hours away and in no position to do anything—except hope she stayed out of trouble.

Twenty-Seven

Morning report had ended, and Tammy sat at her desk twiddling her thumbs. Barkley had instructed her to wait around for her "assignment," without mentioning any details. That alone had others taking bets and offering condolences. Speculation ran the gamut from reopening some long stale cold case to chauffeuring the mayor's second cousin, once removed, on a tour of St. Louis tourist spots. Whatever he had in mind, *she* had a lead on Montez's killer and didn't want to waste time at the precinct.

She saw Barkley park his phone back on its base and stand up. He faced her and motioned for her to join him.

"What's up? Something else new on the Montez Johnson stabbing?" she asked, wondering if the crossed fingers behind her back were noticeable.

"That's for Homicide, not us. You keep your nose out of it." He led her toward the front of the building, while the betting pool gathered in the back.

"But, like I told you, I have a lead."

"Yeah, and I passed it on to Homicide, like *I* said." He opened the door to the lobby and welcomed a middle-aged white lady who definitely looked out of place for the neighborhood. "Ms. Westlake, nice to see you again. This here's the detective I mentioned to you yesterday, Detective

Jahn. She will be more than happy to help you in any way she can. This is Ms. Westlake, from Boston."

Tammy felt a subtle shiver as her sergeant stressed "more than happy." And the woman was from Boston? What was she getting mixed up in?

"Nice to meet you, Ms. Westlake." Tammy extended her hand, while hoping the hesitation she felt hadn't projected into her greeting. She refused to let Barkley have his satisfaction. "Why don't you follow me to my desk, and I can get the particulars of your concern."

"You mean your sergeant hasn't already filled you in? I told him everything yesterday."

Tammy could already see how it was going to be. At least the woman was busting Barkley's chops, not hers. Yet, he didn't look the least bit fazed.

"Sorry, Ms. Westlake, but our paths didn't cross in time for me to fill her in. That shouldn't take long for you. Plus, Detective Jahn will no doubt have specific questions for you."

Nice recovery, Your Daddy, thought Tammy. But then, he'd been around that block a dozen times, and she expected nothing less.

Ms. Westlake looked miffed but followed Tammy to her desk and sat next to it, after Tammy cleared the debris from her chair. The woman looked dour and dressed in a way that made it look as if she'd stepped out of a different era. She needed the "fashion police," not the *real* police of District 5.

"So, please tell me what we can help you with."

Ms. Westlake huffed and with a begrudged attitude, launched into what she pointed out at the beginning was the same story she'd told Barkley. She then added that she had taken it upon herself to visit all three trauma centers and alert them to the possibility that the mother and daughter involved in this AMBER Alert might be checking there for this injured nurse—whose name she didn't know. Big help there.

Once upon a time obtaining a name like that would have been a cinch for the police. Now, with the federal Health Insurance Portability and Accountability Act in place, even the police couldn't get a patient's name without jumping through hoops. HIPAA, HIPAA, hooray! Leave it to the Feds to make our day!

Tammy was about to ask for her credentials but then thought better of it. Certainly somewhere along the line, whether at Barnes Hospital or with Barkley yesterday, someone had verified that she was who she said she was. To ask her again was guaranteed to ruffle her feathers, and Tammy didn't need any more attitude from this lady.

"So, how can I help you exactly? It sounds like you've covered the bases well so far."

"Why, I thought that would be clear. I want you to help me find this girl—and her mother."

Tammy resisted the sigh that formed deep inside. Of course. It would be a cinch to find one mother and child in a metropolitan area of nearly three million people. They might even accomplish that by noon. Right. Only on TV.

"One moment, please. Be right back."

Tammy walked over to Your Daddy's cubicle to find him on the phone. He ignored her until the call was completed. "What?"

"She wants me to help her find a dried pea in a silo of corn."

Barkley smirked. "What, making up your own

metaphors now, Shakespeare?"

"Idiom. That's an idiom."

"Well, don't be an idiom with a 't.' Figure out a way to help her. She's yours for the day." He stressed the words "the day."

"You promised me to her for the whole day?" Tammy knew as soon as she'd said it, that she'd just given Barkley the satisfaction he was looking for.

"Not exactly, but unless you want the assignment extended, you've got the day. Go. I've got work to do, and you do, too." He dismissed her with a wave of his hand.

Tammy returned to her desk to an impatient social worker. Ever since her run-in with those social workers in Racine, the ones who'd wanted to make her a ward of the state for eight months after her grandparents had died, she'd distrusted them. It had taken her close to a year on the GREAT Program to learn to appreciate the two case workers on the team. Still, they had their moments, too. Tammy made a mental note to learn more about the case involving the AMBER Alert.

"Okay, Sarge says you've got me for the day, so, let's head back to Barnes Hospital and see if I can help you find out that nurse's name. That's going to be our easiest first lead. By the way, it might be best if you follow me there. I'd hate to strand you somewhere if I got called out on an emergency."

Ms. Westlake nodded but gave her a look that said, "No fake emergency calls or I'm telling your sergeant." Not that the idea hadn't already crossed Tammy's mind.

An hour later, after great effort at Barnes, they still had no name, but they were assured that Barnes had not admitted anyone, nurse or otherwise, from a helicopter crash within the past week. Following the same trail Ms. Westlake blazed the day before, University Hospital was next on the list.

Twenty-Eight

Amy lifted another forkful of unseasoned scrambled eggs to her mouth, closed her eyes, and savored the bite. She cherished her breakfast, which also included dry toast and apple juice, for more than one reason. Being her first solid food in days, it tasted wonderful, even though she knew that to be an illusion. When you're hungry enough, even the worst food could take on gourmet qualities.

More importantly, the doctor's giving her a full menu meant he was close, if not already planning to discharge her. She had already proven her ability to maneuver on crutches, a skill she had mastered as a teenager with too many sports injuries to count. With that, her orthopedic surgeon had given his blessing to her discharge. Now, the final decision depended on the trauma docs who had overseen her care. She guessed her odds to be 3-in-4 for going home later that day.

She was ready to leave. Yes, the leg injury and requiring crutches would be an eight-week inconvenience, but she had overcome worse. She needed to regain control of her life.

The trauma team came through on its patient rounds shortly after lunch. Her surgeon examined her belly.

"Nice active bowel sounds."

She already knew that. The growling in her gut could have awakened most of the anesthetized patients in the O.R.

"And I see you've had a couple more bowel movements. Any pain?"

"None. At least not in my abdomen. The leg talks to me every once in a while."

"That'll resolve in short order." He reviewed some entries, typed a few lines into her chart on the bedside computer, and concluded by saying, "Time to go home. The order is written. See you in a week at my office. Call, or come to the E.D. if you experience any problems."

"Yes, sir. I'm ready to go and I understand what to watch for."

He smiled and patted her on the shoulder. "Take care of yourself."

The team hadn't finished closing the door on their way out when Amy dialed Macy. "Come get me."

Jeremy followed Westlake back to the Fifth Precinct Headquarters and waited. Although he could handle himself in most situations, he felt uncomfortable parked along the side of the street as he watched the building's front door. He felt as conspicuous as a freshly washed polar bear in a coal mine.

And the longer Westlake remained inside, the more anxious he became. Maybe he should have used the opportunity of the flat tire along the side of the road to reveal himself to her. Yet, that would not have followed the timetable. He would have to stick with Plan A.

He saw that he was being noticed by the "locals"—two small groups of young black men who looked as if they had illegal intentions toward him and his car. Using the internet, he had discovered the evening before that the area around this police station was heavily gang-related. He wanted no such trouble, so he started his car to move back to a less dangerous position.

As he began to pull away from the curb, he noticed Westlake emerge from the building, along with another woman. The second woman escorted Westlake to her car and then walked into the fenced police lot. He drove away from the men he'd seen congregating on the corner nearest to him, to a new spot about a block away where he could still observe Westlake's car. An unmarked police car drove out of the police lot, and Westlake fell in behind it.

He shook his head but had to give her credit for her chutzpah. She had secured the help of a detective after all. He wondered if the police had made any effort to verify her identity or credentials. It would seem they had not. They obviously didn't realize they were assisting a discredited social worker using stolen credentials. He would fix that.

He pulled into traffic and followed from a distance. In short order, he saw that they appeared to be replaying Westlake's movements from the day before, starting at Barnes Hospital. If correct in his assumption, they would move on to Saint Louis University Medical Center. He turned into the big park west of the hospital and found a parking spot as close to the hospital as possible. That made it easy to monitor her movement to or from both facilities.

As he sat there, he turned his attention to his laptop. He drafted a short blog post about Diane Westlake's firing and her missing credentials. In it, he speculated about her keeping them to use surreptitiously. He tagged the O'Malley case, two similar medical kidnapping cases, and the

Massachusetts coordinator for the AMBER Alert system. He knew that the coordinator, a state trooper, kept close tabs on such tags and that his move would bring her into the loop about Westlake. He signed off on the post using his pen name and sent it to a computer at the Boston Public Library that he had previously hacked. Within 30 minutes, his post would go to two internet sites and appear to have come from the library's public network.

He would give his post some time to become noticed. Soon, it would be seen by anyone searching for info on the O'Malley case, as well as the other two cases. However, if the local police officer continued to work with Westlake the next day or the day after, he had an idea how to make sure they knew whom they were working with.

His system alerted him to a change in position of the GPS unit. Westlake was on the move. He monitored her location and confirmed that she now headed toward the Saint Louis University Medical Center.

He started his car and pulled out of the parking spot. He couldn't approach her with the policewoman present anyway, so he headed back to his motel room. He knew where Westlake was staying and could easily monitor her movements. He had another task to tackle, finding out where Amy Gibbs lived.

The early afternoon hours were a lesson in patience for Amy. She had forgotten that the wheels of discharge moved slower than a federal bureaucracy. She had been dressed and packed within 15 minutes of the doctors' leaving her room. Macy had arrived 17 minutes after that. And ever since then, they had tried to locate Nurse Ratched

Junior with her prerequisite discharge papers.

"Do you want me to go stir things up?" asked Macy.

"Again?" Amy shook her head. "I think that just slows her down, out of spite."

"Maybe I could offer to do your discharge. I *am* a nurse here after all."

Amy gave her friend a look. "Would you want Nurse Ratched doing *your* discharges in the E.D.?"

Macy looked as if she favored that idea. "Well, that *is* the one thing that slows us down and takes more time than anything else there. I would love an assistant to do all the paperwork. Maybe they could hire scribes for us."

"Yeah, sure. Until you get named in a lawsuit and discover the scribe didn't cover your tail adequately."

Macy shrugged.

Half an hour later, the nurse stood next to Amy's bed and recited her discharge instructions. After signing off on them, Amy climbed aboard one of the unit's two-wheeled "chariots" and watched the other rooms pass by as an aide pushed her along the hallway to the elevator and then to the front door.

Macy stood next to a silver, four-door Acura TLX and opened the door for Amy.

"Where's your Prius?"

Macy grinned. "You're lookin' at one girl who's steppin' up in this world. I figured I was due a little more luxury. Besides, I got tired of being socially responsible, and my cousin, George, got me this incredible deal."

Amy laughed. "So, you found out what it was going to cost you to get new batteries in that thing. Told you it was going to cost you more money in the long run."

Macy climbed into the driver's seat. "You weren't

kidding." She raised her head and sniffed. "And don't you love that new car smell? Hey, whatcha doing?"

Amy dialed a number on her phone. "Just leaving a message for my dad." She hated lying to her best friend, but Macy didn't need to know about Ruth and Sinead. "Hey, just wanted you to know I'm heading home. Macy's driving. Should be there in 20 minutes. Talk to you later." Now, she could only hope that all was well at her house.

Twenty-two minutes and one near accident on the highway later, Macy pulled into Amy's drive and put the car into park, but her attention wasn't on the car.

"Hey, your front porch light is on. It wasn't on three days ago when I stopped by to get you some clothes."

Amy took a deep breath. Had something happened? Were Sinead and Ruth still here? And was this her way of alerting Amy?

"Umm, I wonder if my dad stopped by and left it on. You know, in case I wasn't discharged until later in the day, and it would be dark when we got here."

Macy shrugged and proceeded to retrieve Amy's crutches from the back seat. Amy was already out and standing next to the car by the time Macy walked to the passenger side.

"I got your stuff. Want me to open the garage door?"

"Let's just use the front door. It'll be easier and I've got my key ready."

"Umm, sure. But you never use your front door."

"That's 'cause I'm usually in my car and parking in the garage. My car's still at work."

Macy didn't look convinced, and Amy held her breath as Macy unlocked the front door and swung it open wide for her. Both looked at the security panel at the same time.

"Your security system isn't armed. I'm sure I re-armed it when I left the other day."

Amy frowned. She started to blame her father but realized that blaming him would be bearing false witness and dishonoring him. To state that she wondered if he had stopped by was one thing. To actually blame him was another. She caught her words before opening her mouth. Why couldn't she trust Macy to see things her way about Sinead and Ruth?

Macy carried Amy's bag to her bedroom, glancing into each of the other rooms as she went. On her way back, she stepped into the bathroom off the hall. Amy heard the toilet flush.

"Ugh, girlfriend, I think you got squatters. And they squatted on that toilet and forgot to flush. Something's going on here."

Amy's heart began to race. "Are the doors locked? Did someone get in while I was gone?" She hobbled to the kitchen windows and checked them. "Locked."

Macy returned from checking the doors and windows. "Everything's locked."

"Amy, I'm pretty sure I armed your system and locked up behind me the other day. Does anyone else know your code?"

"My dad and Richard. I'll, uh, have to check with them both to see if one of them stopped by."

Macy gave her a look. Sure, it was possible that either man had stopped by, turned on the lights, and disarmed her alarm in order to make it easier for her in the dark. She could expect Macy to believe that. However, she had to agree that the idea of either man stopping by, using the john, and not flushing seemed ludicrous. Macy was known to have the gift of suspicion, and her gift was on full display at the moment.

"I think I'll run home, pack a few things, and come back to spend the night. That way I can help you out and make sure you don't have uninvited visitors."

Amy thought of her *invited* visitors.

"Don't be silly. I'll be fine. Besides, you have to work tomorrow and staying here would be inconvenient. My dad'll be back tonight, and I'm sure he'll stop by. He'll help me get my car tomorrow."

Macy didn't appear convinced. Amy had one last trick down her cast.

"Macy, really. I'm going to be boring. Sitting with my leg propped up, catching up on social media, maybe watching a couple of *Downton Abbey* episodes I've recorded. I won't need any help. And if it makes you feel better, I'll get my handgun and keep it under the pillow next to me."

"Well, just the thought of that does *not* make me feel better. We saw how well that worked the last time you used it." Macy shook her head. "Okay, I'll leave you be, but if you need anything, call."

"Promise. Want me to wait on *Downton Abbey* so we can watch it together?"

Amy knew that the simple suggestion of watching that show would make Macy rethink her plans.

"Uh-uh. That's not a show this black girl can even come close to identifying with. I will leave you to your boring evening."

Amy stepped up to her friend and gave her a hug. "Thanks for the ride home and offering to help. I'll be fine. Honest."

"You're welcome. Just let me know when you figure out the mystery here. Something weird going on."

Twenty-Nine

Diane's frustration level still surpassed that of her anxiety, but the latter was catching up. Their visit to Saint Louis University Hospital had provided the same results as Barnes. Nothing. Now, she parked yet again in the lot at Mercy Hospital and waited as the detective pulled into a slot beside her.

She didn't like this driving separately bit, despite the logic of it. Each time they stopped, she expected the officer to greet her by the car and tell her that she'd checked up on her and found out she was using stolen credentials. She envisioned being cuffed on the spot and hauled off to some holding cell to await extradition back to Boston. Once there, the news would make her look crazier than she was beginning to feel.

Mercy Hospital was the final Level I trauma center on the list. The injured nurse had to be here. If not, the list exploded to include eleven more hospitals in the urban area. There was also the possibility that her injuries could require a rehab center for physical therapy. Diane hadn't yet taken the time to count those facilities. And beyond that, if she were to be discharged home before Diane could find her, that made her search next to impossible without a name. At the minimum, she needed a name.

Yes, each stop pushed her anxiety level up a notch. Each negative result increased it by two. She *had* to find this girl. She had to prove to the world that she'd been correct all along that Ruth O'Malley was in danger under the care of her mother. Only then could she hope to get back her job and redeem herself in the eyes of her co-workers and friends.

Tammy pulled into the parking slot next to the social worker's car but hesitated to get out. Never again would she make her sergeant look bad. He had found the perfect retribution in making her babysit a "craaazy" lady all day. She had real police work to do. Even if this mother and daughter were in St. Louis, had they broken any local laws? Did the SLMPD even have any jurisdiction in this matter? And worse, they were no longer within the city limits, so Tammy had no authority here at all. Besides, if the mother indeed had been charged with kidnapping, and transporting the girl across state lines, that was an FBI matter, not one for the local police. So, where were the Fibbies on this one?

Tammy glanced across her car to see the woman emerge from hers. "Craaazy" was being kind. It wasn't so much what the woman said but how she acted. She knew the right words. She knew what buttons to push to get maximum response from the hospital employees they had dealt with so far. Yeah, her words were right on target and smoothly delivered.

But the fidgety hands, the tapping toes, and the back and forth glances with her eyes all told a different story. Her body language screamed "nervous." If Tammy had any reason to suspect drug use by this woman, she'd conclude the lady was hitting early withdrawal. She had seen it on the streets numerous times. Yet, with no hint of illegal substance use, Tammy felt inclined to think this woman was about to lose it mentally. Nervous breakdown. Psychotic break. Her spring wound too tight. Whatever term one might use, this woman was going to snap soon, and if they didn't find this nurse, that event would come sooner, not later. And Tammy needed it to occur later. Much later. After they parted ways.

Tammy climbed out of her car and joined Diana. Together, they walked toward the main entrance. As they came to the door, they stepped aside to let a nurse wheel a patient through the door to a new Acura. Tammy noticed a cast on the patient's leg and smiled in a simple greeting. As soon as they had passed, Tammy and Diane entered the building and walked up to the information desk.

"Hello again," said the volunteer.

Tammy assumed Diane had talked with this person the day before. The woman continued to address Diane.

"We still have your flier and security passed it along to the other information desks, the cashiers in the cafeteria and gift shop, and anyplace else they thought might be helpful. As far as I know, no one has seen them."

Tammy saw a new nervous twitch in Diane. She stepped forward to take control.

"Hi, I'm Detective Jahn, with the Saint Louis Police." She displayed her badge. "Besides looking for the targets of this AMBER Alert, we also need to find the name of the nurse they might be looking for. Is there someone I can talk with about that?"

Five minutes later, they took seats outside the Director

of Nursing's office and waited. Five minutes after that, the D.o.N. ushered them into her office and introductions were made.

"So, I understand you're checking into an AMBER Alert."

Tammy took the lead. "Yes, ma'am. The targets of this alert were identified in Springfield, Illinois, a couple of days ago . . ." She proceeded to fill in the D.o.N. on the details. "We're trying to locate a flight nurse who was involved in a helicopter crash not far from Springfield. We think she might have information on this mother and daughter. The news accounts haven't identified the name of the nurse, and Ms. Westlake here was unable to get it from the company. If you're unable to help us, we will be going there after we leave here."

"And I take it that the two trauma centers in the city were of no help."

"Well, yes and no. Under HIPAA, they would not have been able to provide a name, but they did go so far as to inform us that they had not admitted such a patient, so the issue was moot for them."

The chief nurse looked uncomfortable. If Tammy had a gambling nature, she would bet that the nurse not only knew they'd admitted such a patient but knew the injured nurse personally.

After shifting around in her seat, the director said, "You said the magic word. I'm sorry, but HIPAA really does prevent us from discussing patients. And I'd only be speculating about a patient's reason for admission."

Now Tammy knew the woman to be misleading. A medevac chopper crash with two dead and one survivor would hit home with health care workers, just as the death of a policeman on duty draws together the thin blue line. Even more so at a trauma center where the flight crew would have been known.

"Is there any way you can help us? Ms. Westlake and the Massachusetts Department of Children and Family have a real concern about this young girl."

Ms. Westlake nodded in agreement and started to speak up but stopped. Tammy could see the woman's toe tapping accelerate and felt thankful she hadn't said anything. Although, on second thought, if she had, and had the outburst been wild enough, she might have been able to leave Ms. Westlake to the care of the psych unit and return to her hunt for Montez' killer.

"I did make a couple of calls and security, as well as our volunteer office, assure me that no one coming even close to the description of this mother and daughter have come into the hospital. They all have their workers briefed and alert to the possibility. In fact, not a single child of any age has come into the buildings in a wheelchair in the last day, since we received the alert."

Tammy knew better than to push. She needed cooperation, not forced collusion. She stood to signal that it was time to go. Ms. Westlake didn't take the hint quickly.

"Thank you for talking with us. And, please, if anything should come up, here's my card. Please call me."

"Yes, thank you," added Ms. Westlake, as she finally stood.

Tammy thought Ms. Westlake's words sounded strained, but at least she remained civil. Outside the office, Ms. Westlake began to race toward the front doors. Tammy could barely keep up.

Out in the parking lot, the woman finally stopped

behind their cars but began pacing as Tammy joined her.

"She knows. I know she knows. You could see it written all over her. She could have told us, but she refused. Even though she knows." The words came out like bullets from an automatic weapon.

"Whoa, Ms. Westlake. Calm down."

"Calm down? She could have helped me, us. She has no compassion. She didn't seem concerned about Ruth O'Malley at all. Can't she see we're trying to find a helpless child? Hiding behind HIPAA while that poor girl is in trouble. Indeed."

Indeed? Who speaks like that? wondered Tammy. But then, Tammy was a police officer in the "baddest" precinct in the city. "Indeed" would have been shortened to four letters where she worked.

"Look, I don't think compassion has anything to do with this. I agree. I think she knows, too, but she's stuck behind the law. Do you expect her to violate HIPAA when we don't know whether the O'Malleys are even in St. Louis? If they had been spotted and got away again, then we'd have a stronger case, but we can't confirm they're here."

Ms. Westlake didn't seem any calmer.

"What would happen to you back home if you violated HIPAA with a patient? And I mean knowingly violated it, not accidentally."

The woman looked at the pavement. "I'd be fined and possibly fired."

"And what would happen to the hospital?"

She looked up at Tammy. It appeared Tammy's words were getting through.

"They'd get hit with a big fine."

"How big a fine?"

"Ten thousand to fifty thousand dollars."

"So, would you risk that if you didn't have proof that the O'Malleys are here? I wouldn't."

Ms. Westlake appeared calmer, but it didn't help that they were no closer to finding either party, which got Tammy thinking. She understood privacy concerns, but in the case of this nurse, that hedge of protection seemed overgrown. The news reports hadn't listed her name. Her employee had been tight-lipped with the social worker, although Tammy had yet to try them. The hospital's position she could understand. She wondered if the Illinois State Police would release her name to Tammy.

Diane pounded the steering wheel as she followed the officer out of the hospital property. She had mustered every bit of restraint she possessed not to speak out with that director of nursing. And then this . . . this detective, who had yet to accomplish the simple task of digging up a name, still sought an anonymous nurse, and felt it necessary to speak to her as if she were some pedantic child. Diane wondered if she'd be more successful without this tag-along officer.

Yet, she had to admit that when it came to the nurse's employer, the detective held a greater chance of getting them to cooperate than she did. Begrudgingly, she also admitted to herself that, despite the lack of progress at each hospital, the detective's presence had led to their seeing people in higher authority than Diane alone had been able to see.

She took a deep breath and worked to control her anxiety as she drove. Tears formed in her eyes at the thought that she might fall short in her quest. As she wiped them away, she questioned her motives for coming to St. Louis. She continued to use the child, Ruth, as her reason but now began to sense that the battle was for her own self-esteem. She had been a straight-A student throughout school, had never failed an assigned project, and had always perceived her actions as an adult to be correct. Was this to be her first failure?

She pulled into the MedAir corporate headquarters parking lot and parked next to Detective Jahn. As they had three times before that day, they walked together into the building and presented their case. This time, they remained in the lobby rather than be escorted to an office in the back. Within a few minutes, an athletically-built, middle-aged man with a military-styled haircut approached them.

"Good afternoon, ladies. I'm Craig Sheehan, the C.O.O. here. How can I help you?"

"Good afternoon, sir."

Diane again allowed the detective to make the introductions and present their request. She found the man's strong bearing to be intimidating. The feminist in her didn't like that.

"Do you know for sure that this mother and daughter are in the area?" he asked, at the end of Tammy's presentation.

"No, we do not. But we think the nurse may have had contact with them, and we'd like to ask her some questions. The problem we're running into, is no one seems willing to give us her name or tell us how we might contact her."

"Yes, well, I was on that farm when we found her, and I saw no evidence of anyone else being there. I think you're running down the wrong track. As for her identity, we're not releasing that, and we've asked the media not to force the issue."

"But this is a police issue as well," said Detective Jahn.

"Is it? You have no evidence that the mother is here. No laws have been broken. And you're not exactly in your jurisdiction, detective. I find no compelling reason to break our privacy policy for this."

Diane began to protest, to plea for Ruth, but he raised his hand to silence her. However, raising his hand to her was the final straw. Her ire flared.

"Don't raise your hand to me, sir. I am here to protect a child who is in danger and I find your obstructionist atti—"

The detective stepped between her and the man and stared her down. She backed off and turned away from the others but could feel the flush of heat remaining in her face. The detective turned to the man.

"I'm sorry, sir. *That* won't happen again."

"Thank you, Detective. I was about to tell you that I will call our employee with your request and contact information and leave it up to her as to whether or not she wants to talk with you."

"If you would, sir, I would greatly appreciate it. And again, I'm sorry." The detective handed the man one of her business cards.

Diane could hear the detective whisper, "She's had a bad day. Sorry."

Diane didn't wait for the detective to join her and marched out the door. Why was Detective Jahn apologizing? The woman wasn't being forceful enough to get the answer they needed, so Diane felt the need to step in. She couldn't believe that the detective cut her off like that and made her look like a fool.

Just outside, three people in flight suits walked up to the door. At first, wrapped up in her own anger, she ignored their conversation as they passed by. But then she overheard, "Did you hear? Amy was released from the hospital today. She's due back to work on Monday."

Thirty

Amy gave it an hour and a half before contacting Sinead via text. If Macy had planned on ignoring her request and coming back to spend the night, she would have returned by then. The odds of her coming back during the evening were slim.

Ten minutes after the text, Amy heard the garage door open and a car pull in. She gathered up her crutches from the floor beside her chair and hobbled to the door. She opened it to find Sinead carrying Ruth in her arms, and Ruth crying.

"W-what happened?"

Sinead looked up at Amy with sorrow in her eyes. She moved quickly to the couch in the living room and laid her daughter on the cushions. Amy followed and sat back into her chair, while waiting for Sinead to retrieve the rest of her things from the car. Sinead scurried about and finally paused in front of the couch, closed her eyes, and took a deep breath before sitting next to Ruth's head, which she lifted onto her lap. She began to massage the girl's temples.

"What's wrong? Did something happen?"

Sinead shook her head. "Nothing happened per se. She overdid it yesterday when we came to see you. I had questioned whether or not she was up to it, without her wheelchair, and she insisted on doing it, all the walking. She hasn't walked that far on her own in over a year. The so-called *rehab* unit that I took her from offered her no physical therapy at all. None. They kept telling us her problem was all in her head."

Ruth opened her eyes and looked up. "Yeah, but if I used my wheelchair yesterday, we would have been caught. You said so yourself." She wiped the tears from her cheeks.

Sinead nodded and looked down at her daughter. "True. And I thought you did wonderfully yesterday." She returned her eyes to Amy. "She went to bed earlier last night than usual, which was fine by me. Then, she scared me half to death this morning 'cause I couldn't wake her up. When I finally did, she started crying, complaining about the pain in her legs."

"I'm feeling better now." Ruth tried to sit up, but Sinead gently forced her down.

"Not yet. Let me massage your legs and it's time for more medication."

"Can I help?" asked Amy. "I'm a good massager, er, masseuse."

"Sure. I'll get her pills and some juice."

Amy pushed up from the chair and hopped to the adjacent couch, plopping down next to Ruth's feet. She lifted the girl's legs and slid under them so they'd be in her lap. She began to rub and knead her calves.

"That hurts a little, but that's good, right?"

"Yeah. The pain means we're working out the right spots. Did you know a little pain also triggers the body to move white blood cells and other good things to the hurting area, to help the healing? Well, it does. Helps increase the blood flow there, too." She continued to work Ruth's gastrocnemius muscles, the large muscle in each calf.

"You *are* a good massager. That's feeling better already."

Sinead returned, gave Ruth her pills, and insisted she drink the whole glass of juice, not just enough to swallow the pills.

Amy looked up at Sinead as she returned from the kitchen.

"I took some time to look up what's been published about your case. I think it's a travesty that the court would take your child away because some doctors disagreed on her diagnosis."

"It's been a nightmare," replied Sinead. "And it happens more frequently than you'd think. Doctors make a mistake, and the hospitals cover it up by blaming the parents. A parent wants a second opinion, and the social workers convince the court that the parent is medically abusing the child. A child with a rare disease is recruited to join some study of that disease, and if the parent refuse, the hospital takes them to court and convinces some judge to remove the child from their care. All of these kids become wards of the state, which allows the state to claim more Medicaid money from the Federal government. And as wards of the state, they are forced into these studies or to get immunizations the parents don't want them to have, or whatever."

"It's like parents really have no control over their children anymore."

"They don't. The courts can remove a child from her family on a whim, and no one contests it. In our case, two sets of doctors disagreed. Instead of working together to come to a diagnosis and treatment plan, the second set of doctors convinced the court they were right and to remove Ruth from our care, even though we were taking her to doctors on a regular basis, following their advice, and giving her their prescribed medications."

Tears welled up in Sinead's eyes. "The second group of doctors called it Munchausen by Proxy. They accused me of fabricating or even causing Ruth's problems. Yet, they never charged me with child abuse. We were given no due process under the law. Our first doctors disagreed but were ignored. Before they took Ruth away, she was able to walk, go to school, interact with friends—basically be a normal teenager, with some limitations. In that rehab center, they refused to feed her a proper diet or give her the meds prescribed by her first doctors. She became weaker and weaker. Ended up in a wheelchair, looking like someone in a Nazi concentration camp. And yet, *we* were the ones guilty of abuse?"

The tears flowed freely now. "Can you begin to imagine the anguish and fear of watching some social worker, backed by police, forcibly pull your child from your arms as she's screaming for them to let her go, and carry her to a police car and take her away? And then, we weren't even allowed to visit her for *three* months. When I saw her next, I sat and cried at what they had done to her."

Amy saw that Ruth was also freely crying at that memory. She felt the tears well up in her own eyes as she imagined what that must have been like.

"I knew the only way to save Ruth was to take her. Escape. Put her back on the regimen prescribed by the first doctors and then, when she became stronger, go back and show the court how wrong they were."

"And then I fell out of the sky and ruined your plans."

Sinead looked at Amy with concern. "Amy, don't ever think that way. Ever. *You* didn't ruin anything. The storm did but not you. After that storm washed out the bridge, there was no way we could stay at the farmhouse. If something happened to Ruth, I needed to be sure I could take her for help. I didn't have that assurance with the bridge gone."

Amy's reply was interrupted by her phone. She saw Craig's name and number on her Caller ID.

"My boss, checking up on me." She answered. "Hi, Craig. Yes, I plan to be back at work on Monday."

"That's not why I'm calling."

Amy listened as he described his visit from a Boston social worker and local police detective. What could she tell him? What *should* she tell him?

When he finished, she responded, "Thanks for the heads up, but I, uh, don't have anything to tell them." That was truthful. She hoped that would be enough to convince him.

"I didn't think so. I told 'em I didn't see any signs of anyone else there. Well, tell you what, I'm going to leave that contact information on your desk here, so I can make good what I promised 'em I'd do. And we'll continue to fend off any inquiries about you. However, the funerals for Kent and Johnny are next week. If you're at either or both, the press will notice and most of them know who you are. The families will understand if you're not up to attending."

Amy tried to wrap her head around that potential kink. She had been so focused on getting home, that she hadn't even thought about the funerals. Of course, she would go. How could she not? But then, once her identity was released, how could she continue to keep Sinead and Ruth hidden, too?

Amy looked at Sinead wondering how much to tell the woman. She decided they should know everything. Their freedom and Ruth's recovery demanded as much. She told them what Craig had said.

"She's persistent, if nothing else," replied Sinead. "Well, we probably should move on tomorrow. I don't want to get you into any trouble."

"I'm not worried about that. My dad might stop by tonight, but I know he'll be sympathetic, and maybe he'll have some ideas. My fiancé, Richard, is a bit of a Boy Scout, but I doubt he'd turn you in once he knew the details. Besides, he's out of town for a week, as is the other man I told you about, Lynch. They sort of work together, for the American Party and Bradley Graham."

Sinead's eyes widened. "*The* Bradley Graham? I-I'd love to talk with him. He's in a position to take the whole issue of medical kidnapping to a new level in the public discourse. He could really make a difference for us."

Amy thought about that. The man really might be able to help, but she had never met him face-to-face and could not make that call personally.

"Um, I don't know. I can ask Richard when he gets back, but I know the man is overwhelmed with people wanting his attention. Again, I don't . . . we'll have to play that one by ear."

Ruth's belly growled, and both adults looked at her in sync. The girl laughed when Amy's gut answered.

"Well, it sounds like two of the three of us are hungry," said Amy. "I don't think I have much to eat here. I had planned to go grocery shopping Sunday afternoon. You guys up for pizza?"

"Yeah, pizza," exclaimed Ruth. "I haven't had pizza in months, maybe even years."

Sinead gave her a playful bop on the head. "That's an exaggeration."

"Uh-uh. They never served pizza at that rehab center, and no one would deliver to the farm, even if we'd asked them to, which we didn't."

"And what about on our trip out here?"

Ruth thought about that for a moment. "Oh yeah. I'd rather forget that place. It was awful."

Sinead nodded. "It really was. We were just heading into one of the chain pizza places when a TV there showed our pictures and the AMBER Alert. I simply turned and left before anyone saw us. We found this other place and regretted it all night."

Amy picked up her cell phone. "So, yes or no for pizza. I guarantee you'll love this pie."

With a unanimous 'yes,' she ordered a large deluxe, which arrived about 30 minutes later. The trio moved to the kitchen, and Sinead retrieved sodas from the garage at Amy's direction. They dug into the pie as if they hadn't eaten in days, which for Amy was close to the truth. In short order, they eliminated three-quarters of the pizza and sat back.

"That was delicious," said Ruth.

Sinead laughed. "My pizza connoisseur."

Amy stood, settled onto her crutches, and reached for her empty plate, but Sinead stopped her. "I'll clean up. It's the least I can do."

"Thanks."

She started to move back to the front room, and the doorbell rang. She stopped and glanced back at the others.

Ruth had started to limp toward the bedrooms while Sinead rushed to place their plates in the dishwasher.

A voice reverberated through the front door. "Amy! It's me. I brought you some dinner, from your favorite Greek place."

Macy had returned.

Thirty-One

Three hours earlier, in the parking lot at MedAir, few words had been spoken when the detective joined Diane by their cars. From the look on the woman's face, she was ready to kill Diane, figuratively, while Diane's anger had grown to a point where she wanted to hurt the detective, literally. They parted ways in silence, except for Detective Jahn, whose only comment was that she would be busy the next day, but that if anything came up, she would contact Diane.

A whole day had been wasted, and they were no further along in finding the O'Malleys, or even the name of the injured nurse. Diane's anxiety stretched her like a rubber band near its snapping point. Even at the fast food place where she stopped to grab dinner, her attitude solicited stares from others around her. She didn't care.

Back in her motel room, Diane ate mechanically, not even tasting the food as she chewed. Her mind had become obsessed with her quest.

As her thoughts churned, the nurse seemed like a dead-end. The man, her boss, had told them that he had seen no evidence of anyone else on that farm. Still, why had Sinead O'Malley asked specifically for the injured nurse when she went to that hospital in Springfield? And why hadn't that stupid volunteer remembered the nurse's name? The old woman needed to retire while she could still remember her *own* name.

She jerked to a standing position, nearly spilling her soda across the small table, and began to pace. What could she do? What was her best next move?

Absentmindedly, she turned on the television and discovered a local news broadcast. She let it play in the background as she took another bite of her sandwich and paced. Her mind came to focus on the name 'Amy.' The woman at the company had mentioned "Amy" being released from the hospital. Could it be anyone else? How many employees could a company like that have? And what were the odds that more than one of those employees had been hospitalized at the same time?

She grabbed her notebook computer, turned it on, and set it next to her food as it booted up. As she continued to pace, the newscast caught her attention.

"The funerals for pilot Kent Howard and flight paramedic Johnny Wilson will be held next Monday and Tuesday respectively. . ." The reporter droned on in a recap of the crash and the latest findings of the Illinois State Police and National Transportation Safety Board. By the end of the clip, Diane was ready to slam a chair into the TV. They hadn't mentioned the nurse at all, much less by name. And they didn't state where the funerals were to be held.

But, there was hope. She pulled the computer in front of her and called up her favorite search engine. First, she looked up MedAir, the company. She began reviewing page after page on their website but found no personnel listings except for the founders and chief executive staff. She did, however, find a telephone number that differed from the one she had used before. A thought struck her.

She grabbed her cell phone and dialed the new number. Sure enough, she reached an automated system that offered her the opportunity to access a company directory. Her optimism failed, though, when the system asked for the first three letters of the employee's *last* name. She disconnected and threw her cell phone across the room.

After further scouring the corporate website, she found a PDF fact sheet and opened it. Strike two. The file told her the company operated in ten states and had nearly 3,000 employees. The odds were against her in finding just one employee named Amy, as well as with the possibility that this Amy was the only employee who had been in a hospital in the past week.

She faced one more pitch and hoped this wouldn't be a strikeout. The funerals. She typed in the pilot's name first, and found an article that included info on the man's career and family. Her eyes lit up at the end of the story. His funeral arrangements were listed. She made a note on them in her phone and checked her map for the location. Even better, the cemetery was not far from her current location.

She quickly did a search on the paramedic and was rewarded to a shorter, but as detailed, article on him. It, too, provided information on the funeral.

Now, would the nurse attend one or both funerals? Diane guessed she would. Not only would that be the proper and respectful thing to do, but she assumed the nurse—Amy, if that was her name—would feel an obligation to do so as the sole survivor of the crash. This gave Diane twice the opportunity to spot this link to her quarry. If she missed her at the first funeral, she'd have one more shot.

Tammy stopped just outside of her sergeant's cubicle and took a deep breath. As she debriefed about her day with the social worker, his face had carried that "that'll teach you to mess with me" look. But, by the end of her session, she got the impression she had paid her dues in full. She would *think* twice about making him look bad in the future. Well, maybe for a second or two.

She had the evening off, other than the usual family demands, anyway. What she really wanted to do was call her husband to have him order Chinese, spend a little time with her kids, and settle into a warm bath accompanied by the remaining half bottle of Merlot from the previous weekend.

What she felt obligated to do, however, was find out more about this O'Malley case in Boston, as well as any info she could dig up on that social worker. She sensed her inner vibe saying that chowder head had a crock only half full of baked beans.

She sat in her cubicle staring at a picture of her children. The clock on her computer told her it was past quitting time, but then, detectives rarely had their quitting times etched in stone. She realized she hadn't been home "on time" for over a week. Her kids were going to forget what she looked like if she didn't get moving.

She signed into the department's network and first retrieved the AMBER Alert for this girl. She made a mental note of both the mother's and daughter's physical characteristics. She then printed a hard copy to keep on hand and folded it to a size to keep inside her notebook.

She noted the contact number for the department in Boston and decided to take a short-cut from her usual routine of moving to the internet first by calling the trooper listed as the coordinator for the Massachusetts State Police for an update. She dialed the number on her cell phone, so the answering officer could have her contact number as well.

The AMBER Alert system has led to the recovery of over 700 children since 2001. The program had expanded to all 50 states, plus Puerto Rico and the U.S. Virgin Islands. Each state had a program coordinator, and most news outlets, especially television stations, seemed eager to assist in getting the alerts to the public.

"Trooper Carroll speaking."

"Trooper, this is Detective Tammy Jahn, with the Saint Louis Metro PD. I'm hoping you can give me an update on the AMBER Alert for Ruth O'Malley and her mother. We received the second alert with information that they had been spotted in Springfield, Illinois, but I wondered if there are any new developments. We've been led to believe they might be coming to Saint Louis, and my sergeant tasked me with getting more info."

"Hey, thanks for calling. From the sighting in Springfield, we were thinking they might head to Saint Louis, as well, but then, the next day, we got hits on her credit card in Hannibal and, later, at a truck stop on Missouri Route 6 north of Hannibal and heading west. So, we're not sure about the Saint Louis link at all. One charge was for gas and we're working on what the second charge was for. She bought several items at the truck stop. Do you have something?"

"Sorry, no. They've not been spotted here. Is there

anything else you can tell me about the case?"

"Well, the mother has been formally charged with kidnapping now. This has been such a high profile case that the D.A. held off the formal charges until he had no choice. The press in Boston has been having a field day with this one."

"I'll head to the internet and see what they're saying. Thanks. And if we get anything here, I'll be in touch."

"Thank you. Oh, by the way, this is related indirectly. The social worker who took Ruth O'Malley from her family, by name of Westlake, was fired from D.C.F. in Boston. She's disappeared from the area, and her bosses tell us she took her employee identification with her. She seemed a little unstable to several co-workers when she left. She might be headed your way, too, from the rumors floating around D.C.F. Her boss wants those credentials returned. I know the odds of your running into her are slim, but thought you ought to know."

Tammy wanted to scream "*a little unstable?*" but held her tongue. She would deal with the woman herself . . . and with her sergeant who took the woman's story hook, line, and sinker.

Thirty-Two

Amy stood in the middle of her front room, flustered. Macy had never shown up at her doorstep unannounced. Never. Amy knew her friend imagined that Amy was hiding something, but she must have given her suspicious nature a steroid injection to do this. She even brought food. Typically, her first action when coming to Amy's house was to raid the refrigerator.

When all hints of activity inside subsided, Amy moved toward the door and opened it to her friend. She didn't have to *act* surprised.

"Macy, I, uh, I didn't expect you to come back . . . and with food? Are you feeling okay? You never bring food." She gave her friend a playful smile.

"Like I said, I'm steppin' up. New car, new attitude. I couldn't leave you here all by yourself. I got home and just couldn't settle down, knowing you were here and might need some help."

"I told you I'd be fine. Really."

"Yeah, well. Umm, you gonna block the door all evening or can I come in? Food's getting cold."

Amy hopped back a step and let her friend inside. Macy made a beeline to the kitchen, and Amy said a silent prayer that all was in order there. After closing the door, she followed Macy, only to find her standing just inside the kitchen, staring at the table. Amy followed her gaze to see the pizza box still sitting there, open.

"Girl, you hungry or what? You ate three-quarters of that pizza by yourself? Tonight? Did they starve you that bad at the hospital?" Macy lifted her bags and set them on the nearby counter. "Guess you don't need this Greek stuff. Unless you're still hungry."

"Like I said, I didn't expect you back." Amy glanced about for anything else Sinead might have missed.

Macy eyed the last of the deluxe pie. "You know, I'm not a big Greek fan myself. Mind if I have those last two pieces?"

Amy chuckled. Macy had managed to bring food and *still* raid her refrigerator. "Sure. Help yourself." She started toward the take-out bags. "I'll just put those in the fridge."

"Naw, sit down. I got it." Macy grabbed the bags and walked to the refrigerator. She put the two bags inside but then gazed at something within for a moment before closing the door and turning to face Amy. She gave Amy that questioning look that signaled her gift of suspicion activating. "When did you start drinking milk? You never have milk in your fridge. And it's whole milk at that."

Amy sat down at the table and shrugged without offering an explanation. What could she say? It was there for Ruth.

Macy opened a cabinet, took a plate, and sat across from Amy. Amy watched in amazement as her friend wolfed down the pizza before saying another word.

"I guess someone else I know is hungry, too."

"Man, that hit the spot." Macy sat back, looking satisfied. She surprised Amy by jumping up and grabbing the empty pizza box.

"Hey, where're you going?"

"Just going to throw the box away in the garage."

"Uh, you don't have to do that. Have a seat, or we can go into the front room. I was about to turn on *Downton Abbey*." She hoped that would spur Macy to cut short her visit.

Macy ignored her and walked right to the door to the garage. She disappeared through the door, and Amy's heart flopped. Sinead's car, with its Massachusetts' plates, had now been discovered. What was Amy going to do? How would she explain this to Macy? More importantly, what would Sinead and Ruth do?

Macy walked back into the kitchen and didn't say a word. She picked up her dish, rinsed it, and put it in the dishwasher. Amy watched her closely and Macy's nonchalance puzzled her. Maybe this was a "new" Macy. The old one would have been insisting on an explanation for the car, playing Twenty Questions.

"So, okay, I'll watch one *Downton Abbey* with you. But don't you go telling anyone. All the fanatics at work will start asking me questions. They'll want me to join them for their 'past episodes marathon' coming up. They'll want my opinion of this character and that. I don't want any of that, so don't you dare tell anyone. Got it?"

Amy smiled and saluted. "Yes, ma'am. Got it." She arose and moved into the front room, still puzzled about why Macy had ignored the car.

They watched the recorded show and Macy asked. "Do you want to watch the other one? You said you had a couple of them recorded."

Amy gave her friend the eye. Where was the Macy she

knew and loved?

"Actually, I'm thinking of calling my dad and then going to bed."

Macy waggled her head back and forth. "Well, okay. I'm not going to spend the night like I suggested earlier 'cause I know you really don't want me to."

"And you have to work in the morning."

"Yeah, that, too. I don't want to be wakin' you up at five a.m. So, I'll take off now. Tell your dad I said hi."

Amy nodded and started to rise.

"Naw, don't you get up. I can see myself out and lock the door behind me." Macy walked over to her and gave her a hug. "Call me, if you need anything."

"I will, but—"

"But you'll be fine. Yeah. I got that."

Amy smiled. "Love you, girlfriend."

"Love you back." Macy gave her an unanswered high-five, turned, and left through the front door.

Amy heard the car start up and back out of the drive. She rose onto her good foot, grabbed her crutches, and rushed to the garage. There was no car there. She went to the door of her guest bedroom and knocked gently. No answer. She opened the door to see Sinead and Ruth asleep on top of the queen-sized bed.

She eased the door closed and started back to the front room, wondering, *how did they pull that off?*

Thirty-Three

Jeremy awoke with a start. The previous day had not gone well, and he'd been awake into the wee hours of the morning. He grabbed his cell phone from the nightstand and checked it. The GPS app revealed that Westlake was on the move but apparently only for a late breakfast. On the map, her car came to a stop at a nearby Denny's.

He had a busy day ahead. He still needed to find Amy Gibbs, hoping that in doing so he would also find the O'Malleys. They were integral to his plan.

After using the bathroom, he checked the status of the batteries for his camera and other gear. Those that remained low in charge, he placed back onto their chargers.

He rushed to the motel's breakfast room and grabbed a bagel, cream cheese, and fresh fruit, along with a large cup of coffee. Juggling them all, he returned to his room and renewed his research.

Upon "waking" from sleep mode, the screen on his laptop showed the St. Louis County real estate records website. During the previous afternoon and into the night, he had searched for every possible article and reference to 'Amy Gibbs,' and had been shocked at the amount of material he discovered. It hadn't taken him long to realize that girl found her fair share of trouble. He wondered how she still functioned.

He'd had only one source of trouble in his life, and that episode had robbed him of four years of his life—and his family. He tried to shake the image of his wife, dead on their bed with an empty bottle of pills on the floor, from his mind. She had sent him out to get groceries. An hour later, he returned home to find her. The love of his life, gone forever.

Sometime after midnight, he finally found a reference to Amy's father, a retired Army Lieutenant Colonel A. Gibbs, and a Cessna 172 they co-owned. The reference hadn't helped since "A" could have meant any of a number of first names. He had already discovered more than a dozen "Gibbs" within the county real estate records whose first names began with "A." All except Amy, of course. Why get lucky?

Using the clue of the aircraft, it took him nearly an hour to learn that states have no role in aircraft registration. He found several aircraft title services, all of which charged a fee. Then, he found it. The FAA's registration site. A quick title search revealed over 90 Gibbs as aircraft owners but only half a dozen with a Cessna 172. Of which, only Andrew Gibbs lived in St. Louis County.

By then fatigue had claimed him and he collapsed into bed.

As he now sipped his coffee, he retrieved the real estate data on the property listed to Andrew Gibbs at the address on the FAA registration. No mortgage or liens. No spouse or other co-owner. No references to other properties. No help.

He felt a sudden urgency to find this man as his link to the O'Malleys through his daughter. If that police detective had proven helpful to Westlake, the woman could already be setting up a meeting with the injured nurse. He couldn't afford for her to get there first.

He grabbed the almost fully-charged batteries for his camera and parabolic microphone and installed them. These, along with his laptop, he loaded into the front passenger seat of his car and covered with his coat. He rushed back to the breakfast room, grabbed an apple, bagel, and more coffee, and returned to his vehicle. A moment later, he was on his way to the home of one Andrew Gibbs.

"Amy, I don't know. I'm not comfortable with that."

Sinead paced in the kitchen as Amy's coffeemaker dribbled into the carafe. Amy sat at the table, empty mug in hand. She had slept well for the first time since the accident. She loved her iComfort mattress that had hugged her body all night, cast and all.

"I really think my dad can help. Honest. And I know he'd never turn you in." She paused. "But I won't bring him in on things if you're not okay with it."

Sinead picked up the full carafe and carried it to the table. "I . . . I'll have to think about it. I just think the fewer who know, the better. Besides, we won't stay long. I don't want to get you into trouble."

For some reason, her comment brought Lynch to mind. He used to say that "trouble" was Amy's middle name.

"I won't get into any trouble. We're okay there." She took a sip of coffee after blowing across the top of the hot liquid, and pulled back. "Whoa, that's too hot." She used her tongue to test whether or not she'd burned the roof of her mouth. "I guess I never have the luxury of drinking my coffee right after brewing. By the time I get to it in my car, it's already cooled off."

Ruth walked into the kitchen. "What's wrong?"

"Amy burned her mouth on the hot coffee."

"I'll be okay. Isn't the first time I've done that on something hot and won't be the last, I'm sure." She shifted in her chair and lifted her right leg onto the adjacent chair. "Look, my dad's going to come over so we can get my car from work." She tilted her head and looked at Sinead. "By the way, just where is *your* car? I thought for sure Macy was going to find it in the garage last night."

Sinead smiled. "It's a couple of houses down, on the street, between two pickup trucks so the plates aren't obvious."

Amy nodded. "That was smart."

"I didn't want anyone to find it in your garage. Like I said, I don't want you to get into any trouble. I moved it while you were in the bathroom, before the pizza arrived."

Amy shook her head. "I keep telling you, I won't get in trouble, and your car is probably safe where it is. Those two trucks usually sit there all weekend unless it's hunting season."

Amy's phone rang with a distinctive ring tone. "It's my dad," she said before even picking up the phone. She answered. "Good morning. How was Kansas City?"

"Good morning to you, too. Kansas City was a bust. The guy wanted way too much money for the condition his old 'Vette was in. I gave him an offer. So, how are you doing? I meant to stop in last night, but the hour got too late as I drove back into town. Didja sleep well? Can I get you anything? Breakfast?"

Amy smiled. Her father always took good care of her.

To the point she often worried that he paid too little attention to his own social life and well-being. She'd be getting married soon, and he needed to find someone himself.

"I'm good. About to have breakfast."

"Tell you what, I'll give you time to get ready, and I'll bring some breakfast. Be over there, say, in an hour to hour and a half. Does that work for you?"

"Sure, but I already have something to eat."

"And we can stop for groceries or anything else you need while we're out."

"Okay, see you soon, but I'm already sitting down to eat."

Amy shook her head, unsure whether or not he had actually heard her say she was about to eat. She looked at Sinead as she hung up. "Dad'll be here in an hour or so. Let me know how you want to play this."

Diane finished her Grand Slam breakfast as if the world was to end in 15 minutes and that would be her last meal. She wanted coffee to-go but hesitated in ordering it. She felt so wired already.

What she really needed was to clear her mind. She had been so frustrated by her failed search and so angry at that do-nothing police detective that she hadn't slept, and her mind raced from one complaint to another, like a pinball bouncing between pins in the machine.

She climbed back into her car and headed back toward the Interstate. She decided to simply drive and see where she might end up. She crossed the Missouri River into the next county and saw a sign for Missouri's first capital, St.

Charles. *Why not?* she thought.

Soon she was driving down a bumpy, brick-paved road bordered by old homes, most of which had been turned into quaint shops or restaurants. The place reminded her a bit of Cambridge, more from the age of the buildings than their architecture. She guessed that her own home predated these homes by a few decades. After all, Boston and its surrounding communities were among the oldest cities in the nation. Then she saw a few placards and realized the opposite was true, at least compared to the homes in Cambridge. That surprised her.

She decided to park and walk. The air temperature was warm, although a stiff breeze promised a change in the weather. She noticed the smell of hyacinth in the air. She passed a cute bookstore, a spice shop, and a plethora of gift shops. She resisted the urge to enter each one, not wanting the temptation to buy things with money she really didn't have to spend.

She loved to shop. She hated that she had no job, no income, no security that life would go on as usual. The desire to make things right, to get her job back, surged inside. But how? If she couldn't find the O'Malleys, how could she make that happen?

She stopped in front of one store and window shopped. Just through the glass she saw a rotating rack filled with what looked like old newspapers. She had seen these before. They were duplicates of front pages from historic dates in America's past.

A thought hit her. Newspapers, or at least the modern equivalent. What if she could find articles about MedAir? Surely there had to be some. Press releases. Important cases where they might have been involved in transporting a patient. She had solely focused on the *recent* helicopter crash. Maybe there had been others.

She raced back to her car and reversed her track toward the motel. Once she was comfortably ensconced there, she would move into research mode. For the first time in two days, she could focus.

Thirty-Four

Google Maps on Jeremy's phone led him right to the home of Andrew Gibbs. He parked across and a short distance down the street from the house. There were other cars parked along the street, a fact he found comforting. His car wouldn't stick out and be so obvious among the others.

From the front he couldn't tell if the man was home or not. The garage door was closed and no interior lights were obvious. He glanced up and down the street for any activity and saw no one else outside. No cars had passed since his arrival there.

He reached over to the passenger's seat and picked up the parabolic microphone. He donned the earphones and flipped on the device. After a second glance around his surroundings, as well as into his rearview mirrors, he lowered his window and pointed the dish at the house, aiming for a large front window. Windows transmitted sound much more readily than walls or doors, but you needed something to pick up those subtle vibrations. His microphone was more than capable for the task.

However, unless the conversation happened within close proximity to the window, he wouldn't expect to hear any voices clearly. That was not his desire anyway. He simply wanted to know if the man was home. A television set turned on. A phone conversation. A whistling teapot. He searched for anything to indicate that someone was inside. He knew he could always go knock on the front door on some ruse, but he didn't want to risk being recognized later, should their paths cross again.

As he did so, he continued to scan his surroundings. His listening dish would be obvious to anyone passing by or within sight. He wanted obscurity, not notice.

He saw a car in his mirror, coming up from behind, and quickly lowered the dish. He pretended to be looking at something in his lap as he watched the car pass him. Assured that he was again alone, he returned the microphone to his window and listened, while his eyes glanced about.

There! Maybe not. He thought he heard a voice. He pointed the dish at a different window. Nothing. He aimed once again at the large front window.

Yes. A man's voice, more clearly now. He sounded as if he was on the phone.

He lowered the dish and twisted around to place it on the back seat. He grabbed his apple and sat back to take a bite. Now, all he had to do was wait. The man would lead Jeremy to his daughter. She had, after all, just returned home from the hospital. Why would he not pay her a visit? Jeremy could think of no reason for the man to stay away. They weren't estranged. They co-owned an airplane. So at some point, dad was destined to pay her a visit, maybe buy groceries for her. If not today, then tomorrow.

Amy sat at the kitchen table, with her leg propped up, and watched Sinead prepare breakfast for the three of them. She had offered to help. After all, in two days she'd be "on her own," making her own meals, going to work, and caring for herself in every way.

But Sinead had practically pushed her back into the chair and commanded her to put her leg up. Geesh! Well, perhaps she exaggerated her thoughts. It was nice to have help this morning.

"Almost ready. You really do need some groceries. I had to get creative."

"Smells wonderful, but we're going to have to eat fast. My dad could be here in half an hour."

"Ruth! Oh, there you are."

Ruth walked into the room and sat across from Amy.

"Time to eat," added Sinead.

"I know. Smells good. I'm hungry."

Amy watched the young girl, whose appetite over the previous 16 hours had astounded her. She knew teenage boys could put down some food, and Ruth, it appeared, could hold her own against them. Still, it had been good for her. Just in the week since they'd met, Ruth had lost that gaunt look and again looked like a healthy 14-year-old girl.

Sinead set plates before them and Amy did a double-take. Sinead must have caught her questioning look.

"We call it a garbage plate. You only had a few eggs and, like, three pieces of bacon. I found some slices of red and green pepper, and a small amount of hash browns in the freezer, so I put them all together. Added some onion that I found in the fridge, plus cheese and herbs, and voila, a garbage plate. Hope you like it."

A knock at the front door caught them all with forks half raised. And then the door began to open and Sinead blanched.

"Amy! I'm here. Hope you don't mind my letting myself in."

Her father! Early! And yelling as if she might be in her bedroom or bath.

She looked at Sinead and raised her brow. She whispered, "Sorry. I didn't expect him to show up early. He usually arrives exactly when he says he'll be somewhere." She turned toward the front room. "In the kitchen, Dad."

A moment later, her father rounded the corner and stopped in his tracks. "Oh. You have company. And breakfast." He held up a plastic bag that appeared to hold two carry-out containers. "I stopped at La Bonne Boucheé and got a frittata and almond croissant." He smiled. "Well, I guess we can all share."

"Dad, this is my, um, new friend, Sinead, and her daughter Ruth." Amy doubted the name would mean anything to her dad, but she hated the idea of deceiving him. Plus, she would never lie to him.

Sinead began to stand, but her dad stopped her. "Hey, don't get up. That garbage plate is going to get cold. Nice to meet you both."

Amy knit her brow and looked at her father. "You know about garbage plates?"

He grinned. "Sure. Old army trick to make food stretch in the field." He nodded toward the food with his head. "Go ahead and eat. I'll put my coat up and join you in a sec."

Upon his return, he claimed the fourth chair and opened up both containers.

"This is from Amy's favorite restaurant. Ever been there?" he asked.

Sinead shook her head. Ruth simply looked at her plate and seemed unsure what to say or do.

"Well, here, try some of both. Good stuff."

Amy tried to regain a sense of normalcy to the situation. "These almond croissants are to die for."

Her father cut the pastry into four pieces, which he dished out to the others along with some frittata. He stood and retrieved some utensils for himself, along with a cup of coffee. He returned to the table and looked around. Amy saw what he must be seeing. No one was eating and a nervous tension filled the room. Still, he sat down and seemed normal.

"Go ahead, dig in. You'll love it." He took a forkful of frittata and chewed appreciatively. "So, you said new friends. How'd you meet?"

Amy felt her bite of flaky croissant turn to dry, heavy biscuit and plunge to her gut.

Jeremy settled back into his seat after pulling to the curb in a cul-de-sac across from the home Colonel Gibbs had entered. The man's car remained parked outside. He expected Gibbs to stay awhile, after following him to a local restaurant earlier and then watching him carry a bag of food into this house.

Of course, the big question remained. Was this his daughter's place? And the bigger question, did she know where the O'Malleys were?

He had taken a risk by following the colonel into the restaurant, but the bagel and apple from the motel wouldn't hold him. Plus, the sign over the entrance said it was a bakery as well. How could he resist? He now opened his own carryout container holding a most incredible-looking cinnamon roll. The pastry was one of his absolute favorites.

He thought about it for a moment. Should he ever be put in the position of being asked what he desired for a last meal, this goody would find a place on the tray. Yes, this stakeout wouldn't be so bad after all.

Amy prepared for a lecture. Maybe she deserved one but not for the obvious reasons.

"Dad, I met Sinead last Sunday, on a farm in western Illinois." She let that sink in a bit, and when she saw the questions forming in her father's eyes, she went on to add, "She saved my life from that crash."

Her father started to speak but stopped. A moment later, he said, "But I was told you dragged yourself to that barn, where they found you."

Amy swallowed hard. "Yeah, well, you see . . . there's a catch." She went on to explain what had happened and that it was her idea to stage her rescue in the barn.

The colonel glanced at Sinead and then Ruth. "Thank you for helping her." He turned his gaze back to Amy. "But, you said there's a catch. I didn't hear one in your story."

Amy took a deep breath. "Umm, right. You see . . . um, well, at the time I thought they were hiding from an abusive spouse, and I didn't want to blow their cover. So, I came up with the barn idea, and it was my own clumsiness that led to my spleen injury. And then, a couple days later, in the hospital, I learned who they really are." She paused.

"And that would be . . ." He picked up his coffee and took a sip.

Sinead broke in and told him their story and why they had followed Amy to St. Louis.

"And, well, I gave them access to my house, 'cause they

needed a place to stay. And so . . . here we are, um, enjoying breakfast together, right?"

Her father shook his head slowly and set down his coffee mug. He stood up and walked to the counter and back. He looked at the trio at the table and scratched his head.

"Ladies, this is a *real* problem."

Ruth began to sob and Sinead scooted closer to put her arm around her.

"Ruth, don't worry, I'm not about to turn you in. I think my daughter and I have similar feelings and thoughts about our government's overreach into family matters, our health care, and such. And I'm probably about to step into this sinkhole with you, by not calling the authorities. But, do you know what this means? Amy could be charged with aiding and abetting in Ruth's kidnapping and for harboring a fugitive. There may be other charges I can't even fathom at this point. Your presence here could jeopardize her career, even land her in jail."

"I know," replied Sinead. "I told her we would move on, so we wouldn't get her into trouble."

Her father looked contemplative. "Well, ladies, before we jump into anything, eat up. Let's think on this a bit and see if we can come up with a better plan."

Amy joined the others at picking at her food, while her father finished his meal without hesitation. Maybe he had something up his sleeve. She hoped so, because her mind had gone blank.

As he put down his napkin, he said, "Amy, if you don't mind, I'd like Sinead to help me get your car. I want to talk with her alone for a few minutes. We can do that in the car on our way to MedAir."

That caught Amy off-guard. Sinead, too, looked surprised. In a way Amy felt relieved, though. She had wondered how well she would be able to drive with the cast on her right leg. Her father's suggestion delayed that moment for another day or so.

"I, uh, guess that's okay with me, if it's okay with Sinead."

Jeremy fidgeted in his seat. The cinnamon roll was long gone, and his stakeout had quickly become boring. At least when he'd positioned himself outside Westlake's home in Cambridge, he had had his "toys" to play with and her occasional, one-sided phone conversations to break up the monotony. His parabolic microphone wouldn't pick up much through the walls of the house. It needed a direct line of sight with the speaker to catch anything intelligible.

He glanced at his watch again, thinking he would need lunch soon, but it was only mid-morning. Looking back toward the house, the front door opened, and he watched the colonel leave and head to his car. Right behind him was a petite, black-haired woman. She was too short to be Amy Gibbs, which news accounts had reported at five-foot-eleven.

He wondered who the woman might be. Of course, it could be anyone, another relative, a co-worker, a friend. He grabbed his camera and zooming in with the telephoto lens snapped a shot of the woman before she climbed into the man's car.

He had a decision to make, to follow the colonel again or to stay put. His gut told him to sit still, but he wavered. What if the man was *now* on his way to his daughter's home? He agonized over his decision to stay as he watched the car turn the corner and disappear. In another minute it would be too late to catch up and follow the car.

He was about to switch on his car and chase after the man when he saw the front door of the home open. A woman on crutches, her right leg in a cast, stood in the doorway for a moment and then turned back into the house, closing the door behind her.

This woman was tall. This woman had been injured. This woman had to be Amy Gibbs.

He checked his GPS tracking app and saw that Westlake remained at her motel. Perhaps, the detective had been unsuccessful in helping her. Whatever the case, she remained within his 20-mile radius and hadn't moved.

He still hadn't found the O'Malleys, but, in truth, as he thought about his plan, they became less important to it. Drawing Westlake out now took center stage. He had come near to the end of his timeline.

He had wanted to gloat, to show her that she wasn't going to win this time. He would assure the O'Malleys their freedom to spite her. He wanted to see the look on her face when she realized her mistake, and her loss. Now, without the O'Malleys, maybe the look on her face when she recognized him would suffice.

As he sat in the car watching the Gibbs house, he decided to give it one more day. One more day to find the O'Malleys. Seeing that Westlake remained at her motel, he started his car and drove off. He remained one step ahead of the witch.

Thirty-Five

After a rare, full weekend off, Tammy stormed into the precinct offices and straight to Sergeant Barkley's desk. He wasn't there, so she started her hunt at the break room. He stood next to the coffee maker, filling his large mug for what she knew would be one of his many cups that day.

"We've been played."

He turned to face her. "Oh?"

"That social worker you foisted on me three days ago isn't who she said she is. She was fired from her state's D.C.F. a week ago and has zero official standing."

He stood there, emotionless. "Yeah, so what are you going to do about it?"

"We could arrest her for impersonating a state official. She used up valuable police time here on an alleged official search for this mother and child."

His face took on a peculiar look, as if he questioned the "valuable" aspect of her statement. Tammy grew angry at his chauvinist manner but controlled her temper.

"If that's what you want to do, do it. Just realize the prosecutors are busy and might look the other way on this one."

Was this just another comment to devalue her abilities and time? What if it had been *his* time the woman had wasted? She wanted to punch him.

And yet, as she thought about it, she recognized that he was correct. The local prosecutors would rank this low on their priority list. And if her sergeant wouldn't support her, what chance did she have? She lowered her ire to a simmer.

"You're probably right, but I'm going to contact the Massachusetts D.C.F. and see how they feel about this."

He shrugged his shoulders. "Knock yourself out. But make sure you get to the GREAT Program on time, ya hear?" He turned away and walked to an adjacent counter where someone had left a homemade coffee cake for the officers.

She shook her head. Maybe it really was time to look for a transfer.

Thirty minutes later, she hung up the phone. She had talked with a Commissioner Fitzsimmons, who, while expressing her "grave concern" over the misuse of police resources by her ex-employee, stopped short of asking for her arrest. All she requested was that the woman's state credentials be confiscated and destroyed.

Tammy glanced at the time. She was already 13 minutes late for her duty assignment, what would five more minutes matter.

She dialed the cell number provided to her by Diane Westlake.

"Diane Westlake."

"Ms. Westlake, this is Detective Jahn. I need to meet with you. Just for a few minutes."

"Do you have something for me? A name, address? What have you found out?"

Tammy could hear anticipation in the woman's voice. She also heard fatigue.

"No, I'm afraid I don't have anything new, but I still need to meet with you to discuss something. Are you still at the Quality Inn? I can be there in 20 minutes."

There was a hesitation on the other end.

"What's this about? I was on my way out."

Tammy didn't want to tell her and give her time to skip out. "I'll tell you when I get there. Just sit tight. I'll be there shortly."

She disconnected, collected her things, and ran to her car. Even with a quick stop at the GREAT Program to inform them she had to do something but would return in an hour, she could make it to the motel in 20 minutes. If she hurried.

Diane began to hyperventilate. The detective wanted to see her about something she wouldn't discuss over the phone. What was the saying? You aren't paranoid if they're really out to get you. An image of her being led out of the motel in handcuffs flooded her mind.

She felt her fingers start to tingle and tried to slow down her breathing. Her fatigue didn't help her frame of mind. She had worn out the keys on her laptop searching for information on MedAir that might lead her to a name, to Amy what's-her-name. There had been another recent crash into the lake of a county park, but the victims were never identified by name and apparently, none had died because no funerals resulted.

She even became desperate enough that she tried searching the local paper's archives for "Amy." The 600,000+ results stymied her before she could begin to look through them.

What had the detective said? She'd be there in 20

minutes?

Diane rushed about the room and collected her things. She collected her toiletries as well and packed in haste. There were other motels. She didn't want to see that detective again. Period.

As she opened her suitcase, she pushed her hand under the clothing she had not unpacked until she found what she was looking for. Hard and cold. The old Ruger had been her father's.

She tried to remember the last time she'd tried firing it. She had found it in the house after her mother had passed and took it to an indoor range for instruction. That had been at least ten years earlier. She remembered how to use it, how to line up a target, how to squeeze the trigger, not jerk it. Still, as she recalled from that one day, her target would likely be safe even if the broad side of a barn wasn't.

She inspected the magazine. Three bullets. Three more than she ever hoped to need. She had no intent to shoot anyone, just threaten them. She realized that without the help of the police, she might have to coerce the O'Malleys to go back to Boston with her. To call the local police to assist with the AMBER Alert would also put her in jeopardy of arrest, if indeed that detective had discovered her secret.

She tucked the pistol into her purse. She had a conceal-carry permit in Massachusetts because of her work in sometimes less than ideal neighborhoods, but she hadn't taken the time to rummage through her purse to look for it. She also had no idea if it was valid in Missouri through a reciprocity agreement.

Right now, that didn't matter. She threw her things into her suitcase, closed it, and rushed outside to her car.

She loaded her things into it and drove around the building to the office, where she checked out. A few minutes later, she parked outside a nearby McDonalds and piggybacked onto their Wi-Fi to find a new motel.

Jeremy whistled as he prepared for the day. His discovery of Amy Gibbs' home had been the result of well-reasoned planning and the basic, feet-on-the-ground grunt work of any bounty hunter. His discovery of Sinead O'Malley, however, had been serendipitous.

After leaving Amy Gibbs' neighborhood, he had moved his base of operations to a motel closer to the woman's home. He wouldn't have to sit at the curb, risking detection, or scrutiny by homeowners or the police, and yet, within minutes he could be at the house.

As he settled into the new room, he had downloaded the photos from his camera to his laptop. At first, he paid no attention to them, but one full-face shot of the dark-haired woman attracted him to take a closer look. He pulled it up to fill his screen and it hit him. Sinead O'Malley had dyed her hair. He would not have recognized her in passing on the street, but magnified on his screen, he had no doubt. The faint birthmark on her left cheek became clear then. Truly serendipity.

He checked the tracking app and saw that Westlake had left the motel where she'd been staying. He wondered why. What did that mean? By zooming in on the map, he saw that she parked at a McDonalds. Breakfast again? Didn't the woman like the breakfast provided by the establishment? He would have to pay attention to her movements.

He walked out to his car and took off toward his day's first stop. A short drive later, he pulled into a lot where a red-and-white-striped pole rotated as a symbol that the barber was open for business. After a short wait, he climbed into the chair and held out the photo he had taken out of his car.

"I want a full shave and my hair back to this cut, like in the photo."

"Yes, sir."

Jeremy knew this would take a little while. He hadn't cut his hair and had only occasionally trimmed his beard since his wife's death. The picture took him back seven years. The occasion had been their annual family photo for their Christmas letter. In it, they all smiled, he, his wife, Marie, and their three-year-old daughter, Christine, sitting on daddy's lap awaiting the bribe of a peppermint stick if she cooperated. She had.

He cherished this photo and again gazed at the bright twinkle in Marie's eyes and that perfect smile, as piles of hair collected on the barber shop's floor. Today was Monday. Wednesday marked a special day. With a bit of luck, he might make it special once more.

I'll see you soon, Chrissy, he thought.

Thirty-Six

Diane found another inexpensive motel not far from the airport. That seemed to be a logical place to locate, just minutes from all but the most southern parts of the St. Louis metro area. She had learned that the helicopter that had gone down had flown from the corporate headquarters' helipad just 20 minutes west. Mercy Hospital was six minutes southwest, and the two inner city trauma centers were 20 minutes southeast. The cemetery for the afternoon's funeral sat less than ten minutes due west, just off the Interstate.

She hadn't come prepared to attend a funeral, so her first stop before securing the room had been a shopping mall called the Galleria. She had purchased an appropriate outfit there.

Now, she sat in her new room and waited. She had two hours to kill before heading to the cemetery, but the waiting seemed to be doing *her* in.

Tammy steamed. She had arrived at the motel only to find that the social worker had bailed on her just minutes earlier. She groused about it all the way back to work at the GREAT Program. Her sour mood must have been evident as she walked into the building.

Sam Wellston met her outside their shared office. "Hey, what's up?"

"You don't want to know. Seriously."

"Yeah, well, Your Daddy was calling here for you. I think he was checking up on you."

"Not surprised. It's all his fault I'm late, but he'll never admit that." She could see the curiosity in his eyes. Unlike on television, detectives on the street didn't have partners. So, as mentors with the program, they expected nothing more. Still, she had always wondered what working with a partner might be like, and he was the closest she would come to that.

"Don't worry, I covered for you." A mischievous smile now dominated his face. Maybe having a partner was overrated.

She chuckled. "I bet you did. I don't even want to know what you told him."

"Really? I was nice about it."

She gave him a look.

"Hey, I told him the truth, that you were at a motel—for a hooker's convention." He grinned.

She punched him in the shoulder. "Not nice."

"You know my mom's a hooker, right? She's made some beautiful rugs."

She punched him again. Harder. He laughed.

"That's true. Honest. So, really, what's going on?" he asked.

She scrutinized his face. Was there some other motive to his asking? He'd never been buddies with Barkley, so maybe he wasn't going to stab her in the back. She decided to trust him and told him about her "special" assignment from Barkley the previous Friday. She made a point of not saying anything that might come back to haunt her. She followed up by telling him what she'd discovered about the errant social worker and the events of the morning.

"So, she skipped out, eh?"

"Yeah. Probably worried that we're on to her. That, in and of itself, doesn't concern me. I can put the word out that she's using false credentials, so if she tries to get help from another department, they'll be forewarned. But I have a greater concern. She didn't seem stable to me on Friday. I'm worried about what might happen if she finds this nurse. She could just flip out on her. She almost did with that exec at MedAir."

Sam nodded. "Sounds a bit crazy. She'd fit in, here, in this precinct."

"No, a lot crazy. I'm thinking I need to find this nurse and warn her."

Sam waggled his head noncommittally. "Don't go hunting for her now. We have work to do and you don't want to get on Barkley's permanent sh—, well, you know, his naughty list."

Tammy wanted to chuckle. Sam was no different than any of the other guys in the precinct when it came to rough language, except around her. He always seemed to catch himself from using even the mildest vulgarity when with her. As if she had never heard the words before. She appreciated it.

"You're right, but first chance I get, I need to call that guy at MedAir and alert him."

Amy dressed quietly in her room. She had mentally prepared herself to return to work today but felt relief when Craig had called saying that non-emergent operations had been canceled until Wednesday, to allow people to attend the two funerals. Until now, her mind had been so preoccupied by her own medical concerns, by Sinead and Ruth, and by her father's comments that she could face serious charges for hiding them, that she'd had little time to reflect on the idea of returning to work, much less on the fact that two colleagues of hers, one of whom had been a friend as well, were about to be interred.

She hadn't flown with Kent Howard before that day. He'd been flying for some overtime and was normally based with their Potosi, Missouri squad. Still, she had seen him around headquarters after becoming the training officer. She knew he'd flown in Desert Storm and one subsequent tour in Iraq. He left behind a wife and three older, teenage kids, two sons and a daughter. The eldest, his daughter, was a freshman at Mizzou.

Tomorrow's funeral for Johnny Wilson would be harder. They had worked together for a time and joined together in various social events with co-workers, from Happy Hours to holiday parties. She had even been to his wife's bridal and baby showers. Their two-year-old son promised to be a spittin' image of his old man when he grew up. Now, he'd grow up having never really known and not remembering his father.

The finality of today's celebration of his life didn't make her feel any better. She had promised herself she wouldn't become engulfed in survivor's guilt, and yet, she found her mind wondering how she had survived. She gazed into the mirror over her dresser and wiped away the tears.

As she finished adding appropriate accessories to her

outfit, she tried to decide how involved she wished to get at both events. Certainly, she would talk with the families and express her deepest condolences. But, would she try to explain what happened? What if they asked her how she survived? How could she answer?

There was a knock at her door.

"Amy?" It was Sinead. "Your dad's here."

Her father had tried to convince Sinead to leave during their "talk" two days earlier. He had offered to contact friends in rural Missouri whom he felt would allow them to stay on their farm, but Sinead had refused. She stated they would soon leave for home, and she really didn't want to disrupt Ruth's life with yet another place. Ruth liked Amy and wanted to stay. Her father had relented, but he wasn't happy about it.

"Almost ready. I'll be out in a minute."

Her father had agreed to escort her. As a retired Army aviator, he'd been through more of such funerals than he cared to acknowledge, but still he agreed to go. For today's occasion in particular, she thought that was a good idea. Kent had been military. Her father would be able to help comfort the family in ways she could not.

Thirty-Seven

Amy and her father arrived at Grace Church 40 minutes ahead of the memorial service. Already the parking lot was packed. EMS vehicles from over a dozen services sat in a line behind the hearse and half a dozen cars. Fire trucks, police cars, and personal cars followed. MedAir and their "competitor" had three helicopters on scene to provide a fly-over.

No wonder the service was being held at this church. It was one of a few that could handle such a crowd.

Amy had watched videos of such commemorative processions, honoring first responders. Some were miles long. She had been part of one once, and the memory of sitting with Lynch's parents at the head of that two-mile-long line of vehicles made her heart ache. That time, there had been no body, and Lynch ultimately returned from the dead several months later. Today, the tribute would equal that for Lynch, but this time, there was a body and a finality they could not deny.

Her father assisted her from the car at the front entrance and then went to park. He caught up to her in the lobby.

"They want me to sit up front, with the family. Dad, I-I don't know if I can do that."

"Of course we can. We are here for them, aren't we?"

He had such a way of putting things into perspective.

Amy hobbled her way to the front, accepting nods in greeting from many co-workers. Her father trailed behind. As she approached the front, Craig walked up to her and gave her a hug.

"I'm glad you came. Are you doing well?"

"As well as can be expected, I guess. Um, where should we sit?"

Craig pointed to the front row, which was covered with 'Reserved' signs. "Right here. The family is over there in that side room. They won't come out until just before the service starts. They've asked that you ride with them to the grave site."

Amy wanted to protest. She didn't feel comfortable with that, but her father's words echoed in her mind. She was there for them.

Diane pulled into the church parking lot and felt an immediate sense of defeat. There were hundreds of cars in the lot, not to mention dozens of ambulances, fire trucks, and police cars. How was she going to find someone named Amy in this crowd?

An attendant knocked on her window. She lowered it to speak with him.

"Ma'am, are you here just for the memorial or will you be joining the procession?"

She hadn't thought about that. Even if she could identify this Amy person, how would she be able to find her again? She would need her home address or a phone number. Something.

"Both, please."

"Are you family or a co-worker?" He stepped toward the front of the car and glanced at her license plate. "Well, I guess not a co-worker. From Massachusetts, eh?"

"An old friend," she lied.

"Well, then, why don't you park at the end of that row over there? That guy with the orange vest will direct you." He pointed to another man in a safety vest.

"Thank you."

She powered up her window as she drove toward the next parking attendant. He waved her into a spot. After parking, she climbed out of the car and began to walk toward the front entrance, past car after car after car. *Are all of these cars in the procession?* she wondered. She had passed over 30 vehicles.

Being inside felt just as daunting. Hundreds of people milled about. She looked for a seat where she could easily watch the doors but found the center sections full. She worked her way to the right and found a seat about two-thirds back from the stage.

She sensed that the service was about to begin. People began taking their seats, and a woman with three older children emerged from a side room and progressed slowly to the front row. They were stopped by a dozen people, before that man from MedAir—what was his name?—stepped in and ushered them along, running interference for them. *They must be the pilot's immediate family*, she thought.

The service lasted about an hour and people stood, respectfully allowing the family to leave first behind the closed casket. Diane stood and moved to the lobby area but found herself behind a crowd of well-wishers. She peeked through and around people and saw the family exit the building. Right behind them, a younger woman on crutches followed. Amy?

She pushed forward toward the nearest door and, once outside, watched as the family and the woman on crutches entered a limousine behind the hearse.

"Excuse me," she said to a woman standing next to her. "Who's the woman on the crutches?"

"You know, I had to ask, too. I know the family, but I didn't recognize her. That's the nurse who survived the crash. I didn't catch her name."

Diane nodded, but inwardly she wanted to pump her fist and yell, "Yes!"

She dashed to her car—and waited. By the time she was waved into the line, she started to think the graveside service would be finished before she arrived.

Jeremy avoided the cul-de-sac as he watched Amy's house. He had a concern that his car would be noticed and didn't want to be seen in the same place too often. He had debated renting a different car for the day but calculated that his ordeal would end soon enough. Besides, anyone who might have seen him two days earlier would see a different man this time. He rubbed his bare chin, noting that it felt strange without the beard.

He had stopped by to see if he could verify that the O'Malleys were staying with Ms. Gibbs. After 20 minutes, his visit was validated. A young blonde girl exited the garage's side door and placed a bag into the garbage can. He snapped a photo as she turned toward him.

Blonde? Walking? He had been fooled at first by

Sinead O'Malley but not this time. He viewed the photo in the camera's screen and zoomed in on her face. It was Ruth.

But walking? That was even better than he'd hoped. Not only would he show Diane Westlake that she would lose this case, he would be able to show her she was totally wrong. Under Sinead's care for just a month, the girl had improved to the point of walking on her own. He debated moving his timeline up a day just to see Westlake's face, but no, Wednesday would be the day unless something unforeseen forced his hand.

Moments later, the colonel showed up and assisted Amy to his car. He took a quick glance at the tracking app and saw that Westlake was on the move as well. Discovering her destination would have to wait if he wanted to follow the Gibbs.

He followed them onto the Interstate, across the Missouri River, and off the first exit after the bridge. They led him to a large church, where it became obvious from the assortment of vehicles that the funeral service for one of the flight crew members was to take place. He pulled into a parking slot near the street, away from the building, and idled there.

A knock on his window startled him. He wound down his window.

"Here for the memorial service?" asked a man in a reflective, orange safety vest.

He had to think quickly. "Ah, I'm sorry, no. I think I'm lost."

"Where you headed? I might be able to help."

"Thanks, but you look like you're busy. I've got Google Maps on my phone. It'll just take me a minute to figure out where I missed my turn, and I'll be out of here." He held up his phone.

The man nodded. "Good luck." He walked away toward another car.

As Jeremy lowered his phone, he glanced at the tracking app on the map. Westlake's beacon showed she was right there. He frantically looked about and saw her 40 feet away.

Noooo, he thought. *Not here. It's too soon.*

He ducked down. He couldn't let her see him. There was a chance she might not remember him, but he couldn't take that risk.

After a minute, he lifted his head. She had walked to the front doors and was about to enter. Did she already know about Amy Gibbs? Was she here to confront the nurse? His mind raced from one "what-if" to another, until he realized that while Amy Gibbs might be the link, the O'Malleys were her targets.

He put his car into gear and eased out of the lot. After turning onto the street, he raced toward Amy Gibbs' home. The O'Malleys were there. That's where he needed to be.

Thirty-Eight

Amy talked with Kent's wife and children en route to the cemetery, answering their questions about what had happened a week earlier. She told them of being caught in a wind and of something hitting and damaging their tail rotor.

"I remember hitting the ground and a skid digging into the soft dirt. That's when we began to roll."

She had to think hard about her next words. Did she want to perpetuate a lie?

"The next thing I remember is a woman, helping me from my seat restraint. After that, things are blurry until I woke up in an old pickup truck. Impossible as it seems, the woman had carried me from the crash to the truck. She told me that the others, your husband and Johnny, were dead. I'm sorry. I can't tell you anything more because I don't remember anything more. I do know that your husband was a fantastic pilot and did everything possible to land safely under the circumstances. I-I think his running landing would have been perfect, if the field hadn't recently been tilled to create furrows and soften the ground."

Mrs. Howard took Amy's hand in her own, but gave her a strange look. "A woman? We were told you made it to that barn on your own."

Amy nodded. "I staged it to look that way. You see, the woman was there in hiding, with a daughter. I didn't want to jeopardize their safety. They were willing to come forward, but I stopped them. We've been in touch since, and we've talked about this. I see now that I need to make it clear that she saved my life."

She did see that clearly now. After talking more with Sinead, she realized that had Sinead not cleared the cabin of hazards and helped her out of her restraint, she would have fallen into and impaled herself on the debris by trying to escape the cabin on her own. And if she had stayed in her seat, she would have burned. Sinead knew about the fire and had told her that it started right after she had cleared Amy from the cabin. If she was to appeal to the grace of the judge in Sinead's case, she needed to make it clear that Sinead had gone beyond any responsibility she had and had selflessly gone to Amy's aid after that crash, at some risk to herself.

Much of the remainder of the short trip to the cemetery progressed in silence. Amy had been astounded by the outpouring of respect for Kent Howard. She had no idea how long the procession trailed behind them, but she could hear the helicopters above as they escorted Kent's body to its final resting place. And when they arrived at the cemetery, two fire trucks had hoisted their ladders to form an arch over the entrance, with a large American flag suspended between them.

The graveside ceremony itself was brief but honoring. Amy appreciated being allowed to sit with the family. She didn't think she would have held out until the end on crutches, after all the walking to and from the church, and to the grave. Perhaps the strain had been more emotional than physical. At the end, her father helped her to his own car, and they returned home. Tomorrow would be a repeat of today.

Diane's confidence grew as she drove toward the cemetery, although her fear of missing the service came close to reality. The one and a half-mile-long procession stopped traffic and caught stares from passersby. She knew because she was near the end of the train and witnessed it.

At the cemetery, the EMS and other first responder vehicles were directed along one drive, while the private vehicles were shifted to another. Upon parking, Diane followed the crowd to a point overlooking the gravesite. The family, along with nurse Amy, sat in chairs next to the grave. The service was short and people began to disperse.

Diane became frantic at that moment. She hadn't thought ahead. The family's limousine would be allowed to leave first. Although she had first thought they would drive back to the church to allow the occupants to disperse to their own cars, she now realized they might not. What if they all had come from the family home? She hadn't seen Amy arrive. She very well might have come with the family.

She needed to follow that limo, and she recognized she was in no position to do so if she remained behind a long line of cars waiting to exit the grounds. She struggled to run back to her car, but her heels and the soft ground would not cooperate with each other. Halfway there, she stopped, grabbed her shoes from her feet and then took off. She needed to beat the others to their cars and get close to the entrance to be able to follow that limo.

She managed to get positioned three cars behind the

limo in exiting the cemetery. She sighed in relief. Anticipation lifted her spirit. Within the half hour she would have her answers about the O'Malleys. Maybe, within the hour, she would have the O'Malleys themselves. That posed a new set of difficulties, but she decided to wait until that time to face those.

She followed the vehicle back onto the highway and was not surprised to see that their path followed the funeral procession in reverse back to the church. She had been correct in her thinking. She pulled into a parking spot ten feet away from the limousine and waited for the injured nurse to exit.

She sat there, mouth agape, as the limousine pulled away, leaving the family behind—but no Amy. She laid her head on the steering wheel and cried, as her whole body trembled.

Thirty-Nine

Tammy paced within her small office at the GREAT Program. Four steps forward and four steps back. She had been unsuccessful the previous day in reaching Craig Sheehan at MedAir. Not until after hours and on her way home from work did she learn why—the funeral of their pilot. She'd heard a news report about it on the radio.

Today would also be a write-off, with respect to contacting the man to alert him about Diane Westlake. She wondered how much trouble she would get into by leaving her assigned duties to attend today's funeral for the paramedic. And would it be worth it? Perhaps she was reading more into the situation than truly existed.

Still, that nurse should be made aware that an unstable woman was searching for her, as well as a mother and daughter duo who were likely long-gone from the area, if they'd ever been in St. Louis to begin with. The odds of that had been slim all along.

Of course, she couldn't leave unless Sam was there to hold down the office. And cover for her, even with his made-up excuses.

She glanced at the clock. The late morning funeral was just over an hour away, and he hadn't shown his face there yet. She wondered what concocted story she could give if

Barkley called for Sam, but then she thought, *You're male. Your Daddy won't be checking up on you.*

She sat at her desk and mindlessly thumbed through the stack of papers on her desk. She had a short deadline for the quarterly reports staring back at her, but her mind was far from them. She looked up at the sound of footsteps in the hallway. She could pick out Sam's footfall in a crowd if she had to.

"Boy, do you owe me," he said as he walked into the office and saw her sitting there.

She looked at him, questioning. "And how's that?"

He grinned and pulled a folded sheet of paper from his inside jacket pocket. He tossed it onto her desk in front of her.

"What's this?"

"The answer to your quest." He removed his jacket and sat behind his desk.

Tammy opened the note and read, "Amy Gibbs, RN," followed by a phone number and address.

"How did—"

"Excellent detective work, that's all. I can offer you lessons."

She rolled her eyes and gave him "the" look. "Seriously?" Her closure rate on cases was 30% higher than his. Who would give whom lessons?

"You tried the frontal assault. I did a flanking maneuver. I have a golf buddy who's a paramedic out in Chesterfield. I just called him and asked the question. He was more than happy to oblige."

Tammy smiled. She grabbed the note, stood, and stopped. The woman wouldn't be home if she planned on attending the funeral. She sat back down. *Well,* she thought, *if I can't meet her face-to-face, I can at least warn her by phone.* She picked up her phone and dialed the number on the sheet.

"Hi, this is Amy, at MedAir, and you've reached my office. I'm currently out of the office but will be back . . ." Great, the number was for her office, not her home, and the date she mentioned had been a week earlier, when she would have returned to work had it not been for the accident.

She tried directory assistance, only to learn the woman had an unlisted number. That didn't surprise her, as many first responders followed that practice. Tammy's home number was unlisted as well, by department policy.

She was back to square one. Should she head to the funeral? Yes.

She stood again and grabbed her purse.

"Unh-uh. Where do you think you're going?"

"That funeral. To find Amy Gibbs. This phone number is her office, and I need to warn her."

"Not today, you're not. We have that follow-up meeting with Chief of Staff Raintree in 30 minutes. You skip out on that and you might as well start looking for jobs in Timbuktu."

She closed her eyes and sighed. He was right. She couldn't play hooky on that one, and she'd be tied up the rest of the day. She sat back at her desk.

She gave him her best "pretty please" look, and said, "Hey, tomorrow morn—"

Again, he interrupted, "Yes, I'll cover for you."

Jeremy started awake at the sound of knocking on the

door to his motel room. He sat up and worked to get his bearings. Had he fallen asleep on top of the bed? What had wakened him?

He grabbed his cell phone and checked the GPS app, hoping he hadn't missed his opportunity. Westlake remained stationary at a second motel. He had noticed that she appeared to have changed locations the day before, but found it curious that she relocated near the airport and not nearby. Had she not yet discovered the whereabouts of Amy Gibbs and the O'Malleys? Or was she planning some quick getaway by plane? He couldn't fathom how she would manage that with the O'Malleys.

Another knock on the door. "Housekeeping!"

That's what had wakened him.

He walked to the door and opened it to the length of the chain. "Hi. Sorry. Late night. I won't be needing anything today. Thanks.

The housekeeper gave him a strange look and then nodded. She moved on, pushing her cart in front, as he closed the door.

He walked into the bathroom and glanced into the mirror. No wonder the woman had given him that look. His hair was bedraggled, his eyes bloodshot, and his five o'clock shadow had extended to a 24-hour scraggly growth. As much as he wanted to return to bed, under the covers, there was no point in that futile effort. He'd not be able to go back to sleep.

Passing out, however, was not beyond him. Isn't that how he'd "celebrated" this date each year since his wife's passing? This date, the day before the date of her death, and several days after had been marked by a drinking binge that put to shame sailors on their first night of shore leave after four months at sea. The half-empty bottle of Maker's Mark on his bed stand sat as witness to his destructive tendencies.

This year, however, would be different, thanks to Diane Westlake. And this would be the date, whether today or tomorrow, that she would come to understand the depth of the damage she had done to him and countless others.

He forced himself to shave, shower, and redress despite craving another drink. He rechecked his phone. Westlake was on the move but not in this direction. He watched the changing map on his phone's screen. When she finally stopped, he switched to the Earth view and saw that she had arrived at another cemetery. To him, that meant one thing. She still had not solved the mystery that was Amy Gibbs.

Forty

Diane stepped out from the motel and loaded her things into the front seat of her car. This time she had done her homework and was prepared. That nurse would not elude her today.

She drove past the church where today's service was to be held and saw a repeat of the previous day's event. EMS and first responder vehicles sat lined up to lead the procession. A hundred cars filled the lot. A glance at her watch revealed that the memorial service was about to start.

Today, however, she would precede everyone to the cemetery and claim a spot for fast egress. She wore slacks and sensible shoes, not heels, and she now owned a moderately-priced set of binoculars. She would follow that nurse, no matter what that task entailed.

A man inside the entrance to the graveyard raised his hand to stop her. She pulled up to him and powered down her window.

"Good morning, ma'am. Which funeral are you attending? We're expecting a large procession shortly."

"Good morning. Yes, sir, I know. I know I'm early but I'm here for the Wilson service. I'd be in that long procession, too, but I can't stay for all of it and will need to leave before all those vehicles. Is there someplace I can park where I'll be able to leave, but that's not too far from the gravesite?"

The man seemed relieved. "Oh yes. Thank you. We've been worrying about fitting all those ambulances and cars along the back drives. The more we can park out front, the better." He turned and pointed behind himself, to her left. "If you park right over there, you'll be able to get right out. The grave is actually just over that knoll, the one with the tall monument surrounded by flags." He pointed to a marble obelisk. "The main procession has to go down this main drive and around the back of the grounds to get there. Most people toward the end of the line will actually end up walking a lot farther to get there."

Diane thought that sounded perfect, and a glance at the small hill she'd have to climb revealed an easy trek. "That looks perfect. Thank you, so much."

She pulled off to the left and found a parking spot that would allow her to be first out. She glanced at her watch. Plenty of time to scope out the grounds and return to her car to wait.

The funeral for Kent Howard had not been as awkward as Amy had first imagined. The man's wife had been gracious and kind, showing concern for Amy's injuries rather than contempt for her surviving a crash that her husband had not. That had been Amy's biggest worry yesterday morning.

Today, however, promised to be a hard one. She didn't expect Johnny's wife, Wendy, to harbor any ill feelings toward Amy. They had, in fact, already talked, when Wendy, in the midst of her own grief, had called Amy in the hospital to inquire as to how she was doing. The young woman had even offered her help, as if she wouldn't have her own hands full.

No, the day promised to be difficult because they *had* been close friends. Amy wanted to be able to assist with young Trevor, the couple's toddler, but knew she couldn't while on crutches. Her injury also prevented her from helping with food at the wake, which was to be held at their home in a rural community southwest of St. Louis. Her father had agreed to accompany her to the wake, and he would no doubt find a way to help in her stead. Still, the mismatch of her desire and her infirmity would make a day filled with grief even sadder.

As on the day before, her father picked her up at home and drove her to the church. Again, she was to sit with the family in the front row, although this time Wendy had called to personally ask that of her. And once more, she rode to the gravesite in the limousine at the head of the procession. During that drive, Trevor expressed his fascination with her crutches, oblivious to the somber event around him.

At the end of the short graveside service, Amy took Wendy's hand and cradled it in her own.

"I'm going to catch up with my dad, and we'll head to the house. Is there anything last-minute we can get for you?"

Wendy finished drying her eyes with someone's donated handkerchief. "No, thank you. I think my parents have things under control. Thank you for being with me."

Amy nodded and hugged her friend. "I'll see you at the house."

Diane hadn't needed the binoculars to monitor the interment service. The nurse on her crutches had been easy to follow. She realized what had happened the previous day to make her lose track of the woman. As the event ended and people dispersed, an older man had assisted the nurse to a private car. Perhaps the man was her father, or a co-worker. Whichever, she had seen him the day before and now recognized that he had likely helped her after that service also.

She watched as the man helped the nurse into the car and then stow the crutches in the back seat. She used the binoculars to make note of the brand and model of the car, as well as the license plate. Then she scrambled down the other side of the knoll and to her car. She managed to pull into the line of exiting autos just two cars behind that of her quarry.

Within minutes they entered the flow of cars on the outer ring Interstate and headed south and then southwest on I-44. They passed an amusement park and exited onto a rural road that took them past a rock quarry and pastures with horses. Where in the world did this nurse live? But then, as she thought about it, wouldn't this be an ideal hideout for the O'Malleys?

She reached down under her seat. Her old Ruger remained where she had placed it. She began to think through the timing of what had to happen and the how of it. The timing aspect of things wasn't so bad. She could "claim" the O'Malleys, turn them in, and drive back to Boston without stopping. She didn't look forward to it, but her motivation to clear her name would keep her going.

Then again, being this far out of the city, maybe the

local authorities had no idea who she was. Would the city police detective have contacted other departments about her? Of course, she only speculated that the detective knew about her in the first place. She had never confirmed that suspicion. Maybe contacting the local authorities and having the police handle the O'Malleys' "extradition" would be the better course.

The nurse's car turned onto a smaller lane marked by a "No Outlet" sign and by four postal boxes on a stand near its beginning. Oddly, the car separating her from the nurse's car also made the turn. Diane slowed to turn as well and noted four cars behind her also signaling for the turn. More cars behind those followed suit. She'd been so lost in thought that she hadn't noticed that she was but one of a dozen cars in a line on the same rural road, apparently heading to the same destination. Were all these cars going to the nurse's house?

Of course not. Where was her mind? She really was losing it. These people were going to a wake. What else could explain this caravan to the sticks?

She watched the two cars ahead of her pull into the drive of a modest, two-story home on a large wooded lot. She drove past and turned around at the next driveway, several hundred yards down the road. She returned and parked about 50 feet from the drive. Other cars pulled into the drive, while some parked along the side of the road. Within about 30 minutes, she had counted over 60 people in attendance.

She crouched down into her seat so as to decrease her visibility. She could still see the nurse's car, but if this "party" was to continue past dark, would she be able to see it as it left? And would she be able to follow it again, in the dark?

She groaned. Had she come this far to get thwarted again?

A bright light in her face woke Diane. Headlights from straight ahead. She panicked. How long had she been out? How had she let herself fall asleep? A glance at the clock on her dash told her she had been asleep no longer than 20 minutes, but what if the nurse and the man with her had left during that time. The clock also told her it was after midnight. The odds were good that she'd blown the whole evening's stakeout.

More headlights flashed on. Several cars along the driveway were about to leave. She sighed in relief as more than once, their lights illuminated the nurse's car. She was among the last to leave.

The saving grace to the late hour was that the car was much easier to follow. On the rural roads, she blended in with the other cars leaving the wake, and on the highway she was simply one of dozens of other cars traveling along the same route.

They drove about 45 minutes to a community north of the Missouri River and not far from where the nurse worked. As they exited the highway, she stayed back, hoping to avoid the attention of the man driving. Apparently, she had succeeded. She watched the car turn into a driveway and pulled to the side of the street with her lights out. She watched the nurse climb out of the car and hobble up the walkway. The man offered to help her to the door, but she turned him back. A moment later, she disappeared inside, and the front lights went out.

Diane yawned and tried to think. As she watched the car back out of the driveway, she ducked down to avoid being seen when the man drove past. That rural home made much more sense as a hiding place. The likelihood of the O'Malleys being here plummeted in Diane's exhausted mind. So, that left the question. Where were they hiding?

As much as she wanted to confront the nurse right now and get that answer, she knew this was not a good time. To ring the doorbell or knock on the front door at one a.m. would be to invite a police patrol car to pull up behind her. Besides, in her fatigued state, she had a short fuse, and she knew well enough that the slightest rebuttal by the nurse could lead to consequences that would not be in her favor.

She glanced at the clock and decided. A quick trip back to the motel. Five hours of needed sleep and back to this house. She logged the address into her cell phone so she wouldn't forget it, flipped on her headlights, and drove off.

Forty-One

Jeremy looked at the clock and at the empty bottle on the table. When psychologists say that anniversary dates trigger emotional problems, they could point to him as a textbook case.

He took the wrinkled photo of his wife and daughter into both hands and began to cry. If only alcohol could deaden the pain he felt on this date. He kissed both of their faces and slid the photo back into his shirt pocket, close to his heart.

He knew that this would be the day to fulfill his destiny. The timetable would end today. Last night's panic had eased. He had tracked Westlake to the cemetery only to have her disappear from his GPS system. Panic number one. Had she given up and left town, depriving him of his final satisfaction? Panic number two. Had the GPS battery died? He felt relief when, after midnight, the alert came through that she had reentered his 20-mile radius. No, she had not left town, and no, the battery had not died. He would get his redress.

Panic number three had been the worst. He watched as she closed in on Amy Gibbs' home. He wasn't ready. He hadn't expected her to confront the nurse at that time of the morning. His mind sobered enough to grab his things and rush to the woman's home. As he drove by, he saw Westlake's car, lights out but running, parked 50 yards from Amy Gibbs' driveway. Where was she?

He had pulled around the corner and flipped off his own lights. Getting out of the car and staying in the shadows, away from a corner street lamp, he found a vantage point to watch Westlake. It had taken a few minutes to recognize that she was still in her car. She had remained there and soon pulled away. The tracker showed her returning to her motel. Only then did he feel comfortable returning to his.

Since then he hadn't slept. Of course, on this date, he rarely did anymore. He hadn't passed out either, as much as he would have liked that brief respite from his turmoil.

He stood and walked to the window. Dawn. The sun's rays lit up the high cirrus clouds into vivid pinks and oranges. On any other day, he would have relished such a beautiful sunrise. Today, he had other things on his mind.

He gathered his belongings and stashed all but two items into the trunk of his car. He closed the door behind him, checked out at the front desk, and drove off.

Tammy awoke earlier than usual. Something simply felt, well, off. She had nothing critical going on at work, but her plan was to go to Amy Gibbs' home early. She had reached a receptionist at MedAir the previous day and had been informed that Ms. Gibbs was expected back at work at eight a.m. Tammy planned on being at her home by seven-fifteen to talk with her before she left for work. She had cleared that with Barkley, as well as Sam. Her husband had agreed to handle their kids' morning routine and see them off to school.

Everything seemed organized and settled. Except, it didn't feel that way.

She glanced at the clock. Six forty-five. Taking into account the morning traffic, she needed to leave. She found her spouse in the bathroom, shaving. She leaned up to him and kissed him on the back of the neck to avoid his soapy face.

"Thanks, honey. I hate to leave this to you alone."

He shook his head. "No problemo. It used to be a lot worse when you were on the streets. I'll see you tonight."

She kissed him again and turned to leave.

Amy brushed out her hair and pulled it into a pony tail. She had discovered that her flight suit was a great fit over her cast. The zipper on the lower leg allowed her to slide her cast through without difficulty, and this option sure beat her others.

There was a knock on her bedroom door. She grabbed her crutches and hobbled to the door. Sinead stood there, dressed and smiling.

"Good morning. I fixed you some eggs and toast. Hope that's okay."

Amy smiled. "Sure. Thanks. Usually all I have time for is a breakfast bar and coffee."

"Umm, Amy, I'd really like to thank you for letting us stay here, but we're going to head out shortly after you leave for work. I'll make sure the alarm is set and all that."

"Head out?"

"Yeah. We're heading home. Ruth is doing great, and we miss the rest of our family. Plus, I don't want Jameson sitting in jail any longer. He's already sacrificed a lot to let me do this. You, too. We've put you in jeopardy for too long."

"But, they'll arrest you."

She nodded. "I'm sure they will. But I can make my case and argue against theirs, now that Ruth is up and about again. It's the only chance I have. We can't run forever."

Amy didn't like the odds of Sinead going up against the state, particularly a state that felt it "owned" your children. And yet, Sinead was right. She and Ruth couldn't run forever.

"I understand. Well, I pray that God prepares your path and defends you in your battle."

"Thanks. I'll need his help."

The doorbell rang.

Amy scrunched her brow. She wasn't expecting her father, but she wouldn't put it past him to show up to drive her to work. Sinead disappeared into the spare bedroom.

Amy walked to the front door and opened it, expecting her father saying "Surprise!" Instead, a dour-looking woman stood on the stoop.

"Um, can I help you?"

"You're the nurse from the helicopter crash, right?"

Amy turned her head in a slight nod, wondering where this was going. The woman didn't wait for an answer but barged inside almost knocking Amy down.

"You have no right—"

At that moment, Ruth emerged from the kitchen, saw the woman, and froze. Sinead rushed from the hallway to her side.

The woman scrutinized the two and a mocking smile crept onto her face. "Harrumph. Well, I was about to ask where the O'Malleys were, but looks like I found them."

Amy rushed to place herself between the woman and the other two. "Get out of my house!"

"Not without these two. They're wanted back in Massachusetts."

"Get. Out. Of. My. House. Or I'm calling the police."

"Oh, please do. We'll need them anyway, and you'll be charged as an accessory to kidnapping."

Amy quieted and glanced at the floor. Her father, and Sinead, had been right about the risk she faced in harboring the duo. Then again, this wasn't the first time she'd not listened to him.

She lifted her crutch and poked the woman hard between her breasts, knocking her back a step.

"I said it once already. Get. Out. Of. My. House."

The woman scowled and shook her head. She pulled a handgun from behind her back. Amy stood her ground.

"And just *who* will be facing kidnapping charges?" Amy smirked. "Do you still want me to call the police?" She started to move toward a nearby phone.

The woman shot a round into the ceiling. Amy stopped. She wasn't bluffing, or she was crazy. Or both.

The woman pointed the gun at Ruth. "You two are coming with me. Now."

Sinead, with her arm around Ruth's shoulders, urged her daughter to comply. "We'll come. Please don't hurt anyone."

Amy looked at Sinead. "Sinead, who is this person?"

"Meet Diane Westlake."

Westlake smiled and nodded. Amy recognized the name immediately.

"C'mon, you two. We have a date with the court."

The comment worried Amy. Why did this woman

seem to have no concern about appearing in court after holding them all at gunpoint? She wasn't thinking straight. Plus, she shot a hole in Amy's ceiling. Amy didn't like how two and two were adding up.

Westlake backed out of the door, still holding the gun on the O'Malleys. As the mother and daughter emerged, the woman hid the handgun and pointed with her other hand toward a car parked in the driveway. "Get in front. You're driving," she said to Sinead. "Straight to the police station."

Amy approached the door and emerged outside when Westlake didn't say anything. She quickly scrutinized the car and memorized the license plate. They wouldn't get far. Amy would call the police as soon as she could get to her phone and report the shot fired and the pair taken at gunpoint. If she could get the police on her side before Westlake got there, maybe they stood a better chance. But a better chance at what? Sinead would be arrested one way or the other. Ruth would be taken into custody. And she . . . what would happen to her?

Westlake looked at her. "And if you're thinking of calling the police, don't. These two have ruined my life. If I so much as see lights or hear sirens, I'll testify that you not only harbored them in your house, but that you helped them plan their escape, too."

This time Amy knew this lady was off her rocker.

As Sinead opened the driver's door, another car raced up to the driveway and screeched to a halt at its end, blocking the drive. A man jumped out of the car, ran into the drive, and stood facing Westlake. He looked awful, as if he hadn't slept in days. Who was this? What was going on here?

Amy made use of his distraction to ease closer to

Westlake.

"Let the O'Malleys go, Westlake! Ruth, walk over next to your mom."

The scowl returned to Westlake's face.

"Did you even notice that?" the man asked. "Ruth is up and walking. Does that even register in that pathetic brain of yours?"

Amy could see the anger rising inside the social worker.

"You've lost, Westlake. The court is going to see how Ruth has improved in the care of her mother, and you're going to be ridiculed for your 'it takes a village' attitude. The free press will have a field day with this. And more than losing this case, it proves you're wrong. Everything about you has been wrong."

Amy didn't like the way this man was escalating the problem. He was pushing button after button on this woman, and she was going to erupt.

Westlake spit at him. "And just who are you?" She paused and took a longer look. "Do I know you? Where do I know you from?"

"You don't even remember us, do you? Does this date mean anything to you?"

Westlake appeared to think about that for a moment and then shook her head.

"Does the name Christine Meecham ring a bell?"

The woman blanched.

"Or Marie Meecham?"

Amy noticed sweat emerging on the woman's brow.

"*You* stole our daughter from us when all we wanted was a second doctor's opinion. *You* put her in a foster home where you said she'd be safe from us. Six months later, four years ago today, she was dead. She had been sexually and physically abused in that house. Because of you. My wife went into a depression that no doctor could help. Two years ago today, she committed suicide. All because of *you*."

Westlake's gun appeared and rose toward the man. Amy took a quick hop forward and as the gun fired, bumped the woman with her crutch. The shot went wide.

She looked toward the man to see him move to one knee and retrieve a gun from behind his back in one fluid movement.

"Noooo!" she screamed.

In that split second a single shot rang out. The look of anger on Westlake's face morphed into one of surprise—and pain.

As she again looked toward the man, she heard another voice, a woman's voice, scream, "No! Don't do it!" Amy watched in horror as the man put the gun to his temple.

Traffic had tied up Tammy for a bit longer than she had anticipated, but as she drove down the residential street toward Amy Gibbs' house, she glanced at the clock. The woman would likely still be there.

As she neared the home, she saw several people in the driveway. Some kind of argument seemed to be occurring. As she pulled to the curb about 50 feet away and behind three other vehicles parked there, she recognized Diane Westlake. The woman on crutches could only be Amy Gibbs. And there was a woman and a young girl on the opposite side of the car from Westlake. The O'Malleys? Had they been here all along? Who was the man?

She climbed out of the car and before she could take a step, she heard the man talk about a daughter and his wife. As the impact of what he said hit her, Westlake pulled a gun. The nurse used her crutch to knock the social worker off-balance. At the sound of the shot, Tammy pulled her own gun. Within three more steps on the run, the man had pulled a gun and shot Westlake.

Tammy screamed, "No! Don't do it!"

Was she was too late? Ten feet short of tackling the man, she heard him say, "I'm coming Marie. Daddy's coming Christine." As he placed the gun to his temple, Tammy took a leap she never thought she was capable of doing and hit him with her right shoulder as the gun discharged.

Forty-Two

Amy couldn't have imagined the day getting any worse. During her career as a trauma nurse, she had seen the aftermath of horrible accidents, tragic falls, gang shootings, and more, but she'd never been present during the event. The shootings that took place on her very own driveway had shaken her. Yet, although she, Sinead, and Ruth had not been injured, she worried about Ruth more than herself. She should not have had to witness that. None of them should have.

But her immediate concern was more personal. When had she gone from being a flight nurse to a flight *risk*? The hard bench of the holding cell at her municipality's police department did not favor her injured leg and the officer in charge of the jail had little compassion for her, despite her good standing as a first responder. In reflection though, she realized he probably knew nothing about her, other than the charge she was being held on.

The city detective who had arrived unexpectedly at her home as the shooting occurred seemed more sympathetic. Unfortunately, she was out of her jurisdiction, and once the local detectives confirmed that Sinead O'Malley had a warrant out in Massachusetts for felony kidnapping, Detective Jahn held no sway in the case. After consultation with the local office of the FBI, Amy was taken to the jail pending charges for being an accessory to kidnapping by harboring the O'Malleys.

Her jailer appeared at the door. "You have a visitor. Hands forward."

"What?" She stood at the door to speak to him through the small portal used for meals and communication.

"Like this." He demonstrated putting his hands forward, with wrists touching, into the opening.

She complied and stood there, mouth agape, as he cuffed her. "Really?"

He was not persuaded. "Policy."

The morning's events and the consequences of her actions weighed on her mind. She had wanted to cry but had refused to give in to that inclination. Now, she wanted to laugh at what she knew was about to happen.

The door opened and the officer stepped aside. She didn't move.

"C'mon. We don't have all day."

"Um, not going anywhere without my crutches." She pointed to her leg. She couldn't keep anything that could be used as a weapon. Thus, no crutches in the cell. Policy, although this one she could understand. Kind of. What was the difference between having them in the cell, where she couldn't reach a single officer and had no room to swing at one with a crutch, and giving them to her in the hallway where she actually could use them as a weapon? Well, the man did blame "policy," not logic.

This time the officer looked a bit embarrassed. He stepped away for a minute and came back, carrying her crutches. "Here." She didn't take them and he said again, more forcefully, "Here, take 'em!"

She held her hands out in front and said, "Ahem. And just how do I do that?" She resisted the smirk that tried to cross her face. The officer took a deep breath and sighed before stepping up to her and removing the handcuffs.

She preceded him to a conference room where her father sat waiting for her. She thought about his comments four days earlier. He'd been correct, as usual, but she simply couldn't turn Sinead away. She had decided to stand up for what was right. She hadn't, however, fully thought through what she might face by doing so.

She sat down across from him and waited for him to say something. Anything. The two sat in silence for several minutes.

Finally, he spoke up. "You know, after meeting Sinead and Ruth, I started doing some research on their case, as well as a dozen other cases of medical kidnapping. I know I said you were putting your life and career in jeopardy and that you should send them away before you got into trouble. But I want you to know that I think you did the right thing in helping, the Godly thing. I'm proud of you for that."

A tear came to her eye and she dabbed it away with her sleeve. "Thank you." She had not expected his praise.

"You okay?"

"I guess. Not exactly a comfortable place to spend the day, but then, it's jail, not a motel. Never thought I'd be spending time here."

He placed his hand on hers across the table. "I placed a call to my lawyer, to get a recommendation for a good defense lawyer. Still waiting to hear from him."

The idea that she needed a defense lawyer hit home like their helicopter hitting the earth. The tears welled up freely. Her dad pulled a small packet of tissues from his jacket pocket and handed them to her.

"I stopped by your house. They're done processing the crime scene. That city detective was a big help since she basically witnessed the entire shooting. So, they've released your house back to you and the O'Malley's belongings have been removed. Their car was impounded."

"What about Sinead—and Ruth?"

"Nobody out here would tell me anything, but I called a friend at the county PD. Ruth is in custody of family services . . ."

Amy groaned. That would be the last place the girl would wish to be.

". . . and Sinead has been taken to the county lock-up. The FBI has stepped in and assumed custody since Sinead crossed state lines. My friend couldn't confirm any kind of timeline but guesses that mother and daughter will be returned to Massachusetts this weekend."

"Dad, I need to get out of here. I need to be in Boston for Sinead's hearing. I just have to be there."

He nodded. "We'll cross that bridge when we get to it. First, we have to find you a lawyer."

A knock at the door interrupted them. At first, she thought they'd gone past some kind of time limit for visits, but then realized they hadn't been together *that* long. A familiar face peeked around the door as it opened. Familiar, even though she had yet to meet the man personally.

"Mr. Graham?"

Her father appeared as shocked as she felt. Bradley Graham? The presidential candidate for the new American Party entered the room as two seriously dangerous-looking men stood outside.

He smiled and extended his hand toward her. "Amy, it's a pleasure to finally meet you. And you, sir, are?"

"I-I'm Andrew Gibbs, Amy's father. A pleasure to meet you as well." The men shook hands.

"An honor, Colonel, and thank you for your years of service to our country."

Bradley Graham knew about her father, too? Amy had no idea what to make of this turn of events but suspected Richard had his hand in this. He did, after all, work for the candidate. But then she thought, *How would Richard know what has happened? I haven't talked with him yet.*

"Did, um, Richard ask you to come here?"

He laughed. "No. In fact, he's up to his eyeballs in work right now. The social media software we're installing in the Washington office isn't performing as we had hoped. I don't think he knows about this yet. Aannddd . . . I figured this is something *you'd* want to tell him about."

"So . . ."

"Lynch Cully called me."

Lynch? Of course. She shouldn't have been surprised. With his years in local police work, before the incident with the L.A. Rapist that almost cost them both their lives, he still had a network of comrades whose antennae reached across the metro area. Maybe even the bi-state region. She had no doubt that as soon as the police call went out for a shooting at her address that someone was on the phone to him about it.

But, then, where was Lynch? As Mr. Graham's chief of security, he would be wherever Bradley Graham went.

"Lynch, by the way, isn't here. He's gone on ahead of me to my next stop. He wanted to see you but didn't have the time." He paused. "So, look, I wanted to stop by to give you a heads up. We've got this under control. I have a good friend who's a defense lawyer, and he should be here within the hour. As I understand these things, he'll spend some time talking with you and then arrange for your formal interview with the police, and maybe the local prosecutor. Our goal is to get you home without any charges, but at the least, we want to get you out of here. We'll cover any bail you might need, should it come to that, and work from there."

Amy sat there, stunned. She didn't know what to think, other than to be amazed that this busy man had taken time to get involved on her behalf. Even more, he seemed intent on handling the issue, to the degree he was even willing to extend the bail money if necessary.

"I-I don't know what to say. I will pay back any expenses, of course."

He held up a hand and shook his head. "Not necessary. I highly value both Richard and Lynch, and knowing what you mean to both of them, it's the least I can do for them, as well as for you." He paused for a second. "I'd love to get to know both of you better, but I have to run. I need to be in Austin in time for dinner." He turned to leave but stopped and turned back. "I forgot to tell you the name of the lawyer. It's Robert Sullivan. He should be here shortly. Bye."

Before Amy could say "goodbye," he was out the door. Her mind zoomed in on one phrase, ". . . knowing what you mean to both of them. . ." *Both* of them? How was she supposed to read that? What she meant to Richard was clear. They were engaged, after all. But, just what *did* she mean to Lynch? And for a split second, a second question flitted through her mind. What did Lynch mean to *her*?

She turned to her father and saw him sitting there,

mouth open. He said nothing.

"Dad?"

"He said Robert Sullivan, right? I heard him correctly, right?"

She nodded. "Yeah."

"Do you know who he is?"

She hadn't a clue. "Not at all."

"He's the city's top defense attorney."

This time, *she* was speechless. Would the day's surprises keep coming?

"I could be wrong, but I think a week's worth of his services could probably buy us a new airplane. And I'm sure he has, but I can't recall ever hearing about a case he's lost. Your Mr. Graham sure knows how to pick 'em."

Forty-Three

Tammy sat at her desk fiddling with a pen, her thoughts everywhere but at work. She wanted to go retrieve her kids from school, hug them, spoil them, and take them someplace safe to play. She thought she had been hardened to the worst cases. She'd seen more than enough of shootings, cuttings, deranged behavior, sexual deviancy, and the like. She'd dealt with the bereaved parents of toddlers who had died from senseless gang drive-bys. She thought of Montez dying in her arms.

She thought she had been hardened to the worst. She wasn't.

The thought of what that man must have gone through played over and over in her mind. To have lost his child over something so ridiculous as wanting a second doctor's opinion was awful enough. The torment that must have caused. The hours of grief. The vain efforts to convince the court they had been wrong. The worry over finances, wondering how he could ever pay the lawyers. To feel so powerless. She thought about losing one of her own children under that scenario. Only a year earlier, they had sought a second opinion about the need for a corrective surgery. What if?

But to know that his little girl had been horribly

abused at a foster home of the state's choosing, before dying at the hands of that same abuser was more than she could handle. She couldn't put herself in that place. What parent could? Would she have gone off the deep end, into depression, like his wife had?

And then to lose his wife to suicide. The final straw. The loss of everyone and everything he held dearest in his life. His words, "I'm coming, Marie. Daddy's coming, Christine," echoed through her mind. To have reached such a point of desperation that he wanted to take his own life. And would have, had she not arrived in time.

"You okay?" asked Sam as he walked into their office.

"No, I'm not." She realized he probably meant the flesh wound to her shoulder where the man's gun went off as she struck him and knocked him down. That wound was fine. Just a little sting from it now and then. The emotional toll, however . . .

"Want to talk about it?"

"No, I don't."

Sam turned around and started to leave.

"Sam, I-I'm sorry. I don't mean to take it out on you. My shoulder's fine, if that's what you're asking about."

"Hey, I understand. No problem."

From the look on his face, maybe she had been wrong about his being concerned about her shoulder. Still, she knew he didn't understand. He hadn't been there.

Sinead sat in the jail cell staring at the empty bunks. She felt as empty as the eight-by-ten space with its metal bunk beds and single metal chair, all bolted to the floor. At least she had the cell to herself, for the time being.

She fretted about Ruth. No one would tell her anything about her daughter. Where had they taken her? Had they placed her with some family who would have no idea how to manage her diet or health needs? Had they taken her to Children's Hospital? Maybe that would be a good thing. Maybe they could break the tie, so to speak, between Boston Children's and Tufts. And then, maybe they'd come up with a third diagnosis and muddy the waters even more.

More importantly, she worried about how Ruth would handle what she had witnessed. She needed the emotional support of her mother, her family, not some compassionless foster caregiver or pediatric therapist who would want her to go through daily support sessions.

An hour had made all the difference. Sixty minutes, maybe less. They would have been on the road, heading back to Boston on their own terms. Instead, she was in jail and Ruth was who-knows-where. She lowered her head and cried softly.

Forty-Four

Best lawyer in the city, eh? Home by nightfall. Right. So, why was she now eating a McDonald's Big Breakfast in the holding cell? The meal could have been worse. Amy wanted a shower and clean clothes but not as much as to be released home.

As she understood the law, the prosecutor had 24 hours to charge her with a crime or release her. That time limit was fast approaching.

There was a knock at the door and the hatch opened.

Amy could see a man in a suit through the opening.

"Amy Gibbs, I'm the local prosecutor. I know you're waiting on your legal counsel before giving any statement here, but I'm here to inform you that formal charges of abetting a felony kidnapping have been issued. The FBI has asked that we move you to the county jail and we will comply shortly. We'll let your lawyer know where to find you."

Amy hopped up onto her good leg. She had questions. Questions that would go unanswered as the hatch closed without further words.

She sat down and finished her breakfast. Fifteen minutes later, she heard the now familiar rattle of the hatch reopening. She hopped to it and passed the garbage from her meal through to the officer outside.

"Get ready to move. We've pulled your things together. You're heading to county now."

"But, my lawyer . . . he should be here soon. Can't we wait on him?"

"Sorry. We've got our orders."

What options did Amy have? Resisting would result in additional trouble. She didn't have a leg to stand on, and she cringed as the pun in that thought crossed through her mind.

"Told you!" The taunting voice of Diane Westlake came from the adjacent cell. "I'll be out on bail by lunch. *You're* going to the big house."

The woman had been arrested as well, on misdemeanor gun charges, and placed in the cell next to Amy. Throughout the previous evening she had thrown barb, after taunt, after snide remark toward Amy, until the jailer told her to shut up. At least Amy would no longer be a target for the woman. And she hoped and prayed that Westlake's forecast was just wind.

Twenty minutes later, Amy had been processed into the county jail and now walked toward her new cell. She marveled again at what she had experienced so far through this ordeal. Never in her life had she once thought that this was something she needed to know. She hoped the lesson would end soon.

She passed by one cell on the woman's floor and glanced through the viewing port. Sinead! She slowed down, and their eyes caught each other's gaze for a moment, before the officer told her to move along. In an instant, Sinead's face filled the port, and the look on her face filled Amy with sorrow. Amy already knew that Sinead felt defeated at being caught and from the fear of losing her daughter forever. Now she saw total remorse, for putting Amy behind bars as well.

Amy thought she had died in her sleep and gone to hell. She sat alone in her cell, tormented by the thought of facing time in prison and worse, of losing her career. For as far back as she could remember, she had wanted to be a nurse, to help people. She loved her job, despite the harsh realities of that job at times, of watching others suffer from their own hand and those of others. Was this loss to be her personal demon?

In the darkness, she heard others along the hall crying. Their anguish added to hers. Yet, they could not reach out to comfort each other. Others along the hall chided and mocked the criers for waking them. Some threatened. Yes, this was as close to the Biblical Sheol as she ever wished to encounter.

After such a fitful night, she had no appetite. But she also had no choice when the time came for breakfast. She was rousted from her cell and forced to move into the cafeteria with the others. The guards paid close attention to her, but she surmised that this was due to their concern over another inmate taking and making malicious use of Amy's crutches.

She juggled her tray and the crutches, sat down by herself, and took a few bites. Now, she wished she had that McDonald's Big Breakfast. That would be a gourmet meal compared to what sat on the table before her. She looked about the room for Sinead. She never appeared. Amy wondered if she was allowed to inquire about her but decided not to.

"Eat up. You're wanted in the interview room. Your legal eagle is here."

The guard surprised her from behind.

Amy finished her last few bites and stood up. The officer pointed to the place where her tray needed to go. She complied and followed the woman to a locked door. The door opened and they entered a different hallway. *No cuffs today?* she thought. Had they finally realized she was no threat to them, or was she about to be released? Soon, she sat in the interview room facing Mr. Sullivan for the second time.

"Amy, I'm so sorry this is taking longer than we expected. I never thought you would end up here. Are you doing okay?"

"As well as can be expected after all this wonderful food and trying to sleep on a rock." That came out a little more harshly than she planned. "Sorry, I had trouble sleeping, between their excuse for a bed and my leg. I'm a little cranky."

"Fair enough. I've dealt with a lot worse than cranky."

He paused and seemed to study her face. In turn, she scrutinized his well-coiffed, salt-and-pepper hair, the even tan, and the fine lines beginning to emerge around his eyes. The whimsical, polka-dotted bow tie seemed to belie the fire she saw in those eyes. She hoped he had good news.

"The delay has been the result of jurisdictional issues. The police interview from yesterday was turfed from the county prosecutor to the U.S. Attorney. They, in turn, have been in consultation with their counterparts in Boston."

The man paused as if he was about to deliver bad

news. "And?"

"And Assistant U.S. Attorney Cheever will be here in about 15 minutes to question you directly."

Amy fought letting her breakfast become a big barf at that instant. It was one thing to give her statement to the local detective and quite another to have to talk with a U.S. Attorney. Her thoughts went to Lynch, and how she'd feel more confident if he was with them. And that thought shook her. Why hadn't she thought of Richard? Had she considered Lynch simply because of his years as a police officer and his criminal justice background? Had she?

"Just be yourself. Relax. She's already read your statement to the police and has some additional questions. I think this is a good sign myself. I don't think this is a slam-dunk case for them, and they only take cases they know they'll win."

Amy didn't know if that was as clear to her, but *he* was the defense attorney.

Ten minutes later, a police officer opened the door, and a slim, African-American female who looked to be in her forties walked in. She appeared immaculate in her olive green, skirted suit and close-cropped natural hair. She laid her briefcase on the table and extended her hand.

"Ms. Gibbs, I'm Assistant U.S. Attorney Amanda Cheever."

"Ms. Cheever," said Amy as she stood up.

They shook hands, and the attorney turned to face Mr. Sullivan. "Robert, nice to see you again."

Amy sat back down and placed her hands on the table.

Ms. Cheever pulled a folder from her case, took a deep breath, and let it out. "So, Ms. Gibbs, I believe you know the charge that's pending for your involvement in this case with the O'Malleys. I've read your report and have some questions."

"Yes, ma'am."

"You initially told the people who found you at the farm in Illinois that you somehow managed to get out of the aircraft, fashioned a crutch, and found your way to the farmhouse and barn on your own. That's quite the feat considering your leg injury, but we hear of such things often these days. People are quite resilient and resourceful. And yet, you told the police that Sinead O'Malley actually pulled you from the wreckage and took you to the house, where she administered first aid and cared for you. Would you please explain the discrepancy for me?"

Amy explained how she had been under the impression that Sinead was hiding from an abusive spouse, of her experiences working with battered women in a shelter, and how she came up with the idea of making it look like she had gone to the barn on her own so that Sinead could remain hidden and safe. She mentioned that Sinead had wanted to take her someplace to get care, but that the creek had washed out the bridge, and they were stranded at the house until the water receded.

"Did you know who they were at that point?"

"No. But she acted like someone in hiding, in fear of being discovered. She reminded me of women at that shelter. And despite that, she risked discovery by saving me from that crash and offering to take me for help."

"You say she 'saved' you. Do you think you would have died if she hadn't pulled you from the wreckage?"

"I believe so, yes. She had to clear the cabin of debris in order to help me out of my restraint. In my condition, I think I would have fallen and been impaled on that debris, if I had tried to get out on my own. And there was a fire. She got me out just before it started. If it had been five minutes later, I would have been toast, literally, from what I've been told."

"What happened in the barn?"

Amy explained her actions in the barn, just as she had to the detective. She described hurting herself in her attempts to get into the truck.

"When did you learn who the O'Malleys were?"

"As I recovered in the hospital, I found an email with the renewed AMBER Alert and recognized them."

"Why do you think they searched you out at the hospital?"

"They explained that they became worried when they saw the men carry me out of the barn and I was unconscious. Sinead felt responsible for whatever had happened in the barn because I was protecting her. They needed to find out if I was okay."

"So, at that point, you knew who they were, and, yet, you didn't call the authorities. In fact, you offered them shelter in your home."

Amy took a deep breath. This wasn't going as well as she had hoped.

"True. I had seen, for a brief period at the farm, the love Sinead had for Ruth, and I witnessed firsthand how Ruth was improving in Sinead's care. The court in Boston was wrong in taking Ruth away from her family."

"That isn't your call to make."

Amy nodded. It wasn't. "Also true, but Sinead had no chance of proving that as long as Ruth remained in the care of a rehab facility that wasn't performing any rehab. Sinead's plan all along was to show the court that Ruth would flourish with her family, that she and her husband were not medically abusing their daughter somehow. With Ruth having regained ten pounds, rebuilt her strength to the point of walking on her own, and looking healthier than she has at any point since becoming a ward of the state, Sinead was going to return to Boston on her own, to prove to the court that she knew the proper care for her daughter. If things hadn't gone crazy at my house yesterday, they'd be in Boston today." She shook her head in bewilderment. "I still don't know where those other two people came from."

"Still, as a first-responder you know you have a duty to report certain things. Instead of honoring that commitment, you harbored a fugitive."

Amy didn't have to think through her response to this. "Ms. Cheever, sometimes we have to do the *right* thing, as God would have us do it. God set up society with the family as its hub, not the state. The state was morally wrong in taking Ruth O'Malley away from her parents. If you disagree, then where is the due process for these parents? Isn't that a Constitutional right? And one other thing. Take away the whole family versus state issue. Ignore that part of this case. Would you have turned in someone, someone who is no threat to society, who had saved your life just days earlier?"

At that response, the attorney sat back and stared at Amy. After a minute of silence, Ms. Cheever rose and gathered her materials.

"Ms. Gibbs, thank you. Robert, I'll get back with you within the hour."

Mr. Sullivan stood to watch the attorney leave but said nothing to Amy. His silence spoke for him. She was going to have to get used to orange jumpsuits.

Forty-Five

Amy felt like skipping down the concourse to the boarding gate. Figuring out how to do that on crutches was another matter. Somehow the threat of losing her freedom had made that freedom even more valuable.

Three days earlier, she had faced the Assistant U.S. Attorney and convinced her that prosecution was not that "slam-dunk" case they sought. Her councilor, Robert Sullivan, had told her that the emotional overtones of the case had made it unlikely that a jury would convict, even when instructed to keep in mind only the law. What jurist would not feel the same empathy for Sinead O'Malley as Amy had felt? And who could not identify with honoring someone who had saved your life?

Mr. Sullivan had told her that her own testimony had saved her this time. He claimed to have had no influence on the outcome and applauded her for the actions she took and the reasons she took them. He had even waived his fee.

Now, having yet to return to work, she chose to cash in some vacation time. Craig hadn't been happy about it, but under the circumstances, he, too, appreciated her reason for the time off. Boston, look out.

Fortunately, her Southwest flight out of Terminal 2 didn't require a long walk. Her father had helped her deal with her single piece of luggage, and an airline employee had assured her she would get assistance at Boston's Logan Airport. She had had to use crutches for all of a week and already tired of them. She wanted her independence to rejoin her freedom.

At the gate she sat down and focused on her phone. A flood of emails again threatened to shut down her account. With the backlog in her In-box, she could spend the remainder of the day reading and deleting mail.

"Ms. Gibbs?"

Amy looked up to see Detective Jahn standing next to her, a carry-on bag at her feet and a ticket in hand. She wondered where the detective was heading.

"Is this seat taken?" The detective smiled.

"Detective Jahn, this is a surprise. Please have a seat." Amy shuffled her purse to the opposite side of her chair to give the woman more room.

After settling in, the detective said, "Please, call me Tammy."

"And I'm Amy."

"I heard they declined to press any charges. Good for you."

Amy proceeded to tell Tammy of her 24-hour ordeal. She finished by asking, "Are you going to Boston?"

"I am. I suspect we have the same goal in mind. After spending time with Diane Westlake, I want to testify to her instability. It might help Sinead O'Malley, and others the woman took children from, for the court to know the woman had issues that might have affected her judgment in all her cases. And you and I can both testify to its outcome."

"Unfortunately."

"That man, Jeremy Meecham—his story has haunted

me since the shooting. The pain he must suffer."

They talked more about the incident, which Amy found cathartic. The conversation didn't end with that, however. Amy asked Tammy to be her assistant for boarding since her crutches would put her ahead of the line. Together, they found seats where Amy had room for her casted leg. By the end of the flight, they had discovered half a dozen mutual friends, not least of which was Lynch Cully.

Forty-Six

Amy and Tammy emerged from the hotel, having found rooms there for both of them the night before, and flagged down a taxi to take them to the family court. Tammy had used her position, as well as the fact that both had witnessed the incident with Diane Westlake, to learn when the O'Malley hearings would take place. Jameson was expected to appear first, and everyone expected him to be released, now that his wife and daughter had returned to the city.

They entered the courtroom 45 minutes early and discovered they weren't the only ones who thought they should arrive early for a seat. The place was already standing room only. However, a young woman in the front row caught their attention and waved them forward.

"You must be the women from St. Louis, right? I was told to look for a woman on crutches."

Amy nodded. "That would be us. I'm Amy Gibbs and this is Detective Tammy Jahn."

"Great. I'm Dawn, Mr. Pfeiffer's paralegal. He's defending the O'Malleys. He asked me to save you both seats, so here you go." She pointed to the two chairs next to the one where she had been sitting. "If you don't mind, could I get you to watch my seat for me? I need to go let him know you're here."

"Sure," replied Tammy.

They watched the people in the room and tried to discern each one's reason for being there. The reporters were obvious. Some appeared to be court groupies. The hearing was to be public, due to the intense public interest and despite the reservations of the Department of Children and Family. The judge had asked only one person to see if she had an objection, and Ruth had been enthusiastic in her favor of an open hearing when asked by phone. The judge had not yet seen her.

With five minutes left before the announced start time, three men entered the room from a side door, along with Dawn. Two of the men placed their papers on the table in front of Amy. The third carried nothing but made a beeline toward her. He was about to say something when young voices from the back interrupted.

"Daddy!"

"Daddy!"

A boy and a girl, both younger than Ruth, ran down the central aisle toward him. A broad smile crossed his face, and he stepped to the gate at the end of the aisle. He let them through the gate and scooped them up in his arms, hugging and kissing them both. "Colleen, Kevin. I have missed you both!"

"Do you get to come home today?" asked the little girl.

"I hope so, honey. We'll find out shortly. Tell you what, go back and sit with *Maimeo* and *Daideo*. I have something to do and we start in a few minutes." He let both down and watched them run back to their grandmother and grandfather. He then stepped back over to face Amy and Tammy.

"Ladies, I'm Jameson. I want to thank you both for appearing on our behalf. You can't imagine how good this makes me feel. Mr. Pfeiffer told me what happened with you both. At least, as much as you told him by phone. I hope the court looks favorably at what you have to say."

"We do, too, Jameson. I got to know your wife and daughter pretty well over the course of a few days. I can't imagine how hard this has been for you all."

He nodded and started to reply, but Mr. Pfeiffer stepped in. "I'm Patrick Pfeiffer. Thank you both. I wish we'd had time to prep you for testimony, but under the circumstances, we weren't given that option. Are you ready? Have either of you testified in court before?"

Both nodded.

"Good. I guess I expected that *you* had, Detective. Glad to see you both have some experience here. I don't know what kind of questions to expect from the state, so do your best. Actually, they might protest your testimonies from the beginning. As you probably know, we have this thing called 'discovery' in the legal system. It helps prevent surprises, for everyone, including the judge. They hate surprises more than the lawyers. Anyway, it really doesn't apply for a hearing like this, but he might try to use it as a basis for objecting to your testimony. They might argue that they've had no time to depose you and prepare for your testimonies."

The din of the courtroom suddenly quieted, and Amy looked up, expecting the bailiff to announce the judge. But that wasn't the case. She looked around to find everyone's eyes fixated on the back row, behind the State's table. After a second, Amy saw whom they saw. Diane Westlake.

Obviously, the woman had been correct about getting

released on bail. Yet, Amy had never expected her to have the chutzpah to come to these hearings in person. What did the woman expect? Vindication? Did she come to gloat?

The bailiff got the attention of the court and announced the judge. Judge Waverly entered the room, sat down, and called the hearing into session.

Fifteen minutes later, after some technicalities were resolved, Jameson O'Malley was a free man, his contempt charge dropped. With that decision made, Sinead O'Malley was ushered into the courtroom from the side door. She walked up to and hugged her husband, who then walked to the back of the room, picked up Colleen, and sat down in her chair with her on his lap. Amy smiled as she heard a faint but distinct, "Yay, Daddy!" from the back.

Amy looked about and wondered where Ruth was sequestered. She had thought the girl would be here.

Judge Waverly looked at Sinead and her lawyer. "Mr. Pfeiffer, I've read your request and have to state that this is a bit out of line. The kidnapping charge has become a federal case and no longer falls into the jurisdiction of even the state courts, much less this family court. I'm not sure why you've requested this hearing."

"Your Honor, you're right. This is highly unusual, and this court is not the proper place for this," interrupted the state's attorney.

Amy saw a scowl cross the face of the judge.

"Mr. Wesley, I addressed Mr. Pfeiffer, not you."

"But, Your Honor—"

"*Mister* Wesley! I will not tolerate your repeated interruptions. *Please.* Let the defendant's counsel answer my question."

"But—"

"Do I need to have my bailiff remove you from the courtroom? Perhaps you'd like to take up residence in the cell Mr. O'Malley just vacated."

The state attorney frowned but bowed his head in submission.

The judge turned back to Mr. Pfeiffer. "Mr. Pfeiffer."

"Yes, Your Honor, I know this is unusual. I've asked Boston's Assistant U.S. Attorney to join us." He nodded toward a distinguished-looking man in the first row, behind the State's table. "Thank you for coming, Mr. Jarvis." He turned back to the judge. "My hope is that from today's hearing you'll release Ruth back to the care of her parents, and that, in turn, will make the kidnapping charge a moot issue."

Amy noted the State's Attorney, Mr. Wesley, looked incredulous at that suggestion, while Mr. Jarvis maintained a poker face. Amy began to wonder what good her testimony at this hearing would achieve.

"Your Honor, as you know, Sinead and Ruth O'Malley were discovered in a suburb of St. Louis and returned to the state two days ago. We have with us today, two people from St. Louis who can give this court a first-hand account of what happened there. I realize that Mr. Wesley has not had an opportunity to depose these women. Please understand that I, too, have had no time with them. In fact, I just now met them. They come to this court on their own volition because their experiences with Sinead O'Malley *and* with Diane Westlake, while in St. Louis, led them to do so. I think the court should hear them out."

Mr. Wesley jumped to his feet. "Objection, Your Honor. The State would like time to talk with these new witnesses."

The judge sighed. "I think you'll have that opportunity

shortly, Mr. Wesley. Right here, with all of us. I, for one, would like to hear what they have to say. This is a hearing, not a trial, and *I* would like to *hear* from them."

"Thank you, Your Honor," replied Mr. Pfeiffer. "I'd like to ask Detective Tammy Jahn, of the St. Louis Police Department, to take the stand first."

Tammy talked for ten minutes about her experiences with Diane Westlake and her concern that the woman was unbalanced, although she didn't quite put it that way, with the woman sitting just 30 feet away. Still, when she mentioned that Westlake had pulled a gun and shot a hole in Amy's ceiling, the message came across clearly without sounding slanderous. Amy tried to glance back at Westlake to see her reaction, but the angle was too awkward to do so discreetly.

Mr. Pfeiffer guided her through some clarifications for another five minutes. Mr. Wesley didn't hesitate to jump at her conclusion when his turn came around.

"So, Detective, are you a qualified medical professional? Is that how you came up with your *diagnosis* of Ms. Westlake?" Sarcasm dripped from his use of the word "diagnosis."

Amy tried to hide her smile as she watched Tammy fight to control her eyes rolling.

"Well, sir, how else would you describe someone who used false credentials and then attempted to take the O'Malleys at gunpoint, effectively committing the felony of kidnapping herself? Did she really think that her actions would somehow clear her name? To think that way speaks of an unbalanced mind to me. How about you? And, to answer your question directly, I actually have a degree in clinical psychology and am licensed as such in the State of

Missouri. I practiced clinical psychology for two years before deciding to go to the Police Academy and put my training to a different use."

Mr. Wesley appeared surprised and upset at the same time. Amy was sure that now he really would have liked time to depose them both before this hearing, to avoid just this type of surprise as Mr. Pfeiffer had mentioned. Tammy's testimony spoke well to Diane Westlake's personality at the time.

The judge leaned toward the witness chair and asked, "Could you tell us more about the shooting?"

"Yes, ma'am." She described the scene at Amy's house upon her arrival that morning, relaying the story of Jeremy Meecham both from his words that morning, as well as from what she had learned from news accounts about the case. "Mr. Meecham is currently hospitalized and under close suicide watch."

"I remember that case," said the judge. "It occurred just before I took this bench."

"Your Honor, I'm not trying to tell anyone how to do their job, but I personally would take a close look at *all* of Diane Westlake's cases. I'd hate to see a repeat of the Meecham case."

Amy sensed all eyes drifting toward the back of the room. She wished she had a different seat, so she could join the stares.

The judge looked as if she would take that under advisement. "Thank you, Detective." She looked at both attorneys. "Do either of you have any more questions?" Both men shook their heads. "Detective, you may step down."

Amy took a deep breath as she was called to the stand.

Her testimony took over 20 minutes and rehashed everything she had told the police and Assistant U.S. Attorney in St. Louis. Mr. Pfeiffer followed up with several questions.

"So, have you personally dealt with cases of child abuse?"

"Yes, sir. As an E.D. nurse and as a flight nurse, I have cared for children who were victims of abuse. In every case, a parent or boyfriend was charged with a crime. In this case, to my knowledge, the O'Malleys have never been charged with a crime, or abuse of any of their children. And the other O'Malley children were never taken from the parents."

"That is correct. During your time with the O'Malleys, did you see anything, have any concerns at all, that led you to think Sinead O'Malley was abusing her daughter, Ruth?"

"No, sir. None at all. In fact, quite the opposite. I saw in Sinead O'Malley only love and concern for her daughter's well-being. She told me that her reason for taking Ruth was that her child was deteriorating in the care of the rehab center where Ruth had been placed, and that she couldn't watch her daughter's health worsen any further."

She saw the state attorney begin to protest but refrain from doing so. She realized her last statement was only hearsay, but she wanted to make it known.

"Thank you. Mr. Wesley?" Mr. Pfeiffer sat down, smiling.

"Ms. Gibbs, are you an expert on Munchhausen's Syndrome or Munchhausen by Proxy?"

"No, sir."

"So, you can't really testify as to whether or not Ruth O'Malley was a victim of such."

"No, sir, but I took time to research the topic a bit.

Seems to me that it's a diagnosis no one can ever prove. There's no definitive test. It frequently becomes a case of he-said-she said, and in my opinion,—"

"I didn't ask your opinion," stated Mr. Wesley. "

The judge frowned again. "However, *I* would like to hear your opinion, Ms. Gibbs."

"Yes, Your Honor. I think it becomes an easy diagnosis to abuse if doctors can't find the real cause of a problem, or a state worker wants to prove a point, like Ms. Westlake appeared to do. Medicine has come a long way, but we don't know everything. I had a friend who frequently went to her doctor with abdominal pain. She was referred to her OB/Gyn who thought she might have endometriosis. A laparoscopic procedure failed to find any. She saw a general surgeon who ended up removing her appendix. That didn't solve the pain issue. She had several visits to a gastroenterologist. No progress was made. She was a prime candidate for being labeled with Munchhausen's. It took her seeing an obscure post on the internet, purely by happenstance, to learn she was allergic to yeast. Yeast, of all things. And two common fruits. By eliminating those from her diet, her pain disappeared."

The judge looked contemplative. "What did you see during your time with the O'Malleys?"

"Well, ma'am, I can testify to the improvement Ruth had under the care of her mother. If her mother was using Ruth to get attention, why would she seek to improve her daughter's health? I don't see that as Munchhausen by Proxy." She went on to describe her time with the mother and daughter.

The judge looked at the attorneys. "Any more questions, gentlemen?" Mr. Pfeiffer shook his head.

"I have no other questions, Your Honor." Mr. Wesley, who had been standing while the judge asked questions, now sat down.

Amy sat down, wondering if Mr. Wesley feared another "ambush" and so avoided more questions. She had gotten off light.

Mr. Pfeiffer stood and said, "I'd like to call Sinead O'Malley to the stand."

Sinead took the stand.

"Mrs. O'Malley, I have just one question for you. Why did you take your daughter from the rehab center?"

"To save her life."

Amy glanced at Diane Westlake in time to see the woman sigh and roll her eyes. Hadn't she changed at all?

Sinead continued, "At the center, she lost 20 pounds and became restricted to a wheelchair. They weren't feeding her the proper diet for her condition. I took her to save her life and to prove to this court that the diagnosis from her first doctors was correct. If we waited around for the two groups of doctors to come to agreement, it might have been too late for Ruth. I followed the recommendations and diet that we'd been following before taking her to the E.D. at Children's Hospital."

"So, you resumed your care as prescribed by the doctors at Tufts, the care you were providing *before* Ruth was taken from you. The care the doctors at Boston Children's said *wasn't* appropriate. Correct?"

Sinead nodded and said, "Yes."

Mr. Pfeiffer turned to face Judge Waverly. "Your Honor, I understand you've not had an opportunity to visit Ruth since her return. Do you recall Ruth from your last visit with her?"

"I do. She was frail and in a wheelchair, just as her mother described."

"Well, Your Honor, after a month in the care of her mother, I'd like you to see Ruth O'Malley now."

Amy shifted her gaze toward Westlake again, wishing she could record what was about to come on video.

He nodded to his paralegal standing at the main door to the courtroom. As she opened the door, Amy watched the social worker crane her neck to get a better look. But, it was the look of surprise and then absolute defeat that erupted on her face that caught Amy's attention.

Ruth walked in and stopped, smiling, her complexion glowing. Gasps echoed through the room. She then walked down the aisle, opened the gate and walked up to the bench where she curtsied.

"Good morning, Judge Waverly."

Forty-Seven

Amy spied the copy of *USA Today* that had been slipped under her door as she slept. She picked it up and quietly hobbled to the chair near her bed. She moved the curtain and let the morning light illuminate the pages.

She hadn't slept well. After giving their testimonies two days earlier, she and Tammy found themselves enveloped by the news media. They gave brief interviews with each of the major network stations in Boston, as well as *USA Today* and the local papers. The Assistant U.S. Attorney who had been present at the hearing also requested time to talk with them. By the time they had finished, dinner beckoned.

But that was yesterday's morning headlines, and following a late breakfast, they decided to do some sightseeing. By the time they finished the southern half of the Freedom Trail from Boston Common to Old North Church, Amy had had enough "walking." Yet, more frustrating was the fact that they still had no decision from Judge Waverly. So, between sore arms, an aching leg, and the emotional turmoil from the judge's indecision, sleep had evaded her.

Today's headlines spoke of new tensions in the Middle

East and of more political wrangling in Washington. She scanned the pages of the front section. Nada. Nothing about the O'Malleys.

The phone on the opposite side of the bed rang. She climbed across the bed to answer.

"Hope I'm not calling too early. I've been up for an hour, but I'm so used to getting up for work that I find it impossible to sleep in."

"No problem. I was just reading the paper, looking for something on the O'Malleys."

"Yeah, I looked, too, and didn't find anything. I guess the judge still hasn't decided." She paused. "So, are you up for more sightseeing today? You looked exhausted at dinner last night."

Amy wavered. She'd never been to Boston before and didn't want to miss out on the opportunity to see more of the old city and its history. They would be flying home the next morning, so this was her last chance. "I guess so. I'm tired, but maybe we can go to the harbor and see Old Ironsides. I've always wanted to see that ship and maybe there won't be as much walking."

"You sure?"

Amy shrugged. "I'll manage."

Maybe she could find one of those little scooters to rent. If not, so what. She didn't want to miss out. She could collapse after dinner. They had a supper invitation they couldn't pass up.

By four p.m., they had seen not only the USS Constitution but also Bunker Hill and the sights along the northern half of the Freedom Trail. As it ended up, the day's activities had not been as taxing for Amy, and their location put them closer to dinner.

The taxi took them onto Route 99 and within a reasonable time—reasonable for Boston traffic—they entered the town of Everett, a working-class neighborhood of older two-story frame homes. The taxi pulled up to their destination, and the women emerged onto the sidewalk.

Amy looked up onto the front porch and saw the two younger O'Malley children playing quietly. They slowly ascended the stairs to the porch and were greeted by Jameson's mother. Amy felt downcast by the somber mood surrounding her.

"I hope we're not too early. Jameson said to come around five."

"Not at all, deary. Please. Come in. Let's get you a chair where you can put your foot up." She pointed to an upholstered chair with a hassock. "Can I get you something to drink? We have wine, beer, soda—and of course, iced tea, hot tea or water."

Tammy opted for a beer; Amy, iced tea.

Tammy looked around as the woman went for their drinks. "Awfully quiet here."

Amy nodded. Maybe this hadn't been such a good idea. Yet, Jameson insisted on their joining them for dinner before they left town.

"Here you go." Mrs. O'Malley "Senior" handed them their drinks.

"Thank you, Mrs. O'Malley," said Amy.

"Oh, please. Call me Eileen. My husband is Conan. He'll be back in a minute. Jameson got called into the city but should be back shortly, too. He didn't tell me why."

The women made small talk, but after a bit, that began

to seem strained. Amy felt out of place.

Young Colleen came running through the front door. "Maimeo, come look! Come look!"

The grandmother arose and walked to the front door. "Oh my!"

Amy and Tammy joined her, and the three walked onto the front porch in time to see a Channel 5 news van pull up onto the street. Within minutes, vans from channels 2, 4, and 7 filled one end of the street. It was then that Amy heard car horns blaring in the distance. Neighbors along both sides of the street began to fill their porches and the sidewalks.

Eight-year-old Kevin pointed down the street. "It's Daddy's car . . . and he's leading a parade. Look!"

Amy looked and saw a line of cars coming up from the end of the street opposite the news vans. The lead car pulled in front of the house and stopped. With a grin from ear-to-ear Jameson exited the driver's door and lifted his hands into the air. He stepped around to the front passenger door and opened it. Sinead emerged and pointed to heaven with her right hand.

People from the other cars abandoned their vehicles and surrounded the O'Malley's car. Some held signs saying "Welcome Home." Others whistled and clapped.

And yet, the scene wasn't complete. Then, together Jameson and Sinead opened the back door and helped Ruth from the car. The three stood smiling as the younger siblings ran down the steps to join them—a family united once again.

Afterword

Who doesn't like a happy ending? Unfortunately, hundreds of families and thousands of children are still waiting for theirs.

As I pointed out in the book, these children have been ripped away from loving families by overzealous, sometimes corrupt, social workers employed by their respective states. They claim they are protecting the children. That sounds like something we all want. Right? After all, no one wants to see a child being abused. Those truly engaged in physical abuse are typically charged and tried. However, with the families involved here, there have been no charges. These parents have not been given their constitutionally guaranteed right to due process under the law.

So, why do these state agencies take these children? I mentioned a number of alleged reasons in the story. All seven children in an Arkansas family were removed from their home because a social worker saw a threat to them in the form of a mineral supplement purchased by the father—purchased at a GNC store. He used it to treat a growth on the skin of one child and it caused a chemical burn. Two sisters were taken from their parents in Arizona because the parents refused to enroll them in a medical study at the university—a study in which they would be no more than test subjects. Some might call that being guinea pigs. The muse for this story, as I mentioned, was a girl whose plight began because two sets of doctors disagreed on her diagnosis. Others have been taken because their parents refused to have them immunized, or because their parent wanted a second doctor's opinion. A lawsuit, in progress as I write this, alleges that the child was removed to cover up medical malpractice by a hospital and one of its employed physicians. A 17-year-old girl in Connecticut, just months shy of legally becoming an adult, was taken by force because she refused chemotherapy, a decision her mother agreed with. In Detroit, the Michigan C.P.S. took a daughter from her homeschooling mother for the mother's refusal to give her developmentally disabled child powerful anti-psychotic drugs. They sent a SWAT team to take the girl.

However, the story goes deeper than most reports show. Investigative journalists and others are finally shedding some light on this growing pandemic. Homeschoolers are a prime target, as are the poor who haven't the resources to fight back. Conflicts over immunizations are a common issue. But worse than that, there's growing corruption within the Family Courts and Child "Protective" Services in which social workers are rewarded for taking children and placing them within the foster care system. The federal Adoption and Safe Families Act of 1997 provides money to the state for every child placed into foster care and then adopted out. It also fines states for not moving these children into stable, adoptive homes within a certain timeframe. Social workers are being promoted and given bonuses for their actions. This has pressured the family courts into stripping parental rights from parents who have done nothing wrong, where in the past, parental rights were retained as long as the child was in foster care. In Kentucky, the number of children moved from foster care into adoption in 1999 was 384. By 2005, that number had increased to 902, resulting in over $1M in *bonuses* granted to the state by the federal government. That's above and beyond the $4,000 per child granted to the state just for placing a child in foster care.

The same investigative report, by station WLKY in Louisville, outlined detailed corruption: C.P.S. supervisors changing records, pushing adoptions through instead of seeking reunification of the family, and using retaliatory power. Kentucky's lucrative C.P.S. adoption business includes stories of adopting children to foster families with known criminal records, and even to families residing with convicted sex offenders. One former social worker and whistle-blower refused to ignore allegations of sexual abuse in a foster home and refused her supervisors' request to arrange an adoption for these abusers. The lawsuit that resulted from her being fired cost the state $400,000 at settlement. Another C.P.S. worker witnessed a family "order" a child they wanted to adopt, and well-placed individuals could request and be granted children. For one parent who fought back and won, C.P.S. retaliated by having her relatives' children and her attorney's child taken from them. This corruption has been highlighted, yet little has changed.

Some might think these children are better off having been removed from their allegedly abusive parents. However, studies continue to show that these children do not fare well. In the short term, social workers often fail to investigate the foster homes, as mandated by law, and, as

I've pointed out, even ignore the fact when these homes include criminals and sex offenders. But long-term consequences are as dismal. These children are frequently placed on powerful drugs, with all of the complications those drugs incur. Also, data supplied by the Colorado Department of Human Services shows that only 29% of foster youth in that state will graduate from high school on time. Yet, at least 38% will have been incarcerated at some time between ages 16 and 19. National data is worse. Of those who leave foster care, 43% of women and 74% of men will have been in jail at least once in their lives. In summary, one study showed that children in foster care were three times more likely to become criminals than had they stayed with their "abusive" families.

So, what can be done? Awareness is the first step, and I hope this story has made you aware of this problem. If you want more information, www.MedicalKidnap.com is brimming with reports of individual cases. You can also help spread this awareness through social media. Beyond awareness, I hope you might support efforts in your state to reform the family court system. You might also consider supporting those who are fighting back. The Detroit mom mentioned above is currently suing the state. D.F.S. and the prosecutor there have taken her to court FOUR times, and lost their case four times. Yet, they persist in trying to take this girl from her mother and put the mother in jail. This time she's striking back with a lawsuit of her own, but she needs financial support. The Parental Rights Foundation (www.parentalrightsfoundation.org), founded in 2014, is helping, but lack of funds has this mom's legal team down to one pro-bono lawyer. Other lawsuits are taking place: a large class-action suit in Phoenix, a similar case in San

Diego, and a multitude of smaller cases across the country. The wave of lawsuits is having results. The discovery process of a lawsuit has brought to light the corruption and the threat of financial consequences has state workers concerned. We need to increase the pressure to change this system. I hope you'll help.

SNEAK PREVIEW:

A ZEALOT'S DESTINY

One

Prince Gregory raised his nose in the air and sniffed. He furrowed his brow at the odor and summoned his chief of staff from across the room.

"Is that gas I smell? The rest of the family will be arriving shortly."

Gregory turned 56 that day, and the extended family now began to assemble to celebrate. Some of them had already arrived, and the last thing he needed was to evacuate his home because of some minor gas leak.

The aide sniffed the air as well, and shook his head. "I don't believe so, sir. The exterminators were out this morning while you were in the city. They assured me there would be no residual odors, but I'm afraid they were in error."

The prince looked at his watch and then back toward his assistant. "Are you quite sure? I've never smelled bug spray like this."

The man smiled and looked at his employer. "Sir, can you tell me when you've ever smelled bug spray?"

The prince cocked his head, looked askance, and then smiled. "Right, Geoffrey. Now that you say that, I'm not sure I have. Well, at least since boarding school."

Geoffrey was correct. The Royal Family never had to put up with certain occurrences of daily life. Services such as exterminators, plumbers, and the like worked whatever hours were necessary to avoid inconvenience to the family.

Besides, the Royal Lodge in Windsor Great Park, a 30-room mansion on the Grade II list of royal residences, was in tip-top shape. The prince had spent £7.5 million to fully restore the grand building, its grounds with eight additional staff buildings, and the private chapel. The buildings underwent inspection routinely, and maintenance was scheduled and proactive. The odds of a gas leak were nil.

He walked about the room, sniffing. The odor was indeed faint but seemed strongest near the front hallway.

"My older brother should be here momentarily. His youngest son is escorting, the Queen and they're running late. Please inform security." He reflected on the still present odor. "And, please have someone check the gas lines."

The aide nodded. "Yes, sir. In fact, I will check the basement area myself, for expediency. It might take time to get one of the maintenance workers here, being supper time and all."

"Thank you, Geoffrey."

Geoffrey Hand had been Prince Gregory's Chief of Staff for over 15 years and adored the Royal Family. As a boy, he had daydreamed of being a rugged prince and finding a beautiful princess to take as his bride. Of course, that would never be, but the idea had led him to work hard at school, excel at sports, and join the military for a brief stint.

And yet, it was the one sport he failed to master that caught royal notice. Polo. He nearly fell off the horse with every swing of his mallet. After one disastrous practice match, where he did indeed fall from his mount, he rose from the ground to find the prince offering him a hand up, while calling him the worst polo player he'd ever seen. From there, the friendship grew and this position had been offered him. How could he refuse? Now, he and his wife of 30 years lived on the grounds, and they hobnobbed with royalty . . . within limits. He would do anything for the family.

Geoffrey walked through the kitchen and found the staff scurrying about. They didn't cater to the Queen frequently, so he knew they were seeking perfection. Besides, the entire, immediate Royal Family would be attending. They sought to please more than just Her Majesty.

"Are any of the maintenance fellows still about?"

Simultaneously, half the heads in the room shook negatively.

"Do you smell gas?"

The head cook looked at him askance. "Seriously? We're in the kitchen. Look about. How many gas burners do you see working at the moment? Do we smell gas? When *don't* we smell gas in here?"

Geoffrey chuckled. "Sorry. The prince is smelling gas, and I'm to investigate."

Another cook pointed with her thumb over her right shoulder. "That way to the basement."

He nodded. He knew how to get there. Walking down the hall, he came to the door leading to the basement and stopped. He looked around for other staff members to question about what he had found but saw no one. Of course, it was late and only the kitchen staff remained to prepare for the birthday party and to feed the drivers who would be missing their own meals while carting the family members from place to place.

Again, he turned toward the door and stared at it. Someone had sealed the door with clear tape, like that used for packages. Someone walking past would be unlikely to notice it in the dim evening light. In fact, he had not noted it until grabbing the doorknob and feeling resistance.

Curious, he thought. Was there some reason for this?

He began to peel away the tape, taking care not to damage the paint, if possible. Soon, he freed the door and opened it. Gas! Prince Gregory's nose had been correct. He had to warn them and clear the building.

He turned and found himself facing a member of the security team.

"You there. There's a gas leak. We must evacuate the building immediately. I'll go alert the prince."

The man's hand flew up toward Geoffrey, and a piercing pain shot through his chest toward his back. He looked down to see a narrow blade thrust upward into his chest from just below his sternum. He knew it to be a fatal injury.

The man made two quick, additional movements, and Geoffrey could feel the warmth of his life's blood filling his chest, his breathing becoming difficult. His death would be quick, but he feared for the Royal Family. Were they about to die in a fiery explosion?

His thoughts turned toward his wife and children. He longed to see them one more time, to hold his wife, to tell his kids how proud he was of them. To tell them all how much he loved them.

He could no longer talk, to ask "Why?" Yet, in a flash he understood why. He . . .

"*Allahu akbar*," whispered the man.

The man opened the door, and Geoffrey felt strong hands grab him. The last thing he remembered as he toppled down the stairs was the smell of gas and the door closing behind him.

Prince Gregory paced in the foyer as his extended family gathered in the drawing room. His daughters had been excited to see their cousins. His younger brother and his family had arrived first, followed by his sister and her family. The latest to arrive was his older brother, Peter, the Prince of Wales and next in line to the throne, with his wife. Peter's youngest son, Prince Alexander, was escorting the Queen.

The smell hadn't changed and Geoffrey had not returned. Gregory had not forgotten the plot to assassinate his mother that had led to a drone strike killing two British citizens who had joined ISIS in the Middle East.

"Sir?"

He turned to find one of his security men extending his hand with a note.

"Have you seen Geoffrey?"

"No, sir. Do you wish for me to chase him down?"

"Yes, please."

The prince took the note. His mother had just left Windsor Castle and would be there in minutes. The note also mentioned that Prince Arthur, the Duke of Cambridge, Peter's eldest son and second in line to the throne, and his family would be delayed. No explanation was provided.

He walked into the drawing room and approached Peter.

"Mum is on her way. She should be here within minutes. I just received this note." He handed it to his brother.

After reading the message, his brother nodded. "Morning sickness. This third pregnancy has gotten to Helen more than the first two. Arthur must have anticipated something like this. He had us bring a small gift for you in our car." He looked about for someone on the staff. "Do you know if our drivers are still outside? I'll have James bring it in."

"I believe they've all gone to eat," said his wife.

"Very well. Then, I'll be just a minute. I'll retrieve it and greet Mum at the same time."

The two men walked together toward the front door.

"Tell me, Peter, do you smell anything? Gas, perhaps."

The Prince of Wales stopped and sniffed. "Can't say as I do, but the sniffer isn't what it used to be. Mum's the one to ask. Her nose still seems to pick up everything." The security man opened the door, and the Prince of Wales walked out into the evening chill.

Gregory stood in the doorway and watched his brother. He could see headlights in the distance. A car, presumed to be their mother's, had come through the front gate.

At that moment, he felt a grumble in the floor that preceded a deafening roar behind him. He turned in time to see his home collapse around him and a fireball racing toward him. Unlike in the cinema, he had no time to escape.

A quick note from Braxton . . .

I hope you enjoyed *Wrongfully Removed* and thank you for purchasing it. Please consider writing a review at Amazon, Barnes & Nobel, iTunes, Goodreads, or elsewhere. Reviews are crucial to Indie authors. It doesn't have to be lengthy. Just a couple of sentences will do.

Also, if you'd like to stay informed about my new books, book signings, and more, please sign up for my newsletter. You can do that at my website: **www.braxtondegarmo.com**. As my thank-you for signing up, you'll get a free copy of my eBook *And Then One Day*, a prequel to the MedAir Series. If you ever wondered how Lynch and Amy first met, and what led to their breakup, this is the story you'll want to read.

And did you know you can purchase signed copies of my paperbacks at my website? With shipping included in the price, ordering them directly from me is typically cheaper than ordering them online.

About the Author

Braxton can't lay claim to wanting to be a writer all his life, although his mother and seventh grade English teacher were convinced he had what it would take. A bachelor's degree in Bio-Medical Engineering led to medical school and a residency in Emergency Medicine. He served for a decade in the U.S. Army Medical Corps with tours such as the Chief, Emergency Medical Services at Fort Campbell, KY, and as a research Flight Surgeon at Fort Rucker, AL. Who had time to write?

By the 1990s, as a civilian, his professional and family life had settled down, somewhat, and his mother once again took up her mantra, "Write a book. You're a good writer." In 1997, a Valentine's Day writing contest convinced him that maybe he could write fiction. He spent the next fifteen years learning the craft of writing.

Now, twenty-plus years after that first hesitant start, he has sixteen novels published, as well as non-fiction books and a children's book, and can't find enough time to write. As a Christian, he writes "true-life" Christian fiction (suspense and thrillers) that many call "cutting edge," as he's not afraid to take on such issues as human trafficking, racism, and more. His characters are real-life as well, with all the flaws and blemishes real people have. As such, his books are never likely to gain acceptance by the Christian Bookseller Association. But then, he never intended to tell stories just to the choir.

Books by Braxton DeGarmo:

<u>Still Here Series:</u>
The End Begins - 1
The Shaking - 2
The Beasts – 3
The Trumpets – 4
The Mark - 5

<u>Non-fiction Study Guides:</u>
Still Here! Surviving the End Times
Still Here! The Apocalypse is Now
Still Here! Countdown Revelation

<u>MedAir Series:</u>
Looks that Deceive – 1
Rescued and Remembered – 2
The Silenced Shooter – 3
Wrongfully Removed – 4
A Zealot's Destiny – 5
Kidnapped Nation - 6
The Khmer Connection - 7
Resurrected Trouble - 8

<u>Seamus O'Connor Thrillers:</u>
The Militant Genome
Ten Seconds 'Til

<u>Other Books:</u>
Indebted

<u>Children's Books:</u>
The Toucan Who Can Can-can